PRAISE FOR TAHOE PAYBACK

"AN ENGROSSING WHODUNIT" — *Kirkus Reviews*

"ANOTHER GREAT TODD BORG THRILLER — *Book Dilettante*

"FAST PACED, ABSORBING, MEMORABLE" — *Kittling: Books*
*Borg's Tahoe Mystery series chosen by Kittling: Books as ONE OF THE TEN
BEST MYSTERY SERIES*

"GRIPPING SCENES AND CATCH YOUR BREATH MOMENTS"
— *Gloria Sinibaldi, Tahoe Mountain News*

PRAISE FOR TAHOE DARK

"ONCE AGAIN, BORG HITS ALL THE RIGHT NOTES FOR FANS
OF CLASSIC DETECTIVE FICTION in the mold of Dashiell Hammett,
Raymond Chandler, Ross Macdonald, and Robert B. Parker."
— *Kirkus Reviews*

"I CAN'T RECOMMEND THIS SERIES HIGHLY ENOUGH... THEY.
ARE. THAT. GOOD." — *Kittling: Books*

"TAHOE DARK IS PACKED WITH ACTION AND TWISTS. THE
SURPRISES JUST KEEP ON COMING...THE FINAL SCENE IS AN-
OTHER TODD BORG MASTERPIECE." — *Silver's Reviews*

"A COMPLEX, INTRIGUING, NAIL-BITING THRILL RIDE TO THE
VERY END." — *Tahoe Mountain News*

PRAISE FOR TAHOE BLUE FIRE

"A GRIPPING NARRATIVE...A HERO WHO WALKS CONFIDENTLY
IN THE FOOTSTEPS OF SAM SPADE, PHILIP MARLOWE, AND
LEW ARCHER" — *Kirkus Reviews*

"A THRILLING MYSTERY THAT IS DIFFICULT TO PUT DOWN
...EDGE OF YOUR SEAT ACTION" — *Silver's Reviews*

PRAISE FOR TAHOE GHOST BOAT

"THE OLD PULP SAVVY OF (ROSS) MACDONALD...REAL
SURPRISE AT THE END" — *Kirkus Reviews*

"NAIL-BITING THRILLER...BOILING POT OF DRAMA"
- *Gloria Sinibaldi, Tahoe Daily Tribune*

"BORG'S WRITING IS THE STUFF OF A HOLLYWOOD ACTION BLOCKBUSTER" – *Taylor Flynn, Tahoe Mountain News*

"ACTION-PACKED IS PUTTING IT MILDLY. PREPARE FOR FIRE-WORKS" – *Sunny Solomon, Bookin' With Sunny*

"I LOVED EVERY ROLLER COASTER RIDE IN THIS THRILLER 5+ OUT OF 5" – *Harvee Lau, Book Dilettante*

PRAISE FOR TAHOE CHASE

"EXCITING, EXPLOSIVE, THOUGHTFUL, SOMETIMES FUNNY"

– *Ann Ronald, Bookin' With Sunny*

"BE WARNED. IT MIGHT BE ADDICTING"
- *Gloria Sinibaldi, Tahoe Daily Tribune*

"OWEN McKENNA HAS HIS HANDS FULL IN ANOTHER THRILL-ING ADVENTURE" - *Harvee Lau, Book Dilettante*

PRAISE FOR TAHOE TRAP

"AN OPEN-THROTTLE RIDE"
- *Wendy Schultz, Placerville Mountain Democrat*

"A CONSTANTLY SURPRISING SERIES OF EVENTS INVOLVING MURDER...and the final motivation of the killer comes as a major surprise. (I love when that happens.)" – *Yvette, In So Many Words*

"I LOVE TODD BORG'S BOOKS...There is the usual great twist ending in Tahoe Trap that I never would have guessed" – *JBronder Reviews*

"THE PLOTS ARE HIGH OCTANE AND THE ACTION IS FASTER THAN A CHEETAH ON SPEED" – *Cathy Cole, Kittling: Books*

"AN EXCITING MURDER MYSTERY... I watch for the ongoing developments of Jack Reacher, Joanna Brady, Dismas Hardy, Peter and Rina Decker, and Alex Cross to name a few. But these days I look forward most to the next installment of Owen McKenna." – *China Gorman blog*

PRAISE FOR TAHOE HIJACK

"BEGINNING TO READ TAHOE HIJACK IS LIKE FLOOR-BOARDING A RACE CAR... RATING: A+"

- Cathy Cole, Kittling Books

"A THRILLING READ... any reader will find the pages of his thrillers impossible to stop turning"

- Caleb Cage, The Nevada Review

"THE BOOK CLIMAXES WITH A TWIST THE READER DOESN'T SEE COMING, WORTHY OF MICHAEL CONNELLY"

- Heather Gould, Tahoe Mountain News

"I HAD TO HOLD MY BREATH DURING THE LAST PART OF THIS FAST-PACED THRILLER"   *- Harvee Lau, Book Dilettante*

PRAISE FOR TAHOE HEAT

"IN TAHOE HEAT, BORG MASTERFULLY WRITES A SEQUENCE OF EVENTS SO INTENSE THAT IT BELONGS IN AN EARLY TOM CLANCY NOVEL"

- Caleb Cage, Nevada Review

"TAHOE HEAT IS A RIVETING THRILLER"

- John Burroughs, Midwest Book Review

"WILL KEEP READERS TURNING THE PAGES AS OWEN RACES TO CATCH A VICIOUS KILLER"

- Barbara Bibel, Booklist

"THE READER CAN'T HELP BUT ROOT FOR McKENNA AS THE BIG, GENEROUS, IRISH-BLOODED, STREET-WISE-YET-BOOK-SMART FORMER COP"

- Taylor Flynn, Tahoe Mountain News

PRAISE FOR TAHOE NIGHT

"BORG HAS WRITTEN ANOTHER WHITE-KNUCKLE THRILLER... A sure bet for mystery buffs waiting for the next Robert B. Parker and Lee Child novels"

- Jo Ann Vicarel, Library Journal

"AN ACTION-PACKED THRILLER WITH A NICE-GUY HERO, AN EVEN NICER DOG..."   - *Kirkus Reviews*

"A KILLER PLOT... EVERY ONE OF ITS 350 PAGES WANTS TO GET TURNED... *FAST*"
- *Taylor Flynn, Tahoe Mountain News*

"A FASCINATING STORY OF FORGERY, MURDER..."
- *Nancy Hayden, Tahoe Daily Tribune*

PRAISE FOR TAHOE AVALANCHE

ONE OF THE TOP 5 MYSTERIES OF THE YEAR!
- *Gayle Wedgwood, Mystery News*

"BORG IS A SUPERB STORYTELLER...A MASTER OF THE GENRE"
- *Midwest Book Review*

"EXPLODES INTO A COMPLEX PLOT THAT LEADS TO MURDER AND INTRIGUE"
- *Nancy Hayden, Tahoe Daily Tribune*

PRAISE FOR TAHOE SILENCE

WINNER, BEN FRANKLIN AWARD, BEST MYSTERY OF THE YEAR!

"A HEART-WRENCHING MYSTERY THAT IS ALSO ONE OF THE BEST NOVELS WRITTEN ABOUT AUTISM"
STARRED REVIEW - *Jo Ann Vicarel, Library Journal*

CHOSEN BY LIBRARY JOURNAL AS ONE OF THE FIVE BEST MYSTERIES OF THE YEAR

"THIS IS ONE ENGROSSING NOVEL...IT IS SUPERB"
- *Gayle Wedgwood, Mystery News*

"ANOTHER EXCITING ENTRY INTO THIS TOO-LITTLE-KNOWN SERIES"   - *Mary Frances Wilkens, Booklist*

PRAISE FOR TAHOE KILLSHOT

"BORG BELONGS ON THE BESTSELLER LISTS with Parker, Paretsky and Coben"   - *Merry Cutler, Annie's Book Stop, Sharon, Massachusetts*

TAHOE SKYDROP

by

Todd Borg

THRILLER PRESS

For Kit

ACKNOWLEDGMENTS

Twice in the past, I've participated in character-name auctions. As part of a charity fundraiser, people bid for the right to have their name used for a character in my novel. This year, two separate fundraisers auctioned off names in the book that follows.

The first took place at the Carson City Library year-end gala fundraiser. Lucy LaMotte won that auction. The money goes to the Friends of the Library.

The second fundraiser was at the Left Coast Crime convention, for which I served as Toastmaster, and which took place in Reno. Nina Mazzo won that auction, and the money went to the Women and Children's Center of the Sierra.

My thanks to both Lucy LaMotte and Nina Mazzo. I hope you enjoy the characters that resulted.

Once again, my editing experts are Liz Johnston, Eric Berglund, Christel Hall, and my wife Kit. While I get all the credit for mistakes - and trust me, there were lots! - these fantastic editors get all the credit for the fixes. I am indebted to them more than I can say.

Artist Keith Carlson produced another spectacular cover. In addition to encouraging people to reading the book, it will no doubt entice some to go out and try paragliding!

As for all the other stuff that helps an absent-minded writer ignore the real world long enough to write a novel, Kit provides double what I need.

Thanks to all.

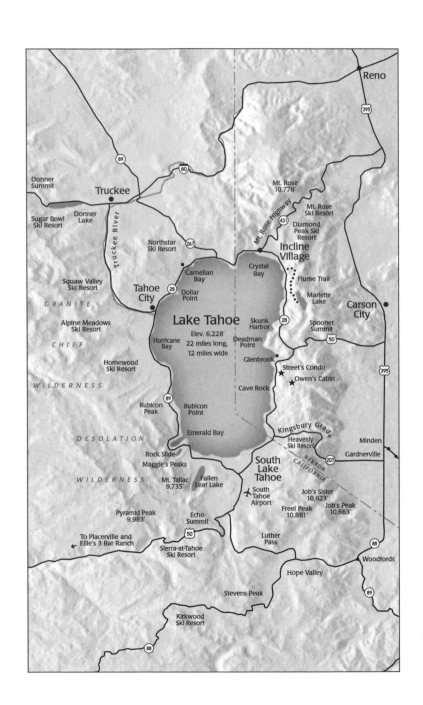

PROLOGUE

As Yardley LaMotte looked out the open door of the helicopter, he knew he wasn't a natural predator. But Yardley was smart. He could, with simple mental study, figure out how to kill.

Yardley was the majority owner of Tahoe Robotics, a new tech company. He was, at his core, not the least bit like a murderer. He was a software engineer. Brilliant. Innovative. He wrote computer code. Yardley almost couldn't believe what he was about to do. But even a squirrel fights back when a fox grabs it. And if the squirrel is particularly wily and can bite the fox's throat, the fox can die.

Yardley was the opposite of an athlete. But because he weighed over 300 pounds, he had some advantage when it came to grappling with anyone in the small space of a helicopter. If he could pull a man down, get his weight on him...

Yardley had already used a series of carefully worded emails - an offer proposed, an enticement formulated - that convinced the man to come along in the helicopter.

After they lifted off, the man, Isak Henriksson, spoke in imperfect English. "I have never taken the ride on the helicopter."

Because all their communication had been by email, LaMotte had never spoken to him in person. LaMotte was surprised by Henriksson's accent.

"Anders had much less accent," LaMotte said.

"He is from Stockholm years ago," Isak said. "I only have come since he is died. To finish his things."

"And call in the debt I had with him," Yardley said, his voice bitter. "Yes, the note had an acceleration clause. And yes, I'm behind on payments. But I'm trying to adjust to Anders' sudden death. To also have to pay back the loan in thirty days, it's too much. That's why I've made you such a generous offer."

"The fast payment on the loan is correct, ja? You miss the payments, the loan is due. Because your debt is now to belong to me, I am to get payment. It isn't personal. It is just business. In the contract."

Yardley realized he shouldn't be surprised at how much Isak Henriksson was unlike Anders Henriksson. Brothers are often very different.

Anders Henriksson's business was investing in new tech companies. He'd made huge profits by identifying promising startups and providing them with seed money. The attraction to new entrepreneurs was that they needn't prepare a complex presentation to pitch to venture capitalists. Anders Henricksson made it easy. He sat down with the young software wizards, talked about their goals over coffee, had them sign some papers, and then wrote them a huge check, often at their very first meeting. It was the bold, impulsive, and large loan that got them to agree to extreme interest rates.

Of course, Anders asked for every conceivable kind of collateral: houses, cars, stock, whatever the borrower had. That, combined with his great skill in identifying and approaching potential borrowers, ensured that he didn't lose too big a percentage of his loans.

Anders' financial and people skills had served him well.

In contrast, his brother Isak Henriksson's mistake had been to move too fast. First, he emailed Yardley to tell him about Anders' sudden death. Then, without giving Yardley even a day to absorb the news, he told Yardley LaMotte that he was going to call Yardley's loan because of late payments.

It was just business.

But to Yardley, it was personal. In making a full payment demand, Isak Henriksson said that if Yardley LaMotte didn't repay the entire loan according to the terms in the contract, Isak would come after all the collateral Yardley had put up. Isak intended to foreclose on Yardley's house in Truckee and on his cars. He even threatened to take Yardley's personal belongings.

Fortunately, Yardley had put much of the money from Anders' loan into a piece of real estate using a limited liability company for ownership. Not only couldn't Isak touch that, he didn't even know it existed. It was Yardley's secret nest egg and getaway.

"The open door is big danger, ja?" Isak said.

The man's headset mic was sensitive enough that Yardley heard Henriksson's voice wavering. Yardley looked up as the man gestured toward the open door on the port side of the helicopter. It was a slider that made a large opening.

"You get used to it," Yardley said. "We have to have it open for the scanner." That wasn't true. With luck, Henriksson wouldn't figure it out.

So far, Yardley's plan was working. Bringing the scanner and his laptop with the robotics software was part of the enticement.

Anders had put up $4 million. Half of that was to purchase 10% of the company's stock. The other half was a loan. Yardley's offer to Isak was to roll the $2 million loan over into an additional 20% equity in Tahoe Robotics. That would bring Isak's ownership of the company to 30%.

Isak Henriksson had already said by email that he went along with Yardley's offer. He followed up his approval with what was called an Agreement in Principle.

Yardley knew that such agreements were not legally binding. But that didn't matter. All he wanted was to get Isak out of the way. Signing the Agreement in Principle provided a smokescreen to make Isak think he was serious. It was the same as offering to take Henriksson for the helicopter ride to show him the details of their digital scanning technique. It worked. Henriksson was now in the helicopter.

"Do you have other siblings?" Yardley asked. As soon as he did, he realized that the question was too revealing. Isak might suspect Yardley's intentions.

Isak shook his head. "Anders and I had each other only. No children. Now I am to be all alone."

Yardley relaxed. Isak didn't suspect anything. Yardley was a good judge of character. He could tell that Isak was the lazy brother, the man with no plan, no past successes. An opportunistic scammer who saw a chance to hustle a fast buck by calling in this loan.

After Isak Henriksson was gone, Yardley would be free from the loan. And if Isak Henriksson had named heirs - which Yardley doubted - who tried to enforce the loan, Yardley would shut down his company and declare bankruptcy. It was done all the time. You can walk away from most kinds of debt with a simple court action. Legal theft.

It was just business.

Yardley could move across the street and start another company with a slightly different mission that would, nevertheless, make use of Yardley's software. A tech startup was always about the founder's genius, nothing else. People who invested were merely backing the founder's vision.

The helicopter headed south from the Truckee airport and went over Brockway Summit into the Tahoe Basin. The chopper crossed the length of Lake Tahoe, making a slow climb the entire way. The helicopter door was still wide open. Isak shivered. Yardley had enough body mass to stay warm.

Yardley knew the importance of impressions. Looking at a scanner in the lab did nothing. But looking at it from inside a chopper flying with an open door next to Sierra cliffs above 10,000 feet... that was impressive.

Yardley's goal was to get Isak Henriksson to focus enough on the scanning process to unlatch his seat belt and look out the helicopter door.

The helicopter flew over the town of South Lake Tahoe to where Freel Peak and Job's Sister rise up, the highest mountains in Tahoe. Following Yardley's instructions to the pilot, the big bird started tracking across the northeast slopes of Job's Sister at 10,500 feet of altitude. Directly out the open door were the ice-coated, jagged outcroppings rising like the teeth of a saw toward the mountain's summit. The cliffs stretched 400 feet above and

400 feet below the chopper.

The air rushing in the open door was cold, the result of high altitude and the fact that the surrounding mountains were still caked in snow and ice at the end of June. They created a giant air cooling effect. Down in town, 4000 feet below and away from the snow, the day was typical for late June. Sunny skies and high temps in the low 70s. Tourists were beginning to flood into the basin and head to Tahoe's beaches and hiking trails, lake shore restaurants, and out onto boats. But at 10,000 feet, the temperature was in the upper 40s and low 50s.

Yardley was pleased when Isak Henriksson looked away from the open helicopter door as if to concentrate on something less scary. His eyes focused on Yardley's laptop computer.

With that single glance from Isak, Yardley realized the man had bought in psychologically as well as financially.

"You fit the data and software on the laptop in total?" Isak Henriksson said.

Yardley grinned. "Not just on the laptop. It's all on this flash drive, too. Fourteen million lines of code. That way, I can do analysis and make adjustments as we gather data." Yardley touched the tip of his finger to the flash drive and made a nervous chuckle, a laugh calculated to make Isak think that Yardley was just an innocent geek, so taken with his software that he could be easily manipulated by a loan shark. "This computer, hell, just this little red memory stick, is probably worth a billion dollars to the right company. Of course, we're that company, and we're not interested in selling. After Tahoe Robotics finishes developing the software, and we launch our IPO, we'll end up with a market cap of a billion dollars. Maybe more. And you will have thirty percent. Imagine where it can go from there."

"What about the situation of the security?" Isak asked. "It is to be completely safe from the hacking?"

Yardley LaMotte slid his finger tip along the flash drive as if caressing it. "Yeah. But I suppose I should be more careful with this little baby, ha ha."

Isak looked alarmed.

Yardley said, "Of course, this stick is only for use while we're scanning. As soon as we're back on the ground, I'll upload the data. Total security there. Two-part verification with an unbreakable password. After the upload, I'll reformat the stick, which erases it completely. You don't need to worry about security." Yardley almost laughed out loud at the irony of that statement.

The helicopter was a Bell 430, large enough for up to eight passengers in the standard configuration. But this helicopter had been substantially modified for search-and-rescue operations, with sliding cabin doors that could be opened during flight. A special bulkhead wall had been installed behind the cockpit to insulate it from the cold of flying at altitude and in winter. It had been easy to mount the scanner on the bulkhead wall so it could point out the open door.

Next to the scanner was one rear-facing passenger seat. Isak Henriksson sat there, his hand locked, white-knuckled, onto the chair arm for security. Opposite the scanner and Isak's seat was a pair of forward-facing seats. Yardley occupied the one closest to the open door. At the center of the configuration was a table just big enough for Yardley's laptop and the two cans of Coke that always accompanied him like little red pets.

Yardley pointed to the scanner. "This is a combination lidar/radar scanner. In lidar mode, it works very much like radar," Yardley said. "Only, instead of bouncing radio waves off of objects, it uses laser light. Unlike radar, lidar can't see through fog. But when the weather is clear, lidar is way more accurate than radar. With the lidar, we can scan the cliff face and get an extremely detailed, three-dimensional picture of the rocks." Yardley tapped a few times on his laptop keyboard, then turned it so his guest could see the graphic representation on the screen.

"Ursäkta mig," Isak Henriksson said. "I mean to say, excuse me. But the pilot can maybe hear what we... vi ska prata. What we are to speaking? This is your company's proprietär... ?"

"What I'm telling you is confidential, yes," Yardley said. "The pilot can't hear us. He's a good guy and very discreet. But we don't want him telling stories at the bar after work. If I need to,

I can press a button and broadcast to him over his headset. And he can do the same to me if he has an important question. But otherwise, our headsets are disconnected."

Isak Henriksson seemed to relax a bit. He made a nervous glance toward the open door, then looked back to the laptop screen.

Yardley continued. "Using this data, our robot will eventually be able to analyze the cliff the way a human climber would, deciding in advance the best route for climbing. It will even take into account the weather forecast, and the current snowfields and ice falls. At some point in the not-too-distant future, our robot will be able to climb the cliff better and faster than a human." Yardley paused and studied his guest's face as if to see whether he was properly impressed.

The helicopter reached the side of the cliff, then arced away in a banking curve, accelerating enough that the men were pulled down into their seats. Isak Henriksson stifled a gasp, but it was audible in Yardley's headset.

The pilot made a loop, and approached the cliff again, this time seventy-five feet higher. The chopper slowed to its former crawl so the lidar scanner could begin recording another pass across the rock face.

Isak Henriksson appeared to take a deep breath as if to calm himself. "Do you think you will one day create the robot that can climb as the person climbs?" Isak asked. "Or, how is the word, skidåkning down unfamiliar slopes in the unknown conditions? And the robot is to leap over the moguls and the buried tree logs?"

"Absolutely," Yardley said. Although he sounded boastful, his manner was merely supremely confident, a quality many tech wizards possess. Yardley added, "Of course, this is simply about how to develop the technology."

Isak Henriksson made a short, nervous laugh. "Ja, the world doesn't have much the need for robots to climb cliffs. But it will get the attention when people see that the robot can do the work."

"Exactly!" Yardley said. His eyes were wide, almost maniacal. "The whole point of this is what I call Presentation Technology. Pretend you are looking up at a steep ski slope, with a huge mogul field like a thousand snow-covered cars. You see three skiers flying down the slope, legs like pistons, hitting and absorbing the bumps, leaping from mogul top to mogul top, periodically flying into the air and doing a three-sixty spin before landing."

Yardley's eyes were afire.

"Then, as you stare," he continued, "focusing on each skier as they get closer, you realize one of them is a robot. Its shape is somewhat similar to a person, two legs, two arms. But it has no clothes. It is a machine, a plastic-and-fiberglass housing covering the mechanics inside. The robot is the equal of its champion skier companions."

"That would make the real impression to the world," Isak said. "When people can see this, demand for robots will be an explosion. And the many of them will be a customer to Tahoe Robotics!"

"Exactly!" Yardley said.

Yardley looked out the open chopper door then turned to his computer and tapped several keys. "Here, let me show you something cool. Can you see this on the screen?" Yardley turned the laptop to face his guest. Yardley didn't really care if Isak could see the image. All Yardley wanted was to impress Isak enough that the man would unlatch his seatbelt and lean forward to look out the sliding door.

"Now look out at that crevasse in the rocks," Yardley continued. "It's filled with snow. But on the screen, I can make an adjustment that shows the crevasse as if there were no snow."

The man stared out the open door and shook his head. "I don't see the crevasse."

"Oh, the crevasse is too low for you to see it. If you stand up, you'll be able to look down."

Isak Henriksson looked alarmed. He once again locked his hand into the arm rest for support. "But what if the helicopter is to shake? I could fall out the doorway."

"No, you won't. The weather is calm. No turbulence. And your seat is farthest from the open door. Go ahead. Stand up and look down at the snow-filled crevasse. Then see the image I can produce on the screen."

Isak looked very nervous.

"Watch me," Yardley said. "I'll show you how safe this is." Yardley unbuckled his seatbelt, shifted his bulk forward, and leaned one knee to the floor of the cabin. From there, he was able to look out the door and down at the rocks hundreds of feet below. He looked back and smiled to reassure his guest.

As if gaining confidence, Isak slowly unbuckled his belt, reached up, and grabbed two of the overhead grips, one in each hand. He pulled on them as if to test their strength. Satisfied they were solid, he slowly stood up. Isak looked nervous, but leaned his head a bit to the side, looking out the open door.

"I don't see it," Isak said.

Yardley turned again to look out the door. The rocky cliff was just yards away. Yardley leaned farther forward and pointed. "See. Right down there. That long vertical stripe of snow." He pointed at the rocks just outside the helicopter door. As Yardley shifted his position, he saw movement in his peripheral vision. He looked back toward Isak and saw the man reach down with one hand and pick up the laptop.

"Hey! What are you doing?!" Yardley shouted. He lunged for the laptop and grabbed its edge.

Isak pulled back.

Yardley shifted, got a better grip on the laptop, and jerked it away. It came away from Isak too easily and hit the arm of Yardley's seat. Yardley lost his grip. The laptop clattered to the floor of the helicopter, and skittered out the open door, falling toward the cliffs below.

Enraged, Yardley turned back toward Isak. He saw that Isak had the red memory stick in his hand. Isak again grabbed the overhead support.

Hanging on to both hand grips, Isak pulled himself up. He lifted his feet off the floor of the helicopter and kicked out at

Yardley. His shoes hit Yardley's shoulder, connecting hard. The blow drove Yardley toward the open door.

Had Yardley weighed half as much, he would have bounced out the door and fallen to his death. Instead, his bulk was still partially on the cabin floor in front of his seat.

Yardley shouted. "Are you crazy?!"

Isak Henriksson kicked out again.

Yardley lifted his arms in defense.

The man's shoes struck Yardley's forearms, propelling him toward the open door. Yardley hit the frame at the side of the door. The rocky cliffs were just thirty yards out. Yardley wanted to reach for the switch that connected his microphone to the pilot, but he was using all his strength to hold on, trying to stay inside the chopper. He screamed for the pilot. There was no response. The pilot couldn't hear him over the roar of the turbine engine.

Isak Henriksson kicked out again, his shoes striking Yardley's chest, driving him closer toward the opening. It was only Yardley's huge bulk that made him resistant to the move.

Yardley drove his hands toward the seat and grabbed onto its edge. He pulled himself forward, away from the door, and toward his passenger.

Hanging from the overhead handles like a circus athlete, Isak again swung toward Yardley and struck out with his feet, aiming a deadly blow to the head.

Yardley tried to wrench his head back and to the side. The man's shoe grazed his jaw, and Yardley's head struck the edge of the door. He was stunned, but still conscious.

Yardley rolled to the side.

Isak kicked out again. His shoe struck the side of Yardley's chest and slid off under Yardley's armpit.

Yardley clamped down with his elbow, trapping the man's ankle next to him. Yardley twisted hard, pulling on Isak's leg.

Isak lost his grip on the overhead handles and fell. The flash drive he had gripped in his hand slid across the floor of the helicopter.

Yardley kept his arm clamped down and rolled sideways, his

massive weight settling onto Isak's leg. Isak jerked his foot, trying to pull it free at the same time he tried to inch his body toward the flash drive. He stretched out his fingertips, brushed the flash drive, then got it back in his grip.

Yardley pulled on Isak's other leg without success. Yardley knew he would never be able to outmaneuver the other man who was strong despite being skinny. So Yardley rolled farther, his weight rolling over the front of Isak's knee, hyperextending the joint.

Isak screamed. He used one hand to push off the helicopter's floor and try to move away from Yardley. His other hand gripped the flash drive. When Yardley rolled more weight onto Isak's knee, Isak slammed the heel of his fist onto Yardley's face, smashing Yardley's lips over his teeth. Isak shifted his grip on the flash drive, gripping it like a miniature knife. He stabbed the open metal end of the USB port into Yardley's face.

Yardley recoiled as the metal connector cut rectangles in the flesh of his lips. He tried to pull back, tried to roll away.

But Isak kept pounding him, kicking at him, slamming the flash drive down. Yardley felt trapped, pushed toward the open door. Isak Henriksson continued to kick and punch, driving Yardley closer to the door.

Yardley's legs slipped out of the opening, dangling into space. His hips slid closer to the door rim, an inch for each heavy blow that Isak landed.

Yardley tried to focus on getting a grip on the helicopter. But Isak's blows to his face with the flash drive cut deeply. A strip of loose flesh flopped beneath Yardley's nose. The taste of blood was on his tongue.

Yardley realized he was about to tumble out of the aircraft. He noticed Isak's punching rhythm, then opened his mouth just as the fist and flash drive descended again. The flash drive smashed against Yardley's teeth and gums. An explosion of salty blood filled Yardley's mouth.

But Yardley bit down.

Isak got his trapped leg free and kicked more forcefully.

Yardley clamped the flash drive between his teeth and wrestled it from Isak's fist. He used his tongue to push the drive into his cheek just as he fell out of the helicopter and plummeted toward the rocks below.

Jarilyn Beyers was at her new job waiting tables at the upscale piano bar and dinner restaurant on the top floor of one of Reno's hotels. The restaurant was much more complicated than the diner where she had learned the basics of table service. The entrees had to be described in dramatic and sumptuous terms. The specials had to be memorized and repeated back - performed - in front of the chef before she went out onto the restaurant floor. And the wine list alone would require a year of study to develop any serious level of expertise. Yet, in less than a week, the maitre d' had promoted her from slinging drinks on the piano bar side to serving four-star meals on the dinner side.

Tonight she was working the south windows, eight two-person tables with views of Mt. Rose in the distance. The couple at table 7 were discussing the wine. Jarilyn had answered their questions about what went best with the Shetland Lamb, Potatoes Fondantes, and Spring Herbs, and then let them take their time discussing the options. When she had said she'd check back, they asked her to wait because they'd nearly decided.

So Jarilyn stood to the side, waiting. The two men behind her at table 6, who, by their choice of words and the look of their clothes were wealthy beyond anyone Jarilyn had ever known, were engaged in conversation. Compared to the couple discussing the nose traits of pinot noir, the two men were much more interesting.

One of them said, "The strangest thing happened the other day. A colleague told me he was at a computer event and he overheard two people talking. One of them was that client you mentioned, the young man with the robotics company. I recognized the name when he said it, but now I've forgotten. What was it? You said he was a large fellow with a brash attitude."

"LaMotte," the other man said in a faint accent that sounded to Jarilyn a bit like her neighbor, who was from Norway. "Yardley LaMotte."

"Yes, that was the person he heard. Anyway, apparently Yardley LaMotte was saying how sorry he was that you had died! How's that for a wild rumor?"

"Definitely wild considering the fact that I'm sitting here. Was the cause of death mentioned? I'd like to know how I perished, ha ha."

"He said it was a sudden, massive heart attack."

"And how did Mr. LaMotte know this?"

"I guess he's been in contact with your brother."

"It gets better and better. I don't have a brother. Any other goodies?"

"No, that was all my colleague heard. I thought you'd be amused."

"Yes, I'll have to call Yardley LaMotte and let him know I'm still drinking wine, even if he is behind on his payments."

The couple Jarilyn was waiting on spoke up. "We'll take this foothill pinot you recommended."

"Very well," Jarilyn said. "I'll be back shortly."

Jarilyn went back to her duties.

An hour later, the two men at table 6 were ready to leave. Jarilyn brought them the check.

"Please put this on my tab," the man with the accent said. He added a tip, signed the bill, and handed it back to her.

"Oh," Jarilyn said. "I'm new here. I didn't realize we kept tabs."

The man smiled. "I have a special arrangement. Check with François. He'll verify it."

"I will," Jarilyn said. "Thank you. What is your name, please?"

"Henriksson. Anders Henriksson."

"Thank you Mr. Henriksson."

ONE

S treet Casey and I were hiking at 8000 feet when my phone rang.

We'd been following a trail that branches off Blackwood Canyon and goes to Ellis Peak, not far from Homewood on Tahoe's West Shore. Although the lower routes had melted clear, the ground was still soggy. Spot and Blondie explored in the forest, disappearing for five minutes at a time. The dogs would come back, check on us, then charge off again, following scents that were unknowable to us. We focused on the grand views of the lake from the higher elevations. They focused on the movements of coyotes and bear and other critters that humans overlooked.

We hadn't made it to the top of Ellis Peak, having been turned back by a rising wind and stubborn snowfields that had so far refused to go away in the warm, high-altitude summer sun.

In the summer, you can walk on most snowfields without punching through up to your thighs or your neck. But those snowy areas are often on steep, northeast-facing slopes. Unless you wear crampons and carry an ice axe, you're always at risk of slipping and sliding down a slope that might deposit you a thousand feet below in a dark forest where the way out is not clear and a cold night with the coyotes yipping nearby refuses to let you sleep, no matter how cozy the smelly bear cave you're taking shelter in.

I didn't want to risk being stranded. The weather service forecast a major wind event that was to start tomorrow at high elevations and continue for a couple of days. When it came to severe weather, the greatest danger always came from wind because in warm, dry conditions, it could sustain and drive fire. And in cold weather, wind could suck the heat out of your body until you died of hypothermia.

So when the snows got deep, we had paused at 8000 feet and looked at the astonishing blue of Tahoe. When my phone made its disruptive jangle, I thought I should have turned it off. Now someone was interrupting a glorious hike. The readout didn't identify the caller. I wondered if answering would make Street respect me for my discipline about work or disrespect me for not having better priorities on a summer's day off. Man lives by woman's approval.

I tapped the button. "Owen McKenna," I said.

"Uh, hello, Mr. McKenna. My name is Vince. Vince Cooper." The man's voice was deep and resonant like that of a radio announcer. I pictured a guy who looked like Paul Bunyan.

"Hi, Vince, what can I help you with?"

"I got your name and number from a friend. I've, uh... Let's just say I've got a huge problem. But I shouldn't talk about it over the phone. I'm wondering if you can help."

"Maybe," I said. "What kind of problem?"

"Like I said, I'm afraid to talk about it. You'll understand if I can see you in person."

"I won't make an appointment without some sense of the problem. Is this financial? A romantic problem? A physical threat?"

"Physical. It's about my boy. He's... missing. Could we at least meet to talk?"

"Hold on and let me check my schedule," I said.

I looked across the lake, a view that always inspires a reverie. To the far left, up toward Incline Village, were the ski runs of Diamond Peak, still heavy with snow. Narrow, white, S-shaped paths snaked down the mountain and contrasted with the brilliant blue lake. To the far right, forming the backdrop to South Lake Tahoe, were the more numerous ski runs of Heavenly, an alpine calligraphy at 10,000 feet. Heavenly's rounded top shimmered in the summer sun. Straight across the lake, the Carson Range mountains were lower but still covered in snow. If I had my binoculars, I could see the grand estates of Glenbrook, Tahoe's first town, built in the 1860s.

I felt Street looking at me, a question on her face, her gaze switching to the phone in my hand.

"Sorry for the delay," I said into my phone. "I'll be in the Homewood area in an hour or so if that works for you."

"Thank you," Vince Cooper said. "There's the Craft Brew Festival nearby. Can we meet there?"

"Sounds good," I said. "Look for a tall guy with a Harlequin Great Dane."

"And I'm a tall guy who will be wearing a red, flannel cap."

"See you then," I said.

We were back at lake level in an hour.

The brew festival was a long row of tent canopies near Highway 89 not far from the base of Homewood ski area. Regional micro-brewers had set up displays, and they offered samplers of their latest brews. Street ordered a lager, and I ordered an India Pale Ale. There was an area of tables over to one side, and we sat next to some large piles of leftover snow that road crews had pushed off the road and up against the mountain during the winter. The snow piles were dirty and ugly, but they provided a windbreak from the increasing breeze coming down from the mountain.

Spot saw nothing of note, so he circled once, then lay on the asphalt, doing the spread-elbows posture so that his chest provided most of the support and his elbows were mere outriggers. Blondie found a place to curl up nearby.

Street had barely touched her lips to her beer, and I was taking the slow road on my IPA nirvana when I saw a guy who actually looked like Paul Bunyan in a red cap, red flannel shirt, and faded blue jeans over well-worn hiking boots. He was probably in his late thirties, a bit younger than me, and very wide through the shoulders. If he got into some kind of strength competition with a backhoe tractor, I wouldn't know who to bet on. He was scanning the area, when his eyes settled on Spot. He and his female companion walked over to our table. In addition to his size, the man was a singularly handsome guy and as rugged as the men in outdoorsy TV commercials. As he got near our table, the three women at the next table stopped looking at Spot and began staring at the man.

The man's black hair was cut short, and his eyebrows were like toothbrushes darkened with black shoe polish. Although he was a couple of inches short of my six-six, he probably outweighed my 215 by 30 pounds.

The couple slowed as they approached me, perhaps hesitant because Spot was focused on them, his eyes like lasers, his nostrils flexing. They couldn't have known he was only wondering if they came bearing treats.

The man took care to keep some distance from Spot as he stepped closer and reached out his hand.

"You must be Owen McKenna," he said in the radio announcer's voice. "Vince Cooper."

I stood and shook his hand, which made my hand feel delicate. He could probably debark Ponderosa Pine trees with fingers alone.

I introduced Street and the dogs, and Vince introduced his woman companion, Brie Du Pont.

Brie made a polite little nod and murmured something too soft to hear. Hello, probably. She was a soft-looking woman with clean but unkempt brown hair. She wore an old shirt and cargo pants that were worn thin, not from hard use but from age and a hundred wash cycles. Her running shoes were old but looked like they'd never been on any surface more rugged than thick bedroom carpet. Next to the manly man, she telegraphed meek librarian, gawky and fearful. Ms. Du Pont gave Street the furtive, appraising look I've seen before. It was an assessment that in small degree took in Street's graceful, strong thinness and in large degree seemed to consider Street's aura of confidence.

Brie Du Pont made a small smile as she shook Street's hand.

Vince seemed nervous, but I didn't think it was about me. He looked left and right as if worried about a predator.

"Is this an okay time to talk?" he said. Again, he glanced around him. For a guy who didn't look like he would be afraid of anything smaller than a bull, he certainly was uncomfortable.

"Why don't you pull up some chairs?"

The man stared at Spot for a bit, picked up a nearby chair, and set it closer to me than my dog. He gestured to the woman. Brie sat down in the chair. Up close, it seemed her eyes were swollen from crying. She looked very sad and weary. Blondie stood and put her head on Brie's knee. Brie pet her.

A young waiter approached and asked if he could get us anything. Vince ordered a small pitcher of beer and asked for two glasses.

The waiter nodded and left.

Vince said, "Sorry for acting weird. I'm totally freaked out, I'm so scared and worried. I don't know what to do." His voice wavered.

"Why don't you tell me about it?"

Vince took a deep breath as if deciding where to begin, and then spoke in a rush of words.

"Something terrible has happened. I've been threatened and told that I can't talk to the police. So before I tell you, I need to ask if talking to you is like talking to the police?"

"In many ways, no," I said. "I'm a licensed investigator. I used to be a cop. So think of me as a private cop."

"What does that actually mean?"

"It means that, in many ways I'm still an officer of the law. I respect the privacy of my relationship with clients. Our communication is privileged, and I won't betray your confidence. But I also won't keep quiet if I think you're planning a crime that would hurt people."

Vince looked more upset than before. It was as if he'd had an idea that talking to me would make his problem go away. Instead, I started talking about worrisome details. "I thought this was going to be easy." He sounded dejected. "Okay, one more thing. Can I... Sorry, but can I know that neither of you will say anything to anyone else in addition to not talking to the cops?"

Street is always perceptive. I knew she would realize that the comment was largely directed at her. "I never talk about Owen's cases to anyone other than him," she said.

I said, "Street is my partner. You can trust that she, too, keeps everything to herself."

Vince looked at Brie as if for reassurance. "Okay, I'm going to take my chances. My boy has been kidnapped."

TWO

"**Y**our boy is missing?" I said. "How do you know he was kidnapped? Did you get a ransom note?"

"Yes. Well, not really. They're not asking for money. They want me to help them. It's really weird."

"So you got some kind of note," I said.

"Yes. It was a text message from my boy's phone."

Vince pulled his phone out of his pocket, turned it on, pressed a few buttons and turned it toward me. It said,

'Got your boy John. Do exactly as we say, and he won't get hurt. Call us to set up the mountain climb. If you go to the cops, your boy dies.'

"And this text is from his phone?"

"Yes." Vince pointed. "That's his number."

"When did he go missing?"

"This morning. I got a call from the school asking if he was sick because he didn't show up. I told them he left at the normal time. These psychos must have taken him when he was on his way to school. Waiting for the bus or something. An hour later, I got the text. So I asked a friend of mine who used to work at the sheriff's department as an IT person. I asked if he knew of a good investigator who isn't a cop. He gave me your name."

Vince lowered his head to his hands. His breathing was labored. "Please tell me you think my boy will be okay. I can't stand this. They say they'll kill him if I do the wrong thing. I can't breathe!"

Brie reached over and touched Vince's hand.

"Vince, I think you can relax a bit," I said. "I won't sugarcoat this. Kidnapping is serious. But they will keep him alive for the time being. They took him as leverage to get you to do what they want." I said it with more assurance than I thought.

Vince took a deep breath, held it, let it out slowly, then inhaled again as if following a relaxation technique he'd learned.

"His name is John," I said.

"Yeah. Jon with no H. Jon Cooper."

"How old?"

"Eleven. Twelve next month."

"Jon goes to school in the summer?" I said.

"Yes. The summer school is a special computer class," Vince said. He seemed to do better focusing on a subject separate from kidnapping. "He's really good at computers. So he's going to summer school for eight weeks."

"You are his father?"

"Yes."

The waiter appeared and set a pitcher of beer and two glasses on the table.

I turned to the woman. "Brie, what is your relationship to Jon?"

She looked up at me with red eyes. "I'm Vince's girlfriend. Two years, now. Jon is like a son to me. And I'm… I'm practically his stepmother." She looked at Vince. "Isn't that right? Doesn't Jon see me as his stepmother?"

"Absolutely," Vince said. He reached over and gave Brie's knee a gentle squeeze.

"Jon's mother is…" I dropped off.

"Victoria is a flake," Vince said. "She never wanted a child, then changed her mind, then wanted to get married and have a suburban life, then left me and took up with a rancher who raises horses up near Redding. It's easy to see that she'd rather spend time with horses than with her own child. Jon was never more than an inconvenience to her at best."

Thinking about how often children are kidnapped by their own parent, I said, "Do you have custody of Jon?"

"Yes. Victoria was happy not to have legal responsibility."

"What is her current relationship with Jon?"

"Distant but friendly. No closeness. No love. Like an aunt or something. An aunt who comes around just once a year."

"And her current relationship with you?"

"We tolerate each other."

"Brie," I said. "Do you spend a lot of time with Jon?"

"Yes," Brie said. "When Vince is working, Jon goes everywhere with me. In the summer anyway. Even during the school year, I pick him up after school and we're together until Vince gets home."

"What's Jon like?" I asked.

Brie and Vince looked at each other for a moment, a clear indication to me that they were wondering how much of the truth they should tell me.

"He's very smart," Brie said. "He's already written some computer software."

"How does that work?" I asked. "A kid writing software?"

Brie looked at Vince.

Vince said, "We don't actually know much about it. The summer school computer group had a special project at school. A man who owns some kind of computer company came to his school and did a seminar. I later heard from the teacher that the computer guy paid special attention to Jon. After the seminar, the computer guy told the teacher that Jon was really smart and understood something about computer security and stuff the other kids didn't get. Rhythms or something."

"Algorithms?"

"Yeah, that was it. What are those?"

"No idea," I said. "But I've heard the term used a lot." I looked at Street.

Street said, "I don't know much, either, but an algorithm is a basic type of computer process, a set of rules about how the computer processes information. The fact that Jon gets how that works at his young age is impressive."

Vince nodded. "Jon showed me some computer stuff he wrote. These strange letters and symbols and numbers. Like something a robot would write. I can't imagine how anyone would want to do that."

"You sound disappointed," I said.

"Yeah, I suppose I am." Vince paused, thinking. "Jon has never once wanted to do something normal for a boy his age. Camping or scouting or sports. Just this endless geeky stuff. And the weird clothes. The boy won't even wear a normal pair of jeans. Everything has to be certain fabrics. It drives me nuts."

"Vince, you need to try to understand Jon for Jon's sake," Brie said.

"I try! But he's always reading those books. Especially that one about the mystery."

"What's that?" I asked.

"I don't know. Some kind of girly book. A woman trapped in a castle or something." He turned to Brie with distaste on his face. "You're the one who gave it to him," he said like it was an accusation.

"There's nothing wrong with a boy reading books," Brie said.

"Girly books? Hell, yes. It's unnatural for a boy to read girl books."

Brie turned to me. "It's called 'The Mysteries Of Udolpho.' It's actually an important book written by Anne Radcliff at the end of the eighteenth century. It's about a young woman who's held captive in a castle. It influenced Jane Austen. It might be more interesting than normal for Jon because the character who helps the protagonist escape is named Monsieur Du Pont. And my last name is Du Pont."

"What's important is for Jon to grow up and be a man," Vince snapped. Then he shut his eyes and took three deep breaths, calming himself. "I'm sorry. This stress is making me not act normal. He's been taken, and he might get killed!"

"What else does Jon like to do?" I said, trying to direct them away from what was obviously a sensitive subject. "Does Jon have friends?"

"No," Vince said. "Except for two girls who live on our road. But he's not interested in them, like, you know, potential girlfriends. They're more like buddies. They talk about clothes.

And books. Those girls read books about princesses. What kind of boy talks about stuff like that?" Vince said it with disgust.

"He's awfully young, Vince," Brie said. "He'll grow up."

"When I was that age I was building tree forts and playing football."

"It's a new world, Vince," Brie said. She sounded exasperated with him. "Everything is about computers, now. He's going to be one of the kids who run this new world."

"I don't care about that. I can't stand it," Vince said.

"Look, Vince," I said, "let's slow down and back up. Take a moment and drink some beer."

"Right," he said. "I get so bent out of shape trying to raise a boy who isn't, you know, a normal boy."

"There have always been boys like Jon," I said. "He might not be your kind of normal, but that doesn't make him a bad kid. Is he a bad kid?"

Vince thought about it for moment. "No. That's just it. He's a good kid. I never imagined having a boy who won't even play catch with me. But he's still a good kid."

Vince finally lifted the pitcher and began pouring beer into his mug. But there must have been a flaw in the glass because the handle of the pitcher cracked off. Vince still held the handle as the body of the pitcher fell. It hit the edge of the table, shattered into several pieces and beer splashed everywhere. Vince looked shocked. Then I heard a soft, distant crack.

"Run, Street! Behind those tents. Take Blondie."

I leaped out of my chair and onto both Vince and Brie as if tackling them. His chair tipped over backward, and the two of us sprawled in the dirt. Brie tumbled off to the side. Spot jumped up and, nails gouging dirt, scrambled over to us.

"You S-O-B!" Vince shouted. "I'm going to take your head off!"

"Roll away!" I shouted back. "You, too, Brie! Someone is shooting at us!"

THREE

"Get behind that tent! Out of sight from the mountain slope!" I jumped to my feet, grabbed Brie's arm, and pulled her over to the side of the beer vendor tents.

Spot and Blondie ran with us. Blondie looked worried. Spot looked confused about the sudden excitement.

"Hurry!" I shouted at Vince. He joined us in a second. The tent was no protection from a bullet. But it gave us visual cover.

"I don't understand," Vince said. He stood a bit bent and looked up as if objects might fall from the sky and he didn't know what to do.

"Your beer pitcher didn't just break. It was exploded by a bullet. Someone is shooting at us from up in the forest." I knew the tent might provide us some cover. But our presence was putting the beer vendors at risk.

"The shooter might fire again," I said in a low, tense voice. "We have to get out of here. Follow me."

I grabbed Brie's arm and ran. Street caught up to us as we went behind the closest tents and headed for the forest. Vince was directly behind. The other bystanders hadn't reacted. Either they hadn't heard the snapping sound, or they didn't realize it was gunfire.

I purposely ran across a small open area because I wanted the shooter to notice us so he would stop firing into the area with the beer tents. I heard no other bullets or shooting sounds, although bullets could strike dirt and no one would know.

We raced toward the forest. In a moment, we were among the trees. After thirty yards, we were well hidden and unlikely to be found by anyone.

I veered into a dense patch of fir trees and then pulled Brie down to the ground. Vince followed. Spot stood nearby and looked at us, his brow furrowed. I could tell he sensed something serious was going on because he no longer wagged.

Brie was shaking with fear and shock.

Vince said, "What do we do? They must have been watching us. If they think you're a cop, they might kill Jon."

"They won't kill him. They took him to convince you of how serious they are about what they want. The shooter could have killed any of us. We were in full view from anyone up on the mountain. The fact that they only shot the beer pitcher is about letting you and us know that they're watching you, that you can't go anywhere or do anything without them knowing. Now they know you were talking to someone. They may not know who I am, but they probably took my photo with a telephoto lens. It won't take them long before they figure it out."

"What do I do now?" Vince's voice was shaky.

"In the text you showed me, they said you're to call them to set up a mountain climb. Tell me about that."

"I'm a guide. A guy called me yesterday and said he wanted me to teach him and his friends to do ice rappelling. He said his name was Lucas. He had an accent that was hard for me to understand. When I commented, he said he was Swedish. He said they were filming a movie about men who are trapped on a high mountain and have to get off of it during a storm. They knew that the weather forecast said we have a windstorm coming. So they wanted me to take them up tomorrow in the wind."

"Up where?"

"Job's Sister. It's a mountain on the South Shore."

"I know it. The second highest mountain in Tahoe after Freel Peak. They were going to film this?"

"The guy said their cinematographer would be down below at Star Lake and that she had cameras with long lenses. She was also going to be using a drone. But I don't see how a drone could fly in high wind. The whole idea of going up the mountain in high wind is crazy. Even going to Star Lake would be stupid."

I sensed Street tense next to me. Star Lake was near the

mining tunnel where she'd been trapped while a crazed arsonist was lighting the forests on fire.

Vince continued, "So I told them I wouldn't do it. It was too dangerous. Now they've kidnapped my boy. They want to force me to take them up the mountain."

"They kidnapped your boy and shot at you to make it clear that they're very serious about this craziness," I said.

"What should I do?"

"Return their text. Or call them if they left you a number."

"And say what?"

"Tell them you'll do it. You'll take them up the mountain and show them ice rappelling. Either that, or we call the cops and let them see what they can do."

"No. I won't take that risk. They were really clear. If I call the cops, they kill my boy. Anyway, it doesn't make sense," Vince said. "No one would kidnap my boy and then shoot at us just because they want to film a movie during a windstorm."

"They obviously want something else. Something much more important than filming a movie."

"You think the movie story was just a cover for something else," Vince said.

"Right."

"Then how will we find out what they really want? And how will we save my boy?"

"As you hike, you'll probably see something useful. I'll be down below with a scope, watching. Maybe I'll learn something."

"What about Jon?" Brie said. She seemed permanently on the verge of crying. "How can we know he's still alive?"

"They'll keep him alive as long as they need to coerce Vince's help. When they get what they want, they'll have cause to walk away. There won't be anything to gain by harming him, unless they think that he can identify them."

"Will they try to ransom him?"

"Probably not," I said. "It seems that they've chosen you for your mountain skills. They will have seen that you're a hard-working guide and unlikely to have riches they can exploit."

"Where do you think they might be holding him?"

"Typically, kidnappers will hold a child in a place that is hard to find and hard to escape from. And because children can't be reliably intimidated into silence, the place will be far enough away from other people so that if the child screams, he won't be heard."

"So there's no basic way to find him," Vince said.

"Not yet. But by paying close attention to everything you see and hear, you may well get a clue."

Vince looked devastated.

Brie spoke first. "Will you help us through this?" Her tone was one of heartbreak.

"Yes. When Lucas called you, did he give any indication of why that location was important?"

Vince shook his head.

"When you call him, try suggesting that you could show them rappelling in a safer place. If they're unwilling to consider that, we'll know that whatever they want is location specific. It is something connected to Job's Sister."

Vince made a single nod.

"I assume you've climbed Job's Sister," I said.

"Many times."

"From your experience, can you think of anything that makes that mountain special for ice rappelling?"

"No. But it generally has serious ice on the northeast-facing cliffs. And its cliffs are tall. Other than that, there's nothing special about it."

"Is it a good place to learn ice climbing or ice rappelling?"

"No. It's fairly high. It's a long hike to get there. There are dozens of better places to learn."

"Why else would someone want to go to that particular mountain?" I asked. "Have you heard of gold or something else valuable up there?"

"No. I've seen some large quartz crystals, but that's it."

"You said the man who called you is named Lucas?"

"Yeah."

"He leave you a phone number?" I asked.

"Yeah."

"It's almost for certain a burner phone. Let's call it."

"And I'm just calling to say I'll take them up?" Vince sounded very tentative.

"Right. I think you can be straight up with them. You know they have your boy. You'll do whatever you have to to get him back safely. You haven't called the cops."

"But the guy shooting at us. He might think you're a cop, won't he?"

"Maybe. But I'm not. You can tell him the truth. Give him my name. Tell him I'm a private investigator, and you just approached me for advice, so they'll know you haven't called the cops. Tell him I said you should call Lucas and tell him you'll do what he wants. If he wants to talk to me, I'm happy to."

Vince looked skeptical. "Okay, I'll do it. I'll put it on speaker."

He pulled out his phone, scrolled up and down on his screen, tapped a few times, then held the phone in front of him.

We heard the phone ring. It was answered on the fourth ring.

"Hello." The accent was obvious with just one word.

"This is Vince. I'll do what you want. Just don't hurt my boy."

"Your decision is to be very smart. Here is those things you will do. We meet in South Lake Tahoe at the High Meadow Trail above the school for children. You will come alone. You will bring the equipment needs for three men. No electronics, no weapons. We have the scan machine to check. What time will be the start?"

Vince frowned. "I'm thinking. If we want to hike to the summit and also learn ice climbing and rappelling, it will be a long day. We should leave by six a.m."

"Six o'clock in the morning," the man said.

Vince nodded to no one. "Yeah. But you should know there are better places to learn how to rappel on ice. Safer places."

"No." The man sounded firm. "It is to be the Job's Sister."

"I'll be there tomorrow morning," Vince said. "I'll bring the gear."

"Let me talk to the man who is your companion."

Vince frowned again. He slowly handed the phone to me.

"This is Owen McKenna, Lucas."

"You are a cop?"

"A retired cop. I used to be in San Francisco. Now I'm private in Tahoe. I've told no one about this. If you keep your word, I'll not tell any cops."

"If I see any cops, we kill the boy. I am not the joking person."

"I understand you are serious," I said. "I am serious, too. I've advised Vince to do what you say. After Vince does what you want, you will release the boy."

"It depends on how Vince is to teach us. If he is good to our need, we let the boy go."

"He'll be good."

"I am to decide that. Not you. The Brödraskapet has a rule. We live to the honor. But we decide what is the honor. It is my wish that you do not make to change my plan. If you do, I kill the boy. First, maybe I cut the boy's tongue out and send it to Mr. Vince." He hung up.

FOUR

I turned to Vince. "You said this guy referred to other men when he previously called you. Any idea who any of them could be?"

Vince shook his head. "No."

"Just now, he said there are three of them. Does that fit with what he said earlier when he asked you to take them up the mountain?"

"I don't think he said how many of them there were."

"Let me ask a general question about climbing," I said. "Why would someone want to do anything up on a mountain in extremely high wind?"

"No idea," Vince said. "Unless they didn't want to be seen by anyone."

"Just what I was thinking. The weather could keep everyone else off the mountain. You would be up there alone. No witnesses."

Both Vince and Brie made slight nods.

"Have you had any recent disagreements with anyone?" I asked.

"No. Life has been, you know, same old stuff." Vince made the briefest glance toward Brie.

"Tell me about your work," I said to Vince.

"I'm a wilderness guide," he said. "My business is called Tahoe Wilderness Plus. Basically, I take people wherever they want. I show them how to do it. Kayaking. Skiing. Biking. Backpacking. Camping. Climbing. Sailing. One of my most requested skills is paragliding. I take people up on a tandem rig."

"That's the big, curved type of parachute?" I asked.

"It's a big curved canopy. A flexible airfoil. But it's not a parachute. You can't jump out of a plane with a paraglider. You launch paragliders on foot."

"I remember now. You take off by running down a hill. And if you find an updraft, you can fly for miles."

"Yeah. Everything I do is about back-country experiences. I teach them how to navigate. I even explain some star stuff. I carry the food pack, and I cook, too."

"Have you been doing this a long time?"

"Yeah. I grew up in Squaw Valley. In my twenties, I was on the U.S. Ski Team. I raced in the World Cup and won second place in the downhill in Val d'Isère, France. I was a serious water skier in the summer. I raced in multiple sailing events through the Tahoe Yacht Club. I've spent over three hundred nights camping in Desolation Wilderness. I've hiked and skied every Tahoe mountain multiple times. I'm a pretty good rock climber and have done serious climbs in Yosemite. I know mountain biking and hiking. I was a Boy Scout. Bottom line is, if you want someone to show you an outdoors experience in Tahoe, I'm your guide."

"How do you think Lucas found you?"

"I don't know. Maybe he just found my website. Or maybe he asked around. I get a lot of business from locals and past customers recommending me."

"You've had no contact with anyone else in Lucas's group?"

Vince shook his head. "No."

We were silent for a time.

"The man on the phone used a word I didn't recognize," I said. "The brodra… something."

"Oh, yeah. He said that on the phone when I first talked to him, too. I typed versions of it into my computer and found out it's called The Brödraskapet."

"Brödraskapet," I said. "Any idea what that means?"

"Yeah. I looked it up on my computer," Vince said. "It means 'Brotherhood' in Swedish."

"Sounds like a gang," I said.

"That's exactly what it is. Some kind of prison gang in Sweden.

Nothing about this makes sense. I can't believe a Swedish prison gang is in Tahoe."

"Maybe someone is just using the gang name," I said. "They said to show up with the gear for three men. What kind of gear would that be?"

"Crampons. Ice axes. Ropes. Ascenders. Brake bars."

"Okay," I said. "Take them up the mountain. Teach them what they want to know. And try to remember every detail."

Vince nodded.

"I think you should consider letting me assemble a team of men ready to intercept these guys. The team could be disguised as a Search and Rescue team. Once we catch these Brödraskapet guys, we can squeeze them."

"You mean bring cops. But things can always go wrong. You know that. Tell me the truth about what could go wrong."

I thought it would be best to say all my thoughts. "Well, even if we pick up these gangbangers, they still hold your boy. Maybe he's locked in a room somewhere. But it's possible they've got a keeper sitting on him, a guy who could act independently. A guy who isn't just waiting on a communication but maybe is planning to act if he doesn't get a communication."

"So we're trapped," Vince said. "Just as I thought. Unable to do anything."

"Not completely."

"How so?" he asked.

"I can observe. Not the cops. Just me. While you're up on the mountain, I'll be down below in the forest, watching with a telescope. As you know, the summit of Job's Sister is very exposed. The summit and cliff faces below it are visible from the north to northeast from all over the Tahoe Basin. So I'll set up where no one will see me, not the men you're leading, nor the drone cinematographer, if she's even real. When the men come down, I can stay well back and follow them."

Street said, "I can be in my car near where the men will likely come out. It's possible we can follow them right to Jon."

Vince shook his head. "No. They might see you're following

them. That could drive them to kill Jon." He turned to me. "What will you do when you watch me lead the climb?"

"You and I will agree on some hand/arm communications that I can understand from a mile or two away. As long as you're not obscured by clouds, I can get information from you. Are you familiar with any hand and arm signals?"

"No."

"Okay, we'll go over some basics. In conditions of radio silence, they can save your life."

"My boy's life," Vince said.

"Right."

FIVE

"Where do you live?" I asked.

"We live in a caretaker's apartment above a garage north of Homewood," Vince said. "The house at the front of the lot is used as a vacation rental. The owner handles rentals, but I do the maintenance, and Brie takes care of the garden in the summer. In return, we get a break on rent."

"I'd like to come visit," I said.

Vince looked puzzled. "Why?"

"I want to make a general assessment."

Vince frowned.

"In this business, asking questions gets you part of the way toward understanding. Walking the territory, absorbing the mood, ruminating on the problem… Those things can't be quantified or analyzed. But they are beneficial. We can go over signals there."

"Okay." Vince turned to Brie. "Should we go?"

Brie shot a glance up through the forest. Then she looked at Street.

"The shooter is probably long gone," Street said.

"I think Street's right," I said. "The shooter was just trying to scare you. He wanted to make you feel under siege."

"It worked," Vince said.

Vince took Brie's hand and pulled her. "Let's show them where we live. Maybe they'll see something helpful." He turned to me. "It's walking distance."

Street kept Blondie on a leash, and I held Spot's collar as we walked with them to Highway 89, the West Shore conduit for all traffic movement, then turned north. After we walked past Homewood ski resort, Vince and Brie turned down one of the side streets. They walked to a medium-sized house, recently remodeled with exquisite architectural details and fine craftsmanship. It had exposed beams and cedar shakes and was painted in two different soft greens. The window trim was red. The house was a combination of country lodge and Tahoe ski townhouse.

We walked down the short drive to what looked like a country carriage house, finished to match the main house. The lower level was a three-car garage. Nearby, but not blocking the garage, was an old Ford pickup with peeling brown paint, probably thirty years old. Next to it was an old Chevy pickup, green, slightly newer. On the right rear side of the building was a wide staircase that led to the second floor apartment.

Vince and Brie went up at a trot. Both of them still glanced at the nearby surroundings, houses and forest.

Spot paused at the base of the steps and looked at me. I pointed up the stairs. "Go ahead," I said.

Spot went up three steps at a time.

The door was painted the same red as the house trim. Vince pulled out his key and opened it. Spot paused at the door.

"It's okay for the dogs to come in," Vince said.

"I'll keep hold of Blondie's leash," Street said.

I took Spot's collar again.

The apartment was luxurious in design and finish and at least twice the size of my log cabin. The main room was open with living room, dining area, and kitchen designated by design features, rather than walls. The living area had many built-ins made of white oak, book shelves and entertainment cabinets and window cubbies with big cushions for curling up with a book. The kitchen was modern with stainless steel appliances and counters of white synthetic stone.

Despite the upscale interior design, the apartment had a motley collection of furniture like one would find in an apartment shared by twenty-something kids who worked as liftees at the ski resorts. Obviously, the owners didn't supply the furnishings.

Vince turned to look at me, a questioning look on his face. "What do you want to see?"

"I'd like to look at Jon's quarters. Does he have his own room?"

"Yeah." He waved his hand. "Down that hall on the right. First door past the bathroom."

Vince and Brie stood in the kitchen area. Street and I walked down the hall, then turned into the doorway past the bathroom.

I flipped on the light. Spot pulled me in.

Jon's room was small, about 10 X 12 feet, with a single bed on the left and a medium desk on the right with a computer on it. Next to the door was a dresser. Next to the desk was a closet.

Street held Blondie in the center of the room, away from the furnishings.

The bed was made up, the blankets and pillow taut and tucked in. There was a bedspread that came up just below the pillow. It depicted California wildflowers. Printed beneath each blossom image was the popular name and the scientific name of the flower.

The desk and dresser had been painted sky blue, and both had ornamentation in the form of triangular patterns custom painted at the corners with purple paint. The edges of the purple triangles had been traced with gold metallic ink pen.

Next to the desk, lined up on the floor, were two pairs of rollerblades. They looked like fancy models, orange wheels in a row. The wheels showed substantial wear.

There was a bulletin board above the desk, and on it were push-pinned sheets of lined paper with numerals and symbols written in long lists. I didn't know what they meant, but I guessed they were some kind of computer coding.

"Look at Spot," Street said.

He was sniffing one of the dresser drawers, working his nose along the edges.

I opened the drawer. Inside were multiple small jars and bottles. There were butter knives, a set of measuring spoons, some artist brushes. A pint-sized bottle of vodka stood next to a bag of cotton swabs. There was a mortar and pestle.

Street reached in and picked up a small metal pot.

"I recognize that, but I can't remember what it's for," I said.

"It's a cappuccino pot." She sniffed it. "But it doesn't smell like coffee. More like lavender." She put it back.

To one side were several plastic produce bags, sealed with twisties. It looked like they contained dried flowers. The drawer emanated powerful aromas of flowers, herbs, and spices.

Back out in the main room, I said, "Does Jon keep his room so neat? Or do you two pick up after he goes to school?"

"That's Jon," Vince said. "He's always been a neatnik. I can't even sit on his bed after he's made it, or he gets upset that I'm messing up the smooth lines of the blanket."

I nodded. "The dresser drawer that smells like cologne..."

Vince looked off as if staring through the walls. "Jon is into fragrances." Vince's voice betrayed a sense of frustration and tolerance. "He's interested in making cologne and perfume. He's always looking for different scents, mixing them into alcohol. He even has a little pot that he uses to boil off scents. Sort of like a still, I guess."

"Is that the cappuccino pot?"

"Yes. He puts his concoction in the bottom and heats it real slow. I don't know what his technique is. I don't think he knows, either. But, as he always says, he's experimenting."

"What does he put in it?"

Vince made a little roll of his eyes and looked at Brie.

"Practically anything with an interesting smell," she said. "He grinds up flowers and herbs and spices and citrus and wood chips and leather. Sometimes he uses scents from the kitchen. Like vanilla and almond oil. When he's done, he mixes the stuff into alcohol. Except we haven't bought him ethyl alcohol. So Vince lets him use his vodka. It's a brand with very little smell."

"He sounds like a serious young scientist," Street said.

Brie nodded. "Perfume science, computer science. Jon is quite brilliant."

"Do you think this will be his future career?"

"Not if I can help it," Vince said. "He wants to be a doctor.

I'm giving him as much reinforcement for that as I can."

Brie didn't comment.

"I see he's also into rollerblading," I said.

"Yeah. He's got more pairs of inline skates than I can count. It's our largest financial extravagance. He likes to say that blading isn't a sport, it's transportation. When there isn't snow on the ground, he goes everywhere on his blades. He has a backpack that's sized to hold a pair of blades, so when he gets somewhere, he switches to his shoes and puts the blades in his pack. He even keeps a pair in the tool lockers of each of our pickups. He's never without his blades."

Brie said, "Vince, didn't you say he can go faster than you now?"

"Oh, yeah. He blew past me over a year ago. No way could I catch him now."

"What an interesting kid," Street said. "He makes perfume and he's into exercise."

Vince nodded. "I'm very proud of his focus on inline skating. It's the one real boy-type thing he does."

"You also said he's interested in computers."

"Yeah. Although it's kind of funny that his interest is not as high as his ability. I'm not sure how to say it."

"You just did very well," Street said. "Aptitude doesn't always correspond to passion."

Vince was fidgeting. He looked at me. "What about the climb tomorrow?" he said. "You said we should use arm signals."

"Yes. You and I need to have some long-distance communication. You're going up on the mountain in the morning, so right now would be good time for me to show you."

SIX

"These hand and arm signals you mention, is this something police use?" Vince asked.

"Some of them, yes, especially when they're sneaking up on a suspect in hiding. There's a wide range of specialty signals that different organizations use. I like the Army Field Manual signals. I'll teach you some critical ones. The thing we need to remember is that this will be a one-way communication. You can signal me, but I can't signal you. And you won't know if I'm receiving your signal."

Vince thought about it. "So if I want to communicate something, I need to use a signal in a way that the men won't realize what I'm doing."

"Yeah, that's critical."

Vince nodded. "Got it."

I said, "I'm going to find a place in the forest where I'll be largely hidden but have a view of the mountain summit. So remember that you have to be visible to me when you make any signal."

"How will I know when I'm visible?"

"The key will be to stand in a place where you can see Lake Tahoe stretched out to the north. If your view is unobstructed, then I'll be able to see you. And I'll be in place by the time you get to the summit. Try to keep moving when you are not going to make a signal. Then, when you have something to communicate, put one hand on your hip and then hold still for a few moments first. That will be my clue that a signal is coming. I know a photographer who has a spotting scope that I might be able to borrow. But looking through a scope can be very fatiguing. I'll have to look away now and then to keep my eyes from glazing over. So it's easy to imagine you giving a signal at a moment when I'm not looking through the scope. But if I see you standing with your hand on your hip and holding motionless for a bit, I'll know a signal is coming, and I'll keep watching until you give it."

"What if you're not the only person watching me? They could have one of their own watching me from a distance. Like the drone operator he mentioned. She would see my signals, too, right?"

"That's a risk we have to take. Because I'll know by the hand on the hip that your signal is coming, I'll be able to recognize it quickly, so you won't have to hold it long. Also, if a person isn't familiar with hand and arm signals, and if the signal isn't given with dramatic flourish, they probably wouldn't recognize that it is a signal at all."

"Got it. Okay, what signals should I know?"

"The fewer signals we use, the less likely we are to make a mistake, and the more likely you are to remember them. So I'll teach you just a few important ones."

Vince nodded. Brie looked skeptical. Street looked worried as if I were putting too much focus on something that wouldn't be useful.

"First of all," I said, "even though I'll be looking through a telescope, you and the other men will still just look like tiny figures up on the mountain. It would be helpful to know who's in charge. To point out that person, we use the 'leader' signal. With your right arm hanging at your side, put three fingers of your left hand across the bicep of your right arm."

Vince did as I said.

"Now, keeping your right elbow at your side, flex your elbow and swing your lower right arm up and out so that your right hand is pointing toward the leader. You don't even need to look at him. I won't be able to make out how many fingers you have on your bicep. But I'll see the arm point, and that will be enough."

Vince went through the motions twice.

"Good," I said. "The next signal to learn is one most people already know. To communicate money, we generally put our thumb to our fingertips and rub them back and forth. Like this." I held my hand up and demonstrated. Vince and Brie both nodded awareness.

"The problem is that if you hold your hand in front of your body, I won't be able to make out the movement. So you hold your hand up and out to your side. Like this. If from my point of view, your hand is silhouetted by the sky, I can probably make out your movement. If I can't see your thumb and fingers moving, I'll still be able to figure it out."

"Why would I need to communicate money?" Vince said.

"Maybe you won't. But when you consider why someone would go to such lengths to rappel down ice in weather that would keep anyone else off the mountain, money becomes a possible motivator. Maybe there's a bag of money up there in the cliffs."

"How would money get up on the mountain? Fall out of an airplane?"

"Maybe. I was once involved in a murder case where the killer was after some gold coins, eighteen-seventy Double Eagles that had been buried in an avalanche not far from Job's Sister. So anything's possible."

"What if it is treasure but not actual money?"

"Same thing. The money signal will communicate that these men are after lost treasure, so to speak, regardless of its form. And it explains better than almost any other concept why they are going in such inclement weather. They don't want to provide any hint of their activity to others who might also be looking for the money."

Vince said, "Anything else?"

"There is the remote possibility they want to rescue someone who's trapped up there."

"Why wouldn't they just request a search and rescue? Oh, maybe that person has committed a crime and doesn't want anyone else to know that he's up there?"

"Right," I said. "Or maybe there's a wounded person who was the victim of a crime, and they want to go up to finish him off."

I saw Brie wince.

"A good way to indicate there's a live person in trouble is with the hostage signal," I said.

"How do I do that?"

"Reach your hand up and grip your throat. That signifies a victim under serious threat. I'll understand."

I continued, "Another reason they might want such privacy is to cover up a crime or retrieve a weapon used in a crime."

Vince thought about it. "Like if one of them was up on Job's Sister and shot and killed someone, but then dropped his gun. So now he wants to retrieve it so he can't be linked to the crime."

"Exactly."

"Which would imply..." Vince paused, thinking it through. "It might imply that we could be coming across a body."

"Right. In addition to retrieving a murder weapon, they may want to hide the body."

"So what signal would I use for a weapon or a crime?" Vince asked.

"These various things, covering up a crime, retrieving a weapon, finding a body, these are all connected to danger. And there is a signal for danger. For that, you raise your arm up and out, palm down, and draw the edge of your hand across your throat." I demonstrated.

"Like cutting your throat," he said.

"Yeah."

Vince frowned. "I could tell you all of this stuff later, after I get down off the mountain."

"True."

"Unless of course, I don't make it off the mountain. If I've already signalled information to you, you have it whether I die or not."

"That's true as well."

"And if you have the information, it might help you find and save my boy."

"Vince, don't," Brie said. "This is creepy enough without you talking about dying on the mountain."

"I'm just facing reality," he said.

"Anyway," I said. "I will try to find Jon regardless of what happens."

Vince was quiet, maybe pondering the likelihood of dying when hiking a mountain in a windstorm. No doubt, it was significant.

"It's time to leave," I said.

Vince nodded, looked at Brie, and she nodded, too. We all walked down the stairs to the drive.

I spoke quietly just in case anyone was listening. "Your job is to show up at your meeting," I said as we stood next to Vince's old pickup. "I'll be out there in the mountains, watching. Do whatever it takes to make them happy, and give me the appropriate signals. We'll reconnect when you get back home."

Street and the dogs and I walked to where we'd left the Jeep near the beer festival and drove away. We got to the opposite side of the lake an hour and a half later.

I dropped off Street and Blondie.

I called an acquaintance of mine, Ryan Picard, an ornithologist in Zephyr Heights who spent most of his time photographing birds.

"Owen McKenna, here," I said.

"Hey, McKenna, long time. Did you start that life list we talked about?"

"No. A good idea, and I keep thinking about that Painted Bunting you showed me. But I'm not that organized. I'm calling for equipment info."

"Bird stuff?"

"No, it's not. Some men are climbing a mountain. I want to observe them from a distance of one or two miles. I don't need photos. I'm wondering if you have a spotting scope I could borrow."

"At that distance you're going to need a spotting scope with a very long lens."

"Is that something I could borrow from you?"

"Yeah. When do you need it?"

"Tonight, if possible."

Picard was slow to respond. Probably reimagining his evening to consider having me drop by and take up a bunch of time. "You're not trying to do this in the dark," he said.

"No. Tomorrow morning. Early."

"When would you be here?"

"I'm home. Maybe fifteen minutes?"

"See you then," he said and hung up.

SEVEN

I left Spot in the Jeep and knocked on Ryan Picard's door. He opened the door with one hand and held a cup of tea with the other. "C'mon in."

I followed Picard into his cabin, a cozy place in the woods, not as small as mine, and much more refined, but without my view. He had a small fire in the cobblestone fireplace to ward off the chill of a June evening in Tahoe. Unseen stereo speakers filled the air with some kind of lavish baroque music, one of Bach's Brandenburg Concertos, maybe. An unseen cookpot in the kitchen nook enticed with a rich blend of smells. I guessed wild rice and turkey soup.

Picard walked over to a corner room that functioned like a study for photographers.

"You said you want to watch from two miles away."

"Maybe. I'm guessing. I won't know until I start walking around in the forest, looking for a view that suits me."

He walked over to a corner with various gear. "My sense would be to send you out with this tripod-mounted spotting scope with binocular eyepieces. Much easier to look through than the single-eye lens. This model has image stabilization. It's heavy, and it takes some time to get comfortable with it. But this gives you serious magnification and quality lenses."

"Sounds good to me. This setup is probably pricey," I said. "You don't mind me borrowing it?"

"Not if you don't wreck it. And if you do, I still won't mind if you buy me the next higher grade of gear for replacement."

"Should I be asking about the cost?" I said, wondering if I was making a mistake.

"Think late model used car, all wheel drive, like an Outback that doesn't even have leather seats." I assumed he was exaggerating. But maybe not.

"Is that all. What do I need to know about working this?"

"Not much. Zoom is here." He touched a sleeve on the lens. "Focus is here."

Picard went over some additional quirks of the scope. Explaining the tripod took the most time of all, adjusting leg length and angle and the locking lens mount. It took enough time that he finished his cup of tea before he was done explaining.

"Thanks very much. I owe you," I said as he finished showing me how to fit the lens and eyepieces into a custom, foam-lined case. Even the tripod had its own carrier.

A half hour later, we'd loaded it all into the back of the Jeep. Picard gave Spot a pet, and then headed back indoors to refill his tea and resume his quiet evening.

EIGHT

After Spot and I left Ryan Picard's house, I knocked on Street's condo door. She opened it, and the dogs ran into the forest as if they hadn't already spent much of the day hiking. I went inside.

Street had opened a bottle of wine and poured a tiny bit into a glass. The fire was flickering in the fireplace. There were all the makings for an evening of joy, maybe even one of celebration.

But Street looked sad.

She pulled a glass out of her cupboard and poured me some wine. It was a petite sirah from the Fairplay appellation in the foothills below Tahoe. The wine was a deep red bordering on purple. Did melancholy come in colors? If so, red-purple may be one of them.

Street said, "I'm very concerned for all of them. For a kidnapped child... How terrifying. And for Vince to have his boy kidnapped. But oddly, the person I'm most worried about is his girlfriend Brie Du Pont."

"Me, too. They both are obviously sick about the boy's disappearance. But Vince, frightened as he is, is a robust guy, physically strapping and mentally focused. I think he could survive nearly anything. Brie, however, seems to be broken."

"Yeah. Very depressed," Street said. "Anxious, too. She radiates struggle, like she's held together by a single thread. Break it, and she'll unravel."

"I want to call my cop friends to help on this. But I'm bound by Vince's wishes."

Street was staring down into her wine glass. "How could you intervene if Vince hadn't said, 'no cops?'"

"That's one of the frustrations in these situations. There

is no clear legal precedent regarding how to respond to a kidnapping."

Street sipped wine. "When you watch this mountain climb from a distance," Street said, "what are you thinking you'll see?"

"I don't know. It's like a stakeout where you think something might happen. So you get in a position where you can watch. Ryan Picard lent me a spotting scope. I'm hoping to hike to a place where I can see Job's Sister. While it's supposed to be very windy, the sky is supposed to be clear. I should have a view of the entire west ridge that leads to the summit. Hopefully, I can get a clue of why they are going up there."

"Good luck." Street raised up on her toes and gave me a quick kiss, the kind that doesn't linger because it happens during a time of stress.

Spot and I got in the Jeep and headed home, back up the mountain.

As I drove up into the dark forest, I felt the familiar sadness cloak me. It may have partially been that my log cabin, however cozy, was quite dark even with all the lights on. Street's condo, with its white walls, was quite bright even with just a few candles. But mostly, the melancholy came because Street, despite being content in her solitary world, was the light in any setting. Every time I left her and Blondie, I felt that no amount of lumens could push away the darkness.

Spot didn't even turn his pre-sleep circle on his bed. He walked onto it, lay down, and seemed to be immediately asleep. I attempted the same in my bedroom, but struggled with thoughts of a child I'd never met being held captive by a man who spoke with a Swedish accent and didn't hesitate to shoot at people in a crowd just to convince them he was serious in his demands.

NINE

When the alarm went off at 4 a.m., I stumbled around for several minutes before I got the coffee on and splashed some water on my face. I made turkey sandwiches for Spot and me, filled two of my retro canteens, grabbed my binoculars, Ryan Picard's spotting scope and collapsible tripod, Spot's folding camp bowl and put it all into a pack. We got into the Jeep and drove down the mountain through the dark. I turned south at the highway and headed down 50 to the South Shore.

As I drove, I tried to think like the bad guys. I reasoned that, because Vince was meeting the kidnappers at the High Meadow trailhead above Sierra House School, they'd likely place a spotter nearby, maybe the woman who was supposed to be in charge of the camera drone.

It was critical that none of them saw me. So I decided to hike in from a different direction. Instead of working my way up from South Lake Tahoe, I'd drop down from the north, following the Tahoe Rim Trail.

When I got to Stateline, I turned up Kingsbury Grade, drove past my office, and wound up to Daggett Pass. I turned on Tramway and went back to the Stagecoach Base Lodge at Heavenly. The ski resort had closed two months before, and the parking lot was largely empty.

Dawn was pinking the sky as I let Spot out of the Jeep. He trotted around as I pulled on the pack and started across the parking lot. There was an old Forest Service road that climbed out of the parking lot, and the Tahoe Rim Trail branched off from that.

Spot ran ahead. Like all animals, he understood trails. The Tahoe Rim Trail, the TRT, is well constructed and maintained.

Every year, hundreds trek its entire 165-mile length around the Tahoe Basin.

At the end of June, most of the trail had melted clear of snow. However, we'd had a strong winter, and the northeast-facing slopes above 8000 feet were still covered in snow. The TRT makes a gentle curve around Heavenly Resort, staying below the higher ski slopes. When I'd consulted my map, it looked like I would have to hike at least three miles out to get to a good view of the summit of Job's Sister. Because of wrinkles in the mountain topography, the summit would be obscured from much of the trail. I might have to go as far as six miles one way.

As the sun cleared the distant mountains to the east of Nevada's Carson Valley, the wind began to pick up. The last weather report had a high-wind warning and high-surf warning for the Tahoe Basin. The forecast predicted steady East wind of 35 plus and 100 mile-per-hour gusts on the ridgetops and mountain summits. Although many trails within the forest would not experience such wind, it was very dangerous weather to climb in. Vince knew it. Probably one or more of the kidnappers knew it, too. But as we had surmised, that was, no doubt, precisely the point. Privacy in the mountains was found where and when others feared to hike.

Spot kept disappearing around curves. Each time I came back into his sight, he'd be standing like a regal statue, head held high, ears focused, and turned back to look. When I came into view, he'd continue down the trail.

After about two miles, we had our first glimpse of the summit of Job's Sister. Despite the clear-sky forecast, there was a misty haze that seemed to stream from the summit, coming from the southeast and blowing off the cliffs on the north side. From the vigorous, straight plume of mist, I guessed the wind at the summit was blowing at a steady 50 or 60 miles per hour.

Spot and I were sheltered in a forest of giant California Red Fir at almost 8000 feet of elevation. Any experienced hiker would know that to go up an additional 3000 vertical feet and get on an exposed summit would be suicidal. Which was exactly what

Vince and the kidnappers were doing.

I looked at the summit, trying to imagine where Vince would currently be. They'd planned to meet and start their hike at 6 a.m. Depending on their fitness, they could be approaching Star Lake, which is at the base of the cliffs leading to the summit. Because of the way the lake was surrounded by a huge cirque of rock, it would be relatively sheltered from the wind.

I didn't worry that I'd be spotted by the climbing party. They were a long distance from me. As long as I stayed off open slopes, I'd be relatively invisible. Even Spot would be mostly hidden in the trees.

In several places, the trail disappeared beneath snow. Instead of a nicely graded path, there was only a broad slope of snow, inclined at enough of an angle that both Spot and I were at risk of sliding away. I then realized that I'd forgotten my cat tracks, a type of hiker's crampons. Not as serious as what climbers use on a glacier, but very helpful in staying upright on snowy slopes.

Spot was visible ahead of me, traversing the steep snow. Unlike the way I had to angle my boots and dig in the edge of my soles, he merely had to grip with his claws. Having four paws, each with four claws like sixteen-penny nail studs, made his mountain hiking much easier.

Thirty minutes later, we had gone another mile and a half, much of it on snow, and I decided to stop at the next decent view of the Job's Sister summit.

It came five minutes later. There was a slight opening in the trees. The ground was relatively level. A thin forest canopy above allowed the sun to shine in during parts of the day. So the snow was mostly melted. Spot waited for me on the dry forest floor, seeming to appreciate that he could simply stand without gripping his claws to keep from sliding.

Moving back and forth, I found a decent place to view the mountain summit. Despite being somewhat level, the ground was rocky. But when I extended the legs on Picard's tripod, I was able to make it stable. When I was ready and looked at the image, it was as if the tree branches in front of me didn't exist. I had a clear view of the summit of Job's Sister. And with the zoom set on its maximum setting, it was like being only a few hundred yards away. Because the scope had binocular eyepieces, I could look with both eyes, which made it much less tiring than a single-eye scope.

The mountain looked imposing. The cliff rocks were dark and menacing, the snow-filled crevasses slick with ice and frozen, crusted snow. I knew from experience that the blowing mist would have been freezing all through the night and probably still was freezing. The rocks that appeared bare from a distance would likely be coated with transparent ice.

To the left of Job's Sister was Job's, 200 feet lower. Job's loomed over Carson Valley to the east, 6000 feet below. In the other direction, Freel Peak, Tahoe's highest mountain, was on the west, a few feet higher than Job's Sister but not as rocky and with none of the Sister's tall cliffs.

Job's Sister is shaped like a broad cone with a gash down one side. The cliffs line the side of the gash. The rest of the cone has relatively smooth slopes that a backcountry skier could enjoy in good weather, when avalanche danger is low.

The scene was dominated by the constant rush of air movement over the summit, air with enough moisture to be visible. The moisture plume waved like a long, gaseous streamer. The high-speed river of wind came up from Carson Valley to the east, which lay below the mountains. The wind raced up the dramatic rocky summit of Job's Sister and jetted skyward. From my vantage point, it was obvious that anyone who climbed up into that jet of air would risk being blown off the mountain. Perhaps a climber could hug the very edge of the summit and hope that the slope would thrust the gale at least a few feet above the climber's head.

I looked for men moving in the early morning light, but saw nothing. The spotting scope had too much magnification to easily scan. The image would jerk, and it was hard to reposition. So I left the spotting scope aimed and focused on the summit and periodically watched the mountain through my hand-held binoculars. They were much lower magnification. But it was probably enough to look for movement.

It was twenty minutes before I saw the men. They probably hadn't hiked any farther than I had, but I had gained less than 1000 vertical feet hiking to my vantage point because I had started at the base of Heavenly, which was relatively high. In contrast, the men Vince was leading had started lower and hiked much higher. They were now above Star Lake, hiking up the slope to the west of the cliffs. They were approaching 10,000 feet, a rise of over 3000 feet from where they started. That would be like hiking up a 300-story building.

When I looked back through the spotting scope, it was easy to see them. Four men, spread out as they hiked up the steep trail above Star Lake. The lead man seemed larger than the other three, so I guessed him to be Vince. But beyond that assumption, I had no other way to identify them.

On closer look, I saw another clue that the front man was likely Vince. The other three seemed to have darkened faces. I guessed they were wearing ski masks. I was glad to see it because it suggested they intended to let Vince live. Without the masks, Vince would know what they looked like. If he could identify them, it was more likely they would kill him after he'd provided the information and skills they needed.

The men appeared to go slowly up the trail. In reality, they were probably moving at a brisk pace, a strenuous hike up a steep slope, fighting the wind, digging their boots and crampons in to get purchase on the ice and snow. And for all but Vince, they would no doubt be struggling to breathe in the high-altitude air.

At 10,000 feet, the air pressure, and hence available oxygen, is 30% less than at sea level. Living at high elevation, Vince was adapted. The other men would be breathing hard.

Unless they too lived at high elevation.

I noticed that the last two men in the procession had stopped. One of them was making a dramatic gesture, shaking his hand toward the other. It appeared they were arguing. Vince and the other man continued climbing, leaning forward into the wind as they marched up the mountain.

The last two men were still motionless but for their arms. From their motions, it looked like they were seriously angry.

Vince and the other man eventually stopped and turned around, looking at the two men arguing.

One finally lifted both arms up and out, a gesture I took to mean, 'whatever you want.'

Because I was focused on them, I almost didn't notice that Vince had his hand on his hip.

The indication of a coming hand signal.

His left hand went to his right bicep. His lower right arm bent up, and his hand pointed down toward the men who were arguing.

Unfortunately, I couldn't tell which of the men Vince was pointing at because Vince was too far above them. But I could tell that he was not pointing at the man closest to him. So the signal was useful.

The leader of the group was one of the two men farther below.

Then both of the arguing men turned and continued up the trail. Because of their argument, there was a large separation between the first pair and the second pair. But they were all still visible in the scope.

I'd learned something valuable. It was not a harmonious group. There was substantial discord.

Vince came to a stop as he got near the summit. He turned and waited for the others to catch up. As they drew close, he gestured toward the summit, then bent down and appeared to put his hands on rocks. I guessed he was explaining how to proceed when they rose up into the gale.

Vince started climbing again, leaning forward. As he gained another 100 feet, he was so bent that his hands repeatedly gripped trail-side rocks. The men behind him mimicked his movements.

As they finally approached the summit, Vince strayed from the trail, moving closer to the cliff edge, no doubt trying to stay beneath the wind as it blew off the back side of the mountain into the sky. It meant he was closer to the cliffs, but less likely to get caught by the worst of the gale.

Vince came to a stop. The other men slowly joined him, gripping rocks, staying low. No one stood tall.

Vince unhooked something from his belt and held it up. His ice axe. The other men did the same. Vince went through a range of movements, no doubt showing them how to hold the ice axe and how to climb with it. Then he holstered his axe and took off his pack. He pulled out a coiled rope and some other items. He did something at his waist, maybe putting on a gearbelt. Or maybe his gearbelt had been in place all the time, and he was unhooking carabiners or something else.

He held up the coil of rope and pointed to various places on the summit. Then he took the rope or webbing and proceeded to rig rappelling anchors. I couldn't follow the details from my distance, but it looked like he was using two different boulders. He then stepped into the loops of what must have been a rappelling harness. He pointed at his gear belt and appeared to explain how to use the various kinds of hardware. I wasn't a rappelling expert, but I knew that the rappelling brake bar was a critical component.

A brake bar actually has four to six bars that hook across a long, U-shaped piece of metal. The rope from which the climber hangs is woven through those brake bars. By sliding the bars closer to each other, the friction on the rope increases, and the rate of descent slows or stops. By sliding the brake bars farther apart, the friction decreases, and the rope slides through more easily.

Vince seemed to attach his gear, and he backed up several feet, demonstrating how he could go down a steep slope or over an edge and control his descent.

Next, he pointed to his feet and his ice axe. I couldn't see details, but I envisioned crampons on his feet. During Vince's on-mountain instruction, I tried to imagine how hard it would be to learn climbing techniques during a freezing gale, a situation where death was a very real risk.

In time, one of the men began to move back and forth along the top of the cliff. I couldn't tell if he was choosing the best place to go down or if he was just pacing, trying to get up his nerve. It also appeared that he held something in his hand and kept checking it.

The man eventually stopped above a steep crevasse filled with snow. Vince helped him get attached to the gear and rope. The man turned around toward the men as if saying something. Then he started backing up toward the edge of the cliff.

He began to drop down the rock face. He was easy to see, silhouetted against the icy snow that filled the depressions in the cliff.

He tried to keep his feet against the ice and snow. But the snow was too vertical for gravity to give him any traction against it. He lost his footing and began turning in a circle as he hung in space.

TEN

A s the man twisted, his descent stopped. It was a reaction
I knew. Something surprised him, and he slid the bars
closer together. The increased friction on the rope stopped his
descent.

The man's rotation increased in speed, his slow turn becoming
more like a spin. The man resumed his descent, still spinning in
the wind. Eventually, his feet contacted the snow, and he stopped
his spin.

He dropped farther, stopped again. He reached out with his
ice axe, swung it into the near-vertical sheet of snow next to him,
and used the axe to pull himself sideways. He kicked his boots at
the snow, no doubt trying to gain purchase with the toe spikes
on his crampons. Then he pulled the ice axe out of the snow and
quickly swung it farther to the side. He used it to pull himself
sideways again.

It appeared that he was looking around, turning his head one
way and then another. He looked down at his waist, then craned
his neck out and sideways and seemed to look down. Then he
began to lower himself again, easily visible against the white
backdrop of snow. Vince and the other men up on the summit
couldn't see him below. I was probably the only person watching
as he dropped like a lowering spider down to what appeared to be
a large two-tone duffle bag protruding from the snow, partially
hidden by an outcropping of rock.

The man maneuvered himself to get closer to the duffle,
reaching out and pulling on the fabric. He'd pulled himself far
enough sideways that his rope was substantially angled from
vertical. Like a pendulum at the farthest part of its swing, if the
man lost hold of the duffle, or if his ice axe came free of the snow,

he'd swing wildly back the other way. It was a precarious position. No doubt the duffle contained something valuable. Maybe it was full of money.

The man reached for his brake bar, made an adjustment, and dropped down a precise, additional foot. He anchored his knee against the duffle to hold his position and then swung his backpack partly off one shoulder. Despite my distance, the pack was easy to see because it was bright red.

He reached into his pack and pulled out an object. I couldn't tell what it was. He held the object against the duffle bag and moved it around. He made a range of other motions I didn't understand, movements that were focused on the duffle bag.

To relieve my eye stress, I pulled away from the scope to blink and rub my eyes. Looking back, I saw movement above the man. Vince was walking away from the cliff edge, behind the other men. He put his hand on his hip. Then he reached up and seemed to grip his throat.

The hostage symbol, used to communicate a man in danger.

In a sudden sickening moment, I realized it wasn't a duffle bag. It was a human.

ELEVEN

All indications suggested the human was dead, a body that had spent some time in the cliffs of Job's Sister. And now the man dangling below the cliff was doing something to a human body.

Why?

The man looked like he was shifting the body. Lifting or prying. Perhaps the body was wedged in place. Another possibility was that the body was in a precarious position such that the wrong movement might make it fall farther down the cliffs. Maybe the man was trying to free the corpse. At over 10,000 feet of elevation, this corpse would be frozen solid. Even if he could free the body, it would be rigid and very difficult to move.

The man continued to make small motions. But his purpose wasn't clear.

After a few minutes, the man again pulled the object from his pack. And again he moved it around near the corpse and then put it back in the pack.

He resumed movements. Next, he pulled his axe out of the snow, holstered it, and moved his knee from its anchor position.

Like a pendulum freed, he swung away from the corpse, left and right, several times.

When you have a rope hanging down from a cliff, or even a building, there are several ways for a climber to ascend the rope without needing excessive strength.

Climbers going up a rappel rope use a prusik knot or a mechanical ascender. The ascender has a clamp that allows a rope to slip through in one direction. But if the rope is moved the other direction, the clamp shuts tight. The prusik knot is less fancy, but it accomplishes the same thing, gripping a rope with enough friction to keep it from slipping through unless the prusik knot is loosened.

The basic principle for climbing a rope is to have two ascenders on the rope, one above the other. Each ascender holds a loop of webbing. In the most basic version, the climber puts his feet in the lower loop and stands up. He raises the upper ascender and loop, then sits in that upper loop. With his weight off his feet, he raises the lower ascender and its loop, then once again stands up with his feet in the lower loop.

The process looks and feels somewhat ungainly. But it's reliable, efficient, and a skillful climber can go up almost as fast as walking up a staircase.

After ten minutes, the man was up over the edge of the cliff. He used his hands to pull himself farther up the rope, away from the precipice.

The three men stood near Vince. It looked like they were talking.

I got the sense they'd achieved their goal.

Until they began fighting.

After a few moments, one of the men pointed down below the cliff, then bent his elbow, shaking his fist in a strong motion suggesting anger. The man standing in front of him gestured back, pointing his hand at the other man's face. The first man turned again and walked away with a jerky movement as if he were stomping. He turned around and came back. The two men grabbed each other, grappling and turning. They fell to the snowy ground, rolling and hitting each other in a violent fight. One man seemed to be victorious. He got up and walked away, leaning into the wind.

Vince went over to the man on the ground, got down on his knees, and tried to help the man up. It took some effort with the wind, but Vince put the man's arm over his shoulder and stood up, lifting the man.

The victorious fighter seemed enraged. He ran toward them and threw himself at them like in an angle block in football. Vince and the man he was helping were slammed downwind.

They weren't pushed off the cliff but a bit to the side where the steep snow-covered slope stretched down to the west for miles. With the wind pushing them, they slid fast as if the snow were as slick as ice.

The two men accelerated, two dark marks on the white mountainside. At first, they seemed a pair, moving together. Then the one on the right seemed to shift. I saw his arms reach out. The main portion of his body formed a kind of a curve. His speed immediately slowed. It was a classic glissade, a kind of controlled slide down a steep snowfield that a skillful mountaineer can use to quickly descend.

Without being able to see the details, I knew that Vince was sitting on the snow, his legs bent a bit in front of him, heels lightly digging into the icy, snowy surface, and his arms holding his ice axe. Despite being under control, Vince was moving fast. I knew he'd be holding onto the head of his axe with his dominant hand. His other hand would be gripping the handle near the pointed end.

Vince would dig the head of the axe into the snow. More pressure meant more braking. The results were clear from a distance. Vince slowed himself, making a rapid but controlled descent.

The other man may have still had his axe. But he had no skills. He sped up on the steep, icy slope. They were both still far above treeline with no obstacles to catch and slow a person. I couldn't tell the other man's speed, but I guessed he was going 60 miles per hour or more when he hit the first ridgeline that threw him into the air. His body flipped over in the air. Even from my distance, his landing looked violent, and he may have landed directly on his head. After his impact, he looked like a limp rag doll, sliding, bouncing, and flipping over as he rocketed unconscious down the mountain. There was no more tension or rigidity in his body. At one point he went airborne again, did a full backward flip, and then, when he hit, began a rapid tumbling.

I knew the man would likely die before he came to a stop if he hadn't already. Eventually, he flipped and tumbled into a ravine, and I didn't see him again. His body would not be found until the last of the snow melted at the end of summer. Depending on his location, his body might never be found.

Vince kept perfect control of his glissade. He also used his ice axe and his boots to have a small amount of control over the direction he slid. Vince steered himself farther from the cliff. By the time he'd dropped maybe 1000 feet of elevation and approached the treeline, he had steered himself over toward the trail they used to climb up. He came to a stop and stood up.

Knowing he was safe, I turned my scope back up toward the summit.

The remaining two men were moving, nearly running down the trail. After about ten minutes, they'd descended a steep quarter mile and dropped about 400 or 500 feet. I was about to swing the scope down to look at Vince, when the two men did something unusual. They turned off the trail and started moving down toward a hollow, a depression in the area between the two peaks of Job's Sister and Freel.

It didn't make sense. The area they were going to had no trail that I knew of. Because it was in a more sheltered area, the snow was somewhat protected from wind and thus much softer. One can hike down in deep snow, but that same snow may be too deep to hike up. They could easily end up stranded in a wilderness area.

They were also moving into an avalanche track. While the current snow above them appeared stable, high wind can loosen giant slabs and send them down to take out everything below.

I stopped looking through the scope to rest my eyes. A sense of movement in my peripheral vision caught my attention. I lifted my binoculars, trying to put my focus on the movement.

In front of the north side of Freel is a lower mountain called Trimmer Peak. It's not a pretty or dramatic mountain but a steeply sloped, unsymmetrical lump with rocky outcroppings at the top.

The movement I sensed was an aircraft flying in from the west, about 1000 feet below Trimmer's summit. With the backdrop of Trimmer, and Freel behind that, the aircraft looked like a small bug working its way through the air, dominated by the mountains looming above.

I looked through the scope, moving it around, trying to find the aircraft.

There it was.

A large, blue helicopter.

I'm not very familiar with helicopter models. But it looked like a Bell, a turbocharged machine large enough to carry eight or ten people.

It was flying in front of the north slope of Trimmer Peak. The helicopter arced across the front of the mountain on a gradual climb. I estimated its altitude at 9000 feet. As it came around Trimmer, it hugged the slope and continued on toward Job's Sister.

Because of the day's high wind, I assumed any aircraft on its general flight path would stay well below the peaks and fly roughly over me on a path to Carson Valley. But this chopper didn't come toward me at all. Instead, it stayed close to the mountain slope where it presumably had some wind protection. It slowed, still climbing, and headed toward the same depression the men were hiking toward.

I realized it was a pick-up.

The helicopter slowed further as it got closer to the men. It stopped its forward motion and appeared to hover. From my distance, I couldn't see details. But I assumed it was being severely buffeted by the wind. The pilot was no doubt trying to find the most sheltered place to drop down.

There was no easy landing area, and a helicopter couldn't be set down in deep snow, crusted over or otherwise.

I turned the scope toward the men. They were high-stepping their way toward the chopper as it lowered farther.

I carefully swung the scope back toward the helicopter. It looked like the chopper was landing, although I assumed it was actually hovering just above ground.

Through the scope, I could see the convergence of men and

chopper, but I could not actually see them climb into the bird. The distance was too great for such detail.

After another minute, the helicopter rose up into the sky, tilted forward, and then moved off to the west, back where it had come from, in the relative safety of the wind shadow from Freel Peak. The chopper arced around Trimmer Peak, then curved south toward Armstrong Pass and Hope Valley beyond the pass. It disappeared from my line of sight.

I turned my scope back to where I'd last seen Vince.

It took some searching. I eventually located him hiking down through the snow, a lone figure on a big mountain. He'd done his job. But the kidnappers still had his son.

TWELVE

With the remaining two men escaping by helicopter, there was no point in continuing along the Tahoe Rim Trail. There would be no one to follow and no license number to find.

So I returned the way I'd come.

When Spot and I got back to my Jeep, I tried calling Vince's cell phone. The cell coverage wasn't sufficient.

When we got to the bottom of Kingsbury Grade, I stopped at my office and tried Vince again using my landline. He answered.

"I'm very glad you made it out," I said. "You are obviously a pro with your axe on a glissade."

"That's just basic stuff everyone in the mountains should know," he said.

"I saw your hand signals. You did a great job. What I don't understand is why the rappelling man was going down to the body, and what the fight was about?"

"It seemed like Lucas got something valuable off the body," Vince said. "Then they were arguing about it. You must have seen the guy who lost control on his glissade?"

"Yeah," I said. "Brutal."

"What was the deal with the helicopter?" Vince asked.

"I don't know, but I can maybe track it. I'll make some calls."

"I did what they wanted and took them up the mountain. So they should let Jon go. I already tried calling the number. But no one answers!"

I could hear Vince breathing hard. "Give it some time," I said. "They may be heading toward wherever they're keeping him as we speak."

After a moment, Vince said, "I still don't see why they wore masks to keep me from seeing them. They were willing to push one of their own off the mountain. They could have done the same with me."

"True, but you know how to glissade to safety. You'd be hard to kill, Vince."

Vince didn't respond.

"I'll see what I can learn," I said.

"You'll call as soon as you know anything?" Vince sounded distraught.

"Count on it."

Vince and I hung up, and I called El Dorado County Sergeant Bains.

"Hey, McKenna," he said when I identified myself. "Always a pleasure. Unless of course you're reporting a crime."

"Kind of." I told him about watching some climbers who found what appeared to be a dead body on the cliffs of Job's Sister, which was followed by the climbers fighting and one of them blowing off the summit and down the west slope.

"The first body appears to be stuck on the cliff face just north of the summit. The person who blew off is in a ravine to the west of Star Lake. No doubt he is dead as well, or will die from exposure shortly. Technically, that would put both bodies in El Dorado County. I thought you should know."

"Do you know the names of these guys?"

"No. I watched them from about two miles away."

"Lucky for me they didn't go off the summit the other direction. Then it would be Alpine County's problem. Now I get to have all the fun. When was this?"

"This morning at about eight a.m."

"There's a gale at high altitude. What were climbers doing up there in this weather?"

"My question, too," I said. "One more thing. Two remaining climbers hiked down to a hollow between Job's Sister and Freel

Peak, where they were picked up by a blue helicopter."

"Interesting. When the weather clears, we'll have one of our volunteer citizen spotter pilots fly by and take a look. I'm curious what you were doing two miles away when you saw this. It would be hard to see men from such a distance."

"I was out hiking with a spotting scope."

"Looking for birds?"

"Sure, why not?"

"Meaning something else," Bains said. "When will you tell me?"

"As soon as my client gives me permission."

We clicked off.

Next, I called Douglas County Sergeant Diamond Martinez. He answered.

"Any chance you're on patrol?" I asked.

"Sí. I see from the readout, you're at your office. I'm not far. Should I stop by?"

"Please."

Spot and I went out to the parking lot and waited. I didn't want to request a visit and then make the visitor run up my office steps.

I saw Diamond's patrol vehicle come up from down on the highway. He pulled into the office lot and rolled down his window. I leaned my elbow on the sill. Spot pushed his head in next to me so that we were both encroaching on Diamond's space.

There was a Starbucks coffee in the dashboard cup holder and a paper bakery bag on Diamond's lap. Diamond was reaching into it.

"It's good to give yourself a treat occasionally, no?" I said.

Diamond lifted out a huge cinnamon bun.

Spot stared at the bun, his nostrils flexing.

Diamond lifted the bun. "Isn't a treat. It's a scientific experiment," he said, his voice excessively serious.

"How's that?"

"I'm going to use Skinnerian psychology to attempt behavioral modification."

"Skinnerian?"

"B.F. Skinner. Famous psychologist. He formulated the principles of operant conditioning."

"What's that?" I asked.

"The way reward and punishment influence behavior."

"How does the experiment work?"

"My question is this," Diamond said. "If a cop does a really good job, and then the cop gets a reward, will that cause the cop to do an even better job?"

"And the cinnamon bun will be the reward in this experiment," I said.

"Sí."

"Have you chosen a subject for this experiment?"

Diamond said, "I was worried about a potential risk to someone's ego if it went badly, so I thought it would be safest if I put myself at risk first."

"So if you do a really good job, you will reward yourself with that huge cinnamon bun."

Diamond nodded. He still looked very serious.

"All in the name of scientific inquiry," I said.

He nodded again.

"And you will subject yourself to this experiment without complaint or compensation just because of your moral virtue?"

"Something like that." Diamond took a big bite out of the bun.

Spot was watching the way all Great Danes look at cinnamon buns. He ran his tongue around his jowls.

Diamond leaned away just a little. "Hound is close enough that he could grab this bun out of my hand. But he won't, right?"

"Dane owners know to never say won't when it comes to stealing cinnamon buns."

"What if I gave him a piece?"

I shook my head. "He knows it's not his, so he's not drooling.

As soon as you break that boundary, the drool will flow like Yosemite Falls until the bun is gone. You'd have to get your sheriff's vehicle steam cleaned."

Diamond looked at Spot. "Sorry, Largeness." He put the bun back in the bag and set it on the passenger seat.

I said, "I've got a question."

"Sí."

"I have a client and a case that I can't talk about specifically. But the general concept is that a guy is in big trouble. Someone close to him is at risk in a threatening way. The threatening agent says that if my client goes to the cops, the person close gets killed."

"You're talking about a kidnapping," Diamond said. There was no question in his voice.

"I'm wondering if you've heard of any bad guys using a blue helicopter for a getaway vehicle? Possibly a Bell? Something with enough oomph to do a pluck-and-lift of two men off a mountain at ten thousand feet in a major windstorm?"

"Did you say oomph?" Diamond asked. He frowned.

"Yeah, that would be a technical term referring to a combination of horsepower and pilot chutzpah."

"Shakespeare, you ain't," Diamond said.

"So when your Skinnerian conditioning needs you to earn another cinnamon bun, you could work on your helicopter getaway merit badge."

"I'll ask around," Diamond said. "Put my investigation skill set to work."

"Investigation skill set," I said. "Sounds impressive."

"Give me a chance to use my secret decoder ring," Diamond said. "I'll call when I learn something."

I gave the top of his vehicle a soft smack with my open palm, and he gave the old Douglas County SUV enough gas to make the wheels scrape sand on the parking lot as he drove away.

Spot and I got in the Jeep and drove home.

I'd just walked into my cabin when the phone rang.

I picked it up. "Owen McKenna."

"Found it," Diamond said.

"No wonder they made you sergeant."

"Got a report here says the chopper went AWOL from a Reno charter company three mornings ago and was found an hour ago on a ranch just out of Markleeville in Alpine County. A kid was out on horseback checking fence lines for downed trees."

"That's cool. Ranch work on horseback. The Markleeville location fits, because after the chopper lifted off Job's Sister, it flew them around the north side of Trimmer Peak toward Armstrong Pass. It makes sense that they would head to Hope Valley and maybe continue on to the more deserted territory of Alpine County. Where's the pilot?" I asked.

"No one knows."

"No passengers, either?" I asked.

"Empty as a showroom model. The sheriff's office report said it was in perfect condition except for one of the leather seats in back had torn stitches and a seam had been pulled open. A stress tear of some kind." Diamond paused. "Tell me about the men on the mountain."

"Except for my client, I don't know who they are or what they were doing. But one of them rappelled from the summit of Job's Sister. It looked like he found a body on the cliff below."

"That's El Dorado County, right?"

"Yeah. I told Bains."

"Ready to reveal your client?"

"I can't say anything about him, yet. Client-detective privilege. But soon. I only saw these guys from the Tahoe Rim Trail a mile or two away. When the bird went AWOL from Reno, what was it doing?"

Diamond said, "The charter log showed that the chopper was under hire by the owner of a Truckee company called Tahoe Robotics," Diamond said. "The wife of the owner reported him missing two mornings ago."

"A computer company," I said absently, thinking about how Vince and Brie had said that Jon was into computers and writing software.

"Yeah," Diamond said. "I guess any robotics company would involve computers."

"Did anyone reveal why the robotics guy was chartering the chopper?"

"There's some other details in the flight log. Something about digital scanning of a cliff face. There is also mention of something called density altitude. But that's probably just pilot stuff, right?"

"Yeah," I said. "Density altitude is a measure of atmospheric pressure that helps a pilot determine how much lift they will have. It lets them know how high they can fly. When the helicopter disappeared, was the original destination Job's Sister as well?"

"Yeah."

"Any chance you got names?"

"Sí." I heard him flip another page. "Missing Tahoe Robotics founder is Yardley LaMotte. His wife is Lucy LaMotte."

"Contact numbers?"

"I don't see that here. I ain't your secretary, either," Diamond said. "Already did most of your job for you."

"An important part, yes. Thank you very much, honorable and distinguished sergeant. Before you go, does the report say anything about the make of the chopper?"

"Let me read. It says it's a Bell Four-Thirty model. Oh, here's one more thing that's a bit interesting."

"What?" I said.

"One of the deputies had a crime scene kit when the sheriff's team went to look at the helicopter. Apparently, she's quite the expert with fingerprints and such. Turns out the chopper was wiped down. No prints anywhere."

"Interesting," I said.

"Gotta go." Diamond hung up.

THIRTEEN

I Googled Tahoe Robotics and found that the company had a minimal website. The home page showed a picture of a cartoon robot. In the balloon above its head were the words, "To be human, or not to be human. That is the question." Below the cartoon was a P.O. box number in Truckee, a phone number with a 530 area code, and a form for sending a message to the company without being able to access the company's email address.

I dialed the number first.

"Good afternoon, Tahoe Robotics, Marie speaking," a young woman said. She spoke with crisp elocution. Or maybe it was just a well-spoken robot outfitted with a young woman's voice.

"This is Owen McKenna calling to speak with Lucy LaMotte, please. I misplaced her home number, so I thought I would try Yardley's office."

"I'm sorry, Ms. LaMotte can't be reached at this number."

"What if it's important?"

"I'm sorry, sir. I don't have Ms. LaMotte's number." There was an edge of frustration in her voice.

"I wondered if you were a robot," I said, hoping to provoke her into helping me. "But you are a bit brusque and hence not very robot-like. In any case, Lucy will want you to break the rules and connect her to me."

"Sir, I'm just doing my job." Now she was upset. Good strategy for the robot designers.

"Can you send her a message, please?"

"No, not really."

I wasn't getting anywhere with this woman. "Not really?" I said. "Another good response for a robot. Imprecise, and thus it makes you seem very human. Or what would robots call it?

Humanoid? Anyway, you seem quite real. Well done. However, a real person would send Lucy a text while we're talking. So if you want to really nail reality, text Lucy and tell her there's a law-enforcement guy on the line who has information about Yardley. Information she will want to know."

"I am real, Mr. McKenna."

"Most robots just call me Owen. You can have Lucy call me at this number. Of course, robots don't have feelings, so at this point you'll probably just decide to hang up on me. Either way, I'm sure your skills include capturing the number from incoming calls. Or you can have Lucy email me at..."

The line went dead.

How rude and very unlike an unflappable robot. This is where artificial intelligence needs to go if it wants to fool us. Making robots that get huffy and flustered. Future robots should make lots of mistakes, then yell at you, and then hang up on you.

I hung up my phone and it rang. Wow, that was robot-fast.

"Owen McKenna," I answered.

"Mr. McKenna, this is Lucy LaMotte calling. My husband's secretary says you are quite rude and that I shouldn't return your call."

"Sorry. Marie was, how shall I put it, not overly solicitous."

"She was designed that way. Yardley's business is focused on replicating human behavior."

"Marie is a robot?" I said, revisiting what I'd said and thought.

"That's what I just said." Now it was Lucy who sounded brusque. "I'd like you to tell me why you wanted to reach me," she said. "And trust me, if this is some kind of sales call, you'll want to hang up right now or you'll regret it. I have certain... resources."

"Thanks for calling, Lucy. Don't worry, I'm not selling anything. I got a little brusque with your, um, secretary because she wouldn't let me talk to you. I'm sorry. I'm an ex-cop-turned-private investigator working on a case that intersects with your husband's disappearance. The key to his disappearance may also be the key to my case."

She paused. "You and the other police still don't know where Yardley is?"

"Correct."

Lucy didn't immediately respond. "I'm still listening," she eventually said.

I said, "From the evidence, it's possible that Yardley was last seen in a helicopter flying near Job's Sister, one of the mountains at the South Shore. A couple of hours ago, that chopper was found sitting in a field on a ranch in Alpine County just south of the Tahoe Basin. The chopper was in good shape, but it had been wiped of fingerprints. There was no sign of your husband or the pilot."

"How do you know this?"

"A cop friend at the Douglas County Sheriff's Office told me. Sergeant Diamond Martinez."

"Is Douglas County where that mountain is?"

"No. Job's Sister is on the border of El Dorado and Alpine Counties. But cops talk. It's common to share information."

"And how could your case connect to my missing husband?" She was wary. Always a characteristic of a smart, sensible person.

"I have no specific idea unless your husband had dealings with the Brödraskapet."

"What's that?"

"A Swedish prison gang."

"You're joking, right? Yardley is a robotics techie. He doesn't operate in any circles that would bump up against a prison gang."

"My case involves some men who recently spent some time on the summit of Job's Sister. We think they might be involved in the gang. We assume, but don't know for certain, that they were involved in a crime of some kind."

"What kind of crime?"

"I don't know. May I come and talk to you?"

"Can you give me names of actual police officers who would

vouch for you?"

"About a hundred, yeah. Cops from all the Tahoe counties, plus Reno, Truckee, Carson City. Cops dating back to my time as a cop in San Francisco."

Lucy was silent for several seconds. "Do you know the Tahoe Donner neighborhood?"

"Yes, I was there on a case a couple of weeks ago."

Lucy gave me her address and said she'd be around for the next few hours.

I told her I was on the East Shore and it would be an hour or more before I could get there.

We hung up.

I called Street.

"I know you're always looking for new places to run, so I thought I'd call. I have an appointment in Tahoe Donner. It might take awhile. But it's a beautiful day for a drive."

She paused. "Yes, I think that would be good. Blondie can use a run as well."

As we drove toward the North Shore, I told Street about my morning, filling her in on Vince's hike with the men but leaving out some of the more stressful details, or at least my conclusions about what the men were doing.

"The wind didn't stop them?"

"No. But it blew one of the men down the west slope of Job's Sister."

"Is he okay?"

"I don't think so. But it will probably be a long while before anyone finds him."

I also explained about the helicopter, originally hired by a robotics company, now sitting on a ranch in Alpine County.

"Why do you think the helicopter came to rescue the other two?"

"I don't know. I'm going to meet Lucy LaMotte, the wife of the robotics company owner. Hopefully, I'll learn something from her."

It was a gorgeous sunny day for a drive. Despite the high wind at high altitude, there was very little wind at lake level. We passed several long lines of parked cars on the edge of the highway a few miles south of Sand Harbor. The road is a long way above the lake and is separated from the water by many acres of steep forest. There are no obvious trailheads signalling access down to the water or up to the Tahoe Rim Trail along the ridgeline at the top of the mountains to the east.

Street said, "Look at the tourists going by us. They're craning their necks as they drive, looking for the source of attraction."

"Anyone would wonder why so many people have parked in what seems like the middle of nowhere. But of course they don't put up signs pointing toward the nude beaches down below."

"One of the lesser known aspects of the Nevada State Park system," Street said. "It's a don't-ask-don't-tell, and keep-your-phone-camera-in-your-bag system."

There was a clear dichotomy among the people getting out of their vehicles. The locals know to slather sunscreen on everywhere and wear hiking boots and shorts until they get down to the water. The tourists, who are merely following rumors, get out of their cars wearing flip flops and bikinis. And they're the ones who show up at Urgent Care that evening or the next day hoping for relief from sprained ankles, bleeding lacerations from Manzanita leg scrapes, and second-degree, high-altitude sunburns in places where most people never get burns.

I went around the North Shore to Kings Beach, turned right on 267, and went up and over Brockway Summit. When we got to Truckee, I drove west out Donner Pass Road, turned north on Northwoods Blvd., and drove up into the Tahoe Donner subdivision, which holds the unusual distinction of being one of the largest homeowner associations in the country. It includes thousands of houses in the Sierra forest, mostly vacation homes, empty most of the year.

The house that belonged to Yardley and Lucy LaMotte was not notable, even though it was larger than most of the Tahoe Donner houses. It had a simple roofline and water conservation landscaping of stones and cobbles and sparse plantings. The drive was lined with bushes and some lights on two-foot-tall posts, obviously designed by an architect who didn't know that they wouldn't be visible during the five or six months of snow season each year. While nice, the house was very modest by the standards we've come to expect from our tech wizards. Perhaps Yardley and Lucy had yet to achieve the gold strike of an Initial Public Offering that would throw hundreds of millions of investor dollars their way. Or maybe they were too busy to engage in the expected, ostentatious material world.

We parked, and Street let Blondie out of the back.

"Probably best to leave His Largeness to sleep. He already put in several miles of hiking this morning. Do you have a plan?"

"A few years ago, I ran on some of the trails around here with a friend. I'm planning to explore them again. If you come out and don't see me, call my cell and I'll tell you where I am."

"Got it." I kissed her, and she took off running. Blondie, like so many rescue dogs grateful for their new owners, kept perfect pace at Street's side.

"Behave, Largeness," I said as I left Spot. I knew my words would serve no real purpose. But I always clung to the hope my dog would be more inclined to make good choices if he knew I was paying attention to his presence.

The doorbell struck a couple of grand chords of a choral group singing Mozart's Requiem. I was impressed but then realized that for the generation that makes sport of choosing ringtones for their phone, a doorbell in a smart house could be programmed the same way.

The door had no peephole. But of course tech people had hidden webcams that were probably sending images of visitors' faces to facial recognition software. A synthetic voice would probably announce my presence to the home's occupants. Marie's cousin, perhaps.

There was a whoosh of weather stripping as a woman in her twenties opened the door. She emanated intelligence and cynicism and something else that seemed negative. Anger maybe.

"You must be Owen McKenna," she said.

"And you, Lucy LaMotte. Pleased to meet you."

We shook. Her grip was strong but shaky as if she had a tremor of fear.

"Come inside and we'll talk," she said.

I followed her through an entry of terracotta ceramic tile on which lay a thick, eight-by-twelve foot rug with a pattern of blues, browns, grays, and greens, a likely abstraction of the Tahoe landscape. Like Reno to the northeast, Truckee identified with Tahoe even though it was a substantial distance from the lake.

Lucy LaMotte walked into a large open room with a kitchen on the right side and a living room on the left. The living room had thick forest green carpet on which sat arrangements of overstuffed leather furniture. Centered on the left wall was a fireplace with a shiny black granite hearth and mantle. To the side of the fireplace was a built-in compartment, lined with stone and filled with split logs. The far wall was all glass facing the forest. To the right, the kitchen had more of the terracotta ceramic floor but was tied to the living room with black granite counters that matched the fireplace hearth and mantle.

Between the living and kitchen areas was a casual dining area with reclaimed hard pine flooring coated in gloss so thick that the flaws in the wood looked great and not like flaws at all.

"Coffee?" Lucy said.

"Please."

She poured two mugs, set them on the heavy, plank dining table as polished as the floor, and then brought over a plate of cookies that appeared homemade.

"Have a seat," she said.

I sat.

Still standing, Lucy sipped coffee with an appraising manner as if to check taste or temperature. I sipped as well. But I'm not discerning. If it's black and warmer than tepid, I'm happy.

"Jean, the neighbor lady likes to bake," Lucy said. "Jean is a widow and not in the best financial shape. So Yardley has the snow service do Jean's drive along with ours. She repays us with cookies. I should decline them, but she's so sweet."

Lucy was silent for a moment and looked awkward as she stood there. Then her face darkened, and her eyes brimmed with tears.

"I'm so worried," she said, her voice rising to a higher register. "This isn't like Yardley. He has a lot of faults. And sometimes he goes away for most of a day and no one knows where. But he's never just disappeared for days at a time." She picked up a cookie and put it whole into her mouth. The move had a touch of desperation as if food might draw her focus away from her worst fears. She chewed and swallowed and drank coffee. Then, with no advance indication, she blurted, "Do you think he's dead? It's been three days, and he's made no contact! I've read about missing people. After a certain length of time, the odds of them still being alive are very small."

As she said it, I thought about Jon Cooper, already missing for more than 24 hours.

"Let's not lose hope, yet," I said. "There could be any number of explanations for his absence. For one thing, the helicopter was fine. The fact that there was no crash and the helicopter was set down in a remote area suggests that someone - Yardley or the pilot - made a specific plan for something that required a change in the flight plan. There was no sign of violence."

"I don't know what to think," she said. "I feel like I've handled so many things badly."

"This is a very tough time for you," I said.

Lucy looked straight at me, her eyes seeming to harden. "I don't want anything bad for Yardley. He's been a good financial provider. At least, until recently. But the truth is he's also a jerk. A self-focused bully. Unfaithful, too."

There was movement in the hallway that entered at the side of the kitchen.

I turned to see an older woman appear. She had a pleasant countenance, with short, white hair and pronounced cheekbones. She looked very much like an older version of Lucy although much thinner. "Lucy! How dare you say that," the woman said in a soft voice. But as she made her protest, something in her tone made me wonder of she didn't partially agree with Lucy.

"Face the reality, mother. Yardley may be generous to you, but he's universally abusive and ungracious to me and to his employees. I don't want him to suffer if he's had some terrible accident. But that doesn't change who he is. I'm just facing reality."

"You're not looking at the big picture, Lucy. Yardley is a genius who's going to change the world. You have to give people like him space. You need to be tolerant of their flaws in order to let them shine."

"Mother, stop at once! I will not hear any more of this." Lucy lowered her face to her hands. "He even made me sign a pre-nup! And now he told me that he took out some kind of crazy loan and pledged our house as collateral. You know what his last words to me were when he left the house three days ago? He said the house was being foreclosed and we might lose it! What kind of a great man is that?!"

"Okay," the older woman said. "I'll just grab a glass of wine and melt back into my quarters, out of sight and out of hearing range." She opened the cupboard, pulled out a glass, held it under the spout of a wine box I hadn't seen, and pressed the button to fill it up. When she was done, she looked at me. "Sorry I didn't get a chance to meet you, mister."

"Oh, I'm sorry," Lucy said. "I'm terrible. Self-focused and vindictive. Mom, meet Owen McKenna. Owen is some kind of cop, and he's looking into what happened to Yardley. Owen, meet my mother Emily Taylor."

I stood up and shook the woman's hand.

The woman turned and disappeared back down the hallway.

FOURTEEN

Lucy stared down the hallway after her mother. "There is a woman who is blind to the ways of powerful men, her husband - my father - and her two brothers who are now all dead, gone to their graves with her full support in spite of their uncountable, never-ending transgressions. And now she's blind to her son-in-law. She's never faced the truth. She even supported Yardley when he said that getting really fat had the upside of setting himself apart from a world full of ordinary people. And what did my mom say? 'Yardley, you do whatever it takes to focus on your genius.' Can you imagine that? And then she started baking him pies. Every time we saw her, she gave him a fresh-baked pie. Apple. Pumpkin. Pecan. And after dad died and Yardley moved her into our house, she has baked him a pie every week."

Lucy started crying.

I realized her tears weren't just for Yardley. They were for the multiple downsides of life, the loss of innocence, the loss of youth, the loss of friendship. The potential loss of a husband and, maybe even more, the loss of the dream of what married life might have been.

Lucy wiped her face with her palms and carefully ran her finger tips under her eyes.

I waited.

She finished her coffee, set down her cup, and looked at me, a steady gaze, pretty blue eyes peering out through puffy red eyelids.

"You said you were working on something that might connect to Yardley."

"Possibly. I can't talk about that case. Not yet, anyway. But

I bring it up because it has the possibility of revealing what happened to Yardley."

"What do you currently think happened to Yardley?" Lucy frowned.

"I don't know. But I might be able to learn why he went missing. Once we know that, his whereabouts might become more clear. I have questions I'd like to ask you."

"I'd like to pay you."

"Thanks, but Yardley's disappearance is something I want to find out about for the other case I'm working on. The client on that case is paying me."

"If you learn something useful or even if you don't, I still want to pay you for your efforts on my behalf."

I made a single nod. "I'll accept payment for anything I do that I wouldn't do on the other case."

"It's a deal." Lucy seemed less upset as we moved toward solving the puzzle of what happened to her husband.

"From what the helicopter charter company said, Yardley hired the helicopter. Why would he need a helicopter?"

"He uses the helicopter to make digital scans of mountains. The data he acquires will one day help his robots to move around on those mountains, climbing them, or skiing them, or whatever else suits him."

"He's really into mountains?" I asked.

Lucy looked at me with disappointment. I'd obviously missed the point.

"Scanning mountains is just one kind of what Yardley called demonstration technology. You dream up a new idea. Then you figure out a way to demonstrate the possibilities."

I nodded.

"So let's say you develop a new set of math formulas that allow a robot to study a surface and infer aspects of that surface that aren't readily observable," Lucy said.

I nodded again.

"You could tell people about it, and they would get it to some extent. But if you want people to really understand it, a better way is to demonstrate it. In Yardley's case, his latest innovations allow a robot to look at a mountain cliff, make judgements about the size and scope of the cliff, the kinds of rock, the presence of other factors that might be relevant like weather or temperature, which might lead to slippery ice. The angle of the sun at any given time of any given day, which might melt the ice. From a lay perspective, if Yardley told about this analysis, it would be boring and hard to grasp. Maybe even from a scientific perspective as well." Lucy paused and drank coffee.

I was getting a lot of nodding practice.

She continued. "Now what if Yardley produced a robot and it ran up to the base of a vertical cliff and climbed it fast, no protection or equipment like what climbers use, and no slow study and planning before the climb?"

This time I made a little smile. "Such a demonstration would blow people away," I said.

"That's what the helicopter is about. The actual AI science isn't about helicopters or scanning or mountains or cliffs."

"AI?" I said.

"Artificial Intelligence."

"Ah," I said. "Demonstration technology."

"Exactly. Anyway, most other software companies are focused on looking at AI from, let's say, the left side. Yardley is looking at it from the right side."

"So Yardley rents a helicopter primarily to develop demonstration technology," I said.

She nodded. "Yardley has scanners on the helicopter and uses them to make digital maps of the mountains. He points them at some surface, whether a building or a mountain or maybe a tunnel, and it scans the surface in three dimensions. You end up with a digital file that you can feed into a robot so the robot knows the territory. It's all part of the process of developing the AI."

"Helicopters must be awfully expensive," I said.

"I don't really know. I assume so. The charter company is in Reno. They fly corporate execs to the airport, do aerial filming for TV and movies. They have a pilot who flies search and rescue missions in the Sierra. Apparently, the guy knows all the mountains that Yardley studies."

"I'd like to learn more about this," I said.

"You think it has bearing on what may have happened to Yardley?"

"Maybe. Would it be okay with you if I visited his company?"

She paused. "It's been three days and no one has heard anything from Yardley. I've filed a missing persons report with the sheriff's office. And I've called them repeatedly. But they haven't found anything. So I don't think I'm overstepping my bounds to say, sure, go visit his company and see what you can learn."

"Do they have local offices? Where would I go?"

"Tahoe Robotics is in an old building in Truckee. Do you know the train station?"

"Yeah."

"Tahoe Robotics is just up the hill from there and down a block or two. It's an old, renovated brick warehouse. But it still looks like an old place. It's even got the old sign of the previous business, a drygoods shipping company. So don't let that fool you." She turned, opened a kitchen drawer, pulled out a card, and handed it to me. "Here's the address."

"Can you call them and tell them I'll be visiting?"

"Yes."

"Does Yardley have his office there? Or is it here at home?"

"It's there."

"I'd like to look at Yardley's stuff. His files and such. Would that be okay?"

"Yes. It's one of those new open-layout places. Everybody in one big room. The idea is that constantly mixing it up with everybody else is good for creativity."

"Where is his desk?"

"In the right, rear corner. He originally wanted to be in the center front of the room. He thought of himself as the conductor of the business, with all the people radiating out from him like an orchestra. But I convinced him he had to have at least a little bit of privacy for talking on the phone and such."

"Who should I talk to when I go there?"

"Well, you will first meet Marie. Although she's a robot, you will quickly come to think of her as, simply, Marie. She is the chief usher. Her job is to meet and greet and handle the phones and guide visitors to their appointments. After Marie, you'll meet a woman named Sal. She's what Yardley calls his Stage Manager."

"Like an office manager?" I asked.

"Yeah, I suppose so. Basically, her job is to say no to all the people who want access to the company. I'll make sure she says yes to you."

"Anyone else I should know?"

"Well, you might meet Tapper Logan. He's Yardley's right hand man. They call him the concertmaster, like the first violin in the orchestra. He's the guy who implements many of Yardley's objectives. He's real smart, although I have to say I don't like his style."

"What about it bothers you?"

"I'm not sure. I think there's a little voice in my head that says not to trust him. Frankly, he's a jerk. Worse than Yardley in most ways."

"How?"

"He thinks he's the smartest person who ever walked the planet. And it's true he's very smart. But he's insufferable. And unless he wants something from you, he treats you like a pesky insect, something to swat away. So when you try to talk to him, be aware that he will want you to go away. And if you don't, he'll try to smack you down."

"Anyone else who would be a good source of information?"

She thought about it. "Actually, the person who knows almost as much about Tahoe Robotics as anyone else, doesn't work for the company. William Lindholm was the first investor. He's been a mentor to Yardley. He put in money back when the company was just an idea in Yardley's head. He and Yardley talked concept and strategy. It wasn't about how to make amazing robots. It was more about humanity's future and how robots would fit into that future. Change that future. Maybe overwhelm that future. Mr. Lindholm won't know the details about how the company runs, but he probably has a better big-picture understanding of Tahoe Robotics' mission than anybody outside of Yardley."

"Where does he work?"

"In San Francisco. I haven't been to his office. Somewhere downtown, I think. But Yardley took me to his house once. It's in Sea Cliff near the Presidio, above China Beach. An amazing place with a view of the Golden Gate. When you go out on the deck, you can see down to the crashing waves on the beach below."

"Wealthy guy?" I said.

"Yeah. He's a venture capitalist. From what I've seen, he has more money than God."

"I don't know when I'll be in San Francisco next, but could you call Lindholm and make an introduction for me?"

"Sure. You might not have to go to The City anyway, because Mr. Lindholm has a place on Donner Lake. Now that it's summer, he'll probably be up here a lot. I'll leave your name with Evelyn, the woman who runs his office."

"His Stage Manager?"

Lucy made a little smile, the first since I'd stopped by.

"Yeah." She opened a kitchen drawer, pulled out a little address book, wrote on a Post-it Note, and handed it to me. "Here's her number."

We talked some more. I thought of a few additional questions, which Lucy answered.

"One more thing," I said. "You mentioned that Yardley and you have some financial worries."

"Of course. It's the nature of new tech businesses. It's always a constant battle to get enough financing to fund your vision and then not go broke. Yardley always says that money to a tech startup is like nectar to a honeybee. You need a constant supply, or you die before you can get back to the hive."

"I don't mean to pry, but money is often at the root of the disappearance of people. So I need to ask, does the struggle to obtain enough funding extend from the business to your personal affairs? From what you said when your mother came out, it sounds like you're in trouble on the house? Have you not been able to pay the mortgage?"

Lucy shook her head in a dismissive way. "No. The foreclosure isn't about paying the mortgage. It is about a much bigger loan from a man in Reno. Yardley pledged our house as collateral. Yardley never talked to me about the details, something that drives me crazy. Because in many respects, I'm better at money management than he is. Apparently, he isn't current on this big loan he took out. The man who lent him the money died. The man's brother inherited the loan, and he is foreclosing on our house and everything else that Yardley used as collateral. Yardley said something about working a deal with that man. But that was right before he went missing, so I never heard what came of that."

"Do you know how much this loan was for?"

"Not exactly. But I think it was a few million dollars."

Lucy stood up and paced around the center island of the kitchen. "Here's what's crazy. And it's something I've seen with some of Yardley's fellow techies. There is no personal financial concern that registers in the mind of a tech entrepreneur. You're not going to fuss about a few thousand dollars for the household bills or even a house when you are running a company that must have millions to fulfill its vision. Yardley got the first trickle of funding from Lindholm. Less than a year later, he got this big loan from the Reno lender. Actually, I think part of it was a loan, and the other part a portion of stock ownership. The loan part is why he had to make repayments. Yardley was holding out for his next level, as he called it. He said that when Tahoe Robotics succeeded at his technology demonstration, he'd go to the next level. He said that when he got to that next level, the next round of venture capital he could attract would be fifty million."

"A lot of money," I said.

Lucy was shaking her head again. "Not to Yardley. He was always focused on the next step. He had a clear vision of an IPO in several years."

"Initial Public Offering," I said.

"Yes. When he reached that milestone, he expected a future company valuation of a billion or more."

"Let me be sure I understand," I said, trying to keep the amazement out of my voice. "Yardley has already gotten millions. He thinks his next round of capital could be fifty million. His projection is for a future valuation of a billion dollars. And he's behind on his loan payments."

Lucy's face darkened. "Yes. I think I made a terrible mistake getting married to him."

FIFTEEN

Lucy shut her eyes and took a deep breath as if resetting her thoughts.

"Tahoe Robotics has great potential. There are now twenty-some employees. The techies at the office are brilliant. There is a possibility that the company will go through the roof. But the reality is that most such companies don't make it. They use up their funds, and their promise never comes to fruition. The company fizzles, and all the investors lose their money."

"Reality can be bleak," I said.

"Yeah." Lucy had stress lines on her forehead to match her tone. She picked up another cookie off the tray and bit off a piece.

"The Reno lender who died," I said. "What's his name? Or his company's name?"

"I'm embarrassed to say I don't know. This is one of the things I can't stand about Yardley. He goes off on his own without ever consulting me about anything. It's not like I'm a bubble-brain idiot. I could be a useful sounding board. Sure, I'm the first to admit I don't get coding and the whole geeky tech world. But I'm smart. I could provide good feedback about a wide range of situations." She paused. "I honestly don't know why Yardley even wanted to marry me. So, in answer to your question, if you talk to William Lindholm, ask him. He will know the Reno lender. Probably personally. Those money people are tight like in any other business."

"Thanks, I'll ask him." I stood up to go. "And you'll call Sal at Tahoe Robotics and ask her to let me look through Yardley's files."

Lucy nodded. "I'll also call Evelyn."

"William Lindholm's stage manager," I said.

Lucy smiled.

I said, "I'm wondering about Yardley's personal ambition."

Lucy frowned. "What do you mean?"

"I assume he is very driven about his company. But is he the kind of person who will do whatever it takes to be successful?"

"You're wondering if he would do something unethical to succeed?"

"Yeah."

Lucy didn't hesitate. "Yes. I've always thought of Yardley as a man of enormous appetites. Money, food, sex, stature in the tech world. He's one of those people you don't ever want to cross."

"Would he bend laws to get what he wanted?"

Lucy paused. "If you pushed Yardley really hard... If he felt like he was trapped in a corner regarding his software, he'd be like a mother protecting her baby. He would kill to survive."

"Has Yardley said anything unusual recently? Has he mentioned any problems or surprises or sudden changes at work?"

"Apart from the problem of the loan, no."

"Any small things that were out of the ordinary?"

"No."

"Has he met anyone new?"

"Just the brother of the Reno lender who died. Yardley didn't talk much about him. I suppose that for all of his robot focus, he was struggling with the idea that a man who inherited an unpaid loan would want to collect on it."

"Did Yardley mention the name of the brother?"

She shook her head.

"Let me know if you think of anything."

I nodded and moved toward the door.

Lucy walked with me. Then she looked down at the floor, radiating discomfort. "May I ask you a personal question, Mr. McKenna?"

"Owen, please. Yes, ask whatever you want."

"When you pulled up, a woman got out of your car and went

running with her dog. Is she close to you?"

"Yes. She's my girlfriend. Her name is Street Casey. She's an entomologist."

"Are you… Sorry, I know this is much too personal. I guess I'm going through a crisis."

"Ask what you want," I said.

"Is your relationship with Street long term? The kind where you might one day get married?"

"I'd like to. But Street is all about being independent. She had a rough childhood. It's important for her to not get too dependent on any one person."

"Do you love her?"

"Yes."

"I noticed… God, I'm so embarrassed to be thinking this."

"It's okay."

"I saw that she's thin and looks very fit."

I paused, wondering about the ramifications of Lucy's questions. "Yes, she's kind of all about fitness."

Lucy looked at me hard. "Is that important to you?"

"It's valuable to me, but not as important to me as it is for her."

"So she's internal about these things," Lucy said. She put a little emphasis on the word internal, as if it gave her a small epiphany. "She stays fit to satisfy her own desires, not yours."

"Definitely," I said.

We said goodbye, and I was walking out to the car when she called after me.

"I just remembered someone new Yardley mentioned. Although I can't imagine how it could matter."

I stopped and walked back to her.

"Yardley goes out to schools now and then and talks to kids about tech careers. I guess some of the local teachers have been referring him to each other. So he goes and makes a little presentation and that's it. He says the kids mostly have no interest. They're too dialed into their phones. But a week ago or so, he had a kid who was really sharp. Sharp enough for Yardley to talk about it later. That's unusual."

"What was the kid's name?"

"I have no idea."

"Do you know what school it was?"

"No. But I think it was fairly close because he probably would have mentioned the drive if the school was on the South Shore or down in Carson City."

"Would anyone at Tahoe Robotics know?"

"Possibly, but I doubt it. Yardley is all business when he's at work."

"Okay, thanks."

"That's not the kind of info you were looking for, is it?"

"On the contrary. It might turn out to be very helpful."

SIXTEEN

When I got out to the Jeep, I dialed Street's cell. She answered huffing.

"Calling for a mileage check," I said.

"Let me look at this ticker on my wrist. It says seven miles."

"Wow. You want me to meet you?"

"What's the alternative?" she asked.

"I go to my next appointment. Either Tahoe Robotics in downtown Truckee or possibly a venture capitalist named William Lindholm who might be in San Francisco or at his place on Donner Lake. It will depend on who is in and who is out."

"Okay, you pursue that. I'm good for another few miles. There's a back road to downtown Truckee. When I get close to wearing out, I'll head there with Blondie and find a dog-friendly coffee shop where I can wait for you."

"I'm pretty sure most places in Truckee are dog-friendly. I'll call after the next stop."

I dialed the number Lucy had given me for William Lindholm. The area code was 415, San Francisco.

"Lindholm Capital LLC, Evelyn speaking," a woman answered. She had the husky voice of a two-pack-a-day smoker.

"Hi Evelyn. My name's Owen McKenna. I'm an investigator calling at Lucy LaMotte's request to…"

"Speak to Mr. Bill," she said, finishing my sentence.

"You are on it. I guess when Lucy asks…"

"I jump," Evelyn interrupted again. "But I want to be helpful. I heard about her situation. I spoke to her yesterday when she called to ask if we'd seen or heard from her husband. It must be so stressful for her to have him go missing. So today I tried to be cheerful for her when she called. You know, get her mind off her worries. It must have worked because after she told me you would be calling, I asked about you, if you could be trusted and such. She said yes. Then she said you seemed like a decent guy and that you were pretty cute, too."

"Cute," I repeated. "Not what your average man shoots for. What about charisma and charm?"

"Hon, at my age, I've learned that the only things that matter are brains and a bank account. In lieu of those, I'll take cute. And charisma and charm? They're nice, but not for the long haul, and they sure don't pay the bills. So we're only left with cute."

"But we're talking on the phone."

"Well, someday you might walk in here and get stuck waiting in the reception room while Mr. Bill swallows up another tech company. Then I'll look at you and imagine what you'd be like if the odds were wrong and you actually had smarts and money."

"Got it," I said. "I don't want to disappoint you, but full disclosure would have me tell you that I don't have money. As for smarts, the available evidence suggests that's not assured, either. As for speaking to William Lindholm now or any time soon, you got odds on that?"

"I'm in San Francisco at Mr. Bill's office. Lucy said you're in Truckee. It happens that Mr. Bill is in Truckee. So I could call him and ask him to give you a moment at Lucy's request. Will that work for you?"

"Yes, please."

"Hold on."

The phone clicked. I waited. Spot snoozed in the back seat. After a few minutes, he began snoring. I turned on the radio. Dialed up NPR. Heard a snippet of news, which, in the last few years, could cause a stroke from temporary high blood pressure. I turned off the radio and enjoyed the pleasure of my thoughts. Which wandered to what Street looked like in her running togs. Were I Shakespeare, I could bang out a sonnet. 'My summer's lease with Street hath all too short a date...'

"Mr. Owen?" The husky voice was back.

"Yes?"

"Mr. Bill said he will be at his Truckee lodge for the next hour or so, and he will gladly grant you a moment."

"A moment?"

"Well, if I were to venture well outside of my purview, I might suggest bringing a fifth of twelve-year-old Macallan single malt. That might buy you several moments."

"This is Truckee," I said. "Craft beer country. Scotch, not so much."

"That you motivated Lucy to call me demonstrates your resourcefulness. I'm sure you'll manage."

"And to what location would I deliver this single malt?"

She rattled off an address. "If you drive out Donner Pass Road along the north shore of Donner Lake, you'll find a poorly marked driveway that angles off to the right and climbs up to what looks more like a small inn in Banff than a vacation home in Truckee."

"Thanks very much, Evelyn." I said.

"Looking forward to looking at you - I mean, meeting you - someday," she said and hung up.

I found a liquor store, acquired the requested libation, and was parked in front of the Mr. Bill Inn twenty minutes later. The house before me definitely had antecedents that reached back to the Banff Springs Hotel. The place was constructed with big log timbers and had a steep copper roof that had long ago developed its green patina. The house was three floors high and had a turret on one end. There was a four-car garage with individual doors that featured beveled, etched glass.

A black Volvo SUV was parked sideways in front of the garages. The black paint had been waxed and polished to a high sheen. The front entry of the house was a floor of slate under a large gable overhang. There was a double front door with each side four feet wide. The doors were made of carved wood that glistened with thick varnish. Each door had a large, beveled-glass window, acid-etched to depict bears playing in the forest.

Spot rose from his slumber and stared at the house, his nose smudging the rear window. Maybe he sensed the unusual smells of money. Or maybe he wanted to frolic with the frosted bears.

I rolled down the window so he could take in the sights and told him to be good.

I got out, walked up three steps to the slate entry, and looked for a doorbell button or door knocker. The closest approximation was a little brass bear sculpture mounted on the wall to the left of the door. I fingered it and found that it was hinged. I lifted the bear to a standing position and heard what sounded like a bear growling inside the house. I turned to look at Spot and see if he was noticing the growl. But Spot wasn't looking toward me. He probably thought that the electronic bear growl was pretty lame compared to his own full-throated roar.

Spot turned toward the garage.

I turned and saw a man in his sixties walking toward me. He had thick silver hair brushed up and back and a silver van dyke beard. He wore a smooth black leather jacket over a black T-shirt and black jeans. The look and style suggested a high net worth. Put the house and black Volvo in the picture, add some zeroes. Factor in a job called venture capitalist, add more zeroes.

"Mr. Lindholm?" I said. "Owen McKenna."

Lindholm nodded, walked up, shook my outstretched hand. "Please call me Bill."

"Single malt delivery service, Bill," I said as I reached out my left hand and presented the bottle.

"Evelyn working her magic again?" he said.

"If making me think that a single malt might buy me several moments of your time is magic? Yes."

"Ah. I pay her a lot. Good to know she's producing a healthy ROI."

"And I'm happy to provide a small part of the return on investment in Evelyn," I said.

Lindholm gave me a slightly longer look. "Always reassuring to have a financially literate visitor," he said.

"Calling me financially literate would be excessive. I've seen money now and then, but mostly from a long distance."

Bill nodded. He held up the bottle. "Let's go in and do a taste test, make sure this stuff is safe to drink." He turned and looked at Spot hanging his giant head out the Jeep's rear window. Spot was panting, giant tongue flopping.

"Your Harlequin is a big boy. Look at that tongue. What's his name?"

"Take your pick. Spot. Your Largeness. Hey You. No. Stop That."

"When I was growing up in Scarsdale, New York, the neighbor lady had a large fenced lawn and a Harl Dane named Nancy," he said. "The neighbor also had a problem with rabbits in her garden. So she made a rabbit trap by burying a garbage can in the ground so that the top of the can was level with the ground. Curious rabbits would jump down into the garbage can. But these rabbits could only jump up about two feet, not quite high enough to get out of the garbage can. After the lady drove off to work, Nancy would trot across the yard toward the garden. I knew that meant that some rabbit was making a commotion down in the bottom of the garbage can. Nancy would get down on the ground, reach way down into the garbage can, and lift out a rabbit. She'd hold it in her paws, lick it and mother it, and then eventually let it go. The rabbit, freshly cleaned, if a bit traumatized, would head back to the garden to collect some dinner. Later, the neighbor lady would come home and check her garden. Of course, she always noticed the amount of vegetables that had gone missing over the course of the day. So she'd check her rabbit trap, see that it was empty, and throw up her hands in disappointment. She never did figure it out."

Lindholm looked back at Spot. "Big carnivore like that, you'd think they'd eat a rabbit."

"Some smaller, less gentle breeds will eat a rabbit," I said. "But a Dane just thinks a rabbit is a surrogate puppy. Or maybe a squeeze toy that makes an interesting noise if you compress it enough."

"Would your gentle boy like to come inside?"

"I'm sure he'd love it."

I walked over and let Spot out of the Jeep. He ran around, nose to the ground, a look I'd seen when he was tracking an animal. I called him, and he took plenty of time to decide it was okay to abandon the wild for the human experience.

I had him sit and shake hands with Bill Lindholm. When Spot lifted his paw and slapped it down onto Lindholm's outstretched hands, I thought he'd knock the man to the ground.

But Lindholm must have remembered the lessons of Nancy. He braced himself, caught Spot's paw with both hands, and gave it a hearty lift and shake.

Lindholm turned and led us in through the front door. Spot looked around, sniffed the slate outside, then the polished oak inside, then turned to look at me.

"What?" I said to him in a low voice. "You want Architectural Digest for your home, find a money man."

The entry expanded to a wider area that opened to the living room on the right and a hallway on the left. There were several pictures of military men in a jungle camp that appeared to date from the Viet Nam era. Perhaps one of them was Lindholm.

There were lots of framed pictures of bicycle racing, several of them closeups of a man in a skin-tight royal blue outfit. The hair was black instead of silver gray, but the resemblance to Lindholm was obvious.

"What's the more challenging pursuit?" I asked. "Racing two-wheelers or investing in tech companies?"

His answer was immediate. "Investing is both harder and less emotionally rewarding, and the competition is more cutthroat. But I'm better at it than I was at racing bicycles."

I was holding Spot's collar. He pulled forward, his nose working hard, still tracking some animal.

"It's okay to let him go," Lindholm said.

"You're sure? Nothing delicate that his tail can sweep off table tops?"

"As long as he doesn't mind a Bear Market, he'll be fine." Lindholm grinned.

I raised my eyebrows.

Lindholm looked over to a large leather chair in the corner of the living room. Taking up most of it was a giant orange cat. "That's Bear Market. When I first got him, I didn't think I could survive his imperious ways. I realized that dealing with his demands was good survival training for whatever calamity could strike in my day job."

Now I understood what Spot had been smelling outside. "You think a dog is safe around Bear Market?"

"That's funny. He's a seventeen pound cat, and you're worrying about your dog? What does he weigh?"

"One seventy."

"So Bear Market is ten percent of your hound."

"A hound who would probably mother a rabbit," I said. "Anyway, the bigger the dog's nose, the bigger the target for the claws of a cat."

Lindholm made a dismissive wave of his arm through the air. "He'll be fine."

I let Spot go. He trotted over toward Bear Market, slowing as he got close. Bear Market opened his eyes, stared at Spot, and decided, as most cats do with Great Danes, that there was no threat. He shut his eyes and appeared to sleep.

Spot stood at a distance, his tail wagging in slow motion. He turned and looked at me. When I didn't react, Spot turned back to the cat. He took one step forward, then stopped. Spot moved his head left and right, sniffing. His head was bigger than the giant cat. But he knew not to go any closer for the time being.

"Come sit," Lindholm said from over at his bar. "I know you have questions about Yardley LaMotte. But first, we'll check out this whiskey you brought."

I turned away from Spot and walked over to where Lindholm stood at one end of the living room. Four small lights with hand-blown glass shades hung over a mahogany bar. Lindholm walked behind the bar and set out four shot glasses.

"You may recall that back in the seventies, the wine world experienced an earthquake of sorts when one of the big, French, blind taste test competitions for wine was won by a California wine."

"I wasn't around at the time, but I remember learning about it later. I think it was a Stag's Leap cab. The French were astonished, right?"

"Yes. Astonished, chagrined, and excited all at the same time. As was the rest of the world. Well, a few years ago, the same thing happened with single malt whiskey."

"You mean Scotch?"

Lindholm made a little shake of his head. "People assume, wrongly, that the words 'single malt' refer only to Scotch. In fact the name Scotch only means whiskey produced in Scotland. But one can use malted barley to produce whiskey anywhere. If a distillery outside of Scotland makes a malt whiskey and doesn't blend it into mediocrity, it is a single malt whiskey even though it can't be called Scotch."

I understood where he was going. "Let me guess, a non-Scottish distiller of single malt whiskey won a blind taste test competition."

Lindholm's eyes were wide, almost demonic. "Yes! It was very exciting." He reached over to his bar, lifted up a bottle, and handed it to me. "A few years ago, the Best In Glass competition for single malt whiskey was won by Balcones Texas Single Malt Whiskey, an outfit in Waco, Texas." Lindholm pronounced the distiller's name as 'Bal Cone Ease.'

"Really. Were the taste testers from Texas?"

"No!" Lindholm was grinning. "They were British! In Britain. As with the French winemakers in the seventies, the Scottish distilleries were taken aback, blindsided."

He opened the Macallan. "You take your medicine neat?"

"Is there any other way?"

Lindholm beamed. He poured a small amount of Macallan into two of the glasses. Then he poured some Balcones into the other two. He pushed two of the shots toward me. "The Macallan is on the left, Balcones on the right. As our palates are fresh, let's try the Balcones first."

I glanced over at Spot. He was still standing in front of Bear

Market, his nose stretched forward, sniffing. Maybe he'd moved a few inches closer. But he was being as careful as if he were reaching out toward a King Cobra. The cat still appeared asleep.

I took a sip of the Balcones. My mouth felt an explosion of taste.

Lindholm took a larger sip, closed his eyes, leaned his head back a bit, moved it in a slight rotation, swallowed, then audibly breathed out and then back in.

"What do you think?" he said. His eyes were afire.

"First, you should know that I'm no connoisseur. I like Scotch - I mean, single malt whiskey - but I don't have the vocabulary to describe it. This has a very distinct flavor, strong, smoky, warm, fills the sinuses."

"Ah," he said again. "You do have a vocabulary for whiskey. We don't need to identify notes of oak and baked pears and chocolate to know what we like. Now try the Macallan."

We each took a sip.

"Well?" he said.

"To my naive sense, I'd say the Macallan is smoother and not as bold as the Balcones."

"Perfect. You can come drink whiskey with me anytime." Lindholm looked at his watch, a large black timepiece that would go with his car. "Now, how can I help you?"

SEVENTEEN

"Yardley LaMotte hired a helicopter to do some kind of digital scan in the mountains, and he never came back. The chopper was found this morning on a ranch near Markleeville in Alpine County." I decided not to add that I'd witnessed the chopper pull two men off a mountain.

"Evelyn told me he'd gone missing," Lindholm said, "but she didn't know about the chopper. How very strange."

I nodded.

"What can I tell you about Yardley and his robotics business?"

"First, what motivated you to invest in Tahoe Robotics?"

"Same thing that drives all of my investments. I saw potential that wasn't funded. I first met LaMotte at a VC conference, and his genius was manifest. I went in as an angel investor."

"What is a VC conference?"

"A gathering where venture capitalists and entrepreneurs meet. This one was in San Francisco, and as always there was a strong focus on tech startups. The techies give the VCs their elevator pitches. It's basically speed dating between people with ideas and people with the money to fund them. Yardley was clearly a force who wouldn't be stopped. I saw money to be made."

"As an angel investor," I said. "What is that?"

"Typically, when a techie believes he or she has a hot idea, they need some initial funding before they can even start their business. So they ask family and friends and maybe former professors. Stanford. Caltech. MIT. And they often get a few thousand to buy office supplies and a dotcom address to put up a starter website. But of course, they soon need much more. So think of angels as the first-round of serious investors, a source of funding that is one step up from family and friends. Angels will put in more money than family, and, like family, an angel will often invest before the business is even officially started. In fact, the business is often dead in the water until an angel investor comes along."

"So you were Yardley's Nancy."

"What? Oh, of course! Yes, I'm a good Nancy, saving helpless critters from oblivion."

"Why are Nancies called angels?"

Lindholm grinned. "There's no set definition for that. But among my colleagues, we use the term angels to describe putting money into an idea that has nothing solid behind it. No product, no test marketing, no sales contracts, no employees, no evidence that the idea can actually be turned into anything. How could we be anything but angels? In contrast, if the company is already going and generating buzz and has a long line of customers waiting to buy, then we have a lot more to go on. When that happens, we approach those companies as traditional venture capitalists. And we will often put millions into them. But as an angel investor, I put my own money into the entrepreneur's business."

"How is that different from a venture capitalist?"

"Venture capitalists work from a large fund, pooled by many investors. The venture capitalist puts a lot more money into a company, typically several million. The absolute risk in dollars is large, but the risk to the individual venture capitalist is relatively small. It's the reverse with an angel. The total money invested is small, but all of it is the angel's personal money."

"How much is one of these small investments?"

"In this case, I put one hundred thousand into Yardley's Tahoe Robotics."

"May I ask, what do you get for one hundred thousand? A portion of ownership in the company?"

Lindholm sipped his whiskey, swirled it around his mouth, swallowed, once again closing his eyes as if eminently pleased. "Twenty percent," he said.

"What made you go ahead with Yardley's business?"

"Yardley had a novel idea of applying the subscription business model to robotics. I'd never heard of such a thing regarding robotics, and I found it exciting."

"What does that mean, subscription business model?"

"You're probably familiar with it. If you watch your movies from Netflix, you pay a monthly fee and can watch as much as you want. Same with getting your music from Spotify. Amazon readers who pay the monthly fee to Kindle Unlimited can read as many books as they want."

Lindholm gestured toward his front door. "My Volvo out there is a subscription vehicle. It's an automotive version of Netflix. Have you ever rented a car with full insurance coverage?"

"No, but I've heard of it."

"It's expensive, but if your time is expensive, it seems cheap. The rental company gives you a car and a key and that's it. If you get in an accident, you can walk away, regardless of who's at fault. A subscription car is like that. I pay seven hundred fifty a month. For that I get the car and all service and all insurance. And after a specified time, I drive it into the dealer and come back out with a new one. It's like leasing a car but with insurance and everything else included. Other than buying gas, I have no variable expenses. And if a problem arises with the car, they take care of it, whether it's mechanical or a computer glitch. My life is much easier."

"This is what Yardley LaMotte is doing?"

"Not yet, but that is the goal. Robots that you pay for with a monthly fee. As the robot software gets more sophisticated, the software downloads are automatic. When your robot acquires a new ability, you don't have to buy a new robot or pay any more money. It's the same as when Netflix expands their movie selection. It's all part of your monthly fee."

"What did your hundred thousand finance?"

"Yardley explained that he needed to buy two kinds of scanners, a radar and something called a lidar. He said that once he had the scanners, he needed very little else, and his monthly burn rate would be under four thousand dollars."

"Burn rate?"

"The outflow of cash just to make his scans and hire a temp a few hours a week to work on the beta version of his software. All the other necessary work would be Yardley writing the software. The temp would be an editor, checking and testing Yardley's code. Of course, these things change rapidly."

"Lucy told me that not long ago Yardley got an influx from another investor."

"Yes. Anders Henriksson recently put up a bunch of money. Four million, if I recall correctly. Although I understand that half was for stock, ten percent of the company. The other half of it was a loan. Yardley didn't want to sell any more ownership position. I found that an interesting development. Yardley probably told him that he'd let go of a ten percent stake only if Anders also floated him a loan. Yardley wants to ride this growth with just me along for the ride. Then, when Tahoe Robotics hits big, he'll have a bigger stake for himself."

Lindholm continued, "I certainly believe in the potential. Yardley has had inquiries from IBM and Google and Amazon. Two of his professors from Stanford have been trying to convince him to go in with them on a concept. He's already gotten some contracts to supply AI software to a Chinese company. Based on that, he's hired two dozen employees or so. I think they'll eventually be the biggest robotics company in the world. My twenty percent could eventually be huge."

"Interesting that you got twenty percent for one hundred thousand dollars and Anders got only ten percent for two million."

Bill Lindholm smiled. "With highly speculative investments, it's all about when you jump in. You probably know that Anders died, right?"

"Lucy told me."

Lindholm said, "I just heard about it from Yardley last week. He'd been contacted by Anders' brother. Apparently, it was a sudden massive heart attack. A real shame. I didn't much care for Anders, but I respected his business acumen."

"Lucy also told me that the brother explained that he was

Anders' heir, inheriting both the ten percent ownership in Tahoe Robotics and the loan. Apparently, Yardley was behind on the payments. So Anders' brother told Yardley he was going to call the loan and foreclose on the collateral Yardley had pledged. That collateral included Yardley and Lucy's house."

Bill shook his head. "I'm shocked. What a heartless bastard. I'm the first to admit that we play hardball in the money business. But surprising Yardley with this news of calling his loan right after telling him that Anders had died... Wow."

"Can you tell me Anders' brother's name?"

"I have no idea. I know nothing about Anders' personal world. We only bumped into each other at various financial events."

"Did Anders just focus on tech companies?"

"No. He was much less narrow about his approach to investing than most of us VC guys. He invests, he loans, he plays with hedge funds. If he sees a way to make money, he'll even bet on horses. We think of ourselves as VC professionals. Anders was just an old-fashioned loan shark. He even said as much when he was in a joking mood. But what a smart loan shark he was."

"Can you give me Anders' contact information?"

"I don't know it. But of course you could call his company. It's called Reno Discovery Group. An LLC like my company. He's in an office building on Liberty Street in Reno, not far from the Nevada Art Museum."

"Will do. Thanks."

In my peripheral vision, I saw Spot jump back from the chair where Bear Market sat like a king on a throne. Spot's tail was wagging fast. I looked over as Spot turned his head toward me. Checking to see if I'd witnessed his altercation.

"I should be going," Lindholm said. "I've got lots to do before a dinner appointment."

"Thanks much for your help."

I fetched Spot from Bear Market's kingdom. As I brought Spot toward the door, I said, "Any chance you've heard of the Brödraskapet?"

"What's that?"

"A Swedish prison gang."

"No. Never heard of them. Why?"

"They may be involved in Yardley's disappearance."

"That's ridiculous. Yardley is a computer nerd. He's probably never even seen a prison or been to Sweden."

"I agree that it seems ridiculous. One more question. I'll be going to Tahoe Robotics to poke around and ask questions. Is there anyone there you know of that I should talk to?"

"Yes, but with a caveat. One of the guys is Tapper Logan. To hear Yardley tell it, Tapper is a brilliant software engineer, and he knows more than anyone else about Yardley's work. But when I met him, I saw a real psychopath. No empathy. No regard for anyone else. A seemingly deadly focus on what he wants at the expense of everybody. In fact, if you suspect foul play in Yardley's disappearance, you might take a close look at Tapper."

EIGHTEEN

I called Street again.

"Mileage reading?" I asked when she answered.

"Hold on. Fifteen. I'm worn out. Blondie, too. I'm just a mile out from the center of town. What's your schedule?"

"Tahoe Robotics awaits. I could be there an hour or so if that works for you. Your call."

"Fine. I'm going to walk the rest of the way. Call again when you're done. We'll meet after."

"Will do."

I drove to Truckee's downtown, a charming and eclectic collection of 100-year-old buildings dating from the town's early days as a major stop on the transcontinental railroad. It took me several minutes of driving up and down narrow streets to find the Tahoe Robotics building. It was an old brick box a few blocks from the train station. There was no parking nearby, so I parked in a city lot several blocks away and walked back.

One of Truckee's trash and recycling trucks was out, lifting a dumpster over its top, beeping as it backed up, revving its engine to go up the steep streets.

I waited as it stopped in the street in front of me and inhaled a monster load of cardboard boxes.

When it continued on, I crossed the street to my destination.

The entrance to Tahoe Robotics was a standard commercial glass door with a sign on the brick wall to the side that said Tahoe Robotics, with a yellow logo of the letters T and R joined together. Above the Tahoe Robotics sign was the old Drygoods sign Lucy had mentioned. I pulled the door open and walked into a large open room about 25 feet wide and 60 feet deep. It had a profusion of desks and computers, maybe half of which were occupied by people. Several of them had dogs. Several of the dogs looked at me. None of the people seemed to notice.

An L-shaped section of benches defined a small reception area. Multiple bicycles leaned against one wall.

The building's interior walls were exposed brick, a rough surface of various reds with even rougher mortar that had oozed out from the bricks here and there back when the building was originally built. The walls were lit with spotlights that made a pattern of ovals that repeated toward the back of the building. One might expect posters or pictures, but these ovals of light illuminated only bricks.

The lights also lit up a series of steel reinforcement plates and rods painted light gray, earthquake-protection retrofitting that all Californians are familiar with.

Near the entrance door was a small counter with a sign-in book, and next to it a short, squat tripod device, about three feet tall. The primary components were made of stainless steel with contrasting parts in shiny metallic red. At the base of each tripod leg was a pair of small wheels like those on a rolling office chair. At the top of the tripod was a red metallic sphere the size of a basketball. Projecting up out of the top of the sphere was a black tube a foot tall. Mounted on the top of the tube was a smaller sphere the size of a baseball. It had what looked like a camera lens embedded in it. Next to the lens was a tiny, blinking, red light.

As I stepped in from the entrance door, the tripod device moved, rotating a bit. Then it rolled over toward me and stopped about three feet away. The small sphere with the lens turned toward me. The red light blinked faster.

"Good afternoon, sir," the machine said in a feminine voice similar to the one used in iPhones. "Thanks for visiting Tahoe Robotics. My name is Marie. I'm the receptionist. What can I do for you?"

I hesitated, feeling awkward. "Hi, Marie. We've spoken on the phone. I'd like to speak to the person in charge, please."

"That would be me," the robot said. "How can I help you?"

Again, I felt strange. When you speak to people, you generally don't have to focus on how you are communicating. But when you speak to a robot, you have to focus just to find words. I remembered talking to a friend who was around when telephone answering machines were invented. She said that when people initially made calls answered by a machine, they often went mute, unable to speak.

After a few seconds of silence had gone by, the robot said, "Don't worry. You can speak to me in normal sentences. I'm pretty good at partial sentences, too. Just don't try to pinch my butt as I go by."

"A cheeky robot," I said. "I like that."

"I'm not a robot in the way you probably think. You may think I have a bunch of pre-recorded statements I summon at appropriate moments. But the reality is, I form my own sentences in a way not unlike the way you form sentences. So it's best to just think of me as Marie. Your thoughts come to you by way of electrical/chemical activity in your brain. My thoughts come to me by way of similar processes. We're more similar than you might think. If fact, it may be that the biggest difference between us isn't our different shapes but simply that my processor and memory circuits are not made up of biological cells like yours."

"And I walk while you glide," I said. "You are certainly smart."

"Thank you. I am the result of the latest advances in machine learning."

"What does that mean?"

"Machine learning refers to when a computer applies algorithms to data, analyzes the results, and then makes its own adjustments about how to proceed with other data."

"That sounds good. But I suspect it's very complicated."

Marie paused, just like a human. "Somewhat. My concertmaster has me focused on speech. Speech recognition is easiest. Speech synthesis in terms of forming speech sounds is also relatively easy. You know these characteristics from your interaction with virtual assistants such as Apple's Siri, Amazon's Alexa, Google's Now, Microsoft's Cortana."

I didn't use any of them, but I didn't say that to Marie.

She continued. "Despite their abilities with speech, free-form conversational skills are much more difficult. We're not there, yet. But I am on the cutting edge of this linguistic frontier. I use a kind of unsupervised learning that involves recurrent neural networks using the Hidden Markov Model."

"Oh, sure, I knew that," I said.

"I'm not excellent with my skills. I'm like an African Grey Parrot. I'm very good at imitating how people talk. But I still struggle with conversation."

"You sound expert in all ways."

"I have great difficulty inferring meaning from creative slang spoken with an unusual accent."

"Me, too. Who is your concertmaster?"

"Tapper Logan. He is a coding genius. He believes I've caught a virus. I sometimes suffer from back propagation problems. Maybe that is the virus."

"What does that mean?"

"Let's just call it getting stuck in a conversational loop."

"I'm curious. As robots get more and more like people, do they begin to look for reward? Does a robot ever get paid for doing a good job?"

"You pose an interesting question. I do not get paid. But perhaps that is coming. When I'm capable, I will prefer a bit of coin. Dollar bills are old."

I pointed at the robot's wheels. "I've used roller skates. They can be quite unstable."

"I hope that doesn't bother you. You can lean on me and I won't move. I'm solid as a rock."

"A rock from a roller. Now I'm all shook up."

"I'm sorry," the robot said.

"Just a pun. It's an Elvis song."

"I don't understand some puns."

"Not the way you roll, huh?"

The robot paused. "I sense that this is your humor. That's great. Probably funny, too. I'll fetch a human. Please give me a minute."

I heard what sounded like a faint telephone ring. I realized that the robot was calling someone from a hidden phone, which of course was just another circuit in its brain. Marie's brain.

"Hello?" came the faint answer.

"Marie calling to request human intervention at the entrance. I have a visitor who could use help."

"With a pun issue," I said.

"With a pun issue," Marie repeated.

"Not the way she rolls," I said.

"I roll very… I roll very… I roll very…" Marie kept repeating the phrase.

"I'll be right there," the faint voice said.

"I roll very… I roll very…"

A small blonde woman with short, straight hair came forward from the center of the room. In a different mood, her eyebrows, which sloped severely downward toward the bridge of her nose, would have made her look stern. Instead, she looked worried. Maybe Marie was her colicky baby. She stepped through a swing gate and popped open a little hinged cover on the back of Marie's basketball sphere chest. The woman flipped some type of switch and the robot stopped saying, "I roll very…" The blinking red light went out.

"I'm so sorry I crashed Marie," I said.

"Don't worry. She caught a cold and that's affected her OS."

"A cold and OS. I'm lost."

"You know how computers get viruses. That traveler malware that came through upset her operating system. Did you say the words 'she rolls'?"

"Yes. Sorry if that was bad."

"The virus created a weird secondary effect and altered her roll response. One of our algorithms needs to be reworked. In the meantime, I'll wait ten seconds and then do a reboot. That will help temporarily. What can I do for you?"

"My name's Owen McKenna. I was asked by Lucy LaMotte to stop by."

"I'm Sal. You must be the person she called about. Lucy said you're an investigator. And I saw your name on Marie's log. She continuously updates my computer."

"Is she really a she?" I asked, feeling silly for asking it.

"I suppose," Sal said. "What makes a she, anyway? And does the he-she thing make a difference if you're not interested in a romantic relationship?"

"Good questions. I don't know the answers. First, I should ask if you've had any word from Yardley."

Sal shook her head. "Nothing."

"Lucy said I should probably start by talking to Tapper Logan."

"Tapper is our concertmaster."

"I heard that from Marie. She also said he's a genius."

Sal sighed and shut her eyes for a moment. "He's indoctrinated Marie with his megalomania." Sal gestured toward the back of the room. "He's back in the rear corner. At Yardley's desk."

I turned and saw a long-haired man in his mid-twenties sitting in a desk chair, leaning back, feet up on the desk, looking at his phone, doing the thumb dance that probably meant he was texting. He glanced up and looked at me across the room, then went back to his phone and renewed his texting, or whatever he was doing, with intensity.

I said to Sal, "I told Lucy that I'd like to look through Yardley's things, and she said I could do whatever I wanted. Are you okay with that?"

"She told me that, too. We, uh, want Lucy to be comfortable. She's not really part of our operation. But we respect that she should have some say in how things proceed in Yardley's absence. So, yes, look around or whatever you do. But may I ask that you just look and not disturb or move things out of place?"

"Of course. What about Yardley's computer? Do you have access to that?"

"Yardley is always leashed to his laptop. It goes where he goes.

So we haven't seen it."

"Right. Does he have non-computer files?"

"You mean paper stuff? Yes, even total techies like Yardley have paper. See those three tall, black file cabinets in the corner? Those are his."

"I might need to take photos of documents if I find anything useful. But you can be sure that I'm not interested in Tahoe Robotics' proprietary information."

"I understand. Do you think harm has come to Yardley?"

"I don't know. I only know what Lucy told me, that Yardley has never disappeared before. Can you think of any reason why he might have gone AWOL?"

Sal shook her head.

"Can you think of anyone who might have wanted to harm Yardley?"

Another head shake.

"Did he have disagreements with anyone?"

Sal made a grimace and looked down at the floor for a moment. She turned a bit as if to face as much away from the others as possible and spoke in a soft voice.

"Yardley had disagreements with everyone. There's no one here he hasn't argued with. Everyone will tell you that he is one of the most difficult people there is. I'm sorry to say that. But Yardley will even acknowledge it. We try to chalk it up to his genius. Yardley calls himself the conductor of this orchestra. But the truth is that most of us think of him more like a feudal lord. A tyrannical feudal lord."

"Is there anyone here who feels he or she really understands Yardley's work? Or maybe a better question is whether there is anyone here who thinks they are as smart as Yardley and as a result might resent his position of authority."

Sal glanced toward the back of the room for just a moment, then seemed to rivet her eyes on me. "You didn't hear this from me, but Tapper has actually said that he knows more about robotics software than Yardley does. And he thinks Yardley is making a significant strategic mistake in how he thinks of robotics."

"Tapper Logan, the young man sitting at Yardley's desk."

"Right."

"What could he know about computer software that Yardley doesn't?"

"Well, his current focus is soft robotics. Tapper thinks soft robotics is the future and that Yardley is hopelessly stuck in the dark ages of rigid robotics."

"Is it possible to explain the difference to someone who doesn't have a Ph.D. in robotics?"

"Of course." Sal set her hand on top of the robot in front of me. It reminded me of an adult patting a kid on the head. "Marie, here, is a rigid robot. Her internal frame is rigid as is her outside. She's like a car. She's very good at what she does. But she can't wriggle her way into tight spaces. And she can't slither down into a hole or climb up a tree. And most of all, she isn't delicate. If I told her to pick up a raspberry, she would. But she isn't able to moderate her strength to any degree, and the raspberry would squish and be useless. In comparison, think of a soft robot like an octopus. A soft robot can potentially do all the things that an octopus can. Softly and delicately."

"A soft robot can pick raspberries?" I asked.

"Yes. Amazingly well. Soft robots can do things the way people can, especially when it comes to gripping things without destroying them. Soft robots can sort eggs as well as delicate fruit. They can fill orders for a wide variety of produce. In the future, soft robots will work with people, helping people move, helping them get dressed, doing jobs that used to require a skilled nurse. Tiny soft robots will help surgeons inside human bodies, crawling through a body to work on an area that needs repair or replacement."

"Interesting. Thanks for the explanation. I'd like to talk to Tapper Logan. Do you need to let him know first?"

"No," she said. "Help yourself. Head on back." Her tone telegraphed dislike for Tapper. I wondered if she hoped that I would bring some discomfort into his world.

"When I'm done talking to Tapper," I said, "is there anyone

else I should talk to?"

"You might want to talk to Andy Strom. He's one of Tahoe Robotics' vice presidents. Tapper has a higher effective rank in the company. But Andy has a higher actual rank."

"That seems peculiar," I said.

"Andy actually had his own startup and sold it to Yardley about six months ago. Part of the deal was a position of vice president in this company."

"What is his focus?"

"You mean like, vice president of marketing? Or vice president of finance?" Sal stopped. I thought I saw a hint of a grin. "Maybe you should ask him."

I raised my eyebrows.

"Andy actually jokes that he's vice president of nothing. That he has a title and nothing more. And, truth be told, he pretty much just comes to work and hangs out and works on his own projects. He's a very creative person. And his contributions to Tahoe Robotics have been significant. But unlike some employees, he never brags or acts important."

"Is he here today?"

Sal nodded. "He's in the other rear corner."

I glanced to the back of the room. "The blond guy bent over his computer keyboard?"

"Yeah. Where Tapper Logan flaunts his bad boy attitude, Andy Strom is one of the studious ones. He keeps a low profile. He's more interested in writing innovative software. Whereas Tapper is more interested in acting the role of software superstar."

"Is Tapper an actual software wunderkind?"

"In his own mind, sure. In other people's assessment, not so much. Tapper spends his day on his iPhone. Andy spends his on his Mac. You can probably guess which guy gets more work done."

"Thanks."

NINETEEN

I walked past Marie and headed back between desks that seemed randomly placed. A Golden Retriever walked up to me, wagging.

"Tanya, come back here," a woman said.

The dog paused but didn't retreat. I was too interesting. I skirted past two desks, one of which belonged to a person with a tape fetish. There were a half-dozen dispensers with every kind of sticky-backed material: Scotch tape in two widths, masking tape, blue drafting tape, narrow striping tape, and two-inch packing tape. Apparently computer geeks still found non-electronic stuff useful.

The next desk was the corner desk where Yardley was reported to work.

I walked up in front of the desk. Tapper lounged in the desk chair, staring at the phone in his lap, his hiking boots up on the desk surface.

I waited a bit. It was obvious I was there, in his field of vision. But he ignored me.

"Excuse me, I'm looking for Tapper Logan. Is that you?"

He still didn't respond.

I said, "Lemme guess. You're watching Youtube videos because you really need the creative inspiration to cope with life as a computer nerd, which is so hard you can barely get through your crushing routine. It would be easier to pick cotton in the sun twelve hours a day, right?"

"Oh, that's good," Tapper said, still not looking at me. "Really inspired. Much better than asking me if I'm hard at work."

"Are you hard at work?"

"No," he said as if it were cool to stake out such a bad-boy attitude. "I'm not paid to work. I'm a two-level coder, paid to think. I'm always thinking hard."

"Thinking about software?"

He tapped on his phone, then swiped three or four times. "Software is such a cute phrase. I write code. Who are you, anyway?" He still hadn't looked up.

"I'm a private cop, hired by Lucy to find out what happened to Yardley. Considering your rude resistance, you are my first clue that something is wrong in this company. Which makes me wonder how hard I'd have to push you to crack your exterior."

"Nice noirish, old guy metaphor. If you were a coder, you'd be one of those point-five-level geek wannabes who spend their time looking for smugs."

I thought about it, trying to discern meaning.

"I'll save you the trouble," Tapper said. "Smugs are the type of coding bugs the only consequence of which is that they're found and identified by people who think they're smart but are, in fact, idiots. So if you want to burn up some more of Yardley's money, keep standing there flapping your mouth. I'll put it on my work log as smug mining. Yardley pays me five hundred per day. You've already spent one hundred of that."

"Have you found out what happened to Yardley?" I asked.

"I didn't know anything happened."

"Would you have your feet up on his desk if he were here like normal?"

"There is no normal for Yardley. Now I should get back to work. You're a pest, and you should go away and leave the smartest one percent of the species to do their work, making a world for the ninety-nine percent whose only care is to walk into Starbucks and buy their lattes by pressing a button on their phone. They don't have a clue what is behind that process. Well, let me tell you, geezer boy, people like me - or maybe I should say, people who want to be like me - are the ones who create that world of convenience. We write the code. The philistines drink the coffee."

"I'm wondering," I said, "if your superior skills make you so resentful of people like Yardley grabbing all the attention, that you would try to undermine his accomplishments. Or maybe even get rid of him."

Tapper Logan looked up at me for a moment. "Yardley LaMotte has no real accomplishment other than being able to win the State Fair hotdog-eating championship. Now, I have more thinking to do, and you are interrupting that."

"Unfortunately, I need you to move so I can look at Yardley's space."

Tapper Logan flicked at his phone as if he were flicking away a bug like me. Or maybe a smug.

"Please," I said.

Tapper looked down at his phone, doing a good imitation of ignoring me.

I turned around and pulled the packing tape dispenser off the desk behind me, then walked around Yardley's desk and stood behind his chair.

Tapper was slow to react, still trying desperately to act the part of the hard guy. I stuck the end of the packing tape onto the chair back and, with looping motions, quickly ran two circles of tape around Tapper's chest and the chair back. While he seemed frozen with shock, I seized the moment to tape his arms to the arms of the chair. His phone clattered to the floor.

Tapper lifted his feet off the desk and stepped down in a feeble attempt to stand up. I bent down and stuck the tape to the vertical chair post. I gave the chair a spin, and held the tape as Logan Tapper went around in a circle, and the tape looped around his feet and the chair's vertical post, trapping him.

"What is this?! What are you doing?! Are you crazy?!"

I set the tape dispenser down, bent over in front of his chest and reached one arm across his body to the far side of his chair. I picked up the chair with him in it and carried him through the office toward the front door.

He screamed at me. "I demand you stop this! This is assault! Kidnapping! I'll have you arrested!" He tried to kick with his legs and pull up with his arms. But the tape limited his movement to jerks.

Everyone in the office stared at us. Several stood up. Two or three dogs wagged vigorously.

No one tried to intervene.

Sal's eyes were wide open as I went past. She looked astonished and more than a little pleased.

It was a little tight getting Tapper and his chair through the narrow opening at the reception area. I noticed Marie's red light was back to blinking.

"May I help you, sir?" she said.

"No thanks. I'm just taking out the trash."

Tapper tried to flex his arm and stretch the tape enough to grab her head, but his hand slipped off.

"You're going down, dude!" he shouted, his voice somewhat muffled by my armpit. "I'm going to sue you until you bleed from your eyeballs."

I turned around and went backward through the front door, pushing it open with my butt.

Out on the sidewalk, Tapper's screaming intensified. "Help! I'm being kidnapped! This man is a violent terrorist!" I shifted my grip so my armpit did a better job of covering his mouth.

My arms were starting to shake from the effort, but I thought I was good for another minute. I walked to the curb, nodding and smiling at the few passersby and one or two drivers who seemed to notice. I watched the traffic, looking for a good moment.

I saw my opportunity in the form of a waste recycling pickup. It had a dumpster on its front end. Its relatively small size allowed it to navigate streets that were too narrow for the big garbage trucks. It was the satellite doing errands for the mother ship. As it crawled past me, I lifted Tapper and his chair and dropped the combo into the dumpster.

When I walked back to the Tahoe Robotics building, all of the employees seemed to be lined up at the front windows, grins on their faces. Marie's little red light was blinking faster than normal.

TWENTY

I smiled at the assembled group, nodded at Marie, and walked back to Yardley's desk. Probably, Sal had told the group the basics, that I was there at Lucy's request, looking for any clue that might tell us where Yardley had gone, and that I would be poking around Yardley's things.

I started with the left-most of three black file cabinets.

The top drawer was filled with legal-sized file folders. They had labels with names that made no sense to an ex-cop. I flipped through some of them. They were filled with papers printed with numbers and symbols. It was like peering into the tomb files of an advanced civilization that had gone extinct. I could grasp that the information contained in the files had order and process and, thus, some kind of value. But it was like looking at a modern version of stones carved with hieroglyphics. An alien world run by an alien government driven by alien power sources and focused on alien goals. None of which could be comprehended by an ordinary human.

I shut the drawer and pulled out the second one, trying not to succumb to the numbness and dislocation that coal miners feel when they take the tour of NASA's rocket science laboratory. I was pretty good with a shovel and pick. But those tools are worthless in the new world.

The second drawer yielded more of the same. I couldn't even discern the subject.

The third and fourth drawers had files with English words in the labels. A significant improvement. But inside the folders were more printouts with numbers and mathematical symbols.

I turned to the next file cabinet.

The top drawer had more of the same.

The middle drawer had more of the same.

The third drawer, way back to the rear, had something different.

There was a folder with a label that was handwritten. It said, 'RE LLC.'

I understood a little about Limited Liability Companies. They were a type of corporation that gave the owner some liability protection. From my limited understanding, they were designed in part to protect owners from frivolous lawsuits. The version I'd heard was the person who buys coffee from a coffee shop, spills it on themselves, and claims they were burned. So they sue the coffee shop owner, saying it's the owner's fault for serving coffee that was hot enough to burn them.

If the coffee shop owner has put official ownership of the shop into an LLC, that helps protect the coffee shop owner from a court settlement that could otherwise decide to award the business owner's entire bank account to the person who spilled the coffee.

I also knew that an LLC obscures the ownership of the entity in question, and it's hard to sue the owner when you don't know who that is. It's also hard to try to take away someone's assets if you don't know what they are.

As I looked at the file, I wondered if the letters RE LLC could refer to Real Estate Limited Liability Company.

If Yardley, or his company, had real estate in an LLC, the second scenario seemed more likely.

I flipped through multiple pages and saw a few things that seemed familiar. I realized that they looked something like the sales contract I'd signed years ago when I was on the SFPD and I bought my cabin in Tahoe as a future summer vacation cabin, unaware that life would change such that I would decide to quit the department and move to snow country to live full time in a garage-less cabin that was half the size of my small apartment in the East Bay. Half the size, but paid for. When I suddenly quit my paycheck, the attraction of no rent or mortgage was beyond my descriptive abilities.

But while the pages I was looking at in Yardley's office had the fine print that specified endless cover-your-ass contingencies common to real estate sales, none of them had any property description or address. And there were no mentions of real estate companies or title companies.

Maybe the pages weren't about real estate at all.

Then I thought about private sales. When people do their property sales through traditional realtors and title companies, the information is shared with endless agencies and websites and databases. Everyone from the Multiple Listing Service to the national Zillow website ends up displaying the information, complete with pictures of the property, address, price asked and price paid. And that information is archived online for eternity.

In an effort to maintain some privacy, many wealthy people sidestep the process by doing things the old fashioned way. A seller and a buyer find each other without engaging sales agencies. Instead, they meet through friends or business associates. A person puts the word out that they are interested in buying or selling something. A meeting is arranged with no intermediary. A deal is made with no broker.

Counties put the basics of real estate sales into the public record. But when no commercial agency is collecting a commission, no one is publicizing the information and using it to brag about their ability to make real estate deals. And if the buyers and sellers are LLCs or other business entities, the transaction avoids notice by nearly everyone.

I shut the file drawer and moved to the bottom one.

That drawer was mostly empty. It had a few files with more pages of fine print. It all appeared to be boilerplate, with inscrutable terms that only a lawyer specializing in contract law could understand. I flipped through the pages and was about to shut the drawer when something caught my eye. I flipped back until I found the page.

It was one of the pages dense with fine print. But there was a section at the bottom that said APN. I thought about my own cabin and tax records and wondered if APN could refer to

Assessor's Parcel Number.

Printed next to it were three groups of three numerals, all in six-point type.

Without making a show, I slipped my phone out of my pocket and took a close-up picture. It wasn't critical that I be surreptitious. But I didn't want to advertise that I'd found something that might be significant.

I put my phone away and continued to look through file drawers. I found nothing else of note.

I moved away from the file cabinets and went through Yardley's desk drawers. The only stuff to see was some desk detritus. A calculator, some pens, three yellow pads of paper, an old iPod and ear buds, a box of paper clips, a mechanical pencil, a spiral notebook with only a few pages left, a coffee cup with the Squaw Valley logo.

I stood up and saw that the other man I'd intended to talk to, Andy Strom, had left.

I walked over to where Sal was working in front of an oversized Mac screen. It had an image of a tree-type flow chart.

"Andy Strom left?" I said.

Sal nodded. "Yeah. Was I supposed to make him wait? Sorry if that screwed you up. He'll be here tomorrow morning if you want. But I don't know how long. Would you like his phone number so you don't waste a trip?"

"Yeah, please."

She wrote it down on her business card and handed it to me.

"Thanks very much for your help. By the way, if Tapper comes back with the cavalry, he can contact me through Lucy."

"Or," she said, thoughtfully, "I might not even be able to remember your name or if Lucy was the person who told me about you. I've been working very hard recently, and my short-term memory has been failing."

"Thanks, Sal."

I left. Back in the Jeep, I called Street.

"You run a marathon?"

"No. My meter says we're only at nineteen miles."

"Wow. Sounds like exercise to me. Where should I find you?"

"I'm here in downtown Truckee. I found a coffee at Dark Horse Coffee Roasters. Now I'm at Word After Word bookshop," she said. "Pull up in front."

"I know where that is. See you there in a few minutes."

I drove down the short hill and paused in front of the store. Street and Blondie pushed out of the door and climbed into the Jeep.

Street held a book in her hand.

"Find a good story?" I asked.

"I hope so. Some mystery that takes place in Tahoe of all places. I'll let you know if it's any good."

Spot seemed interested in various scents he could divine from Blondie's travels. But after 19 miles, Blondie would have none of it. She curled up on one end of the back seat and immediately went to sleep. I drove us all home, telling Street about my visits with Lucy LaMotte and Bill Lindholm and a robot named Marie.

After dropping Street and Blondie off, I went up the mountain to my cabin and called Vince.

"Any communication from the kidnappers?" I asked when he answered.

"None. What about you?"

"Not yet. But I had a question. You mentioned the robotics guy who came to Jon's school. Did Jon say what the man's name was?"

"No. He just said he was kind of a wild man, interesting and smart."

"What school does Jon go to?"

"It's in Truckee. You want the number?"

"Yeah."

Vince gave it to me, and I said goodbye.

As I dialed the school, I thought it would be best if I didn't start them talking about a missing student. Schools are extremely wary of anyone other than parents showing much interest in students. It was probably a moot point anyway, as I didn't expect anyone to be at the school in the evening.

I was wrong. A woman answered.

So I approached it from the standpoint of the missing Truckee businessman.

"My name's Owen McKenna," I said to the woman who answered. "I'm an investigator looking into what I hope is the temporary absence of the owner of Tahoe Robotics, which is not far from your school. The man's name is Yardley LaMotte. His wife Lucy says that he recently gave a talk at a local school, but she couldn't remember which one. We're trying to retrace Mr. LaMotte's steps over the last week or so, and I wonder if it was your school he visited."

"Why, yes, it was just a little over a week ago. The kids loved him. I hope there is no connection between his disappearance and our school?"

"No, not at all. This is just routine legwork, mapping out a person's movements. This information helps. Thanks much."

It was getting late. I thawed out part of a leftover pizza, broke up one piece into little bits, and stirred it into Spot's chunked-sawdust kibble. When I gave him the okay, he lowered his head and looked down into the bowl, his eyelids drooping and his jowls hanging. Then he raised his head and looked at my pizza on the table, large solid pieces.

"What, you feel guilty? I'm forcing myself to eat pure, boring pizza unenhanced by delicious dog food?" Spot furrowed his brow. "I always give you the best in the house because I'm selfless." I pointed at his dog bowl and snapped my fingers. "Go ahead and eat. Don't feel guilty. I'll manage."

Despite his guilt, Spot finished before me.

Next, I pulled out my phone, and looked at the photo I'd snapped of Yardley's real estate file. I expanded the tiny picture until I could see the numbers. I wrote them down and opened my laptop. It took some digging, but I eventually found a property search page on the website for Nevada County, the county that includes Truckee. The search page showed a parcel number pattern that didn't match what I had. It allowed seven digits. My number had nine.

Just to be sure, I typed in the number I'd photographed in Yardley's file.

It produced nothing.

The county just south of Nevada County was Placer County.

After more searching, I found a website page where I could search on parcel numbers. This one took nine digits, just like what I had.

I typed in my number.

It came back with an unusual address:

Rural Route Creek View Terminus

Placer Tahoe Station

Tahoe City, CA   96145

I pulled up a Google Maps page and plugged in the address.

It came up with a message that said it couldn't find the address.

I tried to search for a map on the Placer County website, but there was nothing. I explored every other option I could find but with no success.

It seemed I'd have to drive down to Auburn, the county seat.

Maybe I could eventually find a piece of property that connected to the number I found in Yardley's file. But that didn't seem especially promising.

Instead, I thought it would be better to see what I could learn about the gang members who took Vince's kid.

The Brödraskapet gang.

TWENTY-ONE

I dialed Diamond Martinez.

"Sí," he answered.

"Am I interrupting?"

"I'm making tacos, drinking beer, listening to old Santana records. Of course you're interrupting."

"May I pick your brain about Swedish gangs?" I said.

"If it's okay that I continue working on this taco filling."

"The criminal who is causing my current case…"

"The kidnapper," Diamond interrupted.

"He mentioned a Swedish gang. I'm curious how a Swedish gang could end up doing anything in Tahoe. Naturally, I thought I'd call you."

"Because if I were pale instead of brown, and tall instead of not so tall, and talked with a funny accent, and had an unhealthy desire to eat lutfisk, you'd think I was Swedish, and that, combined with my perspicacity about all things criminal, would make me seem like an information source on Scandinavian crooks."

"Is the lutfisk you mention like the lutefisk Norwegians eat?" I asked.

"Ja, korrekt," Diamond said. "The same, smelly, gelatinous, lye-dissolved fish slime. The Scandinavians beat out even the Scots for worst foods ever invented."

"Wait. My ancestors were Scots and they invented Scotch. How could you slam their tastes?"

"Haggis sausage."

"Oh, that," I said. "Well, what would you do with leftover eyeballs and ears and lips and other such animal parts that don't look so good on a plate compared to a Porterhouse steak?"

"Throw it out," Diamond said.

"Good point. Anyway, only because Mexican cuisine is the best do I forgive your attitude toward my great grandpa's breakfast. So any clue how Swedish gang members could end up in our little mountain paradise?"

"In specific, no. In general, yes." He paused.

I waited.

"Sorry, these cherry tomatoes are slippery," he said over the phone. He made another grunt, which was followed by a loud metallic clink. "There, that'll teach 'em to lie still. Does this outfit have a name?"

"Yeah, although I don't know how to pronounce it. I'll try. They're called The Brödraskapet, with one of those umlaut things over the O."

"I know about them," Diamond said. Then, "Hold on, gotta open this bag of shredded cheddar." In another moment, "I put the phone on speaker. I seem to recall that the Brödraskapet is a prison gang in a maximum security Swedish prison. Bad dudes, from what I hear."

"Anything in particular I should know about them?"

"Just another group of loser guys trying to find direction and making bad choices. These guys set themselves apart by carrying karambit knives."

I said, "Having gone private just a few years ago, I guess I'm already out of touch with the latest trends in nastiness. What's a karambit knife?"

"A wicked weapon developed in Indonesia, illegal in most places, and used by certain military forces. It has a quality that makes it very difficult for a forensic pathologist to identify any cut made by a karambit. I learned about them at a seminar for cops who deal with deadly gangs. The end of the karambit knife's handle has a circular opening that fits over the index finger like a ring. The handle is squeezed in the fist, and the short blade comes out from the fist next to the little finger. So you can stab with it the same way you'd pound your fist on a table. The blade is curved like a four-inch claw. If you hold your fist down at your side, the blade points to the rear and curves down. In many situations, a person can hold it in their fist and no one notices the blade."

"That certainly sounds dangerous."

"No kidding. Like all knives, it can be stabbed into a victim, the power intensified by the finger hole in the grip. But what makes the karambit horrific is that the design is such that one can hold it while punching. And if a punch is modified into a sweeping arc, the trailing blade will cut deeply through whatever it strikes, the most common target being an opponent's neck. There is no practical purpose for a karambit knife beyond killing humans. At the seminar, they showed us some disgusting videos and, afterward, most of the cops who'd watched it looked ill."

"So The Brödraskapet get their tricks from Indonesia."

"You'd think," Diamond said. "But the reality is they probably get their tricks from the same place as most other gang members. It's a terrible blight my people have to face, but almost half of all gang members are Hispanic. Drives me and my Hispanic friends crazy. It's probably the same craziness that good Italians experience when they try to understand why a majority of mafia members are Italian."

I said, "You're saying that the worst gang stuff going is invented by Hispanic crime lords. Other gangs all over the world pick it up from them."

"Right."

"Is this because the Hispanic gangs are so good at what they do?" I asked.

"No. The thing to remember regarding those who adopt other people's behavior is that the appeal of taking on the behavior of a distant and discreet group seems to exist independently of whether or not that behavior has any redeeming qualities."

"You mean, Swedish gangs adopt characteristics of South Central L.A. gangs because they're cool, not because they have any practical value?"

"Yeah," Diamond said.

"Then what about the stolen funds and payoff money that accrues to those who violently intimidate people?"

"Ah, the usefulness of theft. Hard to dismiss that," Diamond said. "But no. It's more of a copycat situation. See it. Copy it. Spread it. Look what that gang over there does. We could do that, too, and then we'd really be scary. Never mind if it's useful or stupid. In fact, as is often the case, the more stupid the behavior, the more it seems to appeal."

"You think gangbangers are stupid?" I asked.

"Sí. Clever, but stupid. If some intelligent alien species ever makes an assessment of humanity, they will focus on the stupid as in, 'Why in the world would such clever creatures do such stupid things?' But of course, it's not just crooks who engage in stupid behavior."

"Is this a dark-thought moment?" I asked.

"Maybe," Diamond said. "But I have some bright-looking taco shells almost ready to come out of the oven. I think they need me."

"Spot would like you to be his keeper," I said.

"When you're done with him, I'll take him. But only if you provide an endowment sufficient to cover his food bill in perpetuity."

"And why would this gang come to Tahoe?" I asked.

"Same reason they go anyplace. It's a ripe new territory."

"So what is my takeaway regarding the Brödraskapet?" I asked.

"Assume the Swedish gang has chosen the worst Hispanic gangs as role models. Conclude that they are therefore very dangerous, very demented, and very lacking in any morality."

"A cheerful thought to take to bed," I said.

"No thought about gangs is cheerful. Not even locking them away, because they organize in prison and take over. Prison wardens everywhere have their hands tied by gangs. In some cases, they work for the gangs and are on their payroll, and the lives of their spouses and children are dependent on their complicity."

"A reassuring thought," I said.

We said goodbye and hung up.

TWENTY-TWO

I got on my computer and Googled "Brödraskapet gang Northern California."

There were multiple websites on prison gangs. One listed the "Top Ten Badass Prison Gangs in California." The Brödraskapet gang was on the list. The website detailed their main focus. Murder, Kidnapping, Extortion, Arms Trafficking. A usual list of fun activities for violent dirtballs. But there was no mention of the gang leader, whether at the international level or the Tahoe level.

I skimmed through some of the websites. Several had links to gun websites where they proclaimed that sales of any weapon were available "no background check and no questions asked."

But if Jon Cooper's kidnapping was connected to the disappearance of Yardley LaMotte, it seemed my case might be about computers or software.

Could the Brödraskapet gang be that sophisticated? Could this entire thing involving Yardley LaMotte be about computer crime? Because Yardley's business was computer-focused, it made sense as a possibility.

The glitch in my comprehension was still that this all required organization and maybe even smarts on the part of the criminals. And what I'd seen and heard of the men who made Vince take them up the mountain revealed a certain discipline but no identifiable smarts. Then I remembered that, during my art forgery case, there was a gang leader who was very bright, never mind the men who did the gang's dirty work. It could be the same with this case, a smart leader manipulating gang members into doing his bidding. But that didn't give me any more useful information. And it didn't seem that there was an official website for the gang.

I drank a beer to clear my head, pacing back and forth across my tiny cabin. Spot looked puzzled at my motion for a bit, then went back to sleep.

Maybe the gang wasn't using the word Brödraskapet. I searched on the English version, The Brotherhood.

Presto. Just to check, I searched the page for Brödraskapet. The Swedish word was down at the bottom in a sentence that said, 'We salute our Swedish Spirit Brothers, the Brödraskapet.'

I went back to the top of the page.

There was a big banner across the top.

THE BROTHERHOOD PRINCIPLES.

Superimposed on the words was the silhouette of a military rifle.

The principles were listed down the left side of the page. There were just four.

1 - Resist Authority: The one-world government is coming. They have already taken your freedom. Next, they will take your guns.

2 - Ready Your Weapons: You will need many, and you will need lots of ammo.

3 - Stockpile Food and Water: Visit survivalist websites for details.

4 - Identify Your Brothers: They are the only ones you can trust when the government soldiers come for you.

The principles were followed by several paragraphs about the evils of government. The focus was partly on survivalist preparations for the coming apocalypse and partly on how criminal activity was the moral obligation of Spirit Brothers.

The website wording said,

'Breaking laws is the only way to undermine the corrupt plutocracy that controls the country.'

I had to read farther to find comments that reminded me of what a plutocracy was: government by the wealthy who, according to the website, controlled everything: business, banking, schools, courts, and government.

I clicked on some links to other pages that ranted in some detail about these subjects.

There was one page that was different.

At the top was the word Marketplace.

It was vaguely like the wantads for jobs in a newspaper. The fine print said listings were free to post, but would be edited to avoid inflaming the socialist stooges who work for the government. Under that, it said respondents' replies would also be edited. It further explained that with all exchanges, neither party's email addresses would be revealed to each other or anyone else, and that all emails go through a Tor network and are untraceable. Correspondents would need to assess their mutual suitability and work out their projects and pay agreements among each other.

There was also a paragraph of qualifiers and disclaimers. The Brotherhood Marketplace assumed no responsibility for anything relative to agreements struck using the website.

The Brotherhood Marketplace said all payments would be made in bitcoin. Employers would pay the Brotherhood Marketplace, and the Brotherhood Marketplace would in turn forward bitcoin payments to vendors, minus a small fee equal to 2% of each transaction.

I scanned some of the ads.

Wanted: Bodyguard. Imposing size and clean-cut style matters more than experience.

Wanted: Safecracker. Business opportunity to make easy money. Huge potential. Must know bank vaults.

Wanted: Hacker, expert in breaking encryption techniques.

Wanted: Enforcer/persuader. Prefer biker look. Must have own weapons manufactured before World War II. No Tactical Tupperware. Weapons that can't be traced preferred.

Wanted: Clean-up specialist who can render a crime scene spotless.

Wanted: Single-engine, float-plane pilot.

Wanted: Military weapons expert. Need to acquire rocket launcher and grenade launcher and all related equipment and ordnance.

Wanted: Actor/impersonator. Must play convincing investment banker with hedge fund experience.

Wanted: Abduction expert. Must have experience. Pay is commission percentage of revenue.

Wanted: Avalanche explosives expert. Focus is small dynamite charges hard to trace. No Plastic.

It was apparent that someone could design and plan a wide range of illegal projects and find people to do the job, all while remaining unknown.

Like the people behind the abduction of Vince's kid. Or the disappearance of Yardley LaMotte.

What a wonderful world of possibilities for those with no ethical compass.

TWENTY-THREE

In the morning, I invited Diamond for coffee at my office. He showed up in his uniform.

I poured him a mug. He sniffed it, then held it out to Spot. "Smell okay to you?"

Spot sniffed it and wagged.

"Okay for the hound, okay for me," Diamond said.

"Last night, I read a Brotherhood gang website," I said. "It has a section where guys advertise their services and can connect with people who want to employ them. The website company explains how they pay them in bitcoin. It's set up so everyone can stay anonymous. I'm curious if you know what bitcoin money is?"

"Kind of. You can just call it bitcoin. It's a type of crypto-currency with no centralized government or major bank behind it."

"I'm not sure I understand what that implies."

Diamond spoke slower. "The way we have a sense of the value of the dollar is that the U.S. Government and the U.S. Central Bank, and a whole lotta other banks and businesses use it and attach dollar amounts to their goods and services. That supports our sense of how much a dollar is worth. But with bitcoin and other such currencies, there's no official government or big bank support. So all we have is business usage to give the currency value."

"Wouldn't that still be a good way to determine value?"

"In the short term, yes, absolutely." Diamond sat down on one of the chairs, leaned back, and put his feet up on the edge of my desk, his ankles resting on the wood, careful to make sure the old surface didn't scuff his shiny shoe polish.

He said, "If you can buy a car or a house or a suit of clothes using bitcoin, then that shows that the sellers who take bitcoin believe in its value. From what I've read, there are other similar currencies popping up every week. However, without the official backing of governments or big banks, the value of bitcoin and other currencies is less stable than dollars. And how much it buys has varied drastically over the years. Bitcoin value has gone down and up with much more volatility than the value of the dollar."

"Does bitcoin come in just coins? Or is there paper money, too?"

"Neither. It's in the cloud. A network of computers spread across the internet."

"Okay," I said. I'd heard about the cloud for years, but the concept still seemed a bit foggy.

"Think of when you see an online banking page that shows your checking account or savings account," Diamond said.

"I don't do online banking," I said.

"Yes, of course," Diamond said. "I keep forgetting the depths of your anachronistic tendencies. Okay, imagine that you did do online banking. You'd go to your bank's website, log in, and then you could look at a page that shows your balance in dollars. You could then go to a site - let's say, the IRS website - and pay your taxes by authorizing the IRS to directly debit your checking account. All this time, you would never actually see dollar bills or coins."

"Ah. I see."

Diamond continued. "So bitcoin is like that. No physical money. Just money in the cloud, money that is not directly connected to dollars or euros or yen. But like other kinds of money, your bitcoin account is accessed with an account number and a password. In essence, you use your computer to point to your little kitty of bitcoins and send some of them to somebody who's selling something you want. As a private detective, you could, for example, decide to take payment for your services in euros or yen in addition to dollars. Increasingly, people are also willing to take bitcoin instead of dollars. Could be, your dentist will one day advertise for patients and use as an incentive the fact that she takes bitcoin."

"You called it a cryptocurrency. What does that mean?"

"I don't know the details. I'm a cop, remember? But I understand that the encryption software - the cryptography - that keeps such a currency secure is very complicated. The fact that the encryption is hard to break gives users a sense of security critical to maintaining bitcoin's value and usefulness."

"So that people can't make counterfeit bitcoins?"

"Yeah. But more details would be above my pay grade," he said. He looked at his watch. "Gotta go."

"Okay, thanks."

After Diamond left, I thought about the people I'd met who were experienced in the computer and financial worlds. People like Yardley LaMotte and his employees at Tahoe Robotics. Angel investor William Lindholm. The lender who just died, Anders Henriksson.

Before I could organize my thoughts, the phone rang.

"I was so busy playing banking professor that I forgot to tell you," Diamond said.

"What?"

"A trucker was coming over Carson Pass into Hope Valley on Highway Eighty-eight. When he got down to the valley floor, he pulled off to relieve his bladder and saw a body lying not too far away. The man apparently looked like he was taking a nap on the meadow."

"But no nap, huh?" I said.

"No. Turns out the guy was the missing helicopter pilot. He worked for the charter company in Reno."

"The same pilot who flew the Tahoe Robotics mission at Job's Sister?"

"Indeed," Diamond said.

"What are we to conclude? That someone tossed the pilot out of his own helicopter?"

"Probably," Diamond said. "And found maybe ten or fifteen

miles as the crow flies from where the helicopter was left in Alpine County. After the autopsy, we'll know for certain that the man died from blunt force trauma caused by a fall from his own helicopter."

"Because the helicopter was found in relatively pristine condition, we can then assume there was another person in his helicopter who was also a competent pilot?"

"Pretty sure about that, too," Diamond said.

TWENTY-FOUR

I'd previously tried to find the property address for the parcel number I'd found in Yardley's file. The number fit a property in Placer county. But the address for that parcel number was Rural Route Creek View Terminus, which did not show up on Google Maps.

I wondered what would come up if I plugged the address into a regular search page rather than a map page.

That brought up no exact match to my search. But it did give me some possible connections. I clicked on several with no good result. So I varied my search, taking out some words, then taking out other words. I came to a hiking website that had faint copies of topo maps, the old kind that showed mine locations, information that has been removed from newer government maps.

Below the image of one map was a description of a hike. Part of the description said to hike up the old Ward Creek View Rural Route. Several of those words were on the address I found for the parcel number.

This time, I went back to Google Maps, found the general location, then expanded it, comparing it to the old topo map on the hiking website. Sure enough, there was a single road on a background of dark green like one would find for National Forest land.

I searched on a topographical map of the area and studied the topo lines for elevation.

The property appeared to be situated on a ridge to the southwest of Tahoe City. The access was a study in privacy. There was a trail on the topo map that appeared to be a Forest Service road. The road went near the Granlibakken Resort, one of Tahoe's earliest ski hills, which was now a resort with an adventure park for people who wanted to test their physical skills, with bridges through the treetops and multiple zip line rides. Outside of the Granlibakken Resort was an area of vacation homes unseen from the highway on Tahoe's West Shore. From that neighborhood emerged a smaller road that twisted around back on itself as it climbed up the slope. And from that road, there was a turnoff to an even smaller road that zig-zagged in switchbacks up to a ridge. The road, a driveway, went along the ridge to a house.

I switched to the satellite view. After it loaded, I zoomed in on the photo.

The house looked sizable from above. It had a roof line with multiple small gables as if each projected over a window on the second floor. The pattern was uniform, with none of the unusual angles common to modern mansions. I switched over to the horizontal view. Nearly all of the house was obscured by trees. But I could make out enough to sense that the house was large and sided with a mosaic of different gray tones, like stone.

I went back to the overhead view and saw that the house had some small yard areas free of trees. It also had a large companion building positioned like a garage. Using the trees for scale, the garage would probably hold three or four vehicles. Zooming to the maximum magnification, I saw a faint fence line tracing an irregular shape in the forest around the house. In places, the line seemed to disappear, obscured from satellite view under the trees. The fence formed a perimeter around the property and crossed the drive at a long distance from the house. At the sides of the driveway crossing were columns, large enough to be visible from the satellite. Anyone who drove up would be blocked well back, possibly distant enough that they couldn't even see the house.

Next, I plugged the address into the Zillow property website. No sales records were available. Yardley had probably acquired the property in a private sale, no multiple listing service, no realtor advertising it with a video tour posted online.

The property appeared to be one of the old summer Tahoe lodges, elegant but rustic, kept in steady private ownership for decades such that almost no one knew it even existed. Even the closest neighbors down below in the Granlibakken area likely weren't aware of its presence on the ridge above. Perhaps they wondered where the occasional vehicle crawling up the rural road was headed. And if a neighbor hiked up the road, they would find everything gated and fenced.

I tried several different kinds of searches using the house's address and also using generic descriptions such as 'stone house on mountain above Granlibakken.'

Nothing came up that was close. I kept varying my search terms, but with no more success. Then I wondered if the Granlibakken Resort existed when the house was built. I searched its history and found out that it only went back to about the late 1940s. Before that, the area was a ski hill and ski jump run by the Tahoe Tavern over on the shore of the lake. So I typed in 'stone house on the mountain above Tahoe Tavern ski hill.'

Scanning down the results, I came to a link highlighting almost those exact words. I clicked on it. It was from a memoir published in 1957, written by Sylvia R. Blomburg. The passage was in a chapter titled Our Magnificent Summers At Tahoe. The passage with the highlighted words said:

One of our favorite activities back in the 1920s, and even before, was to hike up to Stone Lodge on the mountain behind the Tahoe Tavern ski jump. It was a hideaway built by the banker Isaiah Hellman, the first president of Wells Fargo Bank.

Of course, everybody knew Hellman built Pine Lodge, the mansion on the West Shore of Tahoe just south of Homewood. Unlike Pine Lodge, few people knew about Stone Lodge because Hellman wanted it private, his own nirvana away from all of his acquaintances and family except his faithful valet and caretaker, an old man named Ignatius.

I should point out here, that this information comes from Ignatius himself. So if he presented it in a self-serving way to us young girls, that is to be both accepted and excused.

Stone Lodge was a fraction the size of the lakeshore palace. However, it had amazing views! As far as we could tell, Mr. Hellman was never around.

Ignatius let us girls wander around. We would carry sandwiches up the mountain and picnic on Stone Lodge's veranda. We even played on the tire swing just off the patio. Swinging out from the mountain, it felt as if you could drop directly into the magnificent blue of Lake Tahoe.

Sylvia's memoir continued:

Later, we found out that Isaiah Hellman was more than just the president of Wells Fargo. He was also the biggest banker in Los Angeles and ran several banks in San Francisco. He brought the railroad to Los Angeles and owned a huge quantity of land there. More than anyone else, Hellman was responsible for starting USC. And, just like those other Tahoe businessmen, Lucky Baldwin and D.L. Bliss, Hellman also bought a great deal of land in Tahoe.

My friend and I met Ignatius, the caretaker of Stone Lodge, the first time we climbed up the mountain and discovered the house. I remember the date because it was shortly after the Treaty of Versailles was signed, the summer of 1919, at the end of June.

I think it was because the Great War was formally ended that Ignatius - normally a reticent man - was willing to speak of Germany and Bavaria, where Isaiah Hellman and his siblings and cousins were from.

Ignatius explained that Hellman was a Jew, and, like so many Eastern European Jews, had emigrated to America hoping to find a more tolerant place to live, where they could escape the continuous anti-semitism in their homeland. This was back just before the Civil

War. According to Ignatius, Hellman thought America great, and he prospered mightily.

It was Ignatius who let us in on one of Hellman's secrets, what Ignatius called Hellman's Ahab fixation.

I should back up and say that during Hellman's early years in this country, he had reportedly taken interest in the novelist Herman Melville. The reason, Ignatius said - or maybe surmised - was that Melville was one of the few American novelists of any substance who seemed not to harbor any anti-semitism. And when Hellman learned that Melville had even traveled to Jerusalem in pursuit of a greater understanding of Judaism in particular, and of all religion in general, that further piqued Hellman's interest in Melville.

So Hellman read Melville's Moby Dick. In addition to great entertainment, it was useful in helping an immigrant polish his English.

In the novel, a vengeful, crazy, sailing man named Captain Ahab is on a mission to kill Moby Dick, the whale that bit off Ahab's leg a long time before.

Of course, we asked Ignatius what an Ahab fixation was, and he rambled on about how it had something to do with a stereotype called The Wandering Jew. Captain Ahab was Melville's representation of a Wandering Jew, a man who, despite his craziness, has impressive focus and drive and, in his hunt for the whale that maimed him, tenacity. This apparently made Hellman fascinated with the character of Ahab.

Because of our young age and our naiveté, we girls didn't really understand what Ignatius was telling us. But his excitement was obvious. And when he said he'd show us something amazing, but only if we promised to never tell anyone, we became equally excited. So we eagerly said yes.

With his eyes sparkling, Ignatius said that Hellman had little phrases based on Ahab's name. One of them was Alway Have A Backup. If you take the first letters of each word, they spell Ahab. Ignatius said that Hellman had many of these Ahab phrases.

So we asked what Always Have A Backup meant. Ignatius said that it meant never create anything that doesn't have a separate way out, which, I suppose, could also mean another way in.

Of course, as smart young girls, we took this to mean a metaphorical backup as much as anything.

Then Ignatius, eyes sparkling even more, turned and looked at Stone Lodge and said, "Now imagine how an "Ahab" would apply to his lodge!"

We were of course flummoxed.

"Here's a clue," Ignatius said. "Imagine that Mr. Hellman has ridden his horse up the mountain to Stone Lodge. He reaches into his pocket for the key to the door only to discover that he left it down at the lake." Ignatius pointed at the lodge's front door. "As you can see, the door is heavy planks of wood, much too sturdy to force open. Either you'd have to break in a window or consider your trip a loss."

"So the Ahab backup was a spare key?" I said.

Ignatius shook his head. "Consider the scope of the character of Captain Ahab. His mission was huge. Life or death. If Ahab had been searching for a bee that stung him instead of a whale that bit off his leg, then Mr. Hellman might have conceived of hiding a spare key. But Captain Ahab was sailing the world looking to kill the giant whale that maimed him! That kind of scope would suggest that Mr. Hellman's backup was something grand!"

At this, my friend and I were bouncing on our toes. Mr. Hellman's Always Have A Backup concept would have to be very exciting. Something extraordinary.

So we walked over and started looking at Stone Lodge very closely. Its doors and windows and the actual stone walls. My friend even stared up at the roof.

But after a long search, we had no ideas.

"Do you give up?" Ignatius asked.

"Yes, yes," we said.

At that, Ignatius walked over to the wall of the lodge and pointed at one of the windows.

The windows had wooden frames set in the stone wall. All the windows in the lodge had panels of cedar shakes above and beneath the window frames. It was an architectural element to make them stand out from the stone wall. Ignatius motioned us over to one of the windows. With a grand, sweeping gesture like that of a magician, he reached under the window and moved some kind of hidden catch and then pulled out on the cedar shakes below the window.

The cedar shakes swung out all together. They were the covering on a small door!

Ignatius bent over, and stepped under the door as if he were Alice in Wonderland going through the Looking Glass. He seemed to disappear.

My friend and I followed and found ourselves in the living room of the stone house! As Ignatius witnessed our amazement, he made the largest grin. I'll never forget it. He showed us how the inside of the door blended into the woodwork of the living room wall. Then he ushered us back outside and reminded us we were never to tell a soul.

I thought about the implications suggested by a house Yardley had bought but that no one in the company besides Yardley seemed to know about. His wife Lucy had told me Yardley often disappeared for hours at a time.

My guess was that Stone Lodge may have been Yardley LaMotte's personal hideaway just as it had been for Isaiah Hellman. The lodge would provide great privacy even as it perched on the end of a ridge and had a great view of the lake and surrounding mountains.

I decided to see if I could find Stone Lodge.

I got out my topographical maps of the Tahoe Basin. Comparing the Google satellite picture to the topo map, I was able to find the Stone Lodge's likely location on my paper map. By studying the topo lines, which are areas of equal elevations, I could see how steep or shallow the nearby slopes were. It seemed that there was another Forest Service trail a good distance away from the Granlibakken neighborhood. The trail came off the Ward Creek Canyon, a valley where Ward Creek flowed out of the base of Alpine Meadows ski resort. I could park near there, walk up the trail, then bushwhack up the ridge below the house.

Before I left for Stone Lodge, which required another trip around the lake, I wondered if I should detour through Reno and see if I could learn something about Anders Henriksson, the investor/lender who provided financing for Yardley.

William Lindholm had said that Anders' company was Reno Discovery Group. I looked up the number and dialed. A man answered.

"Reno Discovery, Robert speaking."

"Hello. My name is Owen McKenna. I'm an investigator looking into a missing persons case involving a man named Yardley LaMotte. I understand that Anders Henriksson made a substantial investment in Mr. LaMotte's company before Mr. Henriksson died. I wonder if I could…"

"Whoa, Mr. McKenna. Slow down, please. Anders Henriksson didn't die."

"I'm sorry. Maybe I have the names switched. I thought Anders was the one who died. Is Anders the brother?"

"Anders is alive and well. And he has no brother."

TWENTY-FIVE

Rarely am I surprised such that I don't know what to say. But hearing that Anders Henriksson was alive and had no brother required me to take a moment to regroup my thoughts.

"Just to be sure I'm calling the right place, this is Anders Henriksson's company, right? Reno Discovery Group?"

"Yes. Anders is having a cup of coffee and talking on the phone in his office as we speak. Where this rumor about him dying came from is a mystery. But it's not true."

"Perhaps I could speak to Anders," I said.

"Let me look. He's got a full appointment schedule today."

"He also has a two million dollar stake in Yardley LaMotte's Tahoe Robotics," I said, "and I believe he made a personal loan to Yardley for an additional two million dollars. Both the loan and the Tahoe Robotics stock are being appropriated by an unknown man posing as Henriksson's brother. Anders may want to reschedule his appointments."

"Hold on, please."

I held for a minute or so.

"Hello, this is Anders Henriksson."

The accent was very slight. I guessed it as Swedish. Although, had I not known his name, I might not have made such a guess.

"Thanks for taking my call." I reiterated what I'd heard to Anders.

"You have talked to this man who claims to be my brother?"

"No. As far as I know, the only person who has spoken to him is Yardley, and he went missing three days ago."

"I've been meaning to call Yardley ever since I heard this rumor. But I've been overscheduled, and I haven't had a chance.

My mistake not to have made time. How can I help?"

"I'd like to meet and talk. I originally came to this matter on a separate investigation. But I've come to realize that my other case is connected to Yardley's disappearance. I'd also like Yardley's wife and his other investor to meet with us. I believe you know the other man, William Lindholm."

"Yes. A good man. Very cutthroat in business. But honest."

"When could you be available? Sooner is better."

He paused. "Actually, any time today would be good."

"Okay. I'll call the others and try to set something up. Then I'll get back to you."

We said goodbye.

I got busy on the phone and found a time mutually agreeable to the others. The meeting was scheduled for 2 p.m. that afternoon at Lucy LaMotte's house.

Lucy was astonished to learn that Anders Henriksson hadn't died, and that Yardley had been taken in by an imposter. I told her that she'd be able to clear up any confusion when she met Anders.

"Hey, Largeness," I said. Spot had been sleeping. Or at least pretending to sleep. He didn't raise his head, but he turned his ears. It always reminded me of those radar antennas turning above the bridge of a ship. Except a radar antenna never comes with a faux diamond stud at its rim. "A ride beckons, dude. I'm happy to go alone if need be."

Spot seemed to do an instant levitation to a standing position. I took my binoculars and maps, and we left.

When I pulled up to the LaMotte house, William Lindholm's polished black Volvo was out front. As I got out of the Jeep, a silver Audi pulled up and parked nearby in the street. A man got out. He wore a gray suit with a navy pinstripe, and shiny black, pointy shoes that probably cost more than a season pass at Squaw Valley ski resort. Anders' shirt was crisp white and open at the collar. His hair was a shock of red and combed back in a dramatic wave. His appearance, from clothes to hair, was nearly the opposite of my jeans and cotton shirt and hiking boots.

"Mr. Henriksson?" I said. "Owen McKenna. Thank you for coming."

"Happy to clear up this business of me being dead."

We walked together up to the door. Lucy let us in. I introduced her to Anders.

Lucy walked into the living room where her mother Emily Taylor was sitting on the couch holding a cup. Next to her, sitting quite close, was William Lindholm, closer, I thought, than casual acquaintances would sit. A teapot and two other cups sat on the table.

"Hello, Ms. Taylor, Mr. Lindholm," I said. "Emily, this is Anders Henriksson. Bill, you and Anders know each other."

Anders shook hands all around. He was polite but clearly frustrated with social niceties. He telegraphed a strong vibe that life was short and he had important things to do. Having to explain that he was in fact alive pushed his frustration to a high level.

Anders sat on a chair at right angles to the couch where Emily Taylor and Bill Lindholm sat. I sat opposite Anders. Lucy pulled up a dining chair.

After a bit of small talk, I said, "I know you all have busy schedules, so let's get to why I asked you here. As we all know, Yardley LaMotte has gone missing under unusual circumstances. It was not long after he'd been contacted by someone who claimed to be the brother of Anders Henriksson. The supposed brother, whose name none of us knows, told Yardley that Anders was recently deceased, and that he was Anders' heir and had inherited Anders' stake in Tahoe Robotics. Further, he was calling in the loan that you, Anders, had made to Yardley. Now that we know that you're not dead, we have to wonder what the mystery man said to Yardley about your supposed death. Whatever it was, it was convincing enough that Yardley didn't think to call your company and double check."

I turned to Anders and continued, "The only explanation I

can think of would seem to be that the mystery man knew the details of your stock investment and the personal loan you made to Yardley. If those details were accurate and specific enough, that might have been convincing to Yardley. It would seem that those details could only come from someone in your investment company, Reno Discovery, or someone at Yardley's company, Tahoe Robotics. What is your thought, Anders?"

Anders' face seemed to redden. "The people at my company don't know much about my dealings with Yardley. Yes, I have the paperwork in a file. And I may have made a few comments here or there. But while I expect my employees to discuss all of their decisions with me, I don't talk much about decisions I make. None of my people would know enough about my dealings with Yardley to convince him I was dead."

I turned to Lucy. "Lucy, what about Tahoe Robotics? Would the kind of information necessary to fool Yardley be found at the Tahoe Robotics office?"

"You're suggesting someone there got information about the loan and the investment and used that to... what? Hire someone to pretend he was Anders' brother and say that Anders was now dead? And then spin a complicated story about foreclosing on the loan? A story so elaborate that Yardley believed it?" She was vacantly shaking her head. "I suppose it's possible. But that's all I can say. It's supposition. I've never seen any of the paperwork on Anders' and Yardley's financial relationship. I have no idea of where that paperwork is stored." She stopped for a moment, thinking, then turning toward me. "Are you seriously thinking someone would go to so much trouble to try to gain title to this house? I can't believe it. There are so many ways the person could be tripped up, so many details that would have to fall into place before Yardley or I would go to a title company and sign a deed to transfer title on the house. It doesn't make sense."

Bill Lindholm spoke. "I agree. The only believable motivation for a person impersonating Anders' brother and claiming that Anders was dead, is that the person wanted to gain access to Yardley's other assets."

"You're referring to Yardley's business," I said.

"Obliquely, yes. Let's call it his intellectual assets. His software. If someone could acquire that, there would be potential value far beyond any house."

"Yardley has disappeared," I said. "Without Yardley, how would this person gain access to the business and all that it represents?"

"That is a puzzle," Bill said.

"Then let's focus instead on his software," I said. "How could someone use his software?"

I saw Bill glance at Lucy. He said, "From what Yardley told me, the software could, like any creative product, basically be stolen. Of course, the creator of any spectacular content is usually critical to its success. But still, a person could start a new company based on the software and possibly do very well. A software engineer would have to rework it to take out the signature hints of the original writer, in other words, plagiarize it while reconfiguring it to make it look like someone else's work. But I think it could be done. Do you think that's possible, Lucy?"

"I wouldn't know about that," she said. "Yardley has always said that when he looks at old code, he can tell if he wrote it or not. So the style thing could be a problem. I know literature better. If you found a long-lost Hemingway manuscript and wanted to pass it off as your own, you couldn't. You'd have to completely rewrite it. Otherwise, it would only take one or two unaltered paragraphs for people to get suspicious and think it was originally written by Hemingway. Style is a significant component of a creative product."

Bill said, "Then the software would ideally be used in some way that it was out of view from any prying eyes. Especially anyone who knew Yardley's coding characteristics."

"Nevertheless, the software in essence, even reworked, could be very valuable," I said.

"Absolutely," Bill said. "We sometimes hear about a movie or a novel that is the subject of a copyright infringement lawsuit. Novels can be worth money. Movies much more. But software?

Look at how much the big software companies are worth. Google or Facebook or Microsoft. Even Amazon and Apple, with their hardward and distribution facilities, are still, largely, software companies."

"So let's assume the real goal of the mystery man was to steal Yardley's robotics software," I said. "How much do you think it could be worth?"

Anders spoke up. "Yardley told me he thought it was worth a billion dollars. Is that wild exaggeration? Is it even possible? There's no way to know. But the most successful software companies are worth hundreds of billions."

"Let's say I figured out how to steal Yardley's software," I said. "What would I do with it? Would I build robots with it? I don't know the first thing about robots. Or does this innovative software have other characteristics such that it could be used for more than robots?"

Bill shook his head, Anders frowned, and Lucy looked very sad.

It was Lucy's mother Emily Taylor who spoke up. "Yardley told me that the structure of his algorithms was very elegant. He felt that elegance was the essence of his business. Maybe my thought is just a crazy idea from a Baby Boomer who doesn't have a clue about tech. But perhaps someone could steal that elegance, so to speak."

"Mother, you never told me this. How could you know this kind of thing and never mention it?"

"You never asked. To get along in this household, one needs to be seen, not heard. Actually, that's not true. One needs to be neither seen nor heard. Except by Yardley. He listened to me."

Lucy looked like she'd been slapped in the face.

"Did Yardley say anything else about that elegance?" I asked.

"Not that I recall," Emily said.

"Did Yardley give you any kind of idea about what another party would do with his software if they wanted to steal its value?"

Emily made a slow, single shake of her head. "No. We just talked about how beauty can be found anywhere. In nature or art, of course, but also in the mathematical patterns in music. Yardley was interested in fractal patterns in nature, and he said he saw fractal patterns in his software as well. We never talked about such a thing as stealing software. I didn't know that was even done."

"Mother, have I been living in a different house? You make it sound like you have an entire secret relationship with Yardley."

"Someone has to be an audience for geniuses, dear. They are special. They need a sounding board, someone who will listen and then nod and smile at the appropriate moments. I could tell from the beginning that you weren't going to serve in that function. So I've tried to be useful."

Lucy turned red. I couldn't tell if her reaction was embarrassment or anger.

Anders spoke up. "There is a market for anything. If Yardley's software could be scrubbed of his style to eliminate charges of plagiarism, it could potentially be sold to many different companies."

"Or," Bill said, "a person could start a new company. A rival robotics company. The genius of good, innovative software has huge potential."

"So let's say I steal the software," I said. "How do I use it? What would be my next move."

"First, you'd have to get through the security," Lucy said. "Yardley has always been a big believer in security. He has a password on his phone and his computers. He told me he even puts password protection on his backups, like hard drives and those little flash drive memory sticks. The movies make it look like breaking passwords is easy. But Yardley says it's harder than you think. That's why all these scams use phishing approaches. They try to fool you into thinking they're someone they're not so you give them your password. But Yardley says trying to actually figure out a password is hard. So it would be very difficult to use Yardley's software for the simple reason that you'd have to get his password."

"Let's say, I somehow did that. Maybe I got malware installed on his computer that records his keystrokes. Once I can get into his software, how would I use it? How would I sell it? How would I make contacts in the computer industry or the robotics industry?" I was thinking about the Brotherhood website and the Marketplace page where criminals can anonymously offer their services to each other. But I wanted to see what ideas the others had.

"It seems," Bill said slowly, "that the people best positioned to make use of stolen software would be the people who are currently using it. They would know its potential better than anyone else."

"You mean the people who work for Tahoe Robotics."

"Yes."

I turned to Lucy. "Can you add to that line of thinking?"

She looked sick. "I hate to even think it. But the person who most seems like someone with the ability to use the software and also the possible desire to harm Yardley is Tapper Logan."

Lucy looked at me and added, "I heard you had a disagreement with Tapper yesterday."

"Not really a disagreement. You had told me I could look through Yardley's files. When I got there, Tapper was working at Yardley's desk, and I needed to work in that space. So I just helped him relocate to another place. I think all the other employees agreed that the new space suited Tapper's needs better, anyway."

"Oh," she said. "I guess I misconstrued a comment I heard."

"One more question, before we go," I said. "If I stole Yardley's intellectual property and were to arrange to sell it, how would I go about that in a manner that couldn't easily be traced back to me? As an investigator, I know that the money trail is often the easiest and best way to track a theft."

"That's easy," Anders said. "Use bitcoin, and do it through one of the bitcoin laundering networks."

Lucy asked, "How do they work?"

Anders said, "There are lots of ways. For example, you can

use cash to buy prepaid gift cards for thousands of different merchants. Starbucks to Amazon to iTunes. Then you can sell those gift cards for bitcoins. Your name is not attached to the gift cards you bought. When you spend your bitcoins, you do it through a bitcoin mixing service or a Tor network. They are very difficult to trace."

Emily asked, "What's a bitcoin?"

Anders said, "Bitcoin is a decentralized currency, which provides for a decentralized payment system."

Emily frowned.

"Here's a very flawed analogy," Bill said, turning to Emily. "Imagine a Paypal-like payment system. But instead of a currency called dollars, it uses a currency called bitcoin. Then, imagine that there is no Paypal-like company charging a percentage to provide the payment system. It's just a software that allows people to make their own payments to one another with no intermediary."

"What's Paypal?"

None of us responded.

Emily looked chagrined. "Sorry! I guess I should wonder whether I really want to know something before I ask a question! I'll just think of it like a computer payment system. Instead of trading beads or cowry shells, it uses digital currency."

"Perfect," Bill said.

"Where do we go from here?" Anders asked, looking at me.

"We each keep in mind the things we've talked about, the people who had access to information about Yardley's software, and the people who might know how to turn it into money if they got their hands on that software. If you think of anything useful, call me."

We all got up to leave. At the door, I pulled William Lindholm aside.

"Thanks for your help explaining how a company can be formed to utilize software. The bitcoin information was good, too."

"Glad to help any way I can."

I walked with him out the door and down the sidewalk, doing

my best to mosey. "When I was at your Donner Lake place," I said, "I noticed some soldier pics near your bicycle racing photos. Was it Viet Nam where you served?"

"Yup."

"I always heard what a rough war that was," I said. "A lot of soldiers died."

He nodded. "Almost sixty thousand. I was lucky. The ground forces had it the worst."

"You weren't part of ground forces?"

"No, I was a helicopter pilot. Got my training at Fort Wolters, Texas and then spent two tours flying a UH-1C Huey Cobra Gunship over the jungle."

"A guy would develop some serious flying skills doing that," I said.

"Yeah. Those were the days. But I wouldn't go back for anything."

TWENTY-SIX

I thought about what William Lindholm had said as I drove south to Tahoe City. He flew helicopter gunships in Viet Nam. I recalled that those Hueys were built by Bell Helicopters. If one wanted to steal a Bell and fly it away, who better than a pilot with a lot of experience in a similar chopper?

The connection didn't mean Lindholm was the mastermind of an elaborate plot to steal Yardley's intellectual property and kill Yardley if that was part of the plot. Nor did it mean Lindholm was simply a killer who hated Yardley. But Lindholm probably had opportunity. And he may have had motive if he felt that Yardley had cheated him in some way. He could have easily gotten Yardley to let him ride along on the scanning mission. And as the first investor in Tahoe Robotics, he probably knew better than anyone how to sell Yardley's software for huge dollars. Maybe Lindholm already owned part of another company that could use the software. And if the loss of the software meant that Tahoe Robotics collapsed, what better cover for Lindholm? He would only be out his hundred thousand while he could possibly make hundreds of millions off Yardley's creation.

Even if Lindholm wasn't on that helicopter, he might have known other helicopter pilots. Maybe he even trained helicopter pilots. And I thought of one other thing. Lindholm was a Swedish name.

I put those thoughts aside and returned my focus to Vince and Brie and the kidnapped boy, Jon Cooper.

From Lucy's house in Truckee, I headed to Tahoe City and crossed over the Truckee River near the dam. I headed south down the West Shore, then turned west on Pineland and worked my way over to Ward Creek Blvd.

From there, I turned off onto what I thought was the road I'd identified on the maps. It was paved but just barely, broken asphalt from decades before. The path was a little over one lane wide and had enough potholes to slow me down to a crawl. I inspected them as I approached to see if any of them were sinkholes deep enough to swallow a wheel.

I motored over a mile of potholes before I realized it would be faster to walk. So I pulled well off the rough road, grabbed my binoculars and topo map, and Spot and I got out.

The road began to rise as we walked, winding around huge fir trees big enough that the original roadbuilder had decided it would be easier to curve around them rather than mow them down. Or maybe the road builder was Tahoe's first environmentalist who thought trees served a larger purpose than just providing lumber.

After another mile, the road turned to the north, and it seemed it would no longer help me get closer to the house. So I spent some more time studying the map.

Not too far away was an access trailhead that led up toward Stanford Rock and, a bit farther, the Tahoe Rim Trail. While the TRT went less than a mile from Yardley's stone house, that wasn't close enough to help me. I compared the topo lines to the landforms in front of me and made a bushwhack plan.

As I studied the map, I spoke out loud to help me remember. "First, we go up this slope toward the big outcropping on the east-facing slope, then veer to the south toward a prominent east-west ridge, then follow the ridge up to the west until it gets too steep, then circle around counter-clockwise and come up to the house below its north side."

Spot was staring at me. He was used to me talking to myself. But he maybe wondered if this time I'd begun to lose focus. Based on his very slow wag, he possibly anticipated a future with a somewhat demented owner who no longer exercised any discipline or restrictions when handing out treats.

I turned and looked up at the forested slope. Spot turned and looked at it with me.

"Okay, onward and upward."

We did as I'd planned, hiking into a forest of Jeffrey Pine and California Red Firs. We'd gone about two miles up steep slopes and probably climbed over one thousand vertical feet when I paused to breathe. Our path hadn't been very long. Nor had we climbed very high. But hiking without an improved trail requires ten times the effort.

We came to a good-sized, flat rock. I sat on it and breathed some more.

Spot was panting and staring up through the trees.

"You want to lie down and take a rest?"

He ignored me, then stopped panting for a moment, something he did when he wanted silence in order to hear better. After ten seconds, he began panting again.

I was about to stand up and resume hiking when he stopped panting again. He did another thing I've seen many times, where he looks vaguely down at the forest floor, his ears turning this way, that way, adjusting by small degrees, honing in on a sound source. Then he turned his head but stayed looking at the dirt. I stopped my own breathing, mimicking him.

A high-pitched voice carried through on the breeze. "No, I don't know it! You can't make me because I have no idea about it." A child's voice. The kid said something else, but the words were unintelligible, lost in the air currents blowing through the tree branches. Then came a thud that sounded like a window shutting.

I took hold of Spot's collar and tapped my finger on the front of his snout, the signal for quiet. We walked through the forest. Spot pulled forward, eager as always to discover whatever was ahead. He liked to find people in the woods or anywhere else because they usually doted on him. He liked children even better, because they liked to play, often running in circles chasing him, a favorite game for all dogs because it was so easy to evade and dodge people, who, whether young or old or Olympic sprinters in their prime, were always so slow. I took care to pick a route where I saw no sticks that could break with a loud snap.

We went up through the trees at a gradual angle, stepping through the thick duff of fallen conifer needles. We were heading on a traverse course across a slope that was getting steeper, when Spot stopped. His ears twitched, the faux diamond ear stud flickering in the shade of the forest. His head was turned sideways to look up the slope. I looked where he was looking. I saw something hanging from a tree. Two chains, badly rusted. Something dark between them.

A tire swing. The one mentioned in Sylvia's memoir from 60 years ago. Behind the swing was a tall fence, newer than the tire swing by several decades. I couldn't see the house, but the fence suggested it was close.

Again, I touched my finger to the end of Spot's nose, signalling silence. We waited another minute, but there was no more sound.

The slope that rose above us to the tire swing was too steep to easily climb. I gave Spot the gentlest of motions on his collar, and we renewed our traverse across the slope, climbing slowly. I concentrated on not making noise.

The ski runs on the back side of Alpine Meadows came into full view to the north, and I could see a patch of Lake Tahoe to the east. But I still couldn't see any house.

Five minutes later, we came to a huge boulder that projected 15 feet up from the ground. The front side of the rock was vertical. The back side sloped more gently. If I could climb up on it, I could maybe see the house.

We walked to the back side of the rock.

"Quiet," I whispered in Spot's ear. He wouldn't know the word, but it often seemed he understood that whispering was about trying to be quiet.

I scrambled up the boulder and looked through my binoculars.

There was a prominent fence, and behind it, mostly obscured by trees, an old, stately, stone-and-timber-frame lodge.

TWENTY-SEVEN

The walls of the lodge were made of rough-cut granite. The steep roof was interrupted by tall, narrow gables for second-floor windows, just like I'd seen on the Google satellite view. The roof was shingled in heavy cedar shakes that wouldn't pass modern fire codes, but, barring fire, would last for 50 years or more. Because of the lodge's age and remote location, most of the county building inspectors might not even know the lodge existed. And if they did, they may have left it and its wealthy owner alone.

I didn't want to stay up on the boulder with Spot still below me on the ground, because he might bark. I saw an area in the forest up the slope a bit, where there might be a view of the house without climbing up on a boulder. I scooted down and off the big rock and took Spot through the trees, heading for higher ground, walking quietly.

Just as I hoped, we were able to maneuver to a place in the trees where we had a view window through the forest, looking slightly down over the fence.

There were two significant trees within the fence, on the north side of the house. And we were close enough that if anyone came outside and spoke, we'd easily hear them.

From my new position, the house and grounds were more clear.

In the middle of the house was a large granite chimney, suggesting a living room with a dominant fireplace that would compete for attention with the lake views out the windows.

At the end of the house, on the second floor level, was a deck that projected out from the house. It spanned the entire width of the house, perhaps thirty feet across.

Nothing moved. There was no sign of any people.

The window panes reflected sky and forest, and there appeared to be no lights on inside the house. There could be people moving around indoors, and I would not be able to see them.

I sensed a movement up on the second floor deck. I turned to look at it.

Next to the deck was a grouping of large fir trees. Their branches were long enough to reach across one end of the deck and envelope it. Someone up there would feel like they were in a tree house. An entire group of people could be out on the deck and I wouldn't know it unless they moved around. I watched for several minutes. A Steller's Jay flew up from the area where I thought I'd seen movement. I waited longer. Spot acted impatient. He turned and gave me a cold, wet nose poke on the side of my elbow.

"Impatience only accentuates the wait," I said.

He walked his front paws out, lowering his chest, arching his back, then settled down onto the duff of the forest floor.

The fence around the house was constructed of stone-and-mortar columns with solid wood panels between the columns. Each section looked eight feet long. Running along the top of the fence were rows of wire. From my distance, the wires appeared to be somewhat irregular. I realized they were barbed strands.

The fence made an irregular polygon, the number of fence sections for each straight run differing from run to run. The layout of the fence was shaped and constrained by the small size of the ridge-top plateau, maybe a third of an acre in total. On one side of the house, the fence narrowed to a passage, which had a heavy wooden gate where the drive approached the house. Just inside the gate, on the northwest side of the fenced yard was a garage.

I trained my binoculars on the gate and fence and saw something I hadn't seen before.

At the top of several stone fence columns, attached to the metal brackets that held the barbed wires, was a brown box the size of a cigarette package, probably made of plastic. The boxes were small and hard to see. I was pretty certain they housed some kind of motion detector for an alarm. They looked like newer additions to the fence. Under the roof eaves were other little boxes. No conventional approach to breaching the castle gates would go unnoticed and unreported.

In the distance beyond the house, it was all blue looking down through the trees below the house. Not sky blue. The deep ultramarine blue of Lake Tahoe. A view like nowhere else.

From the voice I'd heard earlier, I knew there were people, unless they'd left in the time it took me to hike up. I saw no people and no vehicles, either. Although any vehicles could be inside the garage.

Spot lay near me, but on his elbows with his head up, listening and watching, nostrils flexing continuously. Whenever I stayed quiet and acted subdued, he got subdued as well and seemed to focus on what he could smell and hear and, to a lesser extent, see. In these situations, he is my best sensor. He always notices any slight movement or soft sound long before I do. And, of course, the world of smells is an entire universe of which dogs are especially aware, a world that people are largely unable to even detect.

We stayed still for fifteen minutes before Spot moved his ears to the left, zeroing in on a location. I hadn't heard anything, but Spot's reaction made it clear there were sounds to be heard if one had sound receptors sensitive enough. I lifted up my binoculars for a look.

Around the side of the house, a man appeared. Because of my elevated angle, I could see him from the thighs up, enough of him that the radio on his belt and the gun in a shoulder holster were clearly visible. He was dressed in khaki pants and a white T-shirt, tight enough to show that he spent hours each week working out. I guessed him at 6-2 and 195. His hair was dark blond, cut off short and ragged. He walked fast and with a bit of bounce in his step, like an athlete eager to get out on the field and crush the competition. Maybe it was the bounce that made me notice the second holster on his thigh, a camo tone not easily visible against the khakis. I tried to steady the binoculars to keep my view from jumping. I let out my breath and stayed motionless.

The thigh holster held a knife. I could tell it was no Boy Scout camping knife. It looked like one of the karambit knives that Diamond said were popular with the Brödraskapet gang.

I couldn't tell if the man inside the fence was a military professional, trained as an assassin, or if he was a wannabe, feeling tough as he strutted about with the deadliest knife ever designed. Either way, the knife, more than the gun, indicated that this guy was very twisted, his mental landscape a bizarre, paranoid, and death-focused nightmare.

The man walked to one end of the house, stepped up on some kind of raised platform, and looked over the fence toward where we had just been, down below the tire swing. Had we triggered an alarm? Did sensors in the woods put an alert on their security computer? And if this was the house recently purchased by Yardley LaMotte, what were these men doing here? Had they worked for Yardley?

The man lifted his radio to his mouth and appeared to say something, although I couldn't hear it. Next to me, Spot lay motionless but for his nostrils and ears. He stared toward the man, assessing with dog perception. Could he smell him? Could he pick up information beyond what I could see in my binoculars?

Another man emerged through a different door. He looked equally fit and was dressed the same. He walked over to the man with the karambit knife. They spoke. The second man stepped up on the platform and looked over the fence. As he stepped up, I saw that he too had a gun, this one in a belt holster, parked right behind his radio. I didn't see a knife, karambit style or otherwise.

Despite the weaponry, I had nothing on them. Until I could see a boy and determine he was being held against his wishes, I had no ethical justification to intervene. Add to that the knowledge that if I did intervene, these guys would likely cut my head off, shoot my dog, and drop us in the lake or off the side of a mountain. It was hard to muster any desire to polish my armor, saddle my steed, and rush in to save the world.

There was another sound. Incredibly, a third man, similarly dressed and armed, appeared back by the garage. He carried a small rifle outfitted with a serious scope. He too looked like a fitness model, hard body, stylized hair shaped with gel, muscular walk. The three men together telegraphed private death squad for hire. The third man looked around the landscape as if scanning for intruders.

I remembered watching Vince take three men up the mountain. One had slid and tumbled into a ravine at very high speed. Vince and I had both assumed he'd died. The remaining two men must have thought so as well, as they had been lifted off the mountain by helicopter. The helicopter pilot had later been found dead. Yet now there was once again three men.

One man went inside, and the other two walked along the fence, down the driveway, eventually disappearing out of sight.

I pet Spot to keep him from getting frustrated with being motionless and silent. As if bored now that the men had gone inside, Spot yawned, long and wide, his giant tongue extending and retracting.

"The trouble with stakeouts, largeness," I whispered, "is the boredom. It helps to imagine a big turkey breast on the barbecue, sizzling and popping. Doesn't that help?"

He yawned again. Then I yawned. Scientists have demonstrated that dogs catch yawning from people. Or maybe it's people who catch yawning from dogs.

Fifteen minutes later, I gave up and was turning to leave my observation hideout when Spot's ears twitched again. Then came a noise loud enough for me to hear. I turned back and saw an open door.

A young girl came out. She was small, thin, prepubescent. She paused, squinting in the bright sun and holding her right hand up to shade her eyes. One of the men I'd seen earlier - the man with the most hair gel - followed, prodding the kid with his finger to the girl's back. The girl didn't move. The man behind her pushed her hard enough that she was knocked forward, stumbling for several steps.

"Ouch! Stop that! No matter how much you abuse me, I still can't help you!"

I wanted to charge over the fence and tackle the man. But that would probably get both me and the girl killed.

The girl said, "You can't just hit me!"

"Yeah, I can. You're my prisoner."

The girl walked across the yard. She was slight of build and walked with a fluid movement reminiscent of a cat. She had her shirt tails untucked, and she'd taken the front two and tied them together at her waist. She was about the size of Paco Ipar, a kid I'd helped rescue from killers who targeted him for being Basque. I recalled Paco as being 10 years old. This girl seemed like that. Vince and Brie said Jon was almost 12. Maybe the kidnappers had taken multiple kids. Or maybe this lodge and kid had nothing to do with Jon's kidnappers.

The man behind the girl said, "Why do you walk like that?" With his stylish dress, the man reminded me of a James Bond bad guy. He may have been a Swedish prison gang member, but he sounded like he was born and raised in South Dakota. I wondered what his connection was to the Brotherhood gang.

I cupped my ears with my hands to hear better.

"Walk like what?" the girl said.

"Like a girl. Boys should stand up tall and rugged. Like they're strong and in control. But you tie your shirttails up like a girly blouse. And you walk like a girl. Why would a boy want to act like a girl?"

The child didn't respond immediately.

I tried to figure it out. Was the man confused about the kid? Or was the kid not a girl but a boy? I remembered that Vince had said something that suggested his son Jon wasn't the masculine boy he wanted. Vince thought his son acted feminine.

The kid said, "I don't act like a girl. I am a girl."

TWENTY-EIGHT

The child had a soft voice, high-pitched but not especially so. There was a preciseness to her words. Her simple declaration that she was a girl carried a strong sense of self-esteem and confidence. I'd never before heard anyone of that young age make such a statement. Our perception of gender is so central to how we think of a person that it's startling to consider questioning what we think. Yet the child's conviction seemed clear. And it matched what I thought from the moment she walked out of the house.

I pulled out my phone and took some pictures.

The guard's pejorative view of the feminine aspect to her clothes was ironic because the guard and his colleagues were wearing matching outfits suitable for a precision dance troupe - male or female. And this man had spent more time on his hair gel than most women did styling their hair. How could he express displeasure about this girl paying attention to her clothes and tying up her shirt tails when he and his pals had put so much thought into their appearance?

"They said your name's Jon," the man said.

"I'm changing it to Jonni," the child said. "Not spelled with a Y like the boy Johnny, but the girl Jonni. With an I. J-O-N-N-I."

"I get it," the guard said. "You like boys. You're just another gay boy."

The kid paused. "I like boys. But it's not because I'm gay. I like boys because I'm a girl. Maybe not on the outside. But on the inside, I'm a girl."

"You'll never convince anyone of that," the man said. "It's totally obvious you're a boy. Everyone would think so. And yeah,

I see the lipstick. But that's not going to fool anyone."

Despite my distance, I could see Jonni frown. "I'm experimenting," Jonni said.

"So that explains the curled hair. It was straight yesterday. How'd you do that?"

"There are pens in the desk in the room. I got my hair wet and wrapped it around the pens. The pen clips are like bobby pins."

"It's just play, kid. You'll grow up and realize you're just confused."

"I'm not confused."

It was impressive that Jonni didn't act scared. Maybe she'd gone through so much grief in school that an armed guard wasn't intimidating.

"You're ridiculous," the guard said.

Eventually, Jonni spoke, "If I spoke Russian, and you didn't understand me, would you think I was ridiculous? Or would you just think I was different?"

There was a pause as if the man needed a moment to understand what Jonni had said. "You don't know anything," the man finally said.

"I know I'm a girl."

"Take my advice, kid. All this kind of stuff they show on TV is sick. You should forget about it and just be happy with the way you were born. I'm happy with the way I was born."

"Aren't you lucky," Jonni said.

"It's not luck. It's recognizing who you are and where you belong, not wishing for some other fantasy world where things are easy. Let me tell you something, kid. Life can be hard for boys and men. We don't get to take it easy like girls. Men have to do the hard work. So why don't you man up and face reality, face the hard work?"

"You think treating me like a prisoner is hard work?"

"Watch your mouth kid, or I'll toss you off the mountainside. We're out here for your exercise, so go run around or whatever you do."

"Run around?" Jonni said. "Like in circles? I don't think so."

"Or maybe you don't exercise. Maybe you just play with dolls." The man's tone was scornful.

"In the summer, I skate, and in the winter, I ski. I can probably do both better than you."

"You mean, you skate in the winter."

"No, I mean in the summer. Rollerblades. Inline skating."

"Oh, those skates with four wheels all in a row."

"Yeah. But mostly I just write code."

"What's that mean?"

Jonni didn't immediately respond. "Computer code. I'm learning to write apps for phones."

"Do you know how phones work?" the man asked.

"How they work? Smartphones are computers. Really complicated computers. Asking how they work is like asking… I don't know… How spaceships work. It's not something with a simple answer."

"Well, if you write apps, maybe you can fix my phone."

"It depends. If you broke the glass, I can't fix it. If you've gotten stuck in a coding fault, I can't fix that, either. I don't really know a lot beyond the basics. If you've got spaghetti code, I get as lost as anyone."

"All I know is I tried to watch this video last night and it froze my phone. I can't get calls, emails, nothing."

"Did you reboot?" Jonni asked.

"You mean turning it off? Sure. Just like they told me. Hit the button to turn it off. Then hit the button to turn it on. I get the start screen or whatever you call it. But when I press the little symbols, nothing happens."

"Have you charged it?"

"Yeah. Plugged it in all night."

"Maybe your video downloaded some malware." Jonni paused, then said, "I could look at it."

Jonni immediately sounded different. I thought I detected a calculating tone. "A kid in school showed me a phone hack," Jonni said.

"Hacking means breaking into the phone, right?" the man said.

"Sometimes. It's mostly just doing things in different ways. I'm going to summer school. The focus is computers. We get these rotating teachers who come through the classroom. Business people. One of the teachers said that even though everyone opens a can from the top, you can open a can from the bottom, too. Same thing with turning a phone on. I could try it. But it might mess up your phone."

"How? Could I still get phone calls?"

"Maybe. I don't know. I'm just saying that when you do stuff on a computer, you can't always back-button your way out. There could be, like, permanent consequences."

"Consequences. Is that what happens with boys who want to be girls? They start using words like consequences?"

Jonni looked down at the ground. Her shoulders hunched up and shook. Even from my distance, her body language telegraphed major tension and stress.

"Oh, now you're gonna cry," the man said. "I can't believe this. What kind of a wimpy girl-wannabe are you?"

Jonni seemed to melt, sagging down until she was sitting on the dirt. The man's extreme loutish insensitivity was an assault, and I felt a powerful sympathy for the girl, a kid who was being nice and offering to help. I wanted to charge over the fence and grab the man and shake him. An adult who bullies a child commits an unforgivable crime against the child's soul. Anyone can see that a child, even if they get past it, never loses those scars.

The man seemed to look up as if rolling his eyes and sighing. He turned, looked out at the lake, turned back.

"Anyway, my phone is worthless to me now," the man said. "So if you want to look at it, go ahead." He pulled his phone out of his pocket and held it out.

It was a long moment before Jonni spoke. She reached up to her eyes and wiped away tears, her fingertips tracing her bottom lids. Most boys wipe tears with the heels of their palms. Most girls use their fingertips. It's not something that kids analyze.

"It would take some time," Jonni said, "'cause I'd have to figure stuff out. It would help if I had my own phone. I could Google some workarounds."

"Sorry. The boss has it. Doesn't trust you with it."

"I think I can do a forced shutdown and reboot with a certain sequence of the buttons." Jonni looked around the small, mountaintop yard. She pointed to a tree near the fence. "I could sit there in the shade and work on your phone."

The man looked at the tree and then around at the yard. I guessed that he wasn't worried about Jonni causing a problem or climbing over the barbed-wire-topped fence and escaping. I think the man was worried that his comrades would question whether he was doing his job if his charge was sitting and looking at his phone instead of chasing a Frisbee or whatever they envisioned.

"Okay," he said. "But I have a schedule. I have to bring you inside in fifteen minutes."

Jonni reached out and took his phone. She stood up. "Is this password protected?" Jonni asked.

"No, it's steel-protected." The guard made a quick-draw motion toward his belt and pulled out his karambit knife in a flash of movement. His forefinger was in the circular finger hole, and he held the knife up so the blade flashed in the sunlight.

Jonni flinched from the sudden motion.

The man's schoolyard-bully style was so revolting, I could barely sit still.

Like an old-west gunslinger, the guard shifted his grip on the curved, wicked knife and spun the knife around his finger in a blur, four or five rotations. Then he once again grabbed the grip in the meat of his hand. He made a punching, stabbing motion with the blade.

Jonni cowered from the man.

The man was slipping the knife back into the holster on his thigh when he jerked.

"Dammit!" He grabbed at his thumb with his other hand. The man raised his hand as if to get a closer look and released his grip on the knife.

"Ow!" he yelled, his voice high.

I could see the blood spurting from where I sat.

He grabbed again at his thumb and bent down, holding his wounded hand to his stomach. He was panicked.

Jonni ran over. "Stop moving and lift your hands above your head."

The man ignored her. He was still bent, shaking his hands. Blood sprayed from his motions.

"Listen to me!" Jonni said. "I'm going to be a doctor when I grow up, so I know what I'm talking about! Stop shaking your hands. Sit down." She pulled at his clothes, dragging him down until he was sitting on the ground, leaning back against the outer wall of the lodge.

"Now raise your arms above your head." She lifted on his arms.

He did as instructed.

"You've cut your thumb artery. It's small, but it bleeds a lot. Having your hands above your head will reduce the blood pressure to the wound. Now we need a compress. A strip of fabric. I can cut a piece from your shirt. Is that okay? I'll have to use your knife."

The man nodded. Even from my distance I could see that he was shaking with fear from the sight of his own blood. I thought of charging the fence and grabbing Jonni. But there were still two other men nearby. The wounded man would call them on his radio.

Jonni reached down and pulled the knife from its holster. She stretched his shirt out from his body and used the knife to cut the front of it off. She laid the fabric on the ground, cut three strips, and set the knife down.

"I have to go inside and get one of these wet so we can clean the wound. Is that okay? I'll be back in a minute."

He nodded.

Jonni grabbed the strips and ran inside. A minute later she was back. She stood next to him and reached for his hands. I couldn't see the details of her movements. But in a few minutes, she had his thumb and hand wrapped and bandaged. She'd wiped away much of the blood. She had him continue to hold his hands above his head. She put her hands on his arm, just below his elbow.

"The Brachial Artery is deep in your arm," she said. "It branches just below the inside of the elbow. One of the branches is the Radial Artery where you feel your pulse in your wrist. It goes to your thumb. I'm applying pressure to the Radial Artery to shut off the blood flow."

"You must know a lot about this," he said.

"Three-step standard procedure," she said. "A compress on the wound. Elevate the wound. Apply pressure to the artery upstream."

"What do I do next?"

"You should go to a doctor."

"What if I don't? Will I bleed to death?"

"I doubt it. We've stopped the bleeding. If you stay like this, the clotting will continue. Unless you're taking an anti-clotting medicine. Are you on aspirin?"

"No."

"Good. After maybe ten minutes, you can move around, but you'll still have to keep your arm elevated. Whatever you do, don't remove the compress or the strip bandage holding it in place. If you do, it will tear open the wound again. By tomorrow, you should soak the bandage to loosen the dried blood. Very gently wash the wound, then re-bandage it. Do that for at least five days. If you do as I say, you'll probably heal okay. But I still think you should see a doctor. Now I need you to apply pressure to the artery. Do you see how I'm squeezing your arm?"

"Yeah."

"Do that with your other hand."

He did as she said.

"Okay, hold that position for ten minutes. Now I'll see what I can do about your phone."

She picked up his phone and walked away, taking slow, deliberate steps. When Jonni was ten feet away, she turned and walked to the tree. She sat down on the ground, back to the tree, eyes on the guard. Slowly, she turned her attention to the phone. From my angle, I could see her better than the guard could. With the help of my binoculars, I saw that she held the phone for a minute and then began tapping with her thumbs and swiping at the screen. The guard watched Jonni for a bit. From his position, he probably couldn't see her finger motion on the screen. It would just look like she was still holding the phone. The guard turned and looked toward where the other men had walked. He was probably embarrassed about cutting himself with his knife.

I thought about tip-toeing over to the fence near Jonni. If I could get her to believe my intentions were good, I could maybe lean a downed log over the fence, climb over and get her, climb back, and escape down through the forest. But I knew the alarms would go off. Multiple men who were in very good shape would come after us. Even if Jonni could run very fast, there was little chance we could escape. The men had at least one rifle with a scope.

And if Jonni distrusted me and was resistant, I would have no luck getting her out. They'd likely capture or kill me, and my efforts would ensure that Jonni was kept in a locked room from that point on.

After several minutes, the guard called out. "Any luck on that phone?"

"Maybe," Jonni said. "I was able to do a full shutdown. Now I just need to start in DFU mode."

"What's that mean?"

"It's a kind of safe mode. It's about the firmware. If that doesn't work, I'll try recovery mode."

Knowing nothing about phones other than how to make calls and use Google Search and Maps, I had no idea of what Jonni meant. I wondered if what she said was true or if she was merely throwing out terms to try to confuse the guard. After being kidnapped and treated abusively, anything she could do in retaliation would be justified.

The guard didn't respond. It was obvious he had no idea what

Jonni was talking about.

"How much longer?" he eventually said.

Jonni didn't look up from the phone. Her thumbs made fast, staccato taps. Then she put the tip of her index finger on the screen and moved it back and forth. Whatever she was doing, she was in a hurry. "Probably five more minutes," she said.

"That's all the time we've got. I'm taking you back to your room in five."

The other two men appeared around the corner of the lodge closest to me. They were talking. Because Jonni was farther from them than I was, she couldn't hear them. I didn't think they could see her.

"I can't tell if the kid knows what the password is or if she's playing with us," one of them said.

"He," the other man said. "The kid is a he."

"Seems like a she to me. Anyway, we tried pressuring her. Him. I really scared him last night. I thought he was going to break. But he's a tough nut."

"I'm guessing we'll wear him down. If not, we get rid of the kid."

They walked over to the man who'd been guarding Jonni. One of them pointed to the bandaged wound. They spoke in low tones that I couldn't hear. The guard gestured toward Jonni. The two men nodded, then went inside the lodge.

I wondered why none of them seemed suspicious about Jonni working on the phone. But maybe the wounded man hadn't mentioned it. Jonni was far enough away that the other men might not have noticed.

Jonni seemed to be working on the phone with an intense focus. She tapped the screen. Moved her finger as if swiping different pages.

I got to thinking about what could happen if she could make the phone work. She'd probably want to send a text or an email. I knew that some email systems were set up for use with a specific phone. Jonni's phone had been taken away. But maybe she had a web-based account on Gmail or something similar. If so, she could use any phone to access it. If she didn't have such an account, maybe she could set up a new one while acting as if she was trying to fix the guard's iPhone. Then she could send a "Help, I'm being held prisoner" email to her dad, trying to describe her location. Or she could send a text from the man's account and then delete it so he wouldn't find it in his sent file.

I watched her tap furiously. Two or three minutes later, she stood up and walked over to the guard.

"I think it works now," she said.

"Really? You fixed it? I know that the boys who normally can do this stuff are totally nerdy. So I guess it makes sense that a girly boy like you could do it, too."

"You can probably release the pressure on your artery. But keep your wounded hand above your head for an hour or more. After that you should keep it in a sling or tucked up in your shirt so your hand doesn't hang down low. Otherwise the blood pressure might blow open your wound."

The man nodded and used his good hand to take his phone. He used his thumb to try it.

"My email and phone both seem to work. I guess you're good for something."

The man didn't notice that Jonni wasn't looking at the phone. She'd turned and was looking up under the eave toward one of the motion sensors I'd spotted earlier.

The guard stood up, pocketed the phone, opened the door, and ushered Jonni inside.

TWENTY-NINE

Ileft my stakeout place and hustled down the mountain with Spot. We rushed through the forest. Spot can run downhill at high speed. He got far out in front of me, then turned and looked back up the mountain to see what was taking me so long.

I thought about what I'd seen as I hopped and slid and scrambled down the slope. Why would three armed men be up on a lonely ridge guarding Jonni? Two men, unarmed, would have been sufficient to keep a 24-hour-a-day eye on Jonni. In fact, unarmed men would do a better job, because any hiker coming through the woods who happened to see the armed men would likely report it to the police. Clearly, these men didn't care about efficiency and common sense. They cared about a macho sense of intimidation, even if their subject was a young child. Perhaps the people behind the kidnapping felt that their efforts to acquire a billion-dollar software prize suggested extreme support measures. It's the same principle people miss in countless situations. Anytime you have something very valuable, the more extreme your protection, the more you announce that value to the world. Hiding value in plain sight is often a safer approach.

When the guard talked about a password, it made me wonder if Jonni somehow had the key to the stolen software.

In addition to excessive guard forces, one more thing seemed obvious.

The men I saw were merely enforcers. Their general, the decision maker, was someone else. I had no way of knowing if he was on or off the premises. The man on the phone when we'd been shot at was called Lucas, and he had a strong accent. I'd heard enough words from the men at the lodge to know that none of them had an accent.

A half hour later, Spot and I were down the mountain and climbing into the Jeep. I checked my cell reception. There was none in this remote location.

I drove out toward the highway, checking every half minute. As I thought about what I'd tell Vince, I came to an uncomfortable conclusion. It made sense to tell him his child was okay. But he would be agitated and would demand that I tell him where his kid was so that he could storm the castle. Such an action would be unwise and probably unsafe for Jonni.

Saving Jonni would require a careful plan. We would need to consider all possibilities. If we just charged up the mountain, the guards would intercept us, maybe kill us, and maybe decide that keeping Jonni alive was too much of a risk.

I decided to act in Jonni's best interest, and not tell Vince I'd seen his kid. From what I'd witnessed, I believed that Jonni would still be alive in the morning. With planning, we could figure out the best way to rescue Jonni.

When I came to an area with cell reception, I called Vince.

"Any word from the kidnappers?" I asked.

"No! Those bastards said they'd let Jon go!"

"Let's not jump to any conclusions. They may be arranging the release as we speak." The statement could possibly be true.

"But you don't know that, right? You have no idea." Vince was nearly shouting.

"Correct. I have no idea."

"This is killing me," Vince said. "They might be killing Jon."

"Try to take some deep breaths. I'll call you in the morning."

Vince hung up on me.

I dialed Street.

I thought we should meet in person before I told her what I'd discovered. When she answered, I said, "Checking in to see if you can bear to spend another hour without my voice in your ear."

"No, of course I can't," she said. "Just fifteen minutes alone and I'm bereft."

I visualized a silent film star, a distraught look on her tortured face, her arm up, forearm against her forehead.

"Would a visit be appropriate?"

"You may not believe it, but I opened a bottle of wine, which I could share," she said.

"Really? I'm shocked."

"And I've already had some to drink."

"I'm on the West Shore, so it'll take me an hour or so."

Spot stood wagging as I pressed Street's doorbell. When Blondie barked from inside, his wag went from adagio to allegro, and he turned his head a bit and focused so intently on the doorknob that I thought it would heat up and be too hot to touch.

The door opened, and Blondie pushed past Street and ran with Spot out into the night. Street raised up on tiptoes and kissed me.

"Now you can put your bereftness back in the closet," I said.

"The bereft closet. Everyone should have one to store away loneliness."

"Even so, you like to be alone more than anyone else I've ever met," I said.

"Well, I am an entomologist, after all. If I loved being with people all the time, I would hardly choose to study bugs."

Street turned and walked into her kitchen. "You should have some wine before it's all gone." She set out a glass.

I knew it was a joke. There was a glass on the counter with a tiny pool of red at the bottom, and the bottle next to it was still full. I poured some wine.

"Loneliness versus merely being alone is an interesting concept," Street said.

"One could probably divide occupations by a person's affinity for constant social interaction and human companionship."

"Yes," Street said. "The dichotomy of the people who have

a great need for people and the people who don't. On one side would be hairdressers and camp counselors and professors and doctors and bartenders. On the other side would be the scientists and artists, chemists and foresters and astronomers and poets and painters and composers. Most of the scientists and artists I know prefer work over casual friends. I have no close friends the way you have Diamond to pal around with. The people I connect to best are fictional, played by actors who never come closer to me than the other side of the TV screen. I love that their actions and speech are carefully written and directed and then edited for effectiveness and clarity. Some spontaneity is lost, but there's no wasted time."

"That's probably why you don't like small talk. Takes too much time. You're more production oriented."

Street made a chuckle. "You've noticed? When people start gossiping about celebrities or their neighbors, or chatting endlessly about clothes or their Facebook pages or their selfies or their children's favorite video games or their grandchildren's adorable T-shirts, I find myself thinking I've got so much work I want to do and I'm never going to get those fifteen minutes back in my entire life."

"Yet you're talking with me, sipping wine. I'm a lucky guy."

"Well, I'm not a complete shut-in, and I'm not a misanthrope," Street said. "I like to spend time with you. I'm just an introvert, happy to spend most of my time alone."

"But you are alone by your choice. I'm also largely alone, not by my choice but by your choice. I'm a loner by default."

"You also like to be alone," she said, "puzzling out the calculations of human criminal psychology. Speaking of which, anything new on Vince Cooper's son, Jon?"

"Yes. I didn't know if I should talk about it. He's safe, but he's still captive. It's very distressing to not be able to immediately rescue him."

"I don't understand," Street said.

"He's been taken up to an old stone lodge that was built by Isaiah Hellman on a ridge above Sunnyside. Hellman called it

Stone Lodge, and it's now owned by Yardley LaMotte. I couldn't rescue the kid because there are three armed guards with guns and knives. They are all no doubt twisted. But one of them is a sadist and plays with his knife. He gets a kick out of threatening the child."

Street leaned forward and put her hand on my forearm. "I see what you mean. Instead of relief at learning of his whereabouts, seeing him with the guards and not knowing how to free him is even more stressful."

"The kidnappers stressed that they would kill the kid if we called the cops. So I've been trying to think of a rescue approach. But I've had no luck. I don't want Vince to do something rash, so I haven't told him, yet. I'll tell him tomorrow. Maybe Diamond will have an idea and we can make a plan to save the kid. In the meantime, I'll try to believe he's safe for now."

We sat in silence.

Street said, "I feel so bad for that boy."

"An interesting development," I said, "is that the boy Jon is, at least by some measures, really a girl who goes by Jonni." I explained all the details of what I'd seen.

"How ironic," Street said, "that Jonni can finally be herself in the company of violent men who are holding her prisoner."

"Yeah. It shows that life in a child's own home is not necessarily emotionally safe."

"If a parent doesn't support a child, yes," Street said.

"I'm curious if you know anything about gender stuff."

Street sat on one of the stools at her kitchen counter. "Not much. I read science journals. Some are just about entomology or forensics. But others are filled with a wide range of subjects. As you might imagine, most of the articles are very dry. So dry that even my eyes start to glaze over. But over the years I've been exposed to some of the new knowledge about human sexuality and gender issues."

"Is this thing with Jonni - born like a boy but feeling like a girl at such a young age - common?" I pulled out another stool and sat nearby.

Street made a little frown, thinking, as always, before she spoke. She chose her words carefully.

"I think the best way to put it is that gender is not a black-and-white concept. The idea that you're either a boy or a girl and that it corresponds to your body is naive. Scientists have learned that it's vastly more complicated. Gender is a spectrum of characteristics, some physical, some psychological. We've known some of this for years. And we've seen the gender spectrum in many other animal species as well."

"And this is completely different from homosexuality, right?" I said.

Street nodded. "That's about gender preference in a mate. This is dealing with gender perception of self, the question of 'Am I a boy or a girl or in between?' The range of internal gender issues is very broad. But for the moment, let's use the gay-straight preference concept as an example of how society develops awareness. Not too many years ago, people didn't know how many people in their community were gay because of the stigma and general reticence about the subject. Not even gay people knew how big their group was. Jump forward in time, and we now know that there are a lot of gay people."

"You're saying that we're discovering there are lots of people who are like Jonni, too."

"Yes, definitely. Our society is starting to loosen up a bit. People are starting to reveal their feelings. Not much. But some."

I asked, "Do scientists know what causes these issues?"

"Not comprehensively, no. The causes are broad spectrum as well. For example, if you only look at physical characteristics, most people are born looking like one gender or the other. But a surprising number of people are born with a mix of physical characteristics. In the old days, they called these people hermaphrodites. Sometimes it's caused by a child having two X chromosomes and one Y chromosome, which is one more chromosome than normal and creates both male and female development. But some people with ambiguous physical characteristics have just two sex chromosomes, and their physical ambiguity comes because of developmental reasons."

I was thinking about what Street had said about stigma. "And no doubt that's another area people are reluctant to talk about."

Street nodded. "Exactly. What parent is going to want to share that with their neighbor? 'My child looks sort of like a boy and also sort of like a girl.' The very subject conspires against the bulk of the world's understanding."

Street drank her last drop of wine.

I picked up the bottle, gave her a few more drops, then refilled my glass.

"I don't know how psychology works any more than a layperson," Street said. "However, I have a colleague, Nina Mazzo, who is a clinical psychologist specializing in developmental psychology. She could explain. I've been meaning to check in with her. Maybe this would be a good opener for calling."

"You don't need to do that for me."

"No, it wouldn't be just for you."

"It's well into most people's dinnertime," I said.

"She's in Hawaii. Three hours behind us, adjusting for Daylight Savings time." Street looked at the clock. "Eight-thirty here, five-thirty there. She'll probably just be getting home from work. I remember her saying that she always takes her medicine after work and that her medication of choice was a margarita. I could catch her during her margarita hour."

"Does she have a hus… I mean, a partner? I wouldn't want to interrupt their evening."

"Nina is like me, married to her work. Unlike me, I don't think she has a partner who is willing to put up with her cloistered evenings. We could Skype her."

"Is that one of those video calls?"

Street gave me a look of surprise.

"You know I'm a Luddite," I said.

"And proud of it," she said.

"Sometimes. What do we do? Do we hold your phone camera in front of us?"

Street laughed. "No, we just sit in front of my laptop. I'll show you."

There was a bark at the door, Blondie's call to be let in.

I opened the door. The two dogs rushed in, bouncing and panting. As Blondie ran to greet Street, I grabbed Spot and held him tightly to calm him down. "Remember the poem about the rule of space, Largeness. Outdoors, we fly around. Indoors, we lie down."

I got him to lie on the rug in front of the cold gas fireplace. Blondie lay near him. I went back to Street.

We sat on her couch, and she set her laptop on her thighs. Then she reached up to the top of the screen and removed a piece of Post-it note.

"What's that?" I asked.

"I cover up the webcam when I'm not using it."

"Why not just turn it off?"

"Because a clever hacker can turn it on from anywhere in the world."

"Really? That isn't just urban legend?"

Street laughed. "If so, Mark Zuckerberg, the guy who started Facebook, believes in urban legends. Low-tech tape for the ultra-high tech zillionaire. He says he knows how easily hackers can turn on your computer's camera and then see everything you do. He recommends everyone cover it with a piece of tape when they're not using it. The FBI says the same thing."

"Another reason I haven't fully bought into the modern world."

Street picked up her phone. "I'll send Nina a text, first. She'll let me know if this is a good time for Skype or not."

THIRTY

To set up the call, Street first tapped a bit on her phone. Then she hit send.

In less than a minute, her phone beeped. She looked at it and said, "Nina says this is a good time." She turned and looked at me. "I should maybe warn you. Nina is quite a character, so be prepared."

"I picked that up from the self-medicating reference."

Street tapped buttons on her computer, and then a symbol in the corner of her screen started flashing.

At first there was just audio. Street talked to Nina for a bit, and then Nina must have turned on her camera. Or removed the tape. The screen suddenly showed Nina's face as she sat in front of her computer. She was a large, smiling woman with a substantial, messy helmet of brown hair. In her left hand was a tall glass filled with a green drink and a wedge of lime.

"Hi Nina, thanks for being available," Street said.

"Street, hon, you know I'm happy to talk to you any time. Plus, a shrink like me is always eager to explore the recesses of that science exploratorium you call a brain. Hey, who's the hunk next to you? Turn your computer so I can see him better."

Street shifted the laptop a bit.

"Hi, sugar," she said. "My name's Nina."

"Owen McKenna," I said. "Pardon my awkwardness, but this is the first time I've done - what do you call it - picture talking."

"Oh, I love you already. Street, he is sooo adorable. Picture talking! That makes this whole thing sound delightfully charming. Mr. McKenna, dear, thanks to you, I'm never Skyping again. I'm going to do picture talking. Better yet, I'll make it a verb. I'll picture talk you."

"And I'll picture talk you back, Ms. Mazzo," I said.

"Hey, Owen," Nina said. "I like to speak my mind directly, so I'll just say this straight up. When you tire of that beautiful, skinny woman of yours and you want a woman with serious curves who doesn't keep bugs in jars everywhere, you just picture talk me and I'll pick you up at Honolulu International."

"Got it," I said.

"Sorry, Street, sweetie," Nina said. "Didn't mean to ignore you and talk around you. I got a little brain scattered when I saw your boy pal, there. But I'm back. Totally focused on you. Well, mostly focused. Maybe you should turn your computer away from him. What's happening?"

"Actually," Street said, "I'm calling because of a case Owen is working on."

"Oh! That's right. Owen, Street told me some time back that you're a detective! How romantic is that?!"

"Not very," I said.

"Owen has a client whose child has gender issues," Street said. "I told Owen that if he wants to learn about that, the person to talk to is you."

Street gave a thorough but succinct explanation of what we'd learned about Jonni Cooper.

"We have lots of words for this stuff," Nina said when Street was done. "And it's evolving very fast as society comes to terms with something that should be no big deal. The words change every ten minutes. As of five minutes ago, we used the blanket term gender dysphoria."

"Dysphoria?" I said. "That sounds serious."

"Sorry," Nina said. "We have so many terms we use, and the DSM-Five is always changing them."

"What's that mean?" I asked.

"Oh, sorry again. The DSM is the shrink Bible. Diagnostic and Statistical Manual. And now that I've explained that, you can just forget I mentioned it. Anyway, the terms shift because we develop an increased understanding. For example, think of terms for disability. We've gone from crippled to handicapped to disabled to challenged to a person with disability."

"Different terms that mean the same thing?" I said.

"Maybe, maybe not," Nina said. "From a shrink's perspective, linguistic fluidity can be stylistic, but it can often be very helpful. As people develop and learn new terms, they become more sensitive. When they hear that it is no longer appropriate to refer to someone as crippled, it causes them to stop and think about if and how they put people into boxes. Nomenclature adjustments can contain powerful lessons, teaching us to think more carefully about people who aren't exactly like us."

"Good point," I said.

Nina continued. "So dysphoria is simply a term for the state of being ill at ease, of feeling unsatisfied with life. It comes from the Greek word dysphoros, meaning hard to bear. As it relates to gender, it's just what you'd imagine. Gender dysphoria describes someone struggling with discomfort regarding their gender. They are usually uncomfortable with their bodies. And they often - but not always - feel they are a different gender from the way they were born. In subtle contrast to that, the current popular term of transgender is narrower and is usually used to describe someone who senses a mismatch between the way they perceive themselves and the way they look. But in the case of the person we call transgender, they often feel okay with their bodies. Despite the mismatched psychological gender and physical gender, they may accept their situation and suffer no dysphoria. But having said that, I should let you know that tomorrow the nomenclature will shift again, and we'll be using a new set of terms."

Nina sipped her margarita. But unlike Street's delicate sips, Nina drank with what seemed like lust for her medicine.

"You imply that there are large numbers of people who have discomfort related to their gender," I said.

"Absolutely," Nina said. "It goes to the core of the subject. For example, people can't even agree on what we mean when we refer to a person's gender. Physical? Psychological? A mix of the two? Bottom line is, the old nineteen fifty's movie concept of boy meets girl, boy goes to bed with girl, and then boy sleeps with a smile all night doesn't apply to a surprising number of people."

"Gender dysphoria manifests in many ways, right?" Street said.

"More ways than we can count."

"It's sad that so many people have this problem," I said.

"Yes and no." Nina slurped more margarita. "The truth is that in many cases, the problem doesn't belong to the person affected. The problem belongs to society. Take away society's harsh judgments, and many with gender dysphoria no longer feel there's a problem."

"I'm not sure I understand," I said.

"Sometimes the only problem that people with gender issues feel is their awareness that society judges them harshly. Here's a revealing example. In much of the Polynesian diaspora, Samoa especially, society recognizes three genders. There are men, women, and feminine men. They call the feminine men Fa'afafine, or sometimes Fafa for short. These are people who appear to be physically male, but appear to be psychologically and emotionally female. A common way the Fafa come to be is when a family has a boy who clearly acts feminine. Instead of fighting the child and making him feel bad the way many western societies do, they accept him as a feminine boy. And they raise him to be a feminine boy. They let him or even encourage him - or I should say her - to do what society thinks are feminine activities and dress in feminine clothes and pursue feminine ways. As with all people, the Fafa don't always fit into clear categories. However, it appears that many if not most of them perceive themselves as females. Often the only difference between them and other women is that they have men's bodies. Because of society's acceptance, many Fa'afafine grow up happy and well-adjusted, and they don't feel the stress that so many people in western societies feel. When the Fafa have a sexual relationship with a man, they don't see it as homosexual, and neither does the man. Both people feel it is heterosexual sex, involving a woman and a man. But in this case, the woman has a man's body."

"Fascinating," Street said.

"Yes! Because of the lack of societal judgment, the Fafa don't suffer gender dysphoria! They're fine with their gender as they see it. They're valuable members of society. And society accepts them as they are. In some cases, society celebrates the Fafa and their contributions to their world. They hold every kind of job including high-status jobs, judges and doctors and professors. When it comes to gender, Samoa appears to be a far more successful society than ours."

I said. "Take away society's harsh judgment and people are fine with who they are regardless of how they perceive themselves on the gender spectrum."

"Exactly," Nina said. "Live and let live is a good motto. This is not to say that people with non-mainstream gender are problem-free in Samoa or anywhere else. Like people in any group, some people do better than others. And there are some narrow-minded people and bigoted people even in Samoa, many of whom sometimes discriminate against the Fafa. But the lessons from Polynesia are dramatic and clear. Gender problems don't arise innately from the individual. The problems come from those people in society who, for whatever reason, can't accept that all people are okay, regardless of their gender or sexuality. Of course, society has the right to certain standards as regards not harming others, especially children. But society shouldn't tell an individual how to feel. Remove those pejorative attitudes and people thrive."

"That makes sense," I said. "Why do you suppose society is so harsh on people with non-mainstream gender?"

Nina drank the last of her margarita. "I believe people are narrow minded about sex and gender issues for the same reason they are narrow minded about race and religion and other significant cultural characteristics. It's tribal. Our tribe's way is the right way. That other tribe is scary and probably bad. Open-minded people celebrate diversity and love being around others who don't look like them or act like them or speak like them or dance and sing like them or enjoy the same things they enjoy. Closed-minded people want homogeneity. They want to be with others just like them in every way. They're afraid of people who look different or act different. And they certainly don't want those different people living next door to them or teaching their children. This probably goes back hundreds of thousands of years to when you only trusted people you personally knew, people who lived in the same cave as you, who were, of course, just like you. And you feared people in other tribes. Today, most people find that narrow mindedness wrong. But it still exists. And there are few things that bring it out so much as sex and gender issues."

Nina paused.

"One more question, if I may," I said.

"Do I need to get another margarita first?"

"Maybe. But I'll make it short. These kids who believe that their gender is not what their parents think... How young are they when they come to this realization?"

"To my knowledge, no one has made a definitive study about that. But from my own experience, it's pretty common that kids as young as five or six come to think that. They may not articulate it at the time. But those of us in the therapy business often hear comments like, 'I knew I wasn't oriented according to the way I was born when I went to kindergarten, because that was the first time I spent much time with significant numbers of boys and girls. And it was immediately obvious that I didn't belong in my group. I belonged with the other sex.'"

"Nina," I said, "you've been extremely helpful. I've learned a great deal, and I appreciate it. So much so that we'll picture talk again."

"You're welcome, Mr. Owen McKenna," Nina said. "Remember, Street," she added, "when you're done with him, I get him next."

They said goodbye and hung up.

Street and I sat quietly and sipped more wine.

"A big, serious subject," I said. "Both gender stuff and kidnapping stuff.

Street nodded.

"Maybe we should change the subject," I said.

Street said, "I've often noticed how books and movies depict characters suffering from major stress caused by war or crime or persecution. They show the characters responding with - what's the best way to say it without sounding crass? - bedroom appetites. I suppose its a kind of survival instinct."

I reached over and traced the edge of her face and jaw with my fingertip. "I love it when you bring up my favorite subject without any prodding from me. Is this when I should give you a shoulder rub so I can surreptitiously move your collar a bit to the side to see if the lacy shoulder strap of my favorite peach camisole is visible?"

Street gave me the shy smile that quickened my heart rate and my breathing. "But we should savour this wine, first, don't you think?"

"Yes. It's important to keep honing our vino work ethic."

Street picked up her glass and guzzled another four or five drops.

In an effort to keep us from getting lost in thought about people in serious trouble, I said, "I recall the decoration on your camisole straps. Little stitched loops, right? Floral-like, alluding to future potential discoveries. And the stitching is a contrasting color, isn't it? Lavender against the peach? Am I observant or what?"

"I love you even if you get the details of my garment all wrong."

"I'm distracted, no doubt, by what the garment contains in its embrace."

"The hopeless romantic," Street said.

"I strive for art and romance and fear I achieve neither. But if the highly-educated lady should allow the peasant ex-cop an exploratory voyage, perhaps he would find the truth."

An hour later, before we'd discovered where we'd dropped all of our clothes, I poured my last glass of wine, saving a drop for Street. She took that drop with enthusiasm.

THIRTY-ONE

In the morning, Street had to go to an appointment first thing. So Spot and I drove up to my cabin for coffee out on the deck. I called Vince Cooper.

"McKenna here," I said when he answered. "I found your kid at a remote house. Sh… He's alive and well."

"What?! He's okay? That's fantastic! Let me talk to him."

"I don't have him. He's under armed guard. Three men with weapons. Probably the men you took up Job's Sister."

"Those bastards! Where is he? Let's go get him. I don't care about those men. I'll kick their ass!"

"Slow down, Vince. First, I'm not exactly sure of the location because I bushwhacked there up a mountain through a heavy forest. There was apparently a drive that goes there, but it doesn't show on maps. We'll need to figure out the exact location. Second, the men are heavily armed. Guns and rifles and knives and an attitude that suggests they wouldn't hesitate to use them."

"But Jon's okay, right? They haven't hurt him?"

"Yes, he seems okay. I saw Jon from a distance. I couldn't get close enough to talk. I'd like to come to your place so we can make a plan. I live directly across the lake from you, so I'll be there in an hour and a half. I'll tell you all about it then. In the meantime, I want you to check your email. See if anything has come in from Jon."

"I just was on email. There was nothing."

"It's possible you got an email from an unfamiliar address. Jon doesn't have access to his phone. But he might have been able to use a guard's phone to send an email from a different web-based address. You wouldn't recognize that address as familiar."

"Oh, no!" Vince said.

"What?"

"I may have screwed up big time. I was just purging my junk mail. One of them had that little red priority flag. The subject line said something like 'Extremely Important' with an exclamation point. I thought it was one of those spam sex emails. Maybe it was Jon!"

"Maybe. See if there is a way for you to retrieve that email. Maybe it wasn't completely purged and went into the trash folder instead."

"I'm an idiot!" Vince said. "How could I be so stupid. I'll check again."

The sun was climbing high in the sky as Spot and I showed up at the caretaker apartment where Vince and Brie lived near Homewood. Spot trotted up the stairs to the door, and Vince let us in. Brie stood nearby. She had that happy sad look as if she was so glad I'd found Jonni alive, and yet was still so worried.

Vince looked weary and worn out. No doubt he hadn't had any decent sleep since his kid was kidnapped.

"I checked my email," Vince said as he put on a pot of coffee. "There was no way to retrieve the ones I deleted."

A couple of minutes later, he poured coffee into three mugs. We sat at his kitchen table.

"How did you find the place where they have Jon?" Vince asked.

"The man who went missing and who was probably the body up in the crags of Job's Sister was Yardley LaMotte, the founder of Tahoe Robotics. I learned that Yardley was the visiting teacher who went to Jon's school. Yardley also hired that blue helicopter to take him up to Job's Sister two days before we saw the chopper. His wife gave me permission to go through his files at his office. I found property records for a parcel in Tahoe. By cross-checking parcel maps and old topo hiking maps, I found the place up on a high ridge overlooking Tahoe. Because I didn't want to be obvious, I didn't even attempt finding the trail that would lead to the drive. Instead, Spot and I bushwhacked up the mountain."

"So it's an old cabin?"

"No, it's sizable. Like a lodge. I learned that it was built by Isaiah Hellman, the banker who built the Hellman Mansion back in the early nineteen hundreds. He used the lodge as his private getaway and called it Stone Lodge, much different from Pine Lodge, the Hellman mansion on the lake. Stone Lodge is fenced with stone and wood and barbed wire, and there are alarm systems. There are at least three armed guards. The house itself is stone. The drive has a substantial gate. No one could easily break in, and, if someone attempted it, it would likely put Jon at risk."

"Do you know where he's being held in this place?"

"No. All I saw was the guard bringing Jon outside from one of the side doors."

"Was he okay? Was he afraid?" Vince sounded so worried that I thought he might cry.

"He seemed okay, and he didn't seem scared. In fact, he was feisty and a bit wily." I told Vince and Brie about how Jon seemed to manipulate the guard into letting him fix the guard's phone and how, in the process, he may have been able to send an email.

Vince smiled, a father's pride in an accomplished child. "My boy might not be the rugged outdoorsman I hoped to raise," he said, "but I think he's going to grow up to be a really resourceful person, a good, solid man."

I nodded at the two of them, wondering if it was wrong for me not to tell Vince what was obvious to anyone - including Brie - who spent time with his kid, that the child was more girl than boy. That, in fact, at the emotional core, the child was all girl. I wondered if I was complicit in a kind of fraud by not speaking out on the child's behalf. When does the sin of omission become a sin of commission? Yet I stayed quiet. I was just an outsider. And now was not the time. Despite my observation from the forest, I'd never even met Jonni. Yet, it is sometimes the casual observation from someone outside of the inner circle of family that has the ability to jolt a sense of reality into the closest family members. If a casual outsider can see what's obvious, then wouldn't that help the father face the facts?

Vince said, "How can we find out where in this house he's being held?"

"It won't be easy. There aren't big windows. You can't see inside during the day. And there are probably drapes at night."

Vince slammed his fist down on the table. "I did what the kidnappers asked, and they still have my kid! Why do you think they're still holding Jon captive?" Vince was shaking with agitation.

Brie reached over and rubbed his arm. She likely felt helpless, not having the family stature to state her opinion and have it be taken seriously.

"One of the men said something about a password," I said.

Vince nodded in a distracted way, no doubt thinking about Jon trapped in a lodge. Maybe he was tracking what I was saying, or maybe not.

I continued, "Let me back up. I think these men threw Yardley LaMotte out of a helicopter that was flying over Job's Sister. I believe the men wanted some computer software from Yardley LaMotte. Maybe it was on his person. When they first asked you to guide them up the mountain, you said no. My guess is that the men kidnapped Jon to force you into taking them up the mountain so they could retrieve something from LaMotte's body."

I waited a moment to see if Vince was following. When he nodded, I continued.

"Because Yardley protects everything he does with passwords, the men couldn't utilize or even sell the software. But somehow they came to think Jon might know the password. It could be they mentioned Yardley, and Jon revealed he might know something about it. Jon might have thought that knowledge was a bargaining chip. Another possibility is the men learned that Yardley did outreach to schools and they asked Jon if Yardley had ever come to his school. Jon's answer might have been more revealing than he anticipated. Either way, they probably decided to continue to hold Jon in an effort to learn the password."

Vince still looked distracted. But I think he understood what I was saying.

I added, "The fact that Jon has resisted their attempts at getting information from him has kept him safe."

"I want to break into the house! I'll kill them!"

"Slow down, Vince. This can't be solved by impulsive action. This has to be analyzed and planned."

"But where is the house?"

"Vince, I'll tell you most of what I've learned. But the location is the one thing I won't tell you. Not yet, anyway."

Vince jerked himself to a standing position, knocking his chair back behind him. He looked as stunned as if I'd slapped him. "You know where my boy is, and you're going to withhold that information from me? Damn it, Owen, tell me or I'll knock your head off!" He made fists at his sides, his arms rising slightly, muscles bulging with tension. Next to him, Brie looked frightened, her eyes wide with worry, her frown intense.

I stayed sitting, focused on staying calm and relaxed even though I was ready to jump up. For most aggressors, much of the time, if the guy who is threatened raises his voice or his fists, it will trigger the aggressor's attack. But if the guy being threatened looks like he has nothing to worry about, it will produce a pause in the aggressor's manner and sometimes defuse the situation.

"Look, Vince, you've probably got the beef to kill me with one punch if you can land it. And if I get you in a clinch so you can't get off a punch, you might still kill me. But before I die, I'll be able to apply some of the nasty tricks I've learned over my years of being a cop. And you'll go through the rest of your life blind in one eye, deaf in one or both ears, rasping your breath through crushed trachea, and learning to write with your left hand because your right hand no longer works well enough to pick up a pencil."

Vince snorted like a bull, his chest rising and falling. He was ready to leap over the table, but he stayed put for the moment.

"One more thing," I said. "Consider whose side I'm on. The

answer makes it pretty obvious that I have a good reason for not telling you where your boy might be. I know your instinct would be to rush in. And that will get you shot into pieces and, in this situation, cut into pieces. It would probably get your boy killed as well. However, if we plan this carefully, we might be able to rescue your kid."

Brie reached up and rubbed Vince's back.

Vince stared at me, his eyes narrowed. In time, his breathing slowed. His fists relaxed. He sat back down on the kitchen chair, lowered his elbows to his knees, and hung his head. "Okay," he said toward the floor. "What do we do next?"

"First, we need help. We can't go in alone. I've watched this place and counted three men. All three were carrying guns. One was a rifle with a scope. Two of the men had knives."

Vince said, "Were these guys bulked up? Acted like they were some kind of Nordic killing squad?"

"Yes."

I pulled out my phone and showed Vince the pictures I'd taken.

He pointed. "That's Jon." Vince's voice cracked. "My poor boy. He must be terrified. I can't believe this is happening." He sniffled, wiped his eyes. "His hair looks funny. Like it went curly. And why is his shirt tied up?"

I didn't think it necessary to respond.

"The guys I took up Job's Sister wore ski masks," Vince said. "So I can't say for certain, but I bet these are the guys. There were three of them. The one who was blown off the summit was the most normal of the three. He probably died, so that left two. And now there are three at this place."

"Yeah. I'm guessing the additional man is the helicopter pilot. When you took the men up the mountain, did any of them talk with a Swedish accent?"

"Not that I heard," Vince said. "One didn't talk at all in front of me. And what I heard from the other two was American English." Vince pointed at my pictures. "Do you think there was anyone else in the lodge besides the three men you saw?"

"I don't know. Maybe. All three of these guys spoke American English. It could be these guys are the soldiers, and they're taking orders from a general. Where that general is, I don't know. The general could be the man called Lucas, who spoke with an accent. But Lucas could also be one of these men. His accent might have only been used on the phone. It would fool us into thinking there are more men." I pointed at the picture on the phone. "Either way, the building is a well-fortified house, made of stone, nearly inaccessible. It will take more than two of us to take them."

"Who do you propose to help us?"

"First, I'll give you the standard answer, recognized by all experts as the most sensible thing to do."

"No!" Vince shouted. "They said no cops. If they see a SWAT team show up, they'll gun down my kid. I can tell. I've been with these guys. They have dead eyes. That's what you concentrate on when someone wears a ski mask. Dead eyes. Dead hearts, too. They would kill my boy just to prove that they mean what they say."

Vince was breathing hard.

I waited a minute. "The problem is that this stone house sits at the end of a high-elevation ridge. Because of its setting, it's closer to a medieval fortress than a ski vacation lodge. There is just one road in, and it's gated. The land drops away on either side. Glacial moraine with loose scree. Hard to climb. It would be a slow process. All of the approach areas are visible from the house."

I paused to let Vince visualize.

"However, I think I can get a warrant based on what I saw and photographed. If so, a tactical group could approach at night, take down the gate, maybe even disabling the alarm. They could make a fast entry assault."

"No! These kidnappers would have a lookout. They would hear the cops coming. They'd have plenty of time to kill my boy." Vince was shaking his head. "There must be a way to bribe them. They're ultimately after money, right? So there must be a way to pay them enough to release Jon."

"I've talked to several people connected to Tahoe Robotics, Yardley LaMotte's company. I don't know if Yardley's software was stolen. But I asked them to estimate its value. The number they spoke of was a billion dollars. Even if the kidnappers were willing to accept a payoff, I can't think of a way to get that kind of money."

Vince looked devastated.

Vince thought about it. "So you want to pursue the SWAT team approach."

"Actually, no. I said it was recognized by experts as the best way to go in this situation. As a law enforcement person, it's essential that I tell you what the experts think. But I can still disagree."

"I don't understand," Vince said.

"I think you might be right that they could kill your boy. From what I observed, it seemed that these men have no common sense. The way they strut around, it's like they identify with evil comic book characters simply because it feels cool. And because of the layout of this place, I think an approach with a lot of men coming along the road would cause too much commotion. The house appears to have a secure fence and a good alarm system. Maybe two alarm setups, unrelated. The cops could disarm one and still set off another. Even if the armed men inside don't have a lookout posted, it's still likely they'd be awakened by an alarm."

"You think fewer men is better?" Vince said.

"Possibly. A small, silent team. I think you should be on the team because you would have the best chance of keeping your boy quiet and protected. I would go in with my dog because he's usually a help in unfamiliar circumstances."

Vince frowned. "I don't understand. The bad guys can shoot a dog as easily as a person."

"Actually, they can't. A dog doesn't present anywhere near as much frontal area to a shooter. And they move much faster. It's relatively hard to shoot a dog. Also, a dog doesn't shy away from guns. A dog doesn't have fear. He can be sent to attack a suspect no matter how scary that person is to another person. A dog also becomes a good distraction in case the men have their own dog."

I continued, "The last advantage to a dog is that, compared to us, it can pretty much see in the dark."

"Because of its ears and nose?"

"Yeah. Their hearing is much more acute than ours, and their sense of smell is ten thousand times better than ours."

Vince nodded. "So you and I go in with your dog. That's two of us and one dog against three or more armed killers."

"I'd like to bring my friend Diamond Martinez," I said.

"Who's he?"

"A sergeant with the Douglas County Sheriff's Office."

"I said no cops!"

"He wouldn't come in cop capacity. He'd come as a civilian, dressed in his civvies. And he wouldn't tell the sheriff's office. Diamond and I have an understanding. As far as anyone is concerned after the fact, they will believe that Diamond had to make a last-moment decision to try and help save your son's life. He won't have had time to call in the troops."

"Will he agree to help?"

"I don't know. I think so. He's a good guy, determined to do the right thing in every situation."

Vince held my eyes. "You're saying that if the sheriff later asks about it, the official word will be that Diamond didn't have time to call in backup support."

"Yeah. Plus this target is located outside of Diamond's county. That makes it easier." That probably wasn't true, but I thought it would help Vince go with the idea.

"This all sounds very - what's the word - tentative," Vince said. "And it could result in my son getting killed."

"That's why I gave you the official recommendation to bring in the SWAT team."

Vince frowned and sat in silence for awhile. Eventually, he said, "I can see that an assault by a SWAT team would be best from the standpoint of rounding up the kidnappers. But I also know what they told me. No matter how successful a SWAT team could be, if my kid died, I would… I'd be destroyed."

"It's a tough call," I said.

Vince looked out the window, seeing, probably, not the landscape outside but his boy locked in a room, maybe tied to something to prevent his escape.

Vince said, "You said the only approach to this place is a gated road along a ridge. We're coming up on the first quarter moon, high in the sky at sunset. But if we went at three in the morning, the moon will have set. We could sneak along the road without being seen unless someone had an infrared scope."

"Good thought," I said. "You know your moon phases."

"When you lead wilderness trips, you always know where the moon is," Vince said. "But, whether we go before the moon sets or not, we won't want to stay on the road because it may be monitored, right? Even the forest around the house might be monitored."

"True. But there's probably a way in that won't trigger any cameras or motion sensors until the last moment," I said.

"What would that be?"

"Can you fly your paraglider without a moon?"

Vince raised his eyebrows. "I never thought of that! I could do a skydrop."

THIRTY-TWO

"What's a skydrop?" I asked.

"In our gliding circle, we sometimes talk about what to do when the breeze stops and we lose our ridge lift. If that happens when we're over forest, it creates a dangerous situation."

"Because you have to get down through the forest canopy," I said.

"Exactly. We have to find an opening and do a pinpoint drop out of the sky. So we call it a skydrop."

"Tell me how this could work," I said.

"I could fly my glider into the house's yard. It would be silent. If no one was looking out, I could get right to their door undetected." Vince thought about it, then said, "In answer to your question, yes I could fly without a moon. It's like flying a small plane without instruments. All I need are some ground lights to get a sense of how far I am above the trees."

"What if there were no lights on at the house and you came down toward the trees in the night?"

"Then I could fly directly into a tree and kill myself. Or I could get tangled in a tree and hang and twist in the wind until I'm rescued. If I'm rescued. I suppose I could bring a flashlight. But a regular beam wouldn't be bright enough from up in the sky. If I brought my tactical flashlight, that's probably bright enough to let me see as I'm flying in. But it would negate the whole point of paragliding in at night, right? A super bright light would announce my approach. If the beam shined on any of the house's windows, anyone inside would be instantly aware. It'd be like a spotlight on the curtains or blinds."

"Right," I said. "You'd have to drop out of the sky in complete darkness. So we'll just hope there'll be some lights on at the house." I sipped coffee that had gone cold. "How would you get into the air above the house?" I asked. "You said you can't jump out of a plane with a paraglider."

"Right. Paragliding is a foot-launched sport. You've probably seen parachutes shaped in an arc that are a cross between a paraglider and a parachute. They're pretty maneuverable. But they don't glide like a paraglider. But if you jumped out of a plane with a paraglider, it would rip apart."

"How exactly do paragliders work?" I asked.

"Basically, you get up on a mountain or a dropoff where there's a steady wind coming up from below. Landforms push wind up. The rising air lifts us off the ground. There's different techniques depending on wind direction and speed. But the basic thing is to let the wind fill your glider. It's the wind that makes it hold its shape. Think of a paraglider as a wing made of cloth tubes. The wind blows into those tubes. When the tubes are filled, air pressure makes the glider rise up above your head. You take a few running steps downhill or off a cliff, and then you step off into the air."

"Next question," I said. "Didn't you say that you're an instructor, and you use a tandem glider to carry a passenger?"

"Why didn't I think of that?! You could come with me! I've used a tandem to give lessons many times." Vince stared with wide eyes, not seeing me or Brie but an image in his head.

"Are tandems dark-colored enough to be invisible at night?"

Vince nodded. "Lots of gliders are bright. But the tandem that I use belongs to a buddy in Carson City. He lets me rent it on a per-day basis. It's a deep purple. On a night with no moon, and if there aren't many lights shining up at the sky, it would be invisible. But those conditions would also mean I'd risk killing both of us. Can we find a way to spy on this place from the next ridge over or something? So we can see if there's any lights on at night?"

"Sure. We could hike up at night. But if we wanted to not waste time and go up tonight, then we won't know about lights at night."

Vince paused. "There's a lot of problems with this idea."

"Like what?"

"When you do a wilderness trip, you do exhaustive planning. We're talking about paragliding into a place with armed men, but we have no time to prepare. If we go tonight, how would we do it? What is our plan? What happens if we go in and before we even land, they start firing machine guns at us? And if I am able to land between the trees, how do we get your friend inside the fence? What is the best way to get into the house and find my boy? There's a thousand questions. I think it would be better to sneak up through the woods."

"All good points. But we have to make a compromise. Coming by land, we'll set off alarms. And if they were to anticipate someone approaching, it would be by land. But coming from the sky would mean we'd have surprise and silence on our side. Exhaustive planning is great. But no mission, regardless of how thorough the preparation, goes off without some glitches. Usually, there are many glitches. So we need to balance our desire for preparation with the current risk to your son. The longer we wait to go in, the longer he's at risk."

Vince looked horrified. "Are you suggesting they might think there isn't enough reason to keep holding him? Even if we don't challenge them, they could still kill him?"

"Don't focus on that. But these guys are probably unpredictable." I was thinking of the way the man spun his knife to impress a kid. It was a clear demonstration that the man was a mental infant. "We need to prepare for all the possibilities that are obvious. But our preparations could never be exhaustive. And tackling these guys sooner is better, I think."

Vince swallowed. "I understand. They might have already killed him."

I saw Brie flinch as he said it.

"As far as keeping a hold on me, all they need is for me to believe he's still alive. That isn't the same as him actually being alive, right?"

"True. But try not to despair. He's likely to still be alive for the simple reason that he is probably still resisting their attempts to make him give up the password. I heard him talk to them. One man cut his hand and Jon helped bandage it. Just by his words, I could tell that he's smart enough to know how to play dumb. Even if he knows the password, I think he'll act as if he is still trying to figure it out. Also, keeping Jon alive gives the kidnappers options. He's like a chess piece to them. They can use him for strategic advantage in many ways. But most of those ways evaporate if he isn't alive."

Vince nodded.

"What are the other problems you're thinking about?" I asked.

"We have no time to practice. From what you said, it doesn't sound like you've ever even seen a paraglider up close. How will you prepare? Leaping a tandem rig off a mountain at night is going to be hard. Doing it with someone who's never flown is asking for trouble."

"I'm competent. You'll only need to give me a thorough explanation of the process, and I'll be fine." It was a presumptuous statement regarding how I would perform, but accurate regarding how I approach such tasks. "Tell me what to do, and I'll do it, regardless of whether my stomach is doing somersaults of fear."

"Okay, but we haven't gotten an okay from your friend."

"Diamond," I said.

"Right." When will you call him?"

"If you're okay with this, I'll call him now."

Vince seemed to study my face. He looked at Brie.

She nodded.

"Okay," Vince said. "I'm ready to go."

THIRTY-THREE

I nodded, pulled out my phone, and called Diamond. He answered on the second ring.

"Are you on duty?"

"Sí. Morning shift. Off at two p.m."

"I'm hoping you can help with me with a problem," I said. "Can you talk now?"

"As long as the man on the highway in front of me keeps it below fifty."

I looked at Vince as I spoke to Diamond. "I think I told you in general terms about a man with a serious problem. You figured out that it must involve a kidnapping," I said.

"I remember," Diamond said.

"The man's name is Vince Cooper. He's with me now. I'm going to put the phone on speaker, because he's why I'm calling and he should hear what we say. Vince's girlfriend Brie is also here."

"Okay," Diamond said.

I pressed the speaker button and set the phone on Vince's kitchen table.

"Hi, Diamond. This is Vince."

"Hola, Vince and Brie," Diamond said.

I said, "Vince is a paragliding instructor and a wilderness guide. His son's name is Jon. And you know about Yardley LaMotte?"

"Yardley LaMotte is the Tahoe Robotics guy who went missing," Diamond said.

"Right. Yesterday, I found out that Yardley LaMotte owns a property in Tahoe that no one seems to know about, a property that was built by Isaiah Hellman, the guy who built the Hellman

Mansion. Spot and I hiked up to this little-known property late yesterday and saw Vince's son Jon being held captive there by three men. I believe they are the same men who had Vince take them up Job's Sister. Despite Vince doing as they demanded, they haven't released Jon. My thought is that the kidnappers stole software from Yardley, but they can't get past the software security. I'm guessing that they learned that Yardley taught a computer class at Jon's school. Yardley had told people he met a very bright student there. Yardley's work colleague said that Yardley liked to dangle valuable information in front of the kids to see if any of them would ever catch on. And Vince's kid did. It's possible that the kidnappers haven't let Jon go because they think he can tell them the password to that software."

"And you want my help in what way?" Diamond asked.

"I'd like you to help Vince and me plan an assault on the house where they're holding the boy prisoner. It could get us all killed, including the kidnapped boy. But we might also save the boy and apprehend the kidnappers. I told Vince that experts all agree that kidnappings are best resolved in the traditional way, calling the sheriff and letting them and the FBI orchestrate the troops. But the kidnappers told both Vince and me that if he tells the police, they will kill his boy. He believes them. I believe it's possible, too. Maybe even likely. These guys seem like soldier wannabes who are missing common sense or judgement. At the least, a SWAT assault would place the boy at greater risk in the near term."

"These are the Brödraskapet gangbangers you talked about?"

"Yeah," I said. "Crazies who play with their knives."

"What could we do that would be a better solution than a SWAT team?" Diamond asked.

"We'd be fewer men and thus quieter. We'd be less easy to detect by either electronic or human monitoring. We'd have Spot, whose value is usually significant even if not obvious from the start. If we can get to the kid, Vince would be able to calm and reassure his son and help him get out of the house. Whereas a SWAT team entering a house at night is likely to terrify the boy."

"How do you envision us going in?" Diamond asked.

"The place is surrounded by a fence topped with barbed wire and at least one alarm system. I'm thinking that you and Spot would hike up the road. Then you'd wait in the forest while Vince and I drop over the fence and into the yard by paraglider."

There was silence on the phone.

Eventually Diamond spoke. "Do you know how to fly a paraglider?"

"No. Vince is an instructor. He takes people up on a tandem glider. I would ride with him. The beauty of a paraglider is that it's silent. The soldiers at the house have multiple weapons and are prepared in case of an assault. But they'd never expect it to drop out of the sky. And even if the thought occurred to them, they'd assume any air attack would come by helicopter and be preceded by lots of noise."

More silence.

Diamond said, "Vince, does this crazy idea seem reasonable to you?"

"Yeah," Vince said. "I've taken a lot of beginners up on their first ride. It's really just a matter of sitting in the seat and doing what I say and staying calm."

"You think you can do this, Owen?"

"The life of a child is at stake."

"What is it that you'd expect me to do after you drop in on this house?" Diamond said.

"First, Vince will let Spot and you in the gate, which may be as easy as finding and pushing a button or as difficult as unbolting and disconnecting the motorized arm that pulls the gate open. Or maybe he simply helps you and Spot climb over."

"And then…" Diamond said.

"And then we three and Spot figure out a way to enter the house and free the boy."

"You have a plan for that?"

"Not yet. I've got a few ideas that I haven't thought through. This place is called Stone Lodge. From what I read about it, this place has a secret entrance under one of the windows. It can be opened without a key. The men may not know about it, in which case it might not be barricaded. But whether we can sneak in or have to break a window, we could go in with bear spray canisters and use those to subdue the men."

"Pepper spray," Diamond said. "Poor man's mace."

"Yeah. Maybe you have better ideas."

"Maybe not," Diamond said. "There's a guy in Gardnerville who owes me a favor. He's in the business of buying surplus stuff cheap and reselling it. I caught him selling something he shouldn't have. In return for his testimony in a big case, we didn't fuss about his contraband and merely confiscated it. It included a stack of bear spray canisters. I'll see if I can pick up three of them after my shift."

"Great."

Diamond asked, "When would we do this mission?"

"We'd go in tonight."

"Will there be a moon?"

"There's a first quarter moon at sunset. But we'd wait until after the moon has set. That would be about three a.m. The darkness will give us cover."

There was more silence on the line.

"You think our objective is too ambitious?" I said.

"I don't know," Diamond said. "You're competent in most ways."

Brie and Vince both frowned.

"In what ways aren't I competent?" I asked.

"That time you cooked enchiladas at my house, your ratio of cheese to chicken was off a little bit. And one time when you poured me a beer, the head built up and foamed down the outside of the glass. I got it on my hand and I had to wipe it off on my jeans."

"The world is overrun with seriously flawed individuals," I said.

Now Vince and Brie looked confused.

I spoke to the side. "He's making a joke."

They didn't look reassured.

"If the house doesn't have lights on, we'd be in complete darkness," Diamond said.

"And even if there's an outdoor light," I said, "that would still probably be the best time to go in because the men would be at their groggiest."

There was silence on the phone.

"You're thinking about riding a parachute into a fenced mountain compound protected by armed men, and doing it in complete darkness," Diamond said, "And you've never flown a parachute before."

"A paraglider. It's very different than a parachute."

"But still made of flimsy cloth and held in place with strings, right? Able to collapse and allow people to fall to their deaths."

"Maybe we survive and save the boy. You could be part of this noble rescue."

"Entreaties to my soft emotional interior don't usually work," Diamond said. "Where is this house?"

"On a high, isolated ridgetop west of Tahoe City." As I said it, I saw Vince get more attentive. It was the first he'd heard about the location where his kid was held captive.

"Placer County," Diamond said, establishing jurisdiction. "Are you going to tell Sergeant Santiago your plans?"

My turn to pause. "I would love to but I just discovered the boy's location, and there isn't time. We have to, you know, rush in. You know how it is, making an emergency no-knock entry to save a life, no time to get a warrant or find the help of sheriff's officers."

Diamond said, "And you happened to bump into me in the process, and I joined the mission, and then you bumped into Vince Cooper, and he happened to have a tandem parachute. So he flew with you to the house, and there never was even five minutes to call the cops."

"Right. But it's a paraglider. Parachutes can't fly. They can only drop. Glide a little bit forward as they do so, maybe. But still, they just drop."

"So how do paragliders fly, and how do you get them into the air?"

"Vince, you want to explain that?" I said.

"Yeah. Basically, you go up on a mountain where there's a breeze blowing upslope. You jog down into the breeze, and the paraglider takes off. It slowly glides down into the air. If the air mass is rising fast enough, you rise with it, like a soaring eagle, riding the updraft high up into the sky."

"Got it," Diamond said.

"It's pretty simple," I said.

"I'm so reassured," Diamond said. "Where and when do we meet?"

"You said you're off at two. Vince has to drive down to Carson City to borrow the glider. How 'bout we all meet to discuss strategy at my office at three?"

"I'll get my cape and see you then," Diamond said.

THIRTY-FOUR

I drove to the South Shore to stop at my office and check messages. I saw Diamond's candy-apple-green Karmann Ghia outside the Douglas County Sheriff's Office in Stateline. I pulled in to see if he was in or out on patrol. I found him standing outside the entrance, holding a map, and talking to a deputy. As usual, his dress browns were pressed to perfection, shoes polished to a high sheen. He looked up at me.

"Hey, sergeant. I saw the Green Flame. Thought I'd say hi." Diamond would know otherwise, but it made things seem benign in front of his deputy.

"Hi," he said. He turned away from me, said a few more words to the deputy, then pointed to the map.

The deputy nodded, took the map, and folded it up as he walked away.

Diamond walked over to me. "We're meeting later. What's up now?"

"I was thinking about the Brödraskapet gang, and I wondered if there's anything else you've thought of that I should be prepared for."

"Good to be worried," he said as he walked past the Green Flame. He pinched the sharp crease on one of his uniform pant legs, hitched it up, and sat at an angle on a section of split rail fence that defined the edge of the parking lot.

He said, "After we talked about the Brödraskapet, I looked up some Swedish stuff. Learned about the Svenska language, too. Good to know next time I'm in Stockholm."

"You've been to Stockholm?"

"Never. But Stockholm looks pretty. Kind of place where I could meet a woman named Inge on the shores of Lake Mälaren.

Change my life."

"Inge?" I said.

"Name comes from Ingun, a Goth goddess."

"Which doesn't tell me how tough these Brödraskapet dudes are. These guys who have Vince's kid are scary. Hard bodies. Tough attitude. Like UFC fighters. But is it mostly show? Or do we really need to fear them?"

"Well, I don't know much," Diamond said. "Swedes have always shown great determination. You've probably heard of how the Goths sacked Rome."

"Probably," I said.

"Most historians trace the Goths back to what is now Sweden. Their culture goes back a thousand years before Christ. Then, around the first century AD, the Goths decided to reach out. So they sailed across the Baltic Sea to what is now Poland and from there spread across Europe. A bunch of them became Vikings, went on raids all over the Baltic and North Atlantic, stole women, and took them back home. There were more Swedish Vikings than Norwegian. Lots of different Goth groups emerged. And physically, they have always been an imposing people. Big and tall and pale. Like you, but more muscles for paddling their long boats. There were Goth invasions all throughout Europe. Tough, muscular farmers and boatsmen and warriors."

"Isn't it a reach to assume they were tough and muscular?" I asked.

Diamond shook his head. "Around the time the Goths took Rome in four hundred AD, there was a Greek historian named Eunapius who described the Goths as too big and too heavy but pinched in at the waists like wasps. Sounded like he was describing superheroes."

"I guess that means the Greek guy didn't like them."

"Regular men have never much liked other men who are big and strong and handsome and have narrow waists. You tolerate a superhero if he's vanquishing evil. But you don't want to hang out and drink beer with him."

I nodded.

Diamond said, "So it would be good to be very careful around the Brödraskapet boys."

"You learn anything specific about the gang?"

"I told you I'd seen a video that mentioned karambit knives. I called the guy who put on the presentation and asked him about the Brödraskapet. He said their basic foundation is a set of rules to weed out anyone who isn't the worst of the worst. For example, to become an official Brödraskapet gang member, you have to have been incarcerated in a maximum security prison. You can't have ever complied with a requirement to submit urine for a drug test. You can't have ever informed on another prisoner. And you can't have ever taken part in any rehabilitation program."

"A code of toughness," I said.

"Sí. Stupid toughness," Diamond said.

"Do you know of any useful techniques to use if one were to get in a fight with a guy who uses a karambit knife?"

He thought about it. "Washoe County is the only nearby Sheriff's Office with anything approaching big-city experience, what with Reno and Sparks. You could call them. Do you remember Sergeant Lori Lanzen in Incline Village?"

"Yeah," I said. "She came to that crime scene in Incline Village where I was nearly killed."

Diamond nodded. "I've heard in the past that Washoe County Sheriff's Office sometimes utilizes a Bay Area weapons trainer who retired to Washoe Valley. If you called Sergeant Lanzen, she could probably give you his contact info. Maybe he could help." Diamond looked at his watch. "Lots I gotta do. See you at your office at three."

"Thanks."

I went back to my Jeep, endured Spot's cold, wet, nose on my neck, and called the Washoe County Sheriff's Office.

The person who answered the phone made it sound like he was putting me through to Lanzen, but all I got was her voicemail. I left a thorough message.

I headed toward home and had just driven through the Cave

Rock Tunnel when my phone rang.

"Owen McKenna."

"Lori Lanzen returning your call. Your message said you wanted info on knife fighting?" She sounded incredulous.

"Yeah. Sorry. I realize it sounds kind of out there. I'm dealing with a branch of a Swedish prison gang called The Brotherhood. Or maybe just dirtballs who would like to be a branch of the gang. These particular guys emphasize their wickedness by carrying special blades called karambit knives. Douglas County Sergeant Diamond Martinez told me that Washoe County sometimes consults with a weapons trainer who lives in Washoe Valley. Does that sound familiar?"

"Yeah, I know of him. Kenneth Boomerian. Although he goes by Kenny Boom. Made his living in the Bay Area teaching cops the finer points of shooting. Maybe he knows knives, too, but I haven't heard one way or another. Did Martinez tell you he's retired?"

"Yeah. But maybe he'd be willing to do a little consulting?"

"You'll find out when you call. Let me see if I have his contact info in my phone." After a minute she read off a number. "Tell me, McKenna. Is this gang in Washoe County?"

"Not that I know of. Right now, they're on the West Shore. Placer County. I don't even know if they're officially with the Swedish gang. But they seem to embrace some of the gang's wicked characteristics. And they may have been involved in a murder or two up on a South Shore mountain, Job's Sister."

"El Dorado County," Lanzen said, establishing jurisdiction just as Diamond had.

"Right. If they come to your neck of the woods, I'll let you know."

"Thanks."

We hung up. I was almost home. So I drove up the mountain to my cabin, let Spot out to run, and called Kenny Boom on my landline, which had much better reception than my cell.

THIRTY-FIVE

"Hello?" a man answered in an airy voice like what you'd get from throat damage.

Sergeant Lori Lanzen had said that weapons expert Kenny Boom had retired. Yet the man who answered sounded older than I expected. It didn't matter. An old weapons expert probably knew more than a young one.

"Owen McKenna calling for Kenny Boom, please."

"Speaking. Who's Owen McKenna?"

"I'm a private cop up at Tahoe. Sergeant Martinez of Douglas County referred me to Sergeant Lanzen of Washoe County, saying Washoe County has worked with you. Lanzen gave me your name and number. She said you're retired but that maybe I could ask if you might do a little consulting. I'm dealing with a Swedish Prison gang named The Brödraskapet. They carry karambit knives. I could use some expertise."

There was a long pause. "I've dealt with private cops before. Haven't been real impressed."

"Sorry about that. I'll try not to disappoint. What I'd like is to buy some of your expertise. I'll pay your per diem for an hour of your time."

Another long pause. "You got any qualifications?"

"I can't be bought off. I work with cops, not against them. I've put away some bad guys."

"You ever work in a uniform?"

"Twenty years SFPD. Last several as Homicide Inspector."

"Well, why didn't you say so. What's your schedule?"

"I'm open. Sooner is better."

"Can you come down to Washoe Valley today?"

"I can be there in an hour."

"Make it an hour and a half." He gave me the address.

Spot and I had time to eat some lunch, potato chips and hotdogs and ketchup. I cut Spot's hotdogs into pieces and stirred them into the compressed sawdust dog food with a little added ketchup and broken potato chips. Judging by the rate he inhaled it and his enthusiasm for licking his bowl clean, he liked it even better than I did. As a guilty afterthought and a way to save face with Street should she ask about my lunch, I ate some spinach and cherry tomatoes and carrots before I had two donuts for dessert. Spot didn't want the veggies, but he loved his donuts.

We got back in the Jeep. I went up and over Spooner Summit and down to Carson City. The new freeway routed us around the city, up the rise on the north side of the valley, then dropped down to Washoe Valley. We'd had good precipitation the previous winter, so the on-again, off-again Washoe Lake was full and seemed to be a massive truck stop for birds.

I turned off the freeway, drove along the mountainside to the west, and found Kenny Boom's turnoff a few miles up.

Boom lived in a low-slung ranch house with nut-brown wood siding, a red metal roof, and a wide porch that wrapped around the west, south, and east sides. It looked very stylish and would have fit in Jackson, Wyoming or Sun Valley, Idaho or Aspen, Colorado.

Kenny Boom was sitting on a wooden rocking chair on his porch as we came down the country road. From the distance of his driveway turnoff, I could see he wore blue jeans and a beige shirt, and a wide black cowboy hat. I headed down the gravel drive, the stones crackling under the Jeep tires, and parked. Up closer, his hat was a Cattleman's design, probably a Stetson. His black cowboy boots looked like Western riding boots, with the angled heel and tapered toes. The only thing missing was horses in the nearby pasture.

But the entire valley was filled with horses, possibly outnumbering the human population, so it could well be that he had horses somewhere.

I got out of the Jeep and walked up to the porch. The man got out of his rocker and met me at the porch steps.

Standing on his top step, in his high-heeled boots, he looked down on me as he shook my hand.

"Kenny Boom," he said. "Pleased to make your acquaintance. Come sit awhile and tell me how I can help you."

He parked in his rocker, and I sat on a large wicker chair with a comfortable pad. Without telling him names or any other specific information, I told him about the Swedish gang and the fact that they'd kidnapped my client's kid.

"Our contact said that if this gets reported to the cops, the kid gets killed in retaliation," I said. "I don't know if the threat is sincere. But there have already been two deaths up on a mountain. In my plan to tackle this without bringing in a SWAT team, I will likely confront one or more of these gang members. I've learned they carry karambit knives. Perhaps it's all show. Or perhaps this is their weapon of choice. From what I understand about karambit knives, they can kill and forensics cannot establish the weapon. The blades slice, but they leave no hints as to their origins. So I'm hoping for some kind of preparation before I go in. I could end up in a knife fight. Any tips you can give me would be much appreciated."

Kenny Boom rocked back and forth. He reached a thick, stubby index finger up and scratched his earlobe.

"First, I should tell you that my expertise is firearms. I spent fifteen years as a cop in Oakland, then quit to teach firearms at two different cop schools, then segued into consulting. I've worked for five Bay Area county sheriff's offices and several cities. So if the weapon fires a bullet, I'm your guy. I'm not quite so familiar with knives. However, I've seen what a karambit can do, and anyone who would use one has personality problems."

"Tips?"

"Let's back up. What's your sidearm?"

"I don't carry."

Kenny Boom gave me a blank stare as if he couldn't comprehend my answer.

"Long story," I said.

"Right. Well, what I was going to say is, the best defense against a karambit knife is to have your piece out and cocked, with a round in the chamber and your finger inside the trigger guard. But now that's off the table. So let me start by saying something you probably know if you think about it. The entire concept of a knife fight is bogus. People don't fight with knives. It's not like some dual where the procedure is laid out in advance or a boxing match where the rules are clear and enforced by the referee. The whole point of any knife not used for cooking or cleaning game is that it's carried incognito and employed in a stealth fashion. A guy who wants to attack with a knife keeps it hidden until the time for the attack. Then he brings it out and slashes or stabs in an instant. The victim never sees it coming. No one ever pulls out a knife from a distance, brandishes it as a warning, and then slowly moves in. Maybe in some movies or Youtube videos, but that's not usually the way it is in real life. In real life, if someone pulled out a knife and gave his adversary warning, the adversary would either run out the back door and disappear or pull out a gun and shoot him."

I thought about what he said. "That makes sense. So humor me, please. Let's say I get into a conflict with a man. Even if the man doesn't show his weapon until the last moment, I suspect it exists all along. What might I do to prepare for this?"

Kenny Boom made a big inhalation and let it out in a long sigh as if it were very frustrating to deal with ignorant people like me, ex-cops who should know better.

"Let me review the hierarchy of weapons," he said.

Maybe I frowned at him.

"I realize this is no-brainer stuff that you know," he said. "But it helps to lay it out in a logical fashion. On the spectrum of weapons, let's say the left end is the low-grade stuff. Fists and fingernails and teeth. On the right end is nuclear bombs. A dramatic illustration, but you get my point. Any weapon on the spectrum, wielded with basic competence, takes out the lesser weapon to its left side on the spectrum. When we move away from the far left on the spectrum, away from using our hands as weapons, the very first thing we come to is knives or knife-like instruments. Slashing with a karambit knife is more sophisticated than stabbing someone with a pencil, but the basic principle is the same. It's a lowly, primitive weapon. Why does that matter? Because anyone with a good club takes out anyone with a knife. That's why the knife has to be concealed until it's used. If it's not concealed, the potential victim picks up a baseball bat or even a large, heavy candlestick holder and kills the person with the knife. And so it goes up the hierarchy. A spear, or a bow and arrow, takes out the person with a club. A gun takes out the person with a bow and arrow. You get the idea. So if you are worried about a man with a karambit knife, don't ever waste time wondering how to fight him. Just make sure you have a club. It doesn't matter what kind of club. You know from your cop days the effectiveness of a baton or sap. Think about saps. Short leather clubs that are made around a flexible steel rod and weighted inside with lead. If you have a crazy coming after you, and you don't carry a gun, which would you consider the more reliable and effective weapon to have on your person? A knife? A stun gun? Or a sap?"

"Definitely, a sap," I said.

"So don't worry about how to fight a knife-wielding crazy. If a guy surprises you and sticks you between the fifth and sixth rib and nails your heart, you're dead whether you're packing a nine or a rocket launcher. But if you're lucky enough to see a knife coming, and you have a short sap in the cargo pocket of your jeans, you'll be fine."

I sat a moment absorbing what he'd said.

"So the whole concept of a karambit knife is basically more about intimidation than being an effective weapon," I said.

"Definitely," Kenny Boom said. "Yes, it kills. Yes, it's scary. But it's still a cutting, stabbing instrument that you conceal until the last moment. It's still just a knife. More effective than punching or biting. But not much more effective than a Boy Scout knife. Imagine you have one of these karambit knives and you want to kill a man who has a sap. How do you think it would play out?"

"If the man with the sap saw me pull out the knife, and if he was even half my physical equal, he'd swing his sap and break the arm I was holding the knife with and then break my head."

Kenny Boom leaned back in his rocker. He made a small smile.

"When I walked away from the SFPD," I said, "I left all of my gear with them. As I'm no longer a current peace officer in the state of California, I believe it's illegal for me to carry a flexible sap or an expandable baton."

"Yeah, the rules are crazy. We all - you excepted - carry our guns. And our retired cop IDs mean we don't have to get concealed carry permits for our guns. But most states and cities have laws making it illegal to carry a wide range of weapons, from brass knuckles to ninja stars. Illegal for ex-cops to carry them, too. Why? Because they are lethally dangerous and could be used to kill people." Boom made a little chuckle, and his smile grew a bit wider. "For that matter, the wording of the laws often refers to any item specifically carried to be a weapon. So even a baseball bat could, in certain situations, be looked at in court as a dangerous weapon and thus illegal. But guns, the most dangerous of all, are not only legal, they're celebrated and encouraged. Aren't politicians great?"

Kenny Boom added. "Bottom line is, always remember the lowly club. Most ex-cops I know are creative and resourceful. I'm sure you are, as well." He didn't elaborate, but the intended message was clear.

I stood up. Shook his hand. "Thanks, Kenny. You've been very helpful. How much do I owe you?"

"We'll just call this professional courtesy," he said. "Good luck."

THIRTY-SIX

I drove south to Carson City, stopped at a Lowe's and found the plumbing section. They had a selection of galvanized steel pipe. I looked around for an employee and found a man in his seventies who had the employee badge and apron.

"Can you please help me?" I said. "I'm looking for a section of steel plumbing pipe, threaded on both ends so I can screw pipe caps onto it. Maybe twelve inches long."

"Now that's an unusual plumbing project. Pipe caps on both ends. We usually think of pipe as something that carries water." He gave me a little grin. "Usually a strange request like that suggests you broke something and you're looking for a temporary fix before your wife discovers what you did. But the cap on both ends means you're not screwing the pipe into anything else, like, I don't know, temporarily replacing the broken leg on a couch or something."

"No wife," I said. "Nothing broken, either. Just a quirky idea I had to fix an unusual problem. I won't know if it works until I try it."

"Alrighty, then. Check this out." He took me over to some bins with pre-cut pipe sections. "These pre-cuts come threaded on both ends. Our shortest is three foot long and three-quarter inch on the inside dimension. So I'm thinking, we trim off a one-foot chunk, get out the die, and cut threads on the fresh end. Then we screw a galvanized malleable iron pipe cap on each end. I'd have to charge you for our shop fee, which is a time-based cost. So when we're done, you're gonna think this is the most expensive pipe you ever bought that didn't come from a plumber. How does that sound?"

"Perfect. Is that something you can do today?"

The man looked up and down the aisle, gauging traffic. "Tell you what. I'll let Sandy know I've got a custom pipe order. Right now, I'm pret' near sure she'll be okay with me going back in the shop. But if we get a rush and she calls me out, you'll have to wait while I do the retail thing. Will that work for you?"

"Yes, please. I'll wait as long as it takes."

The man pushed a button on his belt radio, bent his head and talked into a mic clipped to his lapel, got a response, then nodded and let go of the button.

The man pulled a pipe from the bin, pulled a tape measure off his belt and measured off 12 inches. He used the tape measure to make a tiny etched mark on the pipe and handed it to me. "You want twelve inches exactly including the end caps?"

I took the pipe, held it near the little mark. "The measurement isn't precise. Let's make it an inch longer and then the pipe caps will add another half inch or so when they're screwed on."

"Okay. Thirteen inches it is. A good lucky number."

He took the pipe down the aisle, found iron pipe caps, then headed back toward a door at the back of the store. He stopped and turned back to me and said, "For custom jobs, we're supposed to get a fifty-dollar pre-auth on your credit card so we know you won't disappear while we're in the back room. But just between you and me, that's like getting a pre-auth on your Budweiser bump on the way home after work. I don't need to do that, right?"

"Right," I said. "I'll be here when you're done."

He nodded and went through the door.

I spent my time going up the plumbing aisle learning about faucets. I acquired a basic familiarity with kitchen faucets, shower faucets, bathroom sink faucets, bar faucets, and tub faucets. I grappled with the differences between double-handle faucets and single-handle faucets. There was even a section on touchless faucets. That stopped me for a bit as I didn't understand how they worked. But I didn't finish my education because the man came back. He handed me my custom pipe section, thirteen inches of heavy black metal with silvery end caps. It fit the hand well, and had a significant heft. The end caps served not just as additional weight but as a stop to keep the pipe from sliding out of a sweaty hand.

"What do you think?" he asked. "Will this get you out of your bind?"

"It's perfect," I said.

I thanked the man again, and I paid a very reasonable price for it at the cashier. When I was done, I walked out of the store with the plainest, smallest, simplest, and most basic but totally deadly weapon a guy could carry without having to wonder how to load bullets into a magazine. The pipe club fit nicely in the narrow tool pocket on the hip side of my jeans, projecting out just enough to make it easy to grab. It fit my hand. It was light enough to swing easily. It was heavy and dense enough to crush bones.

Hopefully, I'd never need it and soon I would forget which drawer I'd stuffed it into.

THIRTY-SEVEN

Back at my office, I got on my phone to tell Street about our plan. She made the appropriate protests. I knew it wasn't that she didn't trust me or she thought I was rash. She simply cared that I didn't come to serious injury.

When I was done explaining the plan to her, we said our "I love yous," and I hung up.

I called Vince. "Where are you on the tandem glider?"

"I'm currently driving back from Carson City with the glider," Vince said.

"Still on track to meet at my office at three?"

"Will do."

Diamond and Vince were both on time.

They took the office guest chairs, I sat in my squeaky desk chair, and Spot luxuriated on his custom Harlequin camo bed. Diamond slid his chair sideways so he could reach his arm down and pet Spot.

"Walk us through how you envision this going down," Diamond said.

I gave them a rough list of thoughts and concerns, beginning with possible approaches and retreats. How and where one would come in by paraglider. Checking the weather for wind conditions. Paying special attention to any lights, and what we needed in terms of weapons.

"I don't carry a sidearm, as you know, Diamond. Vince?"

"I'm a mountain guide, into nature. Not a hunter. I don't like guns."

I turned back to Diamond. "A good part of me is hoping you'll have your standard assortment of weapons."

He nodded.

"How do you think the timing should work?" Vince asked.

"You said the moon sets at three. Let's plan our approach for three. So we each back up from there. A big variable for us is where we launch from. Do we need to come off the highest nearby peak? If so, the highest one to the south is probably Rubicon Peak at ninety-two hundred feet. But there's no easy trail to its summit. To the north is Granite Chief Peak at Squaw Valley. That's more like nine thousand feet."

Vince was shaking his head. "It's not the height of our launch location. It's whether there's a wind strong enough to produce an updraft we can ride. If we can drive or hike to a location with a good wind, then the elevation doesn't matter, because we can ride the updraft as far as we want."

"Okay," I said. "You know the territory, right?"

"Pretty much."

"You have topo maps?"

"Yeah. I brought them." He held up a cardboard tube.

"Good. Mine are at home. Let's spread yours out."

We got the maps flattened. I found the one that included the territory of Stone Lodge.

"Here's our destination. It's kind of near the end of this ridge." I made a little X on the map with a pencil. "I'm hoping they will have some kind of light on so we can identify the place in the dark. But if not, here's how I think we can find it flying at night. To the west is Twin Peaks, one of the most distinctive mountains nearby, two sharp points not quite nine thousand feet high. If we can fly close to them, we should be able to recognize them even in the dark of a moonless night." I put my fingertip at Twin Peaks. "Following the ridgeline down from Twin Peaks, we get to Stanford Rock, here. From that point, there's a descending ridge that will take us to Stone Lodge, here."

Vince put his big finger at the X I'd made to represent Stone Lodge.

"Vince, once you determine our best launch location, then we can plan a flight path."

He said, "Our current weather pattern has high winds from the southeast at higher elevations and low winds out of the south at lower elevations. If that pattern holds, the best launch point would be at Alpine Meadows ski area, here. We could drive up to the base of the Sherwood Express chairlift and hike up the mountain. South winds would allow us to launch from the ski slope."

"I've been to the front side of Alpine Meadows when I go skiing," I said. "To get there, you drive in from the Truckee River canyon. But the Sherwood Express lift is on the back side of the ski area, up the Ward Creek Canyon. How long does it take to drive up there from where you live?"

He thought about it. "I think it's about thirty minutes."

"And how long will it take to get into the air with me attached?"

"That's a big variable. It depends on the wind. If the wind is good, we'll only have to hike up the mountain for ten or fifteen minutes to get to a clear launch area. But if the wind is weak, we'll be stuck waiting, hoping it picks up."

"Okay. If we successfully launch, how long will it take to fly from that point to the lodge?"

"Again, it depends on the wind. A decent wind gives us good rate of climb. The lodge is only about two miles away as the crow flies from the ski slope. In ideal conditions, we could fly to the lodge in ten minutes. But a wind that dies out means we don't make it at all and we crash-land someplace in the mountains."

"Then let's work the timing from your place. Let's say Diamond and I meet you at your place. I ride with you in your truck to the ski slope. Diamond takes Spot in the Jeep and drives to a place down below the drive that leads to Stone Lodge. We build in a fudge factor of, say, twenty minutes to ensure we can still arrive on time even if we encounter delays."

"Easy for me," Diamond said. "I get up to the gate early, and I hang with hound dog, here, in the dark." He looked down at Spot. Spot's chin was on his bed, between his front paws. Judging by his shut eyes, he was out cold. But from the way his faux diamond ear stud sparkled, he was processing every nuance of our conversation.

I said, "Vince, I can imagine potential delays in getting to our launch and also flying to the stone lodge. So if we get near the lodge early, can we kill time in the sky?"

"First, our goal will be to launch right after the moon sets and then head staight to the lodge. If we need to kill time, and if there is a steady wind, then we can find a ridge-based updraft and ride it for as long as we want. But if we get airborne and then the updraft we're riding dies, then it could be a problem just getting to the lodge."

"I see that as the most important variable. Can you tell by the weather forecast?"

"That will give us an idea, but nothing solid," Vince said. "I can get a winds-aloft forecast. But local conditions vary, so we often don't know if there's enough wind for our trip to go indefinitely, or if it's just going to be a glider ride downhill."

I opened my laptop and went to the national weather website. "When I search on Lake Tahoe, I get a forecast for lake level, sixty-three hundred feet of elevation. It says winds five to ten, out of the south."

"Not enough to fly," Vince said, shaking his head. "We need the winds-aloft forecast. You hiked up to the house. How high do you think it is?"

"If I compare my climb to The Face ski run at Heavenly, it was much more gentle. But I'd guess my total elevation gain was about three-fourths of The Face."

"The Face rises seventeen hundred vertical feet," Diamond said. "Three fourths of that is about thirteen hundred vertical. What do you think your starting elevation was?"

"I drove in on an old Forest Service road past the Granlibakken Resort, and I climbed several hundred feet. So my hike possibly started around sixty-seven hundred feet. If I add thirteen hundred to that, that would suggest the lodge sits at about eight thousand feet." I turned to the topo map. "That fits with the elevation lines on the map. Let me check winds aloft on the aviation weather site." I brought up the relevant information. "They provide a forecast for nine thousand feet. Clear skies, low temp tonight of twenty-two degrees, wind at ten knots out of the south." I turned to Vince. "How does that sound?"

"Possible but not certain," Vince said again. "A five-knot wind won't produce enough uplift unless the landform is shaped just right and it funnels and concentrates the wind. We're unlikely to find that. But if the wind is ten, it might work. Our situation is complicated by the fact that we're both big guys. You weigh what?"

"Two fifteen," I said.

"Okay. I'm two fifty. That means we're hanging four hundred sixty-some pounds from the glider. And local conditions always change. At twelve or fifteen knots, we'd have ideal potential, but we still won't know until we're in the sky. We may get enough lift here and there to make our destination. But there might not be enough to allow us to hang out and circle above. Gliding in the mountains can be unforgiving to the point of deadly. You can't go down in the forest or on a steep rocky slope without serious consequences. We have a saying in the mountains. 'Take your landings where you can get them.'"

"Okay, you're flying the glider. I'm just riding. So I could be on my cell giving Diamond an update as we get closer. I could tell him when we're about to drop in. Whether you think we're going to make the skydrop or not even get close, I could keep him informed."

"Yeah," Vince said. "But you'll have to be real quiet. Some passengers hear the wind in their ears and think they have to talk loud. But if someone on the ground hears voices coming from the sky, it will be way obvious."

"Good point." I turned to Diamond. "When we're about to launch, I'll call you and let you know what our chances look like."

"If you have reception," Diamond said.

"Right. If I don't, then I'll call you once we're aloft. I should have reception from the sky. Once we get close, I'll let you know if it appears that we'll probably make it. Just before we drop out of the sky, I'll call and let it ring once, then hang up."

Diamond reached into his pocket and pulled out his phone. He switched on the mute button. "It's on vibrate, now. Vince will make his best estimate of when he thinks you two can drop out of the sky into the fenced area. At that time, Spot and I will be outside and near the gate."

When Diamond said his name, Spot lifted his head and looked at him.

"Sorry, dude," Diamond said. "I'm not calling you, just referencing you."

"What do we need to prepare?" Vince said.

"Diamond, any update on bear spray?"

"I'll pick them up after this meeting."

I said, "I was thinking that after we sneak into the house, the moment the bad guys show their faces, we fog the place."

Diamond was shaking his head. "They could come out shooting. I have my Sig Sauer. You should have a piece, as well. If that fits with your ethics."

"I wouldn't want to use one. There's a kid in that house."

"But you said these guys carry multiple arms," Diamond said. "You could carry a weapon. Just don't shoot the kid." He looked at me like I was an idiot.

"I would carry one as backup."

Diamond reached down, pulled up his pants leg. He had on an ankle holster with a pistol in it. He unwrapped a Velcro strap, which made a loud crackling noise. He handed the holster and gun to me. "Take this. You come under serious fire, you're going to want it."

I pulled the pistol out of the holster and held it up. "This thing is tiny. It barely weighs more than a large hamburger."

"Less," Diamond said. "It's a Kel-Tec P-thirty-two, six-point-six ounces, seven rounds in the magazine and one in the chamber."

I hefted it, turned it over, aimed it at the wall.

"They call it a P-thirty-two. I call it my Barbie Doll Pea

Shooter," Diamond said.

"It's a semi-automatic, but no safety," I said.

"Correct. It's got a light trigger pull, but it's long. You gotta pull it all the way back. It won't accidently fire even if you drop it."

"Tiny gun, but a thirty-two caliber still packs a punch," I said.

"Sí. Big enough to punch a hole all the way through a guy if you don't hit bones. But it's still just a hole puncher. Makes the target really mad. So it's good to plan on multiple holes. Also, the gun is lightweight so you can expect some kickback. Bottom line is, you might be glad to have a weapon."

I patted my thigh and pulled out my Lowe's club. "I've got this, too."

Diamond reached for it, hefted it, turned it over. "Good as any sap," he said.

Diamond turned to Vince. "What about you? Do you carry?"

Vince shook his head. "No. Like I said, I like nature. Alive. I'm not interested in killing. But I do have a knife." He pointed to a small leather sheath on his belt.

Diamond turned toward me. "Guy lets principles get in the way of shooting people. Imagine that."

"Me, too," I said.

Vince frowned. He wasn't sure if Diamond's dry delivery meant he was kidding or not.

Diamond said, "I also remember confiscating some M-eighties from the bear spray dude. We could use them like stun grenades."

"Do you think they're the old, illegal kind that are really loud?" I said. "Three or four grams of pyro powder in them? Or are they the new pretend ones that are really just firecrackers stuffed into red cylinders to mimic the original M-eighties?"

Diamond shrugged. "They look old, so I'd guess they're the real thing. If we lit them and tossed them indoors through a broken window, the occupants would think they were stun grenades. They'd be cowering before they realized they were just deafened a bit."

"Sounds good," I said. "But I'm hoping we can find the secret entrance and don't have to break any windows."

"Tell us about that again?"

"The guy who built Stone Lodge, Isaiah Hellman, apparently had a thing for backup entrances, and he built one into Stone Lodge. His motto was AHAB, which stands for Always Have A Backup."

"Also the name of the crazed whaler in Melville's book," Diamond said.

"Yeah. Hellman also had a thing for Melville. Something about Melville being one of the only 19th century authors who wasn't anti-semitic. But that's another story. Anyway, AHAB represented something important to Hellman. Maybe focus and drive. The secret door is built under one of the windows. So we'll go along and feel for some kind of latching mechanism. If we find it, we can get into the lodge without anyone knowing."

"Pretty strange," Vince said. "But good for us, if we can find it."

"No ordinary guy, that Hellman," I said. "Another thing I'll bring is small flashlights and large zip ties."

"What's that for?" Vince asked.

"Poor man's handcuffs," Diamond said.

"In addition to our cell phones, we also need radios so we don't have to dial and so all three of us are on at the same time," I said. "Earpieces would be good, too."

"I can get those," Diamond said.

"When do we meet again?" Vince asked.

"I think Diamond and Spot and I should show up at your house at about one a.m. That should give us plenty of extra time."

THIRTY-EIGHT

I met Diamond Martinez on the South Shore at midnight. Because he had agreed to accompany Spot on our mission, he left his wheels at the Douglas County Sheriff's Office at Stateline and transferred into my Jeep.

When Diamond got in the passenger seat, Spot leaned forward from the back seat and got busy with his nose.

Diamond had to reach behind his neck and fend Spot off. "Less enthusiasm would be appreciated, Largeness. Feels like I'm going through the TSA."

I said, "Wearing your dark civvies, I see. Smart."

"Brown clothes, brown skin," he said. "Can't get much more night blending."

"Night blending," I said. "New word coinage?"

"Specialty of Mexicans learning English."

"Seems like you already knew English pretty good," I said.

"Pretty well," Diamond said.

"You got a brown sidearm to be even more blendable?"

"Sí. My Sig Sauer nine has wood grips and the steel has the Nitron finish."

I looked at Diamond's clothes. "Sweatshirt and loose Carhartt pants. So your piece could ride on your ankle, outside of belt, inside of belt, under your arm, small of back... Am I getting close?"

"First and last choice. I'm walking heavy. Carhartts are loose at ankle. Sweatshirt is loose at back. My holsters are level two retention for safety, but I can still clear leather fast enough to burn your average methhead before he puts holes in me."

"Wow," I said. "You gave me your pea shooter. Yet you've still got a back-up gun."

"New Beretta Nano on my ankle."

"But you gave me your ankle holster."

"That's my pea shooter holster. The Nano is in the Nano holster."

"Rambo," I said.

"I'm a cop, what do you expect."

"I'm an ex-cop, and the most dangerous weapon I normally carry is a nail clipper."

"Foolish ex-cop," Diamond said. After a pause, he added, "Although a creative person could get mean with a nail clipper."

"I'll work on that idea," I said.

I drove southwest through South Lake Tahoe, turned northwest on Emerald Bay Road.

The first quarter moon had lowered behind the tallest mountain peaks as we went around the bay. It would set completely in a couple hours. A few boat lights twinkled on the black water fifty stories below.

"The tea house on Fannette Island is a dark shape against a dark background," Diamond said. "Could be a body tied there like that woman you investigated. No one would know until morning."

"As night blending as a Mexican in brown civvies," I said.

We curved around the bay. The high mountains to the west were still cloaked in snow with only the protruding ridges and rocks showing through. Eagle River was a rushing torrent under the highway overpass and over Eagle Falls down toward the Vikingsholm Castle on the water.

"I know you know," I said, "but I should reiterate that you don't have to help us with this."

"Right," Diamond said.

"We don't have a search warrant."

"Sí, mama."

"An illegal entry is a crime no matter how pure our motives," I said.

"Right."

"An armed peace officer like you making a raid in another state and county from his jurisdiction could be prosecuted and even sent to prison."

"Are you done?"

"We could even get killed."

Diamond sighed. "Do you want my help or not?"

"I want."

"Then quit with the warnings. I'm an informed adult, sometimes even lucid. I make my own decisions."

We drove in silence for a minute.

"You haven't seen the kid," I said, "so no dramatic source of empathy there. And you barely met Vince. A guy could wonder about your motivations or even if you're a little bit nuts."

"You should know better than most that cops are all a little nuts. But we still want to do the right thing."

Diamond sounded frustrated.

"Got it," I said. "No more psychoanalysis."

"Finally," Diamond said.

I drove north up the shore and turned off just past Homewood, went back a few blocks and over one and stopped at the house where Vince Cooper lived with Brie Du Pont. The dashboard clock said 1:04 a.m.

We jumped out, me to transfer to Vince's truck, Diamond and Spot to stretch their legs.

Vince came out before we could knock. "Ready?" he said, exuding a tentative, unhappy eagerness like a soldier bracing for a battle that might get him killed.

"Yeah," I said. "Diamond will take my Jeep and my hound. You and I will head on up in your pickup."

"The tandem glider is in the bed," Vince said.

Diamond opened the hatch of the Jeep and reached into the cardboard box he'd set there. "First, you take bear spray. They have clips so you can hang them on your belt." He handed us each an orange can about the same height as a can of beer but a bit narrower. "I should warn you of three things. First, these things shoot thirty feet. When you squeeze the lever, you'll get a fair amount of kickback. So hang on tight. Second, be aware of any breeze. It's possible to send out a serious cloud of toxic spray and have it blow back into your face. You might have to dive down to breathe air off the floor or ground. Third, be aware of the possibility of innocent people. We don't know that everyone in this place is bad. And if you were to fill a room with spray, your kid might choose that moment to enter."

Vince's eyes got wide, and he frowned.

"Better I use my fists," he said.

"Are you a trained fighter?" Diamond asked.

"No, but I can throw a punch."

"No doubt," Diamond said. "But even a light flyweight, if trained and experienced, will dodge that punch and then pummel you to worthlessness."

I turned to Vince. "Remember that the guys I saw had karambit knives. Not many weapons can cut you to pieces as effectively as that."

Vince nodded, his spirit dampened by our comments.

"But stay eager," I said. "We'll subdue these guys." I looked at his cabin. "Does Brie know of our plan?"

"Yes. I told her we'll come back to her first thing. She's pretty stressed out. But I think she'll keep her act together."

"Diamond, as soon as I have cell reception, I'll call and give you an update."

"I'll drive to a close point and park in the forest. I'll have Spot with me."

Spot had picked up a huge Sugar Pine Cone in his teeth. At the sound of his name, he dropped it and looked up at Diamond. Realizing that Diamond wasn't talking to him and wasn't going to throw the pine cone, he lowered his head and stared at the motionless cone as if willing it to move. His jowls drooped. He pawed the cone to one side. When it stopped moving, it stayed stopped, one of the eternal frustrations about pine cones that dogs have to deal with.

Vince spoke up. "I should let you know that the weather

report is still vague regarding wind. They predict unsettled air, which leads to wind here and there in no predictable manner. We could have a breeze or calm. They say we are looking at a return to wind as we approach dawn. We could even get strong wind. But it could change in a minute."

Diamond frowned. "So even if there's enough wind to get into the air, if the wind stops, you come right back down?"

"Yeah. I'll go for altitude gain once we're aloft. If we can get high enough, then we can fly the distance even if the wind stops."

I asked, "What is the altitude we need before the wind stops?"

"The glide ratio on a tandem with two big guys on it isn't good. With clothes and gear, we're a combined four hundred seventy-five pounds. That's over the recommended weight limit. That doesn't mean the glider can't handle us. It just means that performance is degraded."

Diamond was still frowning.

Vince continued. "And we're already in the thin air of high altitude before we even launch. So we'll maybe have a six- or seven-to-one glide ratio."

"Meaning, six or seven feet forward for every foot we drop," I said.

"Yeah. For each thousand feet of altitude drop, we could glide six thousand feet forward. Variable conditions also reduce our effectiveness. The ski runs on the back side of Alpine Meadows are large clearings, and they will get an updraft if the breeze comes from anywhere between southwest to southeast. Those runs catch a lot of sun this time of year, so they should be fairly free of snow, especially on the lower parts. From there, it's only about two and a half miles to the lodge, or about thirteen thousand feet. Divide by six, throw in a fudge factor, and we'd need to start out about twenty-five hundred feet higher than the lodge to make it if the wind dies and we have no more uplift. Better to plan on three thousand feet of altitude above our destination to be certain we're able to glide to the lodge."

"You can also use thermal uplifts when there's no wind, right?" I said.

Diamond said, "No thermal uplifts in the middle of the night."

"I'm ever hopeful," I said, "if ignorant. There's a reason they put engines on planes."

"Also," Vince said, "we estimated the lodge at about eight thousand feet of elevation. If the wind dies, that would only be attainable if we start out at eleven thousand feet."

"Let me guess," I said. "We're not launching from a point as high as the lodge. So we'll actually have to gain more than three thousand feet after launch."

"Right. The slope where I want to take off is lower. Depending on how high we hike up, we may launch from as low as seventy-five hundred feet. So we'll try to find enough of an updraft that we can climb three and a half or, better yet, four thousand feet. If we can find enough wind-driven updraft to do that, we'll get to the lodge. Of course, if we find updrafts along the way, great. But if not, we can still make it if we can get high enough at the beginning."

"Okay," I said. "Once we cross that altitude threshold, I'll call you, Diamond. We won't need to talk, so we'll minimize the chance that someone can hear either of us talking on the phone. I'll just say we have sufficient altitude and we'll hang up."

"Night raptors dropping out of the night sky," Diamond said with a bit of drama.

Vince said, "I've been rehearsing in my mind the plan we talked about. After we land, I'll work my way to the driveway gate and figure out how to open it or breach it in some way so that Diamond and Spot can come inside the fence."

I said, "After you're both in the gate, keep yourselves and Spot in the dark as you approach the house. I'll make a quick trip around the lodge. If I find a guard posted, I'll attempt to disable him before he can sound an alarm. Once the outside of the house seems clear, I'll find you out toward the drive. Based on what we find, we'll decide which way the men are most likely to go when they hear our intrusion. Then we start searching for the AHAB entrance, get inside, and get ready with our bear spray." For Vince's benefit, I added, "When you immobilize someone with the spray, first establish that they aren't holding knives and don't have other weapons on them. When you've patted them down, turn them over onto their stomachs and zip tie their wrists behind their backs." I reached into my pocket and pulled out baggies of zip ties and handed a baggie to each of them.

"Everything we do is aimed at finding Vince's kid," I said. "When we get him, Vince will run with him toward the driveway gate and exit, staying in the trees, out of sight. Diamond and I will deal with the men."

I opened the Jeep and grabbed my jacket. Don't you need a jacket?" I said to Vince. "It will be freezing cold at eleven thousand feet."

"I've got a windbreaker in the truck."

"I almost forgot," I said. I pulled a bag of charcoal dust out of my pocket. "Camo for our faces."

"I'm already dark," Diamond said as I rubbed charcoal on my hands and my face. Vince did the same. I also rubbed charcoal into the white patches of Spot's fur.

"He doesn't mind?" Vince said.

"I've done it before. He likes the attention. And all rubs feel like affection to a dog."

Diamond held out his arms. "Radios and an earpiece with mic that hooks over your ears. This button turns it on. This dial is volume. They're set for the same frequency. These don't work at long distance, like when you're flying. But once we're at the lodge, they'll allow us to talk."

We took the radios and put the earpieces on.

"Testing," Vince said. His voice came through clearly.

I looked at both Diamond and Vince. "Ready?"

"Ready," they said.

I pet Spot, and Vince and I got into his pickup.

THIRTY-NINE

Vince drove too fast. Arriving in one piece was more important than speed. But I understood that trying to rescue one's kid would be so tense that it would be impossible to concentrate on driving moderation.

As we approached Sunnyside, Vince turned off and worked his way back to Ward Creek Blvd. We drove west next to the rushing rapids of Ward Creek, which drains the entire Ward Creek Canyon leading back to the mountains of Alpine Meadows ski resort.

Ward Creek Blvd. turns into Courchevel Rd, which winds up to the Sherwood Express chairlift. There are some nice homes scattered along the road, although, other than a few house lights, it was a dark drive. At the end of the road, we came to the chairlift base station, a huge structure typical of a high-speed lift. It loomed in the dark like an alien spaceship.

Vince parked in the small lot, jumped out, grabbed the backpack out of the pickup bed, and put the straps over his shoulders. I was impressed that a contraption capable of flying two men could fit into such a small pack.

He looked up at the night sky. The moon hadn't set yet, but the sky was already heavy with stars. "I feel no wind," he said. "But I can see some wispy streaks over Cassiopeia. Those are cirrus clouds. I think they usually indicate a coming change in weather."

Vince turned. "Over to the south, there's a clear lenticular cloud stack up above Heavenly, easy to see by starlight. That fits the forecast for continuing winds. The lenticular clouds show that we've still got a steady flow at high altitude. We can simultaneously have calm air down low. What we're hoping for is some turbulence. With strong winds aloft, any disturbance can send ripples of wind down to lower altitudes. But it might not happen."

"Becalmed sailors who have their sails up and ready can catch whatever breeze comes along," I said.

"Right. Luck benefits those who are prepared," Vince said. He looked up at the slopes flanking the Sherwood Express chairlift. "Let's start hiking up the mountain and get ready. A sudden bout of wind might not last longer than a few minutes. If it happens long enough for us to get into the air, maybe we can climb into more wind before the low altitude breeze fizzles out."

Vince led the way. The quarter moon was low in the sky. It didn't shine past the trees to reach the ski run, so we hiked through darkness. Vince took the run that went to the right side of the chairlift. The starlit night wasn't enough to shine light on the run. But we could easily see the path by the way the trees to the side of the run framed the sky.

The run was free of most obstacles, fallen trees being cleared each year by the ski resort maintenance crew. But smaller obstructions were still numerous, waiting to catch our footfalls, twist our ankles, and cause a fall in the dark. So we stared down at the ground, trying with our feeble night vision to divine where the obstacles were. We had flashlights, but we didn't want to turn them on and destroy what little night vision we had.

The weight of the glider probably didn't feel like much to Vince on the flats. But carry any load up a mountain, it turns into work real fast. After we'd marched up a significant slope for a hundred yards, he was huffing fast, loud breaths.

"Time to switch the load," I said. "My turn."

"Thanks, but I'm used to it," Vince said, barely able to get the words out between his breaths.

"Vince," I said. I stopped, figuring he'd realize I was serious, and he'd come to his senses.

He stopped after another few yards. He pulled the straps off his shoulders and set the pack down.

"A ski run is very steep compared to a well-graded hiking

trail," I said.

"Now that you point it out, I realize I've probably never hiked straight up a ski run for any significant distance. This is much harder than taking those men up Job's Sister. That was in thinner air, higher up, but the trail was much more gentle. Here, we keep going straight up. But it doesn't seem like we're getting any higher."

"And the stars above aren't getting any closer, either," I said.

"Funny," Vince said, his voice serious.

"We could take a zig-zag approach," I said as I reached down, picked up the glider pack, and put the straps over my shoulders.

"True. But walking cross-slope with no trail would be risky. Our feet would always be at an angle. That would be asking for a twisted ankle."

"You're right," I said. "We'll continue straight up. But we pause when needed. And we trade off."

This time I led. It made sense that the person with the heavy load set the pace.

After another stretch that probably wasn't as long as the first, I stopped, my lungs burning.

The ski run stretched out into the dark below us. I couldn't imagine how one would launch in the dark when there was no light. But that was Vince's job. I had to accept that he had enough expertise to know how and when to get into the air or, for that matter, know when to call it off. My thoughts went to the way he drove too fast, stressed by the mission, not thinking as clearly as he should.

After another 100 yards, I was gasping for air every bit as much as Vince had. We paused, then switched the glider pack back to Vince.

After another grueling stint, I tapped him on the shoulder. "Back to me," I said.

I'd lost track of how far we'd come. The dark ski run seemed to stretch to infinity. No matter how far upslope we hiked, nothing changed. I struggled to get enough air to haul the glider up the steep slope. I found myself thinking that even if we were able to fly to the lodge, we'd have no more energy after our labors.

Vince stopped and looked around in the dark. "This might be a good place. The slope is steep below us. The ski run is wider below and narrower up above us. That will help funnel any upslope breeze and give it a higher velocity. Of course, right now we have exactly zero breeze." Vince was clearly frustrated.

"Any value in going higher?" I asked.

"Hard to tell. If we went to the top of the ski area, we'd be at eighty-six hundred feet. There could be wind up there that we don't feel here. But the launch area isn't as perfect as where we are right now. If sufficient wind is ever going to come, I think it will catch us here. Also, it's usually gustier at the top. And the wind goes up over one side, pushed up by the ridge. But then it swoops down the other side, just like the air over an airplane wing. If we launched, and the wind was too fast to glide through it, we might find ourselves being blown down the other side of the mountain. The only thing worse than no wind is a down draft."

"That wouldn't be good," I said.

"So this placement on this ski run could be ideal. Once we get into the air, if we stay on this side of the mountain, we won't have to deal with a sudden downdraft. But we need some kind of wind."

"Okay, what can I do to help while we wait?"

"First, we pull out the canopy." Vince unsnapped some reinforcement straps on the glider pack and then opened a zipper that was shaped like a large U. The front flap of the pack opened up. Vince pulled out some fabric, feeling it in the dark. He slid his hand along, found what he was looking for, and handed a bundle of fabric to me. "Here, hold this. This is the left tip of the canopy. Keep a good grip on it while I stretch out the glider."

"Will do," I said.

Vince pulled the glider out and walked across the slope with it. It was so dark it was obvious he was working by feel. He felt with both hands, letting the fabric slip through his fingers, occasionally stopping to reassess what he was feeling and shift the fabric. Every few feet, he arranged some of the thin lines and oriented them down the slope from the fabric canopy. Eventually he set the other end of the canopy on the ground. He was far enough away that I couldn't see or tell what he was doing.

After a minute, he spoke from the other side of the glider. "I've weighted down the right wing tip. You can put yours on the ground and stand on it so it doesn't move as I shape the layout of the glider."

"Got it," I called out. Although, as I set the left wing tip down and stood on it, it seemed that the fabric was grinding onto rocks. I tried not to put too much weight on it. The glider had to work perfectly. I didn't want us hanging from fraying fabric.

I couldn't see Vince in the dark, but I heard him as he moved across the dark slope. Eventually, I figured out he was arranging the glider in a large arc. At one point, as he moved toward what must have been the top of the curve, he was silhouetted against the sky beyond. From his position relative to mine, I saw for the first time just how big the glider was.

"Vince, we may have a problem."

"Hold that thought. I'm coming down."

Backlit by the stars and Milky Way, Vince stepped his way down the ski slope as if he were marching sideways down a long staircase. "What's the problem?" he said as he came near.

"I didn't realize how big the paraglider is."

"Yeah. It needs to be big to fly two of us. What's wrong with that?"

"I thought we'd be able to glide right into the yard to the side of the lodge. But now I'm thinking no way."

Vince was silent a moment. "Then we'll just have to punch a landing, whether the canopy gets hung up or not. I'll try to make it so you and I hit the yard. The canopy will hit whatever it hits. Trees or fence or whatever."

"Give me a worst-case scenario."

Vince didn't hesitate. "The canopy snags in the trees, branches rip the canopy fabric, and we fall to the rocks below and die."

"Break it to me gently," I said.

"That would be hanging from the lines in the dark and getting

- what - shot down by the bad guys?"

"Got it," I said.

"Gentler still would be that we can't get enough altitude to make our target. So we have to put down some distance below the lodge. If that happens, I'll have to take whatever area looks open and out of the trees."

"In the dark."

"In the dark," he repeated.

"Assuming we get some wind and get enough altitude, it's still going to be difficult to find the lodge in the dark. The stars don't provide any light to speak of."

"Actually, even the starlight is helpful. More helpful are the lights at houses and road intersections down below. I can read our location from those lights. I studied my topo maps before we left. As long as we don't get any cloud formation, it shouldn't be too difficult to find the lodge. Your idea of finding Twin Peaks and then working down the ridge from that point should work."

Vince turned around, checking the layout of the canopy.

"While we're waiting," he said, "I'll go over what we're going to do. I've got the glider canopy sitting in an arch shape across the ski run." He pointed to a group of straps and gear that sat on the ground downslope from the canopy. "This is the tandem harness. I'll be in the rear position, while you'll be in front. The harness has loop straps that go around your thighs, a seat of sorts, and straps for your shoulders. While you're standing, the harness feels a bit awkward. But once we're in the air, it will feel like a comfortable seat."

Vince reached down to the ground just up from the harness. "These lines gather together in these bundles called risers. The lines go up to various points on the canopy. Some lines are merely for support. Others that connect to the trailing edge of the wing are designed to be pulled, which bends different parts of the canopy. Depending on where the lines are attached to the canopy, pulling some of them causes the canopy to turn. Others block some tubes causing the glider to lose lift. Pulling those lines is like putting on the brakes, and they make the glider lose altitude faster than normal."

"What do you mean when you refer to tubes?"

"Come up to the canopy, and I'll show you."

We hiked up the slope, walking to the outside of the canopy's width so we didn't tread on the lines. Vince reached down and picked up the edge of the canopy fabric. "The entire canopy is made of fabric tubes. They run the short dimension, from the leading edge of the canopy to the trailing edge. You probably can't see it in the dark, but feel these openings at the front of the tubes? What happens is that as the glider flies, the air going into the tubes creates pressure keeping the canopy in the proper shape. It's a ram air design that creates and maintains the wing shape of the canopy."

"So that's a critical aspect to the design," I said. "Always keeping those tubes filled with air. It sounds quite sophisticated. This isn't just a big kite."

"It's very sophisticated. Computer designed. There are lots of different models. Some go faster, some have better glide ratios. Some allow for very steep banking so a pilot can make tight circles and stay within a narrow thermal updraft. And of course, some, like this tandem, are good for taking up passengers."

"It seems like the paraglider design is inherently very safe. It's like a parachute, right? So if something happens, you can still glide down to the ground. Or am I wrong about that?"

"They are very safe. Even so, we go up with a reserve parachute. Come down and look at the harness."

We hiked back down to the harness. He picked up the left side and a pack that was attached to it. "To the left of my seat is the reserve chute. If something very unusual were to happen to made our glider unflyable, I can pull this reserve chute and we'd drift to the ground on that."

"And, like most parachutes, it won't be as maneuverable as a paraglider, right?"

"Correct," Vince said. "But in all of my six hundred flights, I've never even come close to having to pull the reserve."

"Have you ever done a flight like this? In the mountains, on a moonless night, with little wind, and an unlit target?"

"No. This is new territory. But I'm willing to try it to save my boy. I understand if you don't want to go. He's not your kid. If you want, I can give you the keys to my truck. I can call you when I'm in the air. You could be at the gate with your friend Diamond."

"No, I'm in. I want to be there. Two of us surprising three or maybe more men is much preferable to one person. Speaking of risk, I want to remind you that, the moment we land, we might both get shot to death. It's not too late to back out of this plan and call the cops."

"No. Absolutely not. I've met these guys. They're psycho. I have no doubt they'll kill Jon if we call the cops. I'm worried enough just having your cop friend Diamond along even if he's out of uniform. What if one of these guys recognizes him? We have to get them first."

"Okay. Back to how we launch? Specifically, is there anything I need to do?"

"Yeah. As soon as we start to feel a breeze coming up, we'll get into the harness. So step your legs through these leg loops."

He held them out, I felt in the dark until I had my hands on the straps, then stepped through.

"Now pull the straps to tighten them."

I did as he said.

"Now, arms into the shoulder harness. At the front of the harness is a strap across your chest. Feel it?"

"Yeah."

"Tighten the chest strap just enough to keep the shoulder straps from coming off your shoulders."

"Like the chest strap on some backpacks," I said.

"Yes, exactly."

"Okay. I'm in the harness. Now walk me through the launch."

"When we're both in the harness, you will face down the slope, and I'll be behind you. If the breeze is slight, I'll lift the risers and lines a bit and give them a shake. The breeze will blow into the tubes and the glider will inflate and rise behind us. After it's above us, I'll tell you we're going to launch. Together, we walk or jog forward down the slope. As the glider rises above us, it'll lift us off the ground."

"You said this is how we do it if the breeze is slight. So far it doesn't look as if there'll be any breeze at all. But let's just say the wind comes on strong. Then what?"

"Same as before, except I turn around and face up the hill. I need to do that to make certain I have good control over the glider as it rises. Either way, you stay facing forward."

"The glider could pull hard and fast, right?"

Vince nodded, his head movement barely visible in the dark. "Remember, this baby can lift us and more. Probably five hundred fifty pounds, easy. Maybe six hundred. So as it jumps up into the air, it will want to lift us fast and pull us up the slope. I'll be fighting the pull. But you may find yourself jerked backward a few steps. Once I've got the glider positioned, I'll turn around to face forward like you. We probably won't be able to take more than one step forward before we're lifted up."

"Then what should I do?"

"Once you're sitting in the harness, you'll probably want to adjust the seat and the straps on your thighs. This harness tends to give a guy crotch crunch. But a bit of tugging here and there will make things more comfortable. After that, you just sit back and enjoy the ride."

"Let's say we get a decent breeze," I said. "Rough ETA at the lodge?"

"My earlier estimate of a ten-minute ride was simply to traverse the distance. But first we need to climb to eleven thousand feet if possible. Or as high as possible if we can't go all the way. So most of our time will be spent climbing. But if we have a slow breeze, we may not find enough uplift to climb at any rate. In that case, we won't get there. The middle ground would be an intermittent wind, able to climb now and then, but very slowly. If that happens it could be hours to get there. But if it looks like we'll arrive any time after dawn, we should call it off, right?"

I thought about it. "Yeah. We want to come in under cover of darkness. The best time for any raid is around three-thirty or four a.m. The studies on circadian rhythm show that's when people are least alert, even if they're awake. Are these guys younger than you, or older?"

"Younger. About thirty. Why?"

"That's good. Most guys in their thirties sleep better than older guys. We don't want any insomniacs watching the night sky as we come in."

FORTY

We waited in silence for a few minutes. Vince kept looking at the sky.

"The moon will set in another fifteen minutes," Vince said. "And there's still no wind."

"This requires the patience of a stakeout," I said.

"When you were a cop, did you deal with a lot of real bad guys?" he asked. "I mean the kind of guys who don't value life at all?"

"Yeah. I imagine most cops see the dark stuff. Big city cops more than most, I suppose."

"How do you know when you meet one of them? Like maybe you're bringing in a suspect for questioning. Is there a way you can judge if he's one of the really twisted ones?"

"Hard to tell," I said. "The true psychopaths can be good actors. I've seen some of them spin their psyche eval so well that they convince the police shrink they were merely in the wrong place at the wrong time with the wrong friends. Twice, we caught murderers who'd previously been through our system as suspects and been let go after it had been decided they were low risk. But I've noticed one semi-common characteristic of men who don't value life. Not every last one of them has it, but way more of them have it than what you see in the general population."

"What is it?"

"I think you mentioned it before," I said. "Dead eyes."

"How would you describe dead eyes?"

I thought about it. "No sparkle, no excitement, no worry, no fear, no empathy for others."

"No life," Vince said.

"Right."

Vince looked again toward the dark sky. "The cirrus clouds are gone. The lenticular cloud over Heavenly seems to be dissipating. We may as well settle in. It could be a long wait. Maybe we won't get any wind at all." Vince bent over and felt the ground. "A bit moist with condensation, but not too wet to sit." He found a spot and sat down. The slope was steep enough that his feet were down below him. He rested his elbows on bent knees.

I sat nearby.

"What's this going to be like?" Vince said. "I've never even known a cop. So I have no idea what happens when you bust in on bad guys. Is there anything about it that's predictable?"

"Not a lot. We know they're highly motivated to go to all this trouble. Which means, they'll do whatever it takes to prevent us from disrupting their plan. We also know they felt no remorse about their mate who died on Job's Sister. That doesn't mean they'll immediately shoot, if only because gunshots draw attention. It's more likely they'll try to silence us with their knives. Or a baseball bat." I also thought they seemed like the kind of guys who would use their fists. But I didn't say it because it might give Vince a false sense of security, thinking he could hold his own with his fists.

"Does a guy - you know - tend to freeze up in a situation like this?"

"Some do. You won't because you'll be focused on getting your child out of the lodge."

Vince was quiet.

"How'd you meet Brie?" I said, more to pass the time than anything else.

"I met her on an adventuring trip put on by REI."

"What does that mean, adventuring?"

"I suppose it's a new word. It refers to going out on adventures that give people new experiences and help them build self confidence. REI puts on lots of different kinds of trips. Skiing. Hiking. Kayaking. In the past, they had me guide mountain hiking trips. One day the coordinator at the Reno store called me up and said she was putting together an adventuring trip to focus on Tahoe. She wondered if I could come up with a range of physical, outdoor activities for people who hadn't done much outdoor stuff. Her thought was, if people got outside of their comfort zone and did something they never thought they'd ever do, it would build self confidence. She said the trip would be open to anyone. But she also said she thought most of the people who would sign up would be women.

"Anyway, my first thought was to take them paragliding. But the woman said that was too far out of the comfort zone she envisioned. So we settled on things like bouldering and downhill mountain biking."

"Was this a multi-day thing?"

"Yeah, seven days. A different activity each day.

"Did Brie like the adventure?"

"Mostly, yes. She especially liked ziplining."

"Where you hang from a pulley and ride down a long cable," I said.

"Yeah. At first, she said no way was she going to risk her life flying down a skinny little cable. But after some of the other women went and said it was such great fun, she tried it. She loved it. Not only did she find it really fun, she said it proved to herself she could enjoy doing things she was originally afraid of."

"She seems like a good woman, quiet and thoughtful."

"She is," Vince said. "Best of all, Jon really likes her. They've gotten to be quite close. The only discomfort I have is that it often feels like Brie is hiding something."

"Any idea what?"

"No."

"What about Jon's mother?" I said.

"Victoria has always been a flashy woman - what's the word - charisma like an actress. Lots of guys were envious of me when she took up with me. She's trim and is proud of her physicality. Really vain, to tell the truth. But Victoria isn't anything like what you'd think of as a devoted mother or wife. She's self-focused. Everything is always about herself. She never thinks about other people. She treated me like I was a drag on her life. The same for how she thinks about Jon.

"She always said how much she wanted to have a kid. I got the message that having a kid would make for a lot more excitement than her boring marriage with me. But later I began to think that her desire for a kid was just so she'd have someone totally devoted to her. A kid was just a way to make her feel more important.

"But before she had a kid, she ran away. Later, I found out she was pregnant when she left. She'd always talked about how terrible it would be to have your belly get stretched out. I think she couldn't face the idea that other people would no longer see her as the young, beautiful, party girl, always up for a good time. Being stuck at home with a baby and all the related stress was not something Victoria had ever thought about."

"When did you find out she'd gotten pregnant?"

"After Jon was born! I knew she'd always been impulsive, but this was extreme. She just left me one day. I found a note saying she had to do some soul searching about her future. Then she showed up about nine months later with a baby. 'This is your boy!' she told me, all excited. And when I didn't immediately act all happy, she thought I was a lousy person, like I didn't have what it took to be a father.

"Of course, I had my doubts. So I got some of the baby's saliva and a bit of Victoria's hair and got a DNA test. It turned out that Jon really was our child."

I heard Vince take a deep breath.

"We really struggled after that. She said that every problem was my fault because I wasn't embracing being a dad. I told her other dads have nine months to prepare. I said she couldn't just drop a kid in my lap and expect me to think it was the greatest thing that ever happened to me.

"We were together until Jon's first birthday. Then she left again. She said she wanted to have a real life, an exciting life. She wanted to travel and see other countries and explore her spiritual side. She said she couldn't do any of that with a kid and husband dragging her down.

"So I said, what about me? What about Jon? Where was our

exciting life? And Victoria said I'd get used to it. That I was such a plain guy, I wouldn't know how to pursue an exciting life even if it was handed to me. She said that Jon would manage living with me, and that he probably couldn't keep up with her energy and her appetite for excitement, anyway. So she disappeared again, and didn't show up this time for six years. And you know what her first words to me were when she came back? The words keep ringing in my ears. She said, 'Sorry for taking a leave of absence, Vince, but I just couldn't handle the whole diapering thing. Now Jon is old enough, we could get a sitter and go do fun stuff.'"

"Wow," I said.

"That's what I thought."

After a minute, I said, "Speaking of your kid," I said, "I should tell you what I heard when I was watching over the fence at the lodge. I don't think I'm breaking a confidence."

"What's that?"

"The guard was commenting on your kid's walk, saying it was a walk like that of a girl."

I heard Vince make a big sigh. "That again," he said. His tone was part anger, part sadness.

"Then your kid said, 'I am a girl.'"

Vince went silent as if holding his breath.

"And when the guard used the name Jon, your kid said, 'My name is Jonni.' The guard said it was obvious your kid is a boy. But your kid said she only looked like a boy. That inside, she was a girl."

Vince said, "And now you're calling Jon a she. I can't stand it."

"When she said it, she sounded convincing, Vince. It's clear she has no stake in convincing the guard one way or another. But her simple statement radiated honesty. It didn't sound like an opinion or a trial. It sounded like a fact. At that very moment, she convinced me. That even though she was born looking like a boy, she is a girl."

After a long silence, Vince said, "Most of the time, I've tried hard to be a good dad. But I haven't always been there for Jon.

Sometimes, life has been too much, and I've taken an impromptu leave of absence from fatherhood. I'd call a sitter and go away for a few days. Later, Brie was the sitter. But I've been better the last couple of years.

"But it still hurt Jon. At first, I thought this feminine thing was his way of punishing me for my failures. Then I realized that he didn't mean bad. He didn't want to hurt me. But I still thought my occasional absences from his life, my lack of time with him, the fact that I was often gone working, denied him of a strong male role model. So I blame myself for his confusion. I assume he'll grow out of it."

"I saw my girlfriend Street yesterday evening after I'd seen Jonni at Stone Lodge. We were talking with a friend of hers who's a psychologist. The woman has done work in this area. I think she referred to it as Gender Dysphoria. Without using any names, I asked about the situation."

"A gender shrink. Great. Just what I needed. Probably wonders if I was too focused when I was diapering him as a baby. Or not focused enough."

"No. What she did say is that gender identification isn't a black-and-white issue. It's more of a spectrum. And what's interesting is, it appears that much about gender identification is hard wired. Apparently, those differences are independent of a child's physical characteristics."

"Yeah, but that probably comes from their lifestyle choices. Kids are still born as boys or girls. Either or."

"This psychologist doesn't think so. She said as soon as kids develop a clear sense of their gender, the ones whose perception of gender is different from their bodies sense that difference, too. And this developing awareness of gender happens at an early age, when the kids are too young to be thinking about it as a potential choice. The psychologist said that science is firmly behind the idea that people are born with a built-in sense of how they feel. They don't choose to feel different from their physical characteristics. It's part of their makeup."

Vince didn't reply.

"If you think about it, maybe you can remember the early times when Jonni did or said things suggesting she wasn't a standard-issue boy."

Vince was still quiet. Eventually, he said, "It's true. It goes way back. Playing with dolls, obsessing over clothes, singing along with girl-group pop songs. And the makeup. I never knew where he got the stuff. Girlfriends at school, I guess. He was probably seven when I first saw him in lipstick and eyeshadow. He was so young! I tried to interest him in sports. Softball and such. But the only thing he really took to was rollerblading. I think his drive was to have a way to escape from the bullies who tormented him for acting feminine. He'd only bladed for about one summer when he could go as fast as me."

Vince stopped talking abruptly. After a minute, he continued. "In spite of all the talk about using his blades to escape the bullies, I thought he'd grow out of this nonsense. I guess that didn't happen. But I still can't accept it."

"What if your kid had been born a daughter? Physically a girl."

"Then I would have celebrated having a daughter. I mean, sure, I was glad I had a son. I'd always wanted a son to go camping with, fishing, skiing."

"If you'd had a daughter from the beginning, wouldn't you have gone camping and skiing with her?"

Vince made a short pause. "Yeah. But that would be different."

"Different than skiing with a boy? How?"

"I don't know. I'm just... I guess I'm old fashioned. I thought, I had a boy! It fit the picture in my head. How things are supposed to work. It's not some Biblical picture. It's just the way I was raised. Boys are boys, and girls are girls."

"What if you had a regular son and he turned out to be gay?"

Vince made a little snort. "I'd have a hard time with that, too." He paused. "You probably think I'm backward."

"I don't judge. But I think you should allow yourself to

appreciate your kid. Kids are complicated, and life is confusing. I think you should accept and try to love your kid as the daughter she believes she is."

"That's a tall order," he said.

"Is it? You already said that if you'd had a daughter from the beginning, you would have loved her."

"Of course."

I'd made my point, so I said no more.

Vince stood up, looked at the dark sky. "Feel that?"

"Moving air," I said. "A touch of a breeze. On my right cheek. Which would be out of the west."

"Right," Vince said.

FORTY-ONE

I said, "This ski run points down to the south or even a bit to the southeast, right?"

"Yeah. Let's hope this little breeze out of the west swings around out of the south like the forecast predicted."

"What if it doesn't?"

"Can you see that line of trees to the west of us? The chairlift runs through those trees. And on the other side of those trees is another part of this run. A portion of it faces southwest. A westerly breeze would create an updraft over that run. If it's a strong enough wind, we could use that to gain some altitude."

"But this run doesn't face that way. So how would we launch?"

"Maybe I didn't explain it thoroughly. A glider doesn't need an updraft to simply glide downhill. If the breeze is out of the west and we have no updraft on this run, you and I could still get into the harness, inflate the glider by running downhill, and then take off. Our glide slope isn't as steep as the ski slope. So we could glide out until we're above the trees. When I think we can clear them, we could make a hard turn to the west, and try to get over the trees and chairlift and into the wind on the next ski run. With enough wind, we could start riding the updraft on that slope and begin climbing."

"Sounds a bit iffy," I said.

"It is. But I wouldn't give it a go if I didn't think there was a decent chance of success."

"What happens if it doesn't work?"

"We crash into the trees at the bottom. Or we clear the line of trees between the two ski runs, get over to the other run, and find there isn't enough wind to create an updraft. If that happens, we land on that slope."

"Got it. So what do we do now?"

"We're still waiting." As he said it, the breeze stopped, then picked up with just a bit more oomph.

"Why not launch right now?" I asked.

"The wind is probably strong enough on the other side of the tree windbreak. But I want to wait five minutes to judge whether or not there's any constancy to the airflow." Now that we were no longer talking about Jonni, Vince's voice was stronger and more confident. The insecurities of being a father were replaced by the confidence of a paraglider pilot who knew his expertise was solid.

"I just remembered that I forgot helmets and goggles," Vince said.

"No sweat. If we crash, we'll try to keep from bouncing our heads on the rocks."

"I know you're just saying that. But thanks."

Less than one minute later, the breeze had picked up a bit more.

"Let's get into the harness," Vince said. "This wind system may be fast-growing."

There was a small burst of air. The glider canopy blew across the ground to the side. Some of the lines drew tight and pulled the harness sideways a few feet.

"Hurry!" Vince grabbed the harness. He held out the leg loops on the front part of the harness. "Legs in the loops!" he shouted.

I trotted through the dark. Got my right leg through the loop.

"Wrong leg!"

I jerked my leg out, losing my balance, hopping on the uneven ground. Got the left leg through. Turned. Got my right leg through. I was trying to pull the cinch straps to snug the loops on my thighs when Vince shouted.

"Shoulder straps! Hurry! The wind is rising."

I fumbled the shoulder straps over my arms.

"The canopy is blowing to the other side of the run. Quick, run with me to the right, toward the wind. We can't let the canopy get snared on those other trees."

He had a grip on his portion of the harness. As the lines tugged the harness farther to the left, I leaned to the right. Vince also pulled to the right. There was a snap of fabric, and I felt the canopy rise up above us, pulling us hard toward the trees to the left.

"Harder!" Vince shouted. "Pull to the right!"

I didn't dare take my eyes off the ground. I focused on foot placement, struggling to take steps to the west in an effort to keep the canopy from blowing into the trees to the east.

We'd made just a little bit of progress when Vince stopped pulling and turned toward the canopy.

"Keep pulling into the wind. I'm going to dump air from part of the canopy and try to get it steered away from the trees. When I say go, start running down the ski run. You'll feel the canopy pull you to the left, but resist that and keep running. Ready? Go!"

I took fast steps down the slope, my feet pounding on grassy dirt and rocks. On the fourth step, the harness lifted me up and my foot hit nothing.

We were airborne.

FORTY-TWO

The wind in my face grew. I felt Vince's presence behind me. He was pulling on the lines, steering the glider, trying to keep us from hitting the trees on either side of the ski run. We were facing toward the trees on the right side of the ski run. But that was our flight into the wind. Our actual motion relative to the run was down the slope, what pilots call crabbing, or moving partially sideways into the wind so the overall motion stays straight. Our drop in altitude was faster than I expected. But I was used to planes with engines and propellers pulling up into the sky.

Even as we dropped, I could tell in the dark that the slope dropped at a steeper angle. Because of the steep slope, we gradually became higher above the ground. The treetops were still above us. There was no easy escape from the tunnel of the ski slope lined with trees.

Vince was making grunting noises. Probably it was from stress more than physical effort. I sensed the chairlift base station in the dark at the bottom of the ski run. We were dropping toward it fast. Like any pilot, I was running through worst-case scenarios. Potential landing spots. Potential crash-landing spots.

"Prepare for a tight turn to starboard," Vince said from behind me.

The treetops to our right had dropped down below us, but only by about 30 feet. If we lost altitude in the turn, we'd hit them. It seemed we weren't high enough. But it wasn't my call.

I understood the risk-taking scenario. Make the turn, you might get over the trees and into an updraft. But you might crash.

If you don't make the turn, you might find a last-ditch landing spot and put down without any broken bones. You might also crash. In both those scenarios, you lose any chance of completing your mission because it would take too long to repack the glider and hike back up the mountain. By the time we were ready to take off again, it would be too late because it would be dawn before we could get to the target.

"Here we go," Vince said, his voice crisp.

I looked up at the canopy. I saw the right tip bend down under Vince's pull on the lines. A sizable portion of the glider wing seemed to dump air. The opposite tip was still fully inflated. The imbalance in lift made the left tip of the glider wing rise up. Vince and I were swinging out to the left as the glider made a strong banking turn to the right.

As we turned, we slowed down.

Most aircraft lose overall lift in a steep bank. So the aircraft either loses altitude or the pilot compensates by increasing the throttle. But a paraglider doesn't have that option. So we dropped, losing altitude fast. Vince needed no input from me. I watched silently as we swooped around and down, on a likely collision course with the treetops. I was about to speak as Vince said the words I would have uttered.

"We better straighten our legs and lift our feet." He used the unflappable tone that pilots cultivate. The graver the situation, the calmer you sound.

Vince performed a maneuver pilots call a flair, changing the angle of the glider so it temporarily goes up even as it's about to stall. It's a universal technique designed to slow descent just before touching the wheels to the ground. The downside is that the coming stall can kill you if you are up in the air because the wing loses lift in a stall. So you stop dropping for a moment only to drop very fast afterward. Survival depends on being very close to the ground.

Vince's flair worked. But as we cleared most of the trees and were approaching the other ski run, our feet crashed through some high branches. A taller dead branch snagged in one of the glider lines above our heads and then broke off from the tree, tangled in the line. The blow made the glider lurch. As I looked up in the dark, I could see the broken branch hooked on the line just above our heads. The branch was about four feet long.

The drag from our feet striking the treetops slowed us further, pitching the glider forward. As we glided into a bit of clear airspace, our forward-leaning position made us pick up some speed and prevented us from dropping straight to the ground. But the glider was wobbling from the effect of the branch stuck in the line. The branch waved in the wind, bouncing off the adjacent glider lines. Vince reached up and tried to grab it, but it was just out of reach. So he pulled down on the line that held the branch and grabbed the branch with his other hand to pull it free. But the line was lodged in a fork of the branch. Vince tugged, but it wouldn't come free.

Because we had pitched forward, the glider was in a steep descent. The chairlift was below us, and we were heading toward one of the lift towers. It seemed our downward trajectory was made worse by the branch pulling on the line, deforming the canopy.

I looked back and saw Vince reach up again. There was a glint in one of his hands. His knife. Using his other hand, he once again pulled down on the line that held the branch, made a swipe with his knife, and cut the line above the branch. The loose line flopped free. Vince swiped the knife through the lower part of the same line, cutting it cleanly. He threw the branch and its section of line down to the side.

When I looked up, it seemed totally dark. The moon had set. But I could sense in the starlight a deformation in the canopy above the cut line.

And we were still plunging toward the lift tower.

I anticipated Vince's intentions even as I didn't think it would work.

Just before we were about to crash into the lift tower at serious speed, Vince did another flair, more dramatic than the last. The glider pitched up. The breeze on this other side of the trees made a gust. Vince rode the gust. We cleared the lift tower.

Vince banked the glider to the left and down the next ski run.
But this time was different. As we regained our glide path and
headed down this run, we rose faster relative to the trees. We had
sailed into a powerful updraft created by the wind being driven
up the slope of the land. We quickly gained altitude. While we
were still over the ski slope, Vince turned across the slope and
glided sideways to the wind, still riding the updraft. After several
hundred yards, the mountain changed shape, which might have
eliminated our updraft. So Vince did a tight-banking 180-degree
turn and came back through the updraft, climbing well. Although
the canopy was slightly compromised by the severed line and
probably suffered reduced performance, it still seemed to fly well.
As long as the loose line didn't tangle with the other lines, we'd
probably be okay.

Vince rode the updraft, circling upward like an eagle.

In just a few minutes, we'd climbed above the peaks that made
up the ridgetop of Alpine Meadows. We could see down into
the valley on the front side of the ski resort. The landscape was
sprinkled with lights from ski lodges and vacation chalets. There
was enough snow on the north facing slopes to see the layout
of the mountain in the starlight. The summer crowd hadn't yet
arrived in force, so the valley had a bucolic, country feel, the few
residents asleep, unaware of the drama in the sky above their
beds.

"Nice move back there," I said.

"I can call it nice now that it succeeded," he said. "It was
looking pretty stupid for a minute there."

"What puts you and me more at risk provides the possibility
of putting your kid less at risk. I knew we might get banged up.
But your kid is worth it."

"Thanks." Vince banked around into another steep turn. We
rose into the cold, dark sky.

It was exhilarating, flying through the dark. We were now
over a thousand feet above the ground. The pattern of lights
showed the neighborhoods and streets to the east and far below.
Even in the dark night, the view was dominated by the huge

blackness of the lake, a vast oblong with no lights except from a very few boats that near the shore. No lights shone from the center of the lake because no one had cause to cross the big water at four in the morning.

Vince spoke. "The mountain waves of air pushed up by the ridge lines don't just keep rising straight above the ridge. They flow out like water waves. And just like with water, the air goes up and then down. So to get the altitude we need, we'll need to stay in the updraft part of the wave and stay out of the trough that would be a downdraft. Both parts of the wave move farther east the higher we go. But that's an advantage. Earlier, I'd thought we'd be riding an air wave farther to the north."

"Away from our target," I said.

"Yeah. But with a west wind instead of a south wind, the mountain wave moves toward the lake and closer to the lodge."

I looked around, trying to visualize waves of air, invisible but no less powerful for it. Pilots in planes always try to be aware of air movements. But we don't pay attention at the same level as someone flying a craft that's powered by those silent air movements.

The air had been cold when we first launched. Now, as we climbed high into the night sky, it was getting crispy cold.

"Do you have an altimeter on your wrist?" I asked.

"Yeah. Neither my rate-of-climb indicator nor my altimeter have dashboard lights, so to speak. I'll have to turn on my light to read them. So don't look toward me or you'll lose your night vision."

Light came on behind me and then was off in a moment.

"Our altitude is up to ninety-four hundred feet. So we've come up almost two thousand feet since we hit the treetops. But we've lost our lift. Our rate of climb is down to zero."

"Good work, nevertheless," I said. "I'll call Diamond and let him know we're airborne."

I dialed the number.

"Sí?"

"We've launched. I'll call when we have an idea of our

approach time."

"Got it." He hung up.

Vince said, "We had talked about eleven thousand feet as enough safety zone to get to the target even if the wind stopped. It doesn't look like we'll get even close to that. But with this west wind, we're going to be much closer to the lodge. Maybe we can still make our target even without more altitude."

We were heading southwest. I scanned the vague shapes of the mountains before us.

"Twin Peaks," I said, pointing. "Those two little saw teeth barely visible against the faint backdrop of stars."

"I see them," Vince said. "Now we need to follow the ridge that extends from them to the west. Hold on. Dashboard lights coming."

The light came on behind my head, then went off.

"Hold on for a turn."

Vince pulled lines. We banked into a steep turn to the left.

"Hit a trough?" I said.

"Exactly. It's one thing to lose updraft. But downdraft is something we need to escape. You better call Diamond. We're at ninety-two hundred feet. But our rate-of-climb indicator says we're back to dropping. We may still get to the ridge. It wasn't in our plan, but we've come east from our launch spot. I'd guess we're about two miles northeast of our target. Depending on the mountain waves we're riding, we might be able to head that direction without going for higher altitude. In that case, we could be there in maybe fifteen minutes. Give or take ten."

I dialed Diamond. He answered with the softest of grunts.

I repeated what Vince had told me and added, "We're not confident we'll make it. But you and Spot should head up the mountain now."

"Already most of the way there. Your Jeep is well hidden. Call me when you're sixty seconds out." He clicked off.

We glided through the cold, night air. We didn't talk for several minutes. The stars above were brilliant, and the Milky Way was pronounced, a view across the galaxy through billions of stars so distant they were only visible in their foggy white aggregate. The view was serene and beautiful. But the tension of coming down out of the dark sky to unseen trees and rocks made it hard to breathe.

At one point, I felt us do an elevator drop, stomachs in our throats. Then we stabilized. I didn't have a feel for sink and climb in a glider. But my lay-person's sense told me we were going down much too fast.

I felt us rise for a moment, the glider and harness lifting us up. Another updraft. Vince put us into a tight turn, trying to stay in the rising air. We looped around in a tight bank. But just as quickly, we stopped rising. Vince straightened out and headed toward the distant ridge.

"No more climbing," Vince said. "We're on our last glideslope. Where do you think the lodge is?" Now his voice was tight.

"I can still sense Twin Peaks in the distance to the west. Between Twin Peaks and us is Stanford Rock. I feel like I can see that against the night sky, too. But it may be wishful thinking. The lodge is between Stanford Rock and Eagle Rock, which is much lower. If we can spot Eagle Rock, we can track our eyes toward Stanford Rock and get a sense of where the lodge is."

My phone rang.

"Yeah?" I said in a soft voice even though we were still over one thousand feet up and several thousand feet distant from our target.

"Got a problem," Diamond whispered. "Spot and I are at the lodge, looking over the fence from a distance. There's a German Shepherd roaming the yard. He made the circuit of the yard, following the fence line the way a human would. Now he's in a shaded area. Invisible. To say he looks menacing would be an understatement."

FORTY-THREE

"Any men visible?" I asked.

"No," Diamond whispered. "Probably got the dog so they'd feel more comfortable sleeping."

"Has the dog smelled you? Made any noise?"

"No. I'm downwind of it, so it doesn't sense us yet. Either way, the dog means trouble for us, right? Even if it doesn't attack, it'll bark the moment it senses you coming out of the sky. Or maybe the wind shifts and it smells Largeness and makes a fuss. You got a guess why these guys would bring in a German Shepherd in the middle of the night, the same night we're planning a raid?"

I paused. "Maybe the dog was there before and I just didn't see it. Or someone tipped them to our raid. But there's only us three who know about it directly."

"Indirectly?" Diamond said.

"It could be someone who has been assigned to watch me or Vince and has figured out our plan."

"You got advice regarding the hound?" Diamond asked.

"Hopefully, the wind won't shift, and you'll remain downwind from the dog. If you're quiet, the dog won't detect you. Spot, on the other hand, will smell the German Shepherd because Spot will be downwind. So you might want to put your finger across his nose or your palm in front of his nose. That's the signal to be quiet."

"Will he obey that coming from me?"

"Probably not," I said. "He doesn't obey it coming from me, either, unless he's in a good mood and thinks he's getting a treat. But it's worth a try."

"How will you land in a yard with a German Shepherd inside the fence?"

"I don't know."

"Reassuring," Diamond said.

"Here's an idea," I said. "Remember that time I showed you how to make Spot howl? You make a soft rahr-oooo sound next to his head?"

"Yeah," Diamond said.

"You and Spot wait in the trees by the gate. I'll have Vince give me a sixty-second warning before we land. I'll dial your phone and then hang up. When you get my call, you get Spot to make a howl. The shepherd's job is to bark if he senses a human intruder. But he might not bark if he thinks there's another dog nearby, a friendly dog."

"Sounds risky," Diamond said.

"It will make the shepherd curious, and he'll trot toward the fence wherever Spot is, a bit cautious, but probably not aggressive. I'm hoping that's the exact time when we land."

"Then what?"

"If the shepherd and Spot are sniffing each other through the fence, that will disarm the shepherd's protective instinct. Dogs are social. Given the chance, they all just want to run and play. Meanwhile, Vince and I will jump out of our harness and follow our previous plan."

"You got a likelihood on whether or not you'll make it here?"

I held the phone up above my shoulder, hoping Diamond could hear both of us. "Vince, Diamond wonders our likelihood of making it."

Vince spoke louder than before, but not so loud I worried we'd be heard from the ridge in the distance. "I don't think we can count on any additional altitude gain. I'd give us fifty-fifty odds. But I won't know our exact height above the ground as we come in. It could be we won't be making a gentle circle down to our landing site. We might try a straight shot to the yard, coming in full blast from the side to utilize every bit of whatever altitude we have."

"Okay," Diamond said. "When you're a minute from

touchdown, call and give me two buzzes. I'll see about getting His Largeness to howl." He hung up.

"No point in trying to find any more updraft," Vince said. He put the glider into another bank, turning until we were pointing west toward the ridge where the lodge stood nestled in the trees. "We'll try to make a line drive straight to the yard," Vince said. "It's not looking good." His words didn't waver. But I detected fear in his voice.

"Anything I should do to prepare for landing?" I asked.

"Feel around for your strap adjustments. Familiarize yourself with the buckle locations. Once we're down on the ground, you'll want to get yourself free from the harness fast."

Directly below us was the highway that crawled down the West Shore. I could make out the Sunnyside Restaurant and resort on the water. Its parking lot lights illuminated the cars of guests. Across the highway from Sunnyside, directly below us, was the road up Ward Creek Canyon where we'd driven Vince's pickup and left it at the parking lot in the dark forest below.

The giant black lake was behind us. The mountains were in front of us. I knew Vince's earlier altimeter reading put us a little higher than the mountains. But the peaks of the Sierra Crest looked higher than we were.

In the far distance off to our right was Alpine Meadows Ski Resort, its snowfields visible in the starlight.

Vince tapped me on the shoulder. "Any idea of where Stone Lodge is?"

I scanned the mountains to the west, trying to divine the ridges that stretched our way from Twin Peaks and Stanford Rock. I looked down.

"There's Eagle Rock, south down Highway Eighty-nine. If we draw a line from Eagle Rock to Stanford Rock, the lodge should be…"

I stopped as I saw a faint sparkle of light in the distance at an elevation that didn't seem much below us. I studied it, trying to sense how the ridge dropped below it on three sides.

"That light," I said. "Do you see it?" I pointed toward the

dark mountain ridge just south of Ward Creek Canyon.

"Yeah."

"I think that's Stone Lodge. Head for that light."

"It looks almost level with us," Vince said. "Meaning we won't make it," Vince said. "We'll probably crash on the mountain just below the lodge."

"Okay. Do whatever you can to maximize our chances of making the target. If that makes us come in toward the lodge on the wrong track, so be it. Whatever you have to do is worth it if we can get over the fence. If not, maybe you can crash land close below the fence and we can climb up to it and scramble over it before the German Shepherd knows we're there."

We had another sensation of being in an elevator that goes down fast. The glider dropped for some time before we felt the canopy start pulling back.

The light at the ridgetop lodge was still visible in the distance. It looked about three-quarters of a mile out. As I stared, I could sense our loss of altitude as we glided forward. The lodge light went from looking a bit below us to appearing roughly level. As a pilot, I knew that your eyes can give you all manner of perceptions that are a long way from reality. So I told myself to stay calm and trust the paraglider pilot.

As we sailed through the dark, I was acutely aware of the sound of the wind rushing through the air tubes of our glider canopy. I felt the bracing, icy pressure on my face. The cold scent of pine and fir trees reminded me of the forest in winter.

"We're definitely not going to make it," Vince whispered. "At least not in the traditional way."

"If you've got a non-traditional way," I whispered back, "Go for it."

"There's an aerobatic maneuver you might be familiar with," he said. "Barrel rolls are not just for planes. You can do them in a paraglider."

"You mean rolling us over in a circle."

"Right," Vince said. "Not a forward/backward loop-the-loop like in a Ferris Wheel. But swinging around to the side as we still glide forward."

"So, like a plane, we always face forward, but we do a sideways roll so that we're upside down for a bit."

"Right."

"And why would we do that?"

"If I can time it perfectly, I could possibly do a barrel roll so that we're upside down but at the top of the roll when we get to the fence. That might toss us over the top of the fence and into the yard."

"Upside down," I said.

"Upside down," Vince repeated. "I think getting into the yard upside down is better than not getting in at all."

I thought about it. "Give me a sixty-second warning, and I'll alert Diamond."

We kept gliding forward through the night. The lodge with its single lonely light grew in size. It seemed to get higher above us. I kept reminding myself of how hard it is to estimate angles and distances at night.

The trees went from looking like a soft mat of mountain cover to individual trees, huge and menacing.

"Okay. Sixty seconds," Vince said.

I pulled out my phone and hit speed dial for Diamond's phone. I let it ring twice, then hung up, and tucked my phone back in my pocket.

"Just as I thought," Vince whispered. We'd dropped below the level of the lodge's fence, and we could no longer see the lodge's yard light. We were hurtling toward the dark mountainside on a course that would have us slamming into the rocks and trees below the lodge.

When we were just a few yards away, Vince whispered, "Prepare for the roll."

I sensed a dramatic movement behind me, as if he were pulling on the lines hard enough to rip them off. The glider wing arced clockwise above us. We arced below the wing, lifting clockwise up to the left. I felt a sensation of increased weight. Our rotation began slowly and then sped up.

In front of us was nothing but the blackness of mountain. It seemed the lodge had disappeared above us.

Our barrel-roll rotation increased. I was pressed harder down into the seat of the harness. I had the vague sense of roller coaster rides from my childhood.

I couldn't tell my precise orientation. But it was clear I was swinging clockwise in a grand loop, from six o'clock to nine o'clock, to midnight.

In a sudden moment, I was flung upside down into the air so that I was just above the top of the fence. I couldn't fully understand what I was seeing. But as the glider canopy hit the fence, Vince and I, upside down at the top of our barrel-roll arc, were launched above the fence. I put my hands in front of my head as we crashed onto the hard ground. The lines from our harness to the glider wing seemed tied around our bodies. The light we'd seen when we were up in the sky above was now a single bright flood, mounted above one of the lodge doors. It shined directly into our eyes.

As I tried to right myself and stand up with the harness still attached to me, I was distracted by movement. I turned and saw a large, black German Shepherd racing toward us, a ferocious growl coming from its bared teeth.

FORTY-FOUR

"Incoming dog," I said as Vince struggled behind me. I thought of the bear spray on my belt. But I couldn't do that to a dog. Although I considered myself skillful when it came to grappling with dogs, the shepherd intimidated me. He was only half the size and weight of Spot, but like everyone else, I'd been conditioned to think of a German Shepherd as a potentially dangerous adversary.

A portion of the glider canopy had come over the top of the fence.

I grabbed a wide stretch of paraglider fabric in my hands.

A howl erupted from down toward the driveway gate. It wasn't Diamond. It was the real thing.

Spot.

The German Shepherd jerked to a stop as if he'd hit an invisible wall. He turned and stared toward the howling sound.

Spot's howl stopped.

The shepherd seemed confused.

I felt bad. I never want a dog to lose its confidence, to have doubt and confusion when it's only trying to do its job.

The German Shepherd turned back toward Vince and me. I didn't want Vince to be a target, so I jumped left, then right as if to say come and get me.

The shepherd once again bolted toward me, a new growl in its throat. I waited until the last moment. As the dog made its leap to lock jaws onto my shoulder, I threw the fabric up and out like a curtain, then dropped down and to the side. The dog found itself jumping into an ocean of purple material, obscuring its view. I pulled down on the fabric, drawing it down to the ground, the dog with it.

I didn't want the dog to be afraid, but I also didn't want to get bit through the thin nylon material. In the light from the flood by the door, I could see the shape of the dog wrapped in the paraglider wing. The dog was thrashing, trying to get out from under the fabric. I did a fast crawl over and pulled the fabric around the dog's body. I snugged the fabric tight, then slid my grip up toward the base of the dog's neck.

Like horses and many other animals, dogs, no matter how spirited, respond to dominance. When a dog realizes that someone else is in control, it usually gives in. I held the fabric tight around the shepherd, kept my hands and my body weight firm on the dog's body, holding its neck so it couldn't turn and bite, and talked in a low voice.

"It's okay, buddy. We're just gonna lie here a minute. You and I will get comfortable, and we'll get calm. You're okay. You have nothing to fear from me."

As I spoke, I could feel the dog stop trying to turn and bite me. Its body was still tense, 80 or 90 pounds of solid, quivering muscle. But it understood that it was wrapped and subdued. The dog knew I was in control. It also knew the difference between an angry human voice and a calm and soothing one.

I looked past the dog toward the yard and lodge, wondering if anyone had heard us or the dog. Not far from the floodlight was a curved device mounted under the roof eave. It looked like a motion detector. If so, we were directly in front of it. If the alarm was working, and if there were men in the house, there'd be plenty of action happening soon.

I turned around, facing Vince. He'd unsnapped the buckles holding him in the harness. But one line was still tangled around his thigh. He pulled out his knife and sliced through the line.

"That was impressive flying," I whispered. "Thanks."

"I worried we'd land on our heads. But we're not paralyzed. That's pure luck." He stepped out of the tangle of lines and harness and sheathed his knife.

"Get down to the gate and figure out how to let Diamond in. The only way I can ease up on this shepherd without being his chew toy is if you can get Spot into this yard so he can distract this shepherd."

Vince ran toward the gate.

I lay on the ground, behind the shepherd, my arms holding the fabric around him. He panted hard and fast. But otherwise he didn't struggle. "Good boy," I whispered.

I heard several thumps and then a soft screech of metal. I expected an alarm bell to go off. But all I heard was the sound of Spot running up the drive. Even in the dark, Spot is an unmistakable presence, a white-and-black blur that's unnerving to nearly anyone who doesn't know Great Danes and their size. Except that he was now a charcoal-dust gray-and-black dog.

"Hey, Spot," I said in a voice that was just loud enough for Spot to hear.

He realized I was lying on the ground in the large fluffy pile of paraglider fabric. He trotted over, wagging, trying to figure out why I didn't stand up. I saw his nostrils flex. He stepped closer, discovering I wasn't alone.

"Hold on, Largeness. Let me unwrap your new friend."

Spot lowered his head toward the bundle of fabric next to me, his brow furrowed, no doubt trying to understand what new kind of craziness I was up to.

I shifted my grip on fabric and dog, gradually slipping the fabric down over the shepherd's head. I was careful to maintain my grip so that I didn't risk losing fingers or worse to a confused German Shepherd.

I got the fabric pulled off the shepherd's head. With my hands still on his neck so he couldn't grab me, he strained to lift his head and stare at Spot.

The German Shepherd probably didn't know Danes. But he knew a friendly dog when he saw it. Spot stretched out his front paws, lowering his chest, his tail on high speed.

I kept a firm grip on the shepherd as I pulled at the fabric with my other hand. In another minute, I had the fabric pulled free from the shepherd. Buried in the shepherd's thick fir was a collar I hadn't felt before. Holding the dog by its collar, I got both of us up and out of the paraglider material, and we stood. Spot walked up and sniffed the shepherd, nose to nose.

Many dogs, held by a strange man, would be hyper wary, ready to snap at man and dog alike. But Spot has an ability to make all creatures think that life is for having fun. In a moment, the shepherd seemed to reassess his surroundings. Maybe his job wasn't about tackling burglars who dropped out of the sky. Maybe his job was to run around and play with this new, huge companion.

When I sensed that the shepherd had nearly forgotten about the man holding him, I let go and stepped back.

The shepherd didn't seem to notice me. He walked toward Spot, then made a sudden start, and both dogs took off around the yard playing catch-me-if-you-can.

Diamond and Vince appeared, jogging up the drive as I got loose from the glider harness and lines.

Vince spoke in a low whisper. "I found the crank arm that works the gate, and I pounded out the cotter pin that held it in place. What's next?"

I said, "I'll take the north side of the house, you take the south. Diamond, you stay near the front door in case anyone runs out. Remember, we're feeling under each window, looking for the release catch for a hidden door. Maybe it no longer exists. But if we can get inside without breaking a window and making noise, that will be a huge advantage. Turn on your radios. Use a quiet voice to announce your moves. Stay as silent as possible."

"What about your dog?" Vince said.

"I think he's currently performing the most valuable function he can, keeping the shepherd occupied. Let's go."

I ran around to the north side of the lodge, wondering again why there was no alarm. Perhaps Jonni, using the guard's phone, had been able to turn the alarm off.

The north side of the lodge was away from the light at the front and very dark. I crept along, staying low. There were six windows at even intervals along the wall. All of them were dark, which meant that anyone inside could possibly see out. I walked softly to the side of the first one, reached down below the sill and felt for anything unusual that could be a door release. Nothing seemed obvious. I squatted down to the ground and did a more thorough inspection. All I could feel were the cedar shakes that made up the siding below the window.

I crawled under the window and over to the next. It too felt the same. Yet it was obvious that there could be any number of devices that would not present themselves as an opening into the house. The whole point of a hidden door was to be secret. Perhaps one of the cedar shakes twisted or lifted up to open the door. It would be possible to be at the correct place and still never find the door.

Diamond's voice came in my earpiece. "The dogs just ran by, heading for the north side where you are, Owen. Don't want you to surprise the shepherd and make him bark."

"Got it," I whispered. "Vince? Any luck?"

"I've checked four of six windows. No door."

"Expect the door release to be quite hard to find," I said. "I'm only just beginning my second window."

"Trust me," Vince said. "I checked everything. No secret door."

I was certain that Vince's eagerness to find his kid was making him impulsive.

I felt all over under the second window. Same cedar shakes. I tried pulling and turning each one. I ran my fingertips under the windowsill. No catch or handle or latch. I moved onto the third. Same result.

Vince spoke in my ear. "I'm going to make a circuit of the house and look for any other potential ways in."

I finished checking the windows on the north side. At the end of the house was the second floor deck. I stepped away from the house to get a better look. I knew there'd be a door up on the deck, but I couldn't see it in the shadows. What I could see was another mini deck at the third floor level, above it, projecting out from under the peak of the gable roof. It was what I always called a Bird Deck, with just enough room for two people to look at the sky or the birds. The access must be through the attic. I sensed some kind of light glimmer, like a power line attached to the house under the roof overhang. But when I looked straight toward it, I saw nothing.

Either of the second floor or third floor deck doors might be unlocked. But I couldn't see a clear way to get up to them from the outside. There was a thick group of trees around one side of the second-floor deck. Their branches seemed to reach up to the mini deck on the third. If we couldn't find another way in, maybe I could climb those trees.

"Light just turned on in the house." Diamond's voice in my ear. "Second floor. A third of the way back from the front."

"I see it," Vince said. "I'm moving away from the house to get a better line of sight. Maybe I can see in."

Vince would now be on the north side of the house. I walked around to the south side. No lights there. I walked up to one of the dark windows that Vince had already checked and peered in from the side. I cupped my hands around my face but couldn't see anything. I moved to the next window. Still nothing. If there was a stairway within view, no light spilled down from upstairs. I felt the siding below the window. Ran my fingers along the bottom of the sill. Something felt smooth. I slid my fingertips back and forth. Most of the sill felt like painted wood. But there was a part of the surface that felt smoother. Like a brass inlay, flush with the surface.

I didn't dare turn on my flashlight. I had to operate by feel.

"I can't see anything in the upstairs window," Vince said. "The light went off. Probably a bathroom. Could be Jon. But he usually sleeps through the night."

I hooked my fingernails at the edges of the polished part. Moved them down one edge. Back up the other. The smooth inlay was about three inches long and about a half inch wide. I tried to dig my fingernail in at the end of the strip. There was a little movement. I pulled down. The strip moved. My finger slipped behind it. It pivoted. When I pulled it down 90 degrees, there was a soft chunking sound. Like a door latch releasing.

The left side of the cedar shake siding swung out from the wall of the lodge.

"I'm in," I said softly.

"Where?" came Diamond's voice.

"The hidden doorway is on the south side. Second window back from the front."

"But I checked all those windows," Vince said.

"It was hard to find."

"Crap," Vince said with a sudden exhalation.

"What?" I said.

Vince lowered his voice to a whisper, "A door just opened on the north side of the house." Then, even softer, he said, "A guy stepped out. It's so dark I can't really see him. Now he's standing in the open doorway. Oh, I get it. He's smoking. There's a red glow of his cigarette. What should I do? We could charge that doorway!"

"No," I said. "We want more surprise. The hidden door will do that. When he shuts the door, we'll watch the house for signs of his movement. If we can tell where he goes, we can plan our assault."

Vince didn't respond.

"Vince, what do you see?" I asked.

He didn't answer.

"Vince," I said in an urgent voice. "Diamond, you better go check."

"Roger that," Diamond's voice said in my ear.

As Diamond said it, I heard a muffled yell. The cry lingered like that of a man in agonizing pain.

FORTY-FIVE

"**I** got him!" Vince shouted.

There was a flash from within the house and a huge boom. Apparently, Vince was trying to pull off a lone assault, hitting the cigarette smoker with bear spray and then throwing an M - 80 into the house.

I ducked my head down and went in through the hidden door.

I was in a long living room, dimly lit by light coming down a stairway. Vince was visible through the open doorway across the room. He was twenty feet out from the house, sitting on a man's back, wrestling with the man's arms, pulling his wrists together behind his back. He got a zip tie in place, yanked it tight, then moved to the man's ankles. In a moment, he made a yell of triumph. "Got you hogtied, you sick bastard."

"You are dead meat," came the roar of another man who was leaping down the stairway toward me, a knife in his right hand. If Vince had thought the M-80 would stun him or slow him down, it wasn't working.

I jerked my bear spray off my belt and blasted it toward the dim staircase, aiming for where I thought the man's face might be. He yelled, put one hand to his face, and staggered, temporarily blind, unable to breathe. He collapsed to his knees. One of his hands had a heavy bandage around it and his thumb. The man Jonni had helped.

Vince ran inside. "You got another one of these jerks! I'll tie him, too."

I found a light switch on the wall and flipped it on.

Vince was bending down over the man. "Vince! Stop! He's got a knife!"

Vince jumped back, saw the knife. He kicked the man in the back, knocking him forward onto his stomach. Vince stomped the hand with the knife.

The man howled louder.

Vince stepped on the man's wrist to hold his hand in place, then removed the knife from his hand. He pulled the man's hands together and tied them behind the man's back. "Two blind men tied," Vince said.

Diamond appeared at the open side door. "Movement out here," he said. He shined his light.

"What?" I stepped out into the dark behind him.

Diamond was standing near the man Vince had hogtied.

"I thought I saw someone else near this guy," Diamond said. "Bending over him as if he was reaching into the man's pockets."

I did like Diamond, shining my light around the grounds. I ran over to one end of the lodge and shined my light down the outer wall. I saw nothing.

I ran to the far corner and shined my light in the other direction. Diamond appeared near me, pointing his light into the darkness.

"I see nothing," he said. "I better get back to the two men. You said you saw three men when you were here earlier."

"Yeah. The third man could free the other two. You watch them while Vince and I search the house."

"Remember, you've got my backup," Diamond said, referring to his gun that I was presently wearing on my ankle.

I nodded. Outside in clear air, a gun rules. Inside, in dark rooms, I could stop nearly anyone with bear spray even if I didn't shoot accurately. I didn't even need to look in the room, just reach around the corner and spray. Much harder to hit someone in the dark with a bullet. Not that I wanted to.

I looked at the stairway, then turned to Vince. "I'll go up first. Stay ten feet behind me. Separation makes it harder to kill us both."

Vince frowned. I ran up the stairs. There was a landing where the staircase turned back on itself. I paused on the landing and looked up the second flight of stairs. The source of light was visible, an open door some distance away. Vince was below me. As I took the next steps two at a time, he followed, keeping a short distance between us.

The stairs brought me to a central area from which two hallways led to what were probably bedrooms, each doorway at regular intervals that no doubt matched the intervals we'd seen between the gabled windows outside. The doors were all open and all dark. A perfect setup for a trap. An adversary could be standing in the shadow of a doorway, taking aim, and we could not tell where he was.

I took two steps back down the staircase and spoke to Vince in a whisper.

"There's no sign of activity. Just dark rooms…" My words were interrupted by a sound coming from someplace on the second floor. "Follow me!" I said to Vince.

I ran toward the sound, which I thought came from the hallway that went toward the rear of the house. Near the end of the hall was a narrow stairway that went up toward the attic and what I now knew was the small, third-floor deck. The narrow passage was illuminated by two small wall sconces, one at the bottom of the stairs and one at the top. I couldn't hear anyone moving, but the logical thought was that someone had gone up the stairs. Of course, the lights could have been turned on as misdirection.

Vince came down the hall behind me. He charged past me and ran up the stairs, two at a time. Maybe he heard something I didn't. Maybe not.

I worried that if I too went up, anyone who was hiding on the second floor could go down and possibly escape. I looked up and saw Vince reaching for the door out to the bird deck. He opened it. A man jumped into the opening from outside and hit Vince on his jaw with a blow so hard it had the effect of a battering ram. Vince was knocked back to the side wall.

Vince reached out with his arms, trying to grab the wall and stabilize himself. His attacker, who was substantially smaller than Vince, turned sideways. In one smooth motion, he launched a high sidekick, his upper body bending way down to the level of his waist to counter the motion of his foot, which shot out like a lightning bolt. His foot went high and struck Vince on the crown of his forehead.

I knew it was a misfire in terms of effectiveness, because the upper forehead is one of the most durable places to withstand a hard blow. Nevertheless, Vince's head snapped backward and hit the wooden wall. He staggered, rotated as he collapsed, and fell down the stairs toward me as his attacker went out the deck door.

I made two fast leaps up the steps and caught Vince halfway.

He was a heavy limp weight, and it took all of my strength to slow his plunge and lower him to the floor of the second-floor hallway.

He moaned, indicating he was alive. But he wasn't going anyplace anytime soon. I laid his head down on the floorboards. Blood was oozing from his forehead. I ran up the staircase.

At the top of the steps was a small attic space that had been finished off. There were two windows, each set into gables on opposite sides of the slanting roof. The room was empty. It seemed the room existed only to serve as the access point for the door to the bird deck.

I stepped through the open door out into the darkness. The little deck was vacant. The air was brisk with a slight breeze. But all was dominated by a single tone, a metallic sound, slowly rising in pitch as it grew softer and more distant. Zinging.

I couldn't place the sound, but there was a familiarity to it. I reached up above my head. Waved my arm back and forth through the air. Stepped over next to the deck railing. Waved my arm above my head again. My wrist struck metal. Not a hard edge. Something that wasn't rigid. I wrapped my fingers around the object.

It was a cable. The glint of light I'd seen earlier from down below. The cable vibrated.

I realized it was a zip line.

A groggy voice called out from down the stairway behind me. "Jon? Jon, is that you?" Vince said.

I turned to face where the zip line pointed and cupped my hands to my mouth. "JON?" I called out. "ARE YOU THERE?"

After a long moment came a reply, a child's voice, high in pitch.

"HELP ME!"

The zinging sound faded far away.

I called out again. But there was no reply.

FORTY-SIX

I turned to go back inside and down the stairs.

At the edge of the doorway, some pieces of paper fluttered in the dark. I reached for them and saw they had gotten stuck in a gap where the door moulding had separated a bit from the frame. I pulled the pages out.

My light caught similar pages out on the floor of the deck. Thinking it could reveal something about the kidnappers, I picked them up.

I ran down the steps. Vince was struggling to sit up.

"Where's my boy?" he asked, still groggy.

"There's a zip line attached to the third-floor deck. A man took Jon and they went down the zip line."

Vince leaned over against the wall, despondent. "Do you think they'll kill him now?"

"No. If they wanted to, they would have already done it. They obviously need Jon for something that's valuable to them. Probably the password we talked about."

Vince held his head as if trying to keep it from coming apart.

I helped Vince stand and put his arm over my shoulder. He was heavy, and he wasn't taking much weight by himself.

"Sorry, I'm pretty wobbly," he said.

"I'm amazed you aren't out cold or worse. You took two serious blows."

We worked our way down to the first floor.

The room now had two lamps on, giving a soft illumination to the room. It was a grand lodge room, stone walls, and heavy rustic furniture. Above the fireplace mantle hung the huge bone of a whale jaw. The jaw had very large teeth. Probably from a killer whale.

Diamond was standing guard over the men. One was near the door. The man was coughing and wheezing from the lingering effects of the bear spray. His eyes were shut, swollen and red, streaming tears. The other man was visible out the open door, next to the fence. He too was hacking and gasping for air.

Diamond had added a second zip tie to their wrists and also put two ties on each man's ankles. The man near the door was on his belly, his legs bent up behind him, and his ankles bound to his wrists. Diamond had also attached zip ties from the door hinge to the ties binding the man's wrists and ankles. The arrangement had immobilized him.

The other man was tied in a similar fashion but attached to the fence. Diamond had linked up ties like chain links. The result was effective. The only way either man could get free was if someone cut them loose.

"Nice work," I said to Diamond as I looked at the men. "Jon is gone, taken out of here on a zip line escape from the upper deck."

"Down off into the dark woods," Diamond said.

"Yeah."

Diamond made a nod of understanding. "Where he had left a vehicle. A brilliant escape. No way could anyone keep up with a zip line by running through the woods. And the pursuer would need a vehicle as well."

I said, "Even if the escape vehicle is a mountain bike, the concept makes it so any pursuer ends up stranded in the middle of nowhere."

Vince said, "How far do you think the line goes down?"

"I have no idea. There's one at Heavenly Resort that's over three thousand feet long."

"We could drive down the mountain and try to find a road that would intersect with the zip line," Vince said.

"Maybe. But it's almost certain they're already heading away in a vehicle. Another possibility is this zip line leads to a second line going off in another direction. There would be no way to know the destination of a second line."

"It's my fault, isn't it?" Vince said. He sounded despondent. "I didn't wait to go in with you through the hidden door. I saw the guy smoking, and I blasted him with bear spray. He yelled loud enough to wake anyone up. And then I threw in the M-Eighty. I woke up everybody and made it so they could escape with Jon!"

"They might have already been awake," I said to make him feel better. "Or there may have been a silent alarm that woke them when we landed in the yard."

"I doubt it," Diamond said. "If a guy is sleeping, he'd want a loud alarm to make noise. But I didn't hear anything. So I think those sensors out there are shut off."

"Do you think there's another guy still hiding out here at this lodge?" Vince asked.

I answered. "There's no way to know. But you went up the mountain with three men. One blew off in the windstorm. Two men are tied up here. It's likely the leader was the only one left, and he escaped with Jon."

I took a quick look around, shining my flashlight into several rooms, wondering if I might find anything that would suggest where the man had taken the child. But I found nothing.

Back in the main room, I said, "Let's hurry. We can talk in the Jeep."

Vince walked over to the man by the stairs. "This is for taking my kid." He shot a blast of bear spray in the man's face. The man gasped and coughed and writhed. It was cruel and unusual punishment, but I understood Vince's anger.

Vince went outside, over to the other man, and did the same thing.

As bear spray wafted toward us, we left and hurried away from the lodge, our shadows from the floodlight lengthening before us.

When we got to the gate, I made the wolf whistle that meant treats for Spot.

He and the German Shepherd came trotting around the

corner, tongues out, panting hard from their run. They were side by side as if they'd been best friends forever.

But that didn't mean the shepherd was best friends with me. He hung back, carefully regarding the three of us as Spot came up to me, sniffing the pocket where I keep treats. I gave him one and tossed one to the shepherd.

"Where's your boss, boy?" I said to the shepherd. "Who brought you up here?"

I watched him carefully. A dog who is aware of the location of his master will often betray that location with a glance. The shepherd just watched me, wary, still panting hard.

"Let's see what he does as we hustle out of here," I said.

We went out the dark drive, through the open gate that Vince had rendered inoperable. Vince moved slowly and held his forehead with one hand and his jaw with the other. Spot came along with us. He glanced back toward the shepherd, who was staying in the yard, no doubt waiting for the person who'd brought him there.

"If there is still a man here, he's probably hiding from us," Diamond said.

"It could be. I could send Spot on a search. But I think it's more important we go after Vince's kid."

I turned around as we entered the dark tree shadows, out of line from the flood light at the lodge.

The shepherd was still hanging back, watching us.

"How far is the Jeep?" Vince asked, his pain obvious in his voice.

"Down the drive about three-quarters of a mile," Diamond said. "Maybe more. Parked in the trees."

"You okay with that, Vince?"

"Yeah. It's nothing compared to carrying the glider up the ski run. I'd sprint around the lake if I thought it would help get Jon back."

Spot trotted out in front of us. Like all dogs, he was always waiting for the slow humans. He would also pause at road hazards that were obvious to him, even if unseen by us. As our leader, he would alert if he sensed a person. And because he'd already come up the road, he would be aware of any changes, especially if those changes involved the scent of a person.

Vince spoke between fast breaths. He turned toward the pages in my hand, which must have been catching the dim light. "What's that you're carrying?"

"Some papers got caught in the moulding of the doorway out to the upper deck. I thought they could be the kidnapper's notes."

"What are they?" Vince asked.

I turned them over in the light and flattened out a folded portion. It was a title page of a book. The words were visible. "It looks like it's from a book called, 'The Mysteries of Udolpho,'" I said.

"Oh, that's Jon's favorite book. A cheesy romance that was written centuries ago. Good riddance for him to lose it. The last thing Jon needs is to be reading girl books."

"Your kid will be very sad to have lost it," I said.

"Growing up to be a man means learning to appreciate a man's perspective on the world," Vince said.

After some silence, Vince added, "But you think Jon is really a girl. I get that feeling from other people, too. I can't cope with this."

"Hard to be a parent," Diamond said.

In a minute, Vince turned to Diamond. "What do you think? Do you think it's okay for a boy to decide he's really a girl?"

Diamond was silent. For a man who was better with words than anyone I knew, he still understood the importance of thinking before speaking. "I think your kid sounds very bright and thoughtful and not like someone who comes to opinions without careful consideration."

"Right," Vince said. "But even with the most ridiculous notion, he's still stubborn as hell. He just won't let go of this infatuation he has with being a girl."

"You probably had some stubborn characteristics when you were that age," Diamond said.

"I sure did. I thought I knew everything. And I thought adults got a lot of things wrong. So I think I've got a pretty good grip on how these things work between kids and adults."

Diamond continued. "You've probably never doubted your own gender."

Vince scoffed. "Of course, not. I was a boy's boy from point A. I grew up to be a man. There was nothing to doubt. Ever."

"So what if you'd been born in a girl's body?"

"That's ridiculous."

"Is it?" Diamond asked.

Vince wasn't walking fast. But he slowed down.

Diamond's words weren't that far from things I'd already said to Vince. But they seemed to make a stronger impact.

Diamond and I matched Vince's new pace.

"I've read some stuff about gender," Diamond said. "And what scientists have learned about it."

"What, you're some kind of science expert?" Vince asked, his tone disparaging.

"Ain't no brain scientist," Diamond said. "I'm a cop. But I'm a reader. Turns out that gender is pretty much how you feel."

"What does that mean?"

"That how you feel is more important than how you look."

Vince didn't respond.

Diamond said, "A majority of people were born with a body that conforms to the way they feel about their gender. But it's not a giant proportion. A significant portion of people have bodies and genders that don't match up."

More silence from Vince. "And you're saying my boy is one of those people. That Jon is really a girl because of the way… the way she feels. She was just born with the wrong body."

"Seems like it. And if that's a hard thought to wrestle, you can know that she's got a lot of company."

Vince still had a hand on his head.

"Here's another thing to know," Diamond said. "This stuff isn't black or white. Some people feel like girls, some like boys. Some people are in between in the way they feel. There's a lot of middle ground."

"Jon… Jonni likes boys," Vince said. "If Jon is really a she, then she wouldn't be gay. She'd like boys the same way most girls like boys."

"Could be," Diamond said. "The fact she's trapped in a boy's body makes things difficult." Diamond paused. "But it could be having a mis-matched mind and body, so to speak, isn't that difficult for her. It could be the most difficult thing about the whole situation is your dismissal and lack of acceptance. She might be going through life pretty well except for your refusal to acknowledge what she knows and what her friends know. And probably what your girlfriend knows."

I was sure Diamond didn't mean it to sound harsh. But it sounded harsh.

Vince didn't respond.

There was no more talk as we hustled down the drive. Spot led the way, slowing as we slowed so he maintained the same distance in front of us. He came to a near stop at the three different switchbacks, waiting.

Then Spot turned off the drive.

"Jeep's here," Diamond said. He walked into the trees.

"Good place," I said. "I can see it now. But I never would unless someone pointed it out. Can you drive?"

Diamond looked puzzled.

"Either that, or you take Spot on your lap in the back seat."

"I'll drive."

Diamond got into the driver's seat. Vince took the passenger seat. I squeezed in back with Spot, which he thought was fun because he got to lie on me. He didn't know that his elbow points were splitting my thigh muscles and lighting them on fire.

Diamond turned the headlights on, pulled out, and headed down the rest of the drive. He drove for a bit, then cranked the wheel and made a hard turn around a 180-degree switchback. He sped back up and raced down the dark drive. We came to a neighborhood street. "Which way?" he said. "You want to look for the end of the zip line?"

"No. I'm confident they're long gone from the canyon. Let's head out to the highway."

"My cop sense tells me the man would get off the highway as soon as possible," Diamond said. "He'd assume we might have put out a 'Be On The Look Out' for him."

"You think he'd hole up until the BOLO got old?" I said.

"Maybe. The question is where."

"He might fall back on the same idea that brought him to the Stone Lodge," I said.

"What would that be?"

"Isaiah Hellman's Stone Lodge was accessible through Hellman's AHAB concept. Always Have A Backup entrance. That made it a good place to hide. I think the kidnappers knew about the hidden entrance, because there were no broken-down doors or windows that we saw. There's a possibility that Hellman would have an AHAB entrance at the Hellman Mansion, too. The leader of our kidnappers might also wonder that. He's obviously fairly smart, considering what he's already orchestrated."

"You're thinking that the kidnapper would take Jonni and hide at the Hellman Mansion," Diamond said.

"It makes as much sense as any other idea. Hiding in plain sight until things blow over."

"It seems so unlikely they'd hide there," Vince said. "They give tours there every day. The tour docents will be arriving this morning, in just a few hours. But I guess that would make it a great place to hide, wouldn't it?"

"Yeah," I said. "We should get Brie. She's probably tearing her hair out worrying about Jon."

FORTY-SEVEN

Diamond sped up to the highway, slowed just a bit for the stop sign, then made a right turn. He floored the accelerator. We raced south, heading down the West Shore. Diamond sped up to 65 down the curving highway.

"The turnoff to our house is coming up," Vince said as we went through the Tahoe Pines neighborhood.

Diamond slowed.

"The intersection after this one," Vince said as we sped past a cross street. "Okay, turn here. Then go slow and take the very next right."

Diamond did as told.

"See the house on the corner? Just after the next left is the drive. Coming up. Yeah, here."

Diamond turned in.

"Pull all the way back. Past the house. To the garage behind. We live upstairs."

Diamond braked but hadn't completely stopped when Vince got out.

Vince went up the stairs slowly and deliberately and went inside the apartment.

Vince and Brie came down the steps a minute later. Vince leaned in to the open window. "We can't all fit in your Jeep. It would be good for Brie to ride with you so you can catch her up on what we've been doing. I'll follow you in Brie's truck."

I realized Vince probably didn't want to talk with his head aching.

Brie climbed into the front passenger seat of the Jeep.

Diamond pulled out, worked his way back to the highway, and turned south again.

Vince followed us.

I briefly explained how we'd nearly gotten Jonni before one of the men took her down the zip line. I didn't go into the details of crash-landing the paraglider or using bear spray on men and tying them up.

"You're calling her Jonni," Brie said.

"It was obvious when I first saw her up at the lodge."

She nodded. After a long moment, she spoke. "A well-informed mind is the best security against the contagion of folly." Her words sounded distant.

"Nice choice of words," I said.

"It's Jonni's favorite quote from Ann Radcliffe's book, 'The Mysteries of Udolpho.'"

I didn't tell her that I had the torn pieces of the book in the back seat.

I waited and then said, "I have a hunch that the man who has Jonni might try to hole up in the Hellman Mansion for a few hours. Stone Lodge was built by Isaiah Hellman, and it has a secret entrance. I'm thinking that Hellman's lakeside mansion might have a secret entrance as well."

Although Brie said nothing, her silence was heavy with stress.

Diamond said, "At Stone Lodge, it was a secret door under a window. But at Pine Lodge, there must be a hundred windows. It would be a long search to find it. If it even exists."

"True," I said. "But many of the windows are set in stone walls. There are far fewer windows set in wooden walls, with wooden siding below them. Those are the ones we should focus on."

I added, mostly for Brie's benefit, "But of course, the kidnapper may have taken Jonni far away."

She nodded.

"And if they are here, they could be in any of the outbuildings."

"I understand," she finally said in a low voice.

"But if I were the kidnapper," I said, "I'd go to the place

where people are least likely to search."

Brie said, "The tourist crowds will be coming in a few hours. That would make it a great place to hide. Lots of commotion and distraction."

We came to the West Shore village of Tahoma in a few minutes.

"Sugar Pine Point Park and the mansion will be empty at this time of night," I said. "I think the gate will be open for the campers who pay on the honor system. Let's drive in, lights off, and head back toward the parking lot that's close to the mansion."

"Okay. Left turn coming up," Diamond said.

He swung the wheel, turned off the lights and drove into the entrance road.

"Old Jeep allows one to actually turn off the lights when the car is still running," Diamond said.

"Ancient machinery has benefits," I said.

Diamond cruised back toward one of the rear lots and parked.

We all jumped out. Diamond tossed me the keys.

Spot trotted off. For a dog, the darkness was no obstacle at all.

Vince pulled Brie's pickup next to us and got out, moving slowly so as not to jar his head.

The first hints of dawn were lightening the sky beyond the mountains on the east side of Lake Tahoe. It wasn't yet 5 a.m. We stood in the darkness under a stand of pines. The front door of Hellman mansion was about 100 yards away.

"Remember to whisper," I said to the group. "Because the AHAB entrance at Stone Lodge was below a window, let's focus on the windows at Pine Lodge. We can ignore the ones set into stone and concentrate on those with wood siding below. If there is a secret entrance, it will probably have a mechanism like the one at Stone Lodge. It was a smooth piece of brass that pulled down. I'll take Spot and Brie and go counterclockwise around the mansion. Diamond, you and Vince go clockwise. Do you both still have your radios?"

They nodded.

I whispered, "Vince, a reminder to not act impulsively. We need silence in order to not alert the kidnapper and scare him away."

Although he must have been very tense at the prospect of finding his kid, he nodded. "No need to worry. The kidnapper took the fire out of me."

We separated.

I started running toward the mansion. Spot loped ahead. Brie ran next to me down the park road. Vince and Diamond went the other direction, Vince lagging behind. I hoped he wasn't suffering from a severe head injury. But I knew I couldn't dissuade him from coming with us.

When we got close, I took Spot's collar and walked through the dark around the south end of the mansion. Brie stayed to my side. The building was made of heavy stone walls with smaller sections of wood walls. We focused on the windows with wood siding beneath them. At each pair, I checked one and she took the other.

I felt for smooth brass. I also grabbed shingles just to be sure. I pushed and pulled and twisted, but everything seemed solid. The next few windows were set in stone. I came to a rounded room with more stone walls. The second floor above it, and the conical roof above that, appeared to be wooden. But Hellman wouldn't have placed a hidden entrance up there.

We continued around to the lake side of the mansion. There was a long, covered porch made of wooden walls and many windows. This was the area where I remembered the tour guides took tourists into the house.

We walked up the steps. Brie and I walked around each set of windows, pulling and wiggling at each bit of wood beneath the windows. Then I realized, a hidden door beneath those windows would be too low to get through without crawling on the porch floor.

So I checked to the sides of each window. Brie seemed equally thorough. We'd only finished the second set when Diamond's voice said, "Got something," in my earpiece.

"Come," I said to Brie.

We ran back down the porch steps to the lawn and continued around the house to the large wing projecting off the north side of the mansion. From the tour I took years before, I remembered it as the kitchen wing where the staff worked. It also had the entrances for the staff to come and go.

The dim figures of Vince and Diamond were standing near the middle of the long wooden wall with multiple windows. We hurried over, staying on the yard where our footfalls would be quiet. But there were areas of patio stones. Spot's claws clicked on the stones.

Diamond and Vince were near one of the windows. Diamond was running his hands along the window trim.

"Lots of mossy lichen," he whispered. "It's been torn loose. That suggests that something or someone pulled on this recently. But I don't find a latch."

I reached out and touched the lichen. Ran my fingertips along it in the dark, feeling the material, which was like a very coarse sponge. It was thick and continuous. When I came to a corner, I reversed directions and went back the way I'd come, still feeling, trying to see with my fingers.

As my fingertips went in this new direction, a piece of the lichen sponge seemed to move. Underneath was an edge of wood that felt similar to what I'd found at Stone Lodge. Again, I moved my fingers along the lichen and wood, focusing more on the underside of the windowsill.

There it was, another area of smooth metal. I got my fingers hooked on one end of the metal. I pulled. The latch came down. There was a sound of the mechanism releasing tension.

The door opened.

I reached in through the dark opening and felt something.

"Several inches in, there is an obstruction of some kind in the way," I said.

Vince spoke up, trying to whisper but being too loud. "If the kidnapper opened this and found a cabinet or something in front of the door and he had to push it aside, then, once they were inside, he'd push it back where it had been."

"It might make lots of noise," I said.

"We could go through there fast so the man can't escape," Diamond said.

"But where in the house would we go?" Vince asked.

"If I were hiding here," I whispered, "I'd go to the third floor. That's one of the places not on the tour and off-limits to tourists."

Diamond nodded. "The docents probably don't even go there."

"How do we get up there?" Vince asked.

Brie said, "I don't remember if there is more than one way to the third floor. But I do remember that the big curving staircase at the front of the house only goes to the second floor where Hellman and his family stayed. The third floor was just for the servants. On the inside of this wall is the kitchen area. To the left, where this wing joins the main house, there's the so-called back staircase that goes up to both the second and third floors. It may be the only access to the third floor."

I said, "If we get up there fast and quietly, we can maybe prevent them from running. But if they come down to the second floor, then there are two stairwells. For that matter, it may also be possible to escape out a window. We'll try to be silent," I said. "I'll go up first with Spot. His presence tends to prevent people from bolting. Ready?"

The glow of the coming dawn from across the lake caught their faces as they both nodded. Diamond looked like the practiced, serious professional, his dark face revealing nothing. Vince was much paler, and the growing light lit his skin. He looked very worried, his brow a network of deep lines. I was pretty certain his worry wasn't fear of the bad guys or even violence. Brie looked as anxious as a person can be, as if the fate of her world were at stake. Which it probably was.

I reached in through the secret door and pushed against the obstruction. It slid a few inches, making a scraping noise. Then it seemed to stop. I pushed harder, trying to give it a lifting motion to minimize the scraping. It moved again, this time making a screech so loud it would have alerted anyone in the house to our presence.

FORTY-EIGHT

The cabinet or whatever it was moved a few inches, then hit something again and stopped. It still blocked the opening. Now that its scraping noise had announced our presence, speed was even more important. I pushed harder. It moved again, skipping and scraping louder than before. After sliding about a foot, it jammed again.

I got down on my knees, leaned into the opening, and hit it with my shoulder, forcing it into the room with yet more noise.

When the opening was large enough, I ducked through the low door. Spot followed.

"Let's hurry," I whispered as before.

The kitchen was black as a cave. I flipped on my flashlight and let go of Spot. The stairway was to the left, at the end of the room. I ran toward it. Spot immediately understood my destination, and he ran past me and up the stairs. I heard the others behind me.

At the top of the stairs, I shined my light. The steps to the third floor were to the right. To the other side was the hallway that led to the second floor rooms. I stopped and held my hand out behind me, signalling the others to stop. I turned, put my finger to my lips, and waited, listening.

If the kidnapper had Jonni on the second floor, he would have multiple escape routes, and we'd lose them by running up to the third. But if they were on the third floor, we could catch them.

I heard a scuffling sound. I turned my head, trying to discern the direction. Spot looked up the stairs toward the third floor. That was a solid indication.

"I'll stay on this floor," Diamond said. "You go up."

"Will do," I whispered. I touched Spot on his back.

He trotted up the stairs. Brie pushed past me and ran up the steps. I was behind, and I heard Vince charge up after me.

We got to the top. I found a light switch and turned it on. Dim light lit up the long hallway. I could see at least four doors, bedrooms for the servants 100 years ago.

Brie ran halfway down the hall. "Jonni? Jonni! Are you here? Jonni!"

Spot was down at the last door, sniffing its edges.

The door opened a crack.

"Jonni?" Brie said. "Is that you?"

"Brie!" Jonni pushed out the door and ran to Brie, hugging her hard. "I was so scared!"

"Jonni," I said, "where's the kidnapper?"

"He left me in the room. He said he had to check on something. He said if I left the room, he'd kill me."

"Oh, Jonni, you're safe now!" Brie kneeled down, her head just a little lower than Jonni's, and wrapped her arms around Jonni. "I'm never going to let you go."

Vince and I were still standing at the top of the stairs.

"Jon!" Vince called down the hallway. "I'm here, too. I'm so glad you're okay, boy!"

"She, Vince," Brie said. "Jonni is a she." Brie had a tension in her voice that sounded like anger.

"Think what you want. But he's my boy."

"No, dad," Jonni called out. "I'm not your boy. I'm your girl. Your daughter."

"Jon, now is not the time for this discussion. Let's get out of here before the kidnapper comes back."

"Maybe this is the time to have this talk," Brie said in a tone that suggested she was finding her nerve.

"What does that mean, Brie? And what business is it of yours? Do you even care how I feel? Jon, how do you think your mother would feel if she were here? Come to me, Jon."

Jonni stayed next to Brie. "Dad," Jonni said. "You always think whatever - you know - whatever fits your picture."

"You're not making sense, Jon."

"You have this view of the world," Jonni said. "Everything has to fit your view. Otherwise you push it away. You reject it. Like me, dad. You reject me. You never once wanted to really know how I felt. Mom didn't, either. You always talked about how mom wasn't there for me, how she didn't care. Well, you weren't that much different."

"But I only wanted what I thought was best for you. And Victoria, despite all of her absences, she only wanted what is best for you, too. She's still your mother. Even a flawed mother still knows what's best for her child."

"Really, Vince?" Brie said. "What if I told you Victoria never was pregnant? That she never gave birth? That she went to a fertility doctor to conceive Jonni from her egg and your sperm? What if she was so vain and distracted she hired a surrogate mother to carry the pregnancy and give birth to your child without telling you?"

"That's nonsense, Brie. You're talking craziness."

"No, it's not, Vince. Because I was that surrogate mother. I gave birth to your daughter Jonni. When Victoria went away, it was to hide that surrogate pregnancy. Victoria came to see me just a few times during the entire nine months. I knew from the beginning that Victoria never really wanted a kid. She never wanted pregnancy. She even looked at me at seven months into the pregnancy and said she could never stand to be so fat. She just paid me and the doctors the money and looked the other way. And after I gave birth and she took Jonni, I found out she left you both, giving you the burden of raising a child by yourself. Even though I was supposed to stay away and never tell anyone about it, I started trying to figure out how I could get into your life, how I could have some kind of relationship with the child I understood better than anyone. "

Vince leaned his palms against the wall and then bent his elbows so that his head bumped against the wood. He stared down at the floor. Maybe he was astounded. Or maybe he was just stunned from recognizing what he already knew at some deep level.

Diamond had come up the stairs behind me.

"Jonni isn't from my genes," Brie said. "But she's my child as much as anybody's. I carried her and gave birth to her. I nursed her in the beginning. I'm the only one who has recognized she's a girl at heart. Ask her, Vince. Ask her if anyone knows her as well as I do."

Vince lifted his head and looked down the hall at Brie and Jonni, who had their arms wrapped around each other. His face was wet with tears. He opened his mouth to speak. But no words came out.

"What makes a parent, Vince?" Brie asked. "Is it DNA? Or is it involvement and caring and belief and support and constancy? When Victoria was mostly gone, I was there. When you had your events and incidents, as you called them, episodes that took you away, I was there. When you doubted Jonni's feelings and wishes, I was there for her."

Vince rotated and leaned back against the wall. He slowly slid down until he hit the floor, his legs and knees up close to his chest. He held his head in his hands and leaned his face down on top of his knees. His sobs began low and slow, and then they grew until he was gasping for breath and choking. The big man looked small and helpless.

"I'm so sorry, Jon!" he called out, his words almost unintelligible. He tried to suck air but it was as if he were under water. "No, I'm wrong. It's Jonni. I know that now. It's Jonni. I'm so sorry, Jonni!" Vince's speech was the rage of pain and distress from someone who felt worthless. Vince shouted with a torn, ragged voice, "I'm so, so sorry!"

He lifted his face up off his knees and looked down the dim hallway. His eyes and face were red and swollen. His face was soaked.

Jonni pulled away from Brie and took a tentative step forward. She stopped and looked at Vince. She turned back and looked at Brie. Brie nodded.

Jonni ran toward us. I held Spot. Jonni hesitated near Spot

as if judging whether or not he was safe. Then she kneeled down in front of Vince, and he took her in his arms. She wrapped her arms around his neck, and they cried together.

After a long time with no words spoken, Jonni stood up and turned to me. "You are the man who made this happen, right? You helped my dad and Brie find me. Thank you." She gave me a hug. She was a small person, and her head only reached up to my elbow. But she let her face nestle in the crook of my elbow, and I'd never before felt such warmth from the appreciation of a child.

Spot made a soft, warning growl. He turned and looked behind us, toward the stairs. Diamond and I turned.

A man jabbed a rifle into the hollow at the base of my throat.

FORTY-NINE

The man's rifle was small but had a large scope. It looked
like a Ruger 10/22 Takedown. In the dim light, I could
see that he was the man who slugged Vince before he escaped
with Jonni down the zip line. He seemed like the leader, probably
the man called Lucas. He kept the rifle barrel at my throat as he
reached down and grabbed Jonni by her upper arm.

I saw Diamond tense, his hand moving toward his weapon.

Jonni screamed, "LET ME GO!"

The man held her as he backed away from us. He dragged her
over to the first door in the hallway, pushed it open, and backed
into the room, taking Jonni with him.

"If anyone opens this door, the kid dies." He sounded
desperate. I believed he would follow through on his threat.

He shut the door. I heard a lock click.

Brie ran toward us and stopped next to the door. She went to
grab the doorknob then stopped, holding her hands up as if the
doorknob were burning hot.

"Wait," I said.

Vince was still on the floor. The dim light from the wall
sconces reflected in his eyes. He looked lost and desperate and
helpless, unable to even stand up.

I heard a sliding sound from the room, like a person dragging
their shoe across the floor.

Or a window sliding open.

"They're going out the window," Diamond said. "Vince, you
wait here. Make sure they don't come out as part of a fakeout.
Owen and I will go outside and see if we can find them."

Vince didn't respond. He acted comatose.

I ran down the stairs two at a time. Spot ran past me.

Diamond caught up to me at the second floor. We went down the next staircase to the kitchen and crawled out through the secret entry.

Once outside, I said, "Diamond, you go clockwise. I'll go counter-clockwise."

Diamond nodded and we sprinted away.

When I got to the front of the house, I looked up at the top level. The third floor was mostly within a large roof. The roofline was interrupted with gables, extending over the bedroom windows for both the second and third floors.

The first gable on the third floor would be the room the kidnapper dragged Jonni into.

In the dim, dawning light, it looked like the window was open. But I saw no sign of Jonni or her captor. I made a mental map of how they would have escaped. Below the window was a bit of roof. Below that was another gable and window, this one for one of the second floor rooms. If one scrambled down next to that window, they could get to the eave of the roof. From there it would be a significant distance to the ground. But there was no doubt both the kidnapper and Jonni were athletic enough to make the drop.

They must have moved fast. There was no sign of them.

Diamond came around from the other direction.

"Gone?" he said.

"Yeah. Let's run for the parking lots. You head left, I'll head right. He's got to be nearby, probably about to drag Jonni into a vehicle."

I sprinted away with Spot at my side. The drive from the mansion goes by a sizable parking lot. There were multiple vehicles. But I saw no movement. I continued on toward the next area where I might find cars. I watched Spot's head as he loped along. He always turns to look at anything interesting. But he seemed to focus straight ahead.

My Jeep and Brie's pickup were in the distance. I thought I saw movement to the side. Two people running. A large man chasing a small kid. The man was carrying something long and

TODD BORG

thin.

The rifle.

Somehow, Jonni had gotten away from him and was running for her life. The man was gaining on her.

In an ideal situation, I could send Spot to take down the man. But Jonni and the man were too close to each other. I had no easy way to differentiate them to Spot. And he'd been near both of them in the third-floor hallway, so neither of their scents would stand out as unique.

I sped up my own pace to an all-out sprint. Spot loped next to me. If I timed it well, and if I could run very fast, I could intercept the man like a tackler coming in from the side.

I made like an Olympic sprinter, willing my body to move like that of a 24-year-old champion.

But it doesn't work like that in your 40s. My lungs hurt, and my joints felt stiff, and my speed didn't seem to increase. Nevertheless, I closed in on them. It was still dark out. Maybe the man didn't know I was there.

At the last moment, he sensed my presence. He changed direction like an experienced NFL player, and hit me with just as much focus as I hit him.

The collision was like hitting a tree, the impact brutal. We both bounced away. His rifle flew into the darkness of the forest. We hit the ground in a horizontal position. I sensed him tumbling as I skidded. My thigh took a major blow as I slid on the pavement. But it wasn't a serious injury, and I realized it was because my pipe club in my cargo pocket provided protection from abrasion.

When I came to a stop, I felt dizzy. My head throbbed, my thinking was foggy, and I felt fire on my temple. I realized I'd hit my head and cheekbone.

I tried to turn toward the kidnapper. My vision wasn't clear. The man looked like a wavering spirit floating through jail bars as he pushed himself up and got to his feet. He took a moment to stand with his arms out as if trying to balance. I realized the jail bars were a bike rack. The man once again ran toward Jonni.

I made a feeble attempt at spinning on the ground, swung out my foot, and managed to kick at the man's legs as he ran by. My shoe connected with his shin, a hard blow that felt like I'd kicked a piece of wooden furniture.

The man once again sprawled forward to the pavement. He got his arms out in front of him as he went down, palms grinding to a stop on the asphalt and cushioning his fall. But it looked like his chin hit the pavement, and he was stunned again.

I strained to turn my head and see where Jonni had gone. She was sitting on the ground next to Brie's pickup, pulling shoes onto her feet. I remembered Vince had said she kept a pair of rollerblades in both his pickup and Brie's pickup.

I could hear her whimpers of fear. She did a fast, jerking tug on the laces, tying knots, getting the skates on in what was probably record time.

I pushed myself up onto hands and knees. Hung my head. Tried to concentrate.

Next to me, the man I'd tripped did a slow push-up, got to his feet, and made a little shake of his head as if to remember what he was doing. He looked at me with fury, then looked around as if wondering where he'd lost his rifle. He reached down to the little leather holster and pulled out his karambit knife and advanced on me. Then he sensed movement from Jonni's direction, turned, and saw her standing up on her skates.

Jonni pushed off and started skating away toward the highway. The man must have realized he would never catch her by running after her. He ran over to the bike rack. He scanned the bikes, grabbing at several. They all were locked. He found an orange model with a thin steel cable lock. The lock didn't loop through the wheels but instead went from the frame to a lamppost near the bike rack. The post was 8 feet high. The man lifted the bike up above his head. The bike cable would possibly fit over the light if held just right. But dangling from the bike, the loop caught on the lamp. The man gave the bike a shake and a powerful thrust. The cable went a bit higher but snagged on the edge of the lamp housing. The man swore. He threw the bike up

TODD BORG

with a tremendous effort.

The projecting part of the lamp housing broke off, freeing the cable. The bike arced through the air and crashed to the pavement. The kidnapper ran over and picked it up. The cable lock hung down to the side. The man twisted it and made another loop with the cable. He hooked the loop over the seat so the cable was held up and out of the way of the pedals.

I had gotten to my feet. The world seemed to waver. I was too dizzy to bend down to my ankle holster. With great focus, I pulled my Lowe's sap out of my pocket and stepped toward the man. I concentrated on my balance.

The man hopped on the bike. Almost immediately, he realized the seat was set far too low, so he straightened up and began pedaling while standing.

I lifted my sap, but the man got away from me before I could make a focused effort.

The man was wounded, and his head must have throbbed from bouncing his chin on the pavement. But the advantages of bicycle propulsion made inline skates no contest against a bicycle, even one too small. A bicycle has a leveraged powertrain, allowing any modest rider to achieve high speeds. A skater has to kick and thrust and expend more energy for each incremental increase in speed.

The man quickly propelled his stolen bike up to a substantial speed, and he shot off after Jonni.

Spot was still near, watching me and the man and Jonni as she disappeared into the dark. If I'd been quick to give him a command to take down the man, he would likely have made the distinction between man and child. But I was slow and foggy, and sending a dog to attack requires the same careful forethought as shooting a gun. I also had seen the man's karambit knife. He might be able to slash a dog as it approached next to him on the bicycle. I needed more time to think it through.

I put the pipe sap back into my pocket as I turned and limped toward the Jeep.

"C'mon, boy," I said through clenched teeth. I looked for

Diamond, but he must have been searching through one of the other parking lots. I got to the Jeep, opened the door for Spot, jumped in after him, and started the engine. I didn't know where Jonni and the man had gone other than heading down the drive toward the park entrance and the highway beyond. I followed.

Despite my headlights and the approaching dawn, the road was still quite dark. I flipped on my high beams, but saw no movement ahead. I tried to imagine how Jonni would think.

Rollerblading on a highway was rougher and harder than on a bike path, which is usually smoother. Highways also have cars, making them more difficult to navigate. I guessed that Jonni had gone toward the highway and then turned onto the West Shore bike path. But if so, had she gone north or south?

If it were me, I'd go south. I had a vague sense the path south was more sheltered and would provide more opportunities to skate unobserved in the dark, more places to sneak off the path and hide. I had no clear evidence for my thought, just instinct.

The bike path might have been wide enough to drive on with the Jeep, but that wasn't reliable, especially at night. So I drove past the path to the highway, took a hard left, and headed south, my tires scraping loose sand and road dirt.

At first, I could see neither Jonni nor the guy on the bike. Maybe he'd already caught her and strangled her into giving up the software password. Maybe he was already cutting her into pieces with his lethal knife. But I guessed she had at least a small chance of evading him in the dark.

I tried to call Diamond on my radio. But we were too far apart for any connection.

As I had that thought, a light turned on through the forest to my left. Turning to watch as I drove, I saw that the man on the bicycle had a light he'd hooked to something near his waist. It was a blue-white LED, very bright. It shone a dramatic cone of light down the path. Captured in its glow was Jonni, skating fast, but not fast enough.

She made rhythmic strides, powering forward on her skates. Her speed was substantial. But the dark form of the man coming up from behind on his bike was demoralizing. He was still standing as he pedaled, his feet a circular blur. It was like watching a speeding car on the freeway, overtaking a small underpowered vehicle.

It seemed obvious that Jonni had no chance. From my position on the highway, I tried to see an opening in the trees where I could drive off the highway and crash through to the bike path and get in front of the man. But there was no opening. Even if I could find a driveway crossing up ahead, I would only be able to stop and get out and run back to find Jonni after the man had assaulted her.

Other than the man's belt light, the only other lights were distant street intersection lights. They weren't enough to suggest how I could get to him. But his light showed he had closed to within 20 yards of Jonni, and he was gaining fast. Then the highway veered to the right as the bike path went left. Jonni and the man went out of my sight.

I was approaching a hill, and the bike path builders had decided on a grade that would take the path away from the road. Flooring the Jeep, making it downshift and rev the engine, I raced up the hill.

As the road climbed, it curved back toward the bike path. I scanned the dark forest, fearing the worst. There was nothing.

Then I saw movement. Jonni came into view. The kidnapper was just 10 yards behind, still standing, pedaling hard, gaining on her, his cone of blue light lighting her like she was on stage.

I saw Jonni make a hurried glance behind her. Her eyes visible in the harsh glow.

The bike path began a long, sweeping turn to the left as it started climbing a grade. The man was almost on Jonni. I expected him to leap and grab her at any moment.

Jonni looked back again, probably fearing for her life.

Then I saw something change in her look. For a moment, it didn't seem like she was terrified. It seemed more like a look of calculation. It was similar to the look when she talked to the guard at Stone Lodge, saying she could help the man with his smart phone.

As the man came almost within touching distance, Jonnie bent at the waist, leaning forward. Like a speed-skating Olympian on ice, she put one arm behind her, bent behind her back. Then she began a crossover step as the path began to climb up to the left. It's a turning technique I was familiar with. But I'd never seen it quite this effective.

As Jonni leaned into the turn, each step brought her right foot forward and out. She crossed her right foot over in front of her left. Stepping down onto her right foot, she drove it outward in a strong push. It was a powerful move, one that required strength and focus. But it was a type of turn that could increase a skater's turning speed instead of slowing it.

Jonni exuded power as she stepped into the turn, doing the crossover, stepping forward with her left. She went up the grade fast. Her speed increased with each step.

The man's speed was very fast. But as he got within reaching distance of Jonni, he stopped closing the gap. The man's feet blurred. He was determined to catch and destroy the skinny kid just ahead in his light beam.

But Jonni's speed increased even more. She powered up the climbing turn, maintaining a formidable, rhythmic, driving cadence.

Although I only had infrequent glimpses of her through the trees, Jonni was like a dark wind blowing through the black forest. There seemed no limits to her energy. She went faster and then faster still, pulling away from her pursuer the way the wind pulls away from an old man. In moments, she was 10 yards in front of him. Then 20. Then 30.

As the bike path crested the hill and the man's energy flagged, Jonni seemed 50 yards distant, still accelerating, blowing her pursuer off as if he were a mere pretender. My last glance showed her flashing away into the blackness, far in front of his little blue light cone. It was as if she knew how to crush the monster's spirit, and she was merciless in her domination of him.

FIFTY

I saw a cross street approaching, lit by a lone street light. I slowed the Jeep hard, then turned in and jerked to a stop. I jumped out with Spot.

In the distance down the dark trail, I heard the dramatic wheezing of a man who had pushed himself too far and too hard. A man who thought he knew inline skates were no match for a bicycle. A muscular man who was a likely murderer.

Above the wheezing, I heard another sound from the opposite direction, perhaps along the trail where Jonni had disappeared at high speed on her rollerblades. I didn't register the source of the sound or even the kind of sound. It was just one of those background sounds, a dull thumping in the distance, like what you'd expect if you dropped a log onto the soft duff of an undisturbed forest floor.

I ignored the sound and focused on my task, catching the killer who'd chased Jonni.

I took Spot's collar, and we walked down the path in the dark.

The wheezing grew more intense. When we came to the man, he was standing bent over, his hands resting on his knees. His bicycle was on the ground to the side of the path. The blue light at his waist made a bright circle on the ground.

"You probably won't underestimate Jonni Cooper again, huh, Lucas? Or are you using a different name today?"

"Go to hell," the man said, no accent.

"No, that's your destination. But first you get to enjoy the court system, and the media humiliation, followed by conviction on multiple counts of murder."

"Wrong, tall boy." the man pushed off his knees and stood up straight. He was still wheezing. He held his karambit knife up. It caught just a bit of the light clipped to his belt. The shiny blade gleamed in the night. He looked very threatening. But I saw his eyes staring at Spot.

I had Diamond's backup gun in the holster on my ankle. But I pulled my Lowe's sap out of my tool pocket.

"We can make this easy," I said. "Toss the knife onto the ground. Then turn around, hands behind your back, crossed at the wrists."

"You wish," he said.

"Okay, you want to make this hard. My specialty. I see the blade," I said. "The problem for you is that I come from one side and my hound comes from the other. You should know that we are both proficient at subduing idiots like you. So even if you are very fast and succeed in cutting one of us, we still get you. Last chance. Your choice. Live with the consequences."

The man ignored me and came forward, holding the knife in his right fist.

"Spot, you remember our weapon hand training?" I touched Spot's neck one more time, made my own growl, which usually is enough to get Spot growling. He gave it a good display, a full-throated roar, deep enough to shake the man's chest. Spot lowered his head a bit and stepped toward the man, slowly, like a stalking predator. Spot lifted his lips far enough that his white fangs were visible in the dimmest of light.

I saw the man hesitate. No man is capable of not hesitating in that situation. But he didn't hesitate enough.

Spot was approaching the man's right side. I made a fast jump to my right, which was the man's left side. He turned and swung the knife. Spot grabbed the man's knife hand and, judging by the man's scream, bit down hard.

I grabbed the man's left hand.

Maybe I should have held it steady and called Spot off. But I was incensed that a psycho scumbag would chase and terrify and possibly kill a young kid.

So I pulled on the man's arm, dragging him toward me.

Which meant Spot felt the man was trying to get away. So Spot munched harder. I heard the snap of a breaking bone.

I hit the man with a couple of quick gut punches.

"Spot, let go," I said.

The man collapsed to the ground and lay there sobbing with pain.

"I said we could make this easy." I flipped him over onto his stomach, his arms outstretched to his sides.

"Where's the knife?"

He sobbed.

"Where's the knife?" I said again.

More sobbing. I stepped onto the hand that Spot had crushed, slowly increasing my weight on his broken bones.

The man screamed as if we were stretching him on a rack.

I put more weight on his hand.

He cried harder. "Idropit," he mumbled, drawing out his attempted words like a sobbing child.

"Speak more clearly," I said. "Or I step harder."

"I dropped it!"

I kept my foot on his broken hand while I looked around. "I don't see it. Help me out, here, or you're going to have mashed potatoes where most people have a hand." I put more foot pressure on his hand.

The man squirmed. "I think I fell on it."

I looked at Spot. With no specific command from me, he was watching and waiting for me to lead.

I said to the man, "I'll take my foot off your hand so you can lift up very slowly," I said. "Don't do anything you'll regret."

Of course, the man would know he was facing the worst possible punishment society could give him. There was little beyond pain that would constrain the behavior of a man with nothing more to lose. I was very careful. I took my foot off his broken hand and stepped back in the dim light, giving him a bit of room.

He pushed with his elbow, got himself to a sitting position, looked around in the dark. "Maybe I'm sitting on it." He moved his broken hand to the dirt next to where he sat, and made a little jerk as if to shift his butt over. Then he looked to the side. "I see something over there," he said, looking off the trail.

"Where?"

He gestured with his head. "Under that bush. You could reach it."

I shifted my feet for a better stance. "Reach it for me."

He made a tell-tale shift of weight, started to point with his broken hand.

I suspected it was a distraction. I was ready when he leaned out with a sudden jerk and his left hand shot out in a sweeping arc toward my leg, the karambit blade catching the light. If I'd been a quarter second late, he would have sliced through much of my leg muscle and maybe severed my femoral artery.

I had the pipe club in my hand. When he sliced back the other direction, I swung the pipe. I felt his flesh and bone give way to the metal of the pipe. Even if he hadn't screamed, I would have sensed the damage a small, short pipe can do.

He screamed and let go of the knife. It skittered into the dirt. Maybe his left hand was now destroyed. Maybe he was too dumb to know it. Certainly, he understood there was still the possibility he could kill me and even kill my dog. He swiped his hand toward his knife.

I was so angry and frustrated that I kicked him hard in his mouth, breaking his teeth. The man's head jerked up from the blow. The impact flipped him over onto his back. He fell with a thump, his bloody face pointing skyward.

"I said we could make this easy," I repeated.

Once again, I couldn't see the knife. It didn't seem that he'd gotten it in his hand. But he might have tucked it under him. With the knife's location unknown, we were still at risk. Even if he appeared unconscious, he could be faking it. I slowly walked around him, looking for the knife. There was no sign of it. I even walked over to the bush where he'd claimed to see it. Nothing. I went back to him and poked him with the toe of my boot, lifting his clothes under his sides, his arms. I pushed his bloody head to one side and then the other. Through it all he cried and hollered and moaned. When I used my boot toe to move his legs, he suddenly launched his own kick, a surprisingly powerful and vicious snap up toward my groin.

I jumped back. He missed. I jumped forward and did a heel stomp on the front of his knee. He screamed. I moved forward and did a simple knee drop on the center of his chest. It was a move that can kill. A ruptured aorta is fastest. Punctured lungs with sharp broken ribs is slower. As my knee landed on his sternum, the multiple snapping was pronounced, crisp and loud, sternum and ribs.

Lucas was wheezing and gurgling his breath through blood and saliva and broken teeth.

I got zip ties around Lucas's ankles and, with his arms behind his back, his wrists. Following Diamond's example, I pulled his legs up behind his butt and attached his ankles to his wrists.

I unclipped his belt light and shined it on the ground. The karambit knife reflected the blue light. Holding it in place with my boot, I removed the man's knife holster, snapped the knife into the protective leather sleeve, and slipped it into my pocket.

The man howled as I dragged him off the trail so no one would accidentally run over him.

I turned toward where Jonni had disappeared down the path.

I called out, "Jonni, you can come out of hiding. The man is tied up. He can't hurt you."

There was no response. I waited a bit, then called out again.

But Jonni didn't answer back.

FIFTY-ONE

I recalled a vague memory of a thudding sound that came from down the path.

"C'mon, Largeness, let's go find Jonni."

I trotted down the dark asphalt ribbon. Despite the coming dawn, it was still very dark under the tree canopy. Spot ranged out in front of me, his night perception far better than mine. "Jonni!" I called out in a loud voice. "Jonni, can you hear me? The man chasing you is tied up. You're safe, now. Where are you, Jonni?"

Then I remembered that Jonni had given me a hug. She had nestled her face and head in the crook of my right elbow, her skin and hair touching the fabric of my jacket. A person's head is the best source of their scent.

"Spot! Come here. Spot, come now!"

Spot stopped on the trail, probably wondering what I could possibly want. I ran forward until I came to him.

"Spot, smell this scent." I used my left hand to push his snout to the inside of my right elbow. "Take a whiff, Spot! Do you have the scent? Smell the scent! Okay, find the victim! Find her!"

I did the hand-drop point command next to Spot's head and gave him a smack on his rear. "Go on, run! Find the victim!"

When I push a scent on Spot, he picks up on my eagerness for a scent trail. I also knew the main scent on my clothing was my own. But for dogs, understanding the difference is basic. It's obvious to them they should ignore all the other sources of scent and just look for the scent source that stands out because it is unusual.

Spot trotted down the dark trail. I couldn't see his motions in the darkness. But I knew he'd be air scenting, head held high, nostrils flexing. Dogs find scents where they can. A kid racing by on rollerblades is not going to leave any scent trail on the ground. But a kid who is hiding in the bushes or walking down the highway will leave a scent plume, wafting on the wind, as clear to a dog's nose as a visible, daytime smoke plume is to a human's eyes.

I ran after Spot, trying to keep up with his trot.

We'd gone about 50 yards when I sensed Spot slow and stop in the dark. Before I could get to him, he turned off the trail and trotted into the woods. I tried to follow.

Unfortunately, this area wasn't an open forest that was easy to navigate. Spot went down into a steep ravine. I couldn't see anything more than a vague sense of a mottled light shape. Spot was stepping down through bushes and around boulders. The woods were thick enough that no light from the coming dawn filtered in beneath the trees.

I pulled out my light. It shot a bright cone of white into the woods, lighting up leaves and branches and rocks and tree trunks, but no person.

Spot had disappeared.

"Spot, where are you? Spot, make a noise."

I paused and listened. I heard panting. No movement. But I knew Spot was near.

I pushed through branches, stepping down a steep slope. I scooted over a boulder that perched precariously on the slope. Below the boulder was a tree. Something white moved below the tree.

Spot.

I grabbed a bush below me, holding it as I went around it.

Spot was farther down, sniffing something. When my light shined directly at him, he turned his head and looked up at me. His brow was furrowed. Not the look of curiosity, but one of worry. Just past his head was flash of orange, a jolting color in my harsh light. A round shape that repeated.

I realized I was looking at rollerblades a foot or two off the ground.

I stepped down the slope, pushing past more bushes, and moved my light.

The roller blade wheels were bright orange. And near them was a bright red color. I had to move another branch to see better, but there were still more leaves in the way.

Below the knee came more red. Blood. And next to the red was white. I inhaled as I realized what it was.

Exposed bone.

I scrambled down next to Jonni.

She was moaning. Very soft. It was clear that she was largely unconscious. Her injury was vaguely similar to the man's thumb injury up at Stone Lodge. Except it was much worse.

Where the man had cut his thumb artery, Jonni had struck a broken tree trunk and ripped open her pants and, under it, her knee and lower leg, exposing bone, maybe breaking it. Unlike the cut in a small artery in the man's thumb, Jonni had severed the artery on the inside rear of her knee. The spurting of bright red blood was like a small fountain. It shot a pulsing arc of blood the thickness of a red pencil eight inches into the air.

FIFTY-TWO

I made an involuntary gasp. It was difficult to comprehend her blood loss. The bleeding was severe, the ground below her leg soaked with blood.

I'd had just enough training back on the SFPD to know that this level of blood loss was deadly. And since I heard the thudding sound that must have been her crash down the long, steep embankment, it had been several minutes.

Jonni's blood was thick on the forest floor. As I tried to force myself to focus and think of the appropriate action, it seemed that the pulses of spurting blood were happening at a faster rate, even as the distance it shot was already diminishing.

I knew what it meant. She'd already lost such a significant volume of blood, maybe measured in pints. As a result, her heart was pumping faster and faster in order to try to keep her blood pressure up.

As I struggled to find disciplined thought, words of instruction came to me.

I realized they were Jonni's own words from when she helped her guard with his cut thumb. I repeated her words to focus my concentration.

First, apply a compress.

Second, elevate the wound to diminish blood pressure.

Third, if the bleeding is bad, apply pressure to the artery upstream from the wound.

I needed something to use as a compress.

I unzipped my jacket, reached under it and grabbed my shirt. Without bothering to remove it, I tore it open, buttons popping, and ripped the fabric up from the bottom. Got an uneven strip. Did it again. Another strip. I wadded up one strip to use as a compress and pushed it against the spurting blood. I took the other strip and wrapped it around her leg, holding the compress in place. I needed more material. Using my knee against her wound, I held the compress in place while I tore more shirt fabric and wrapped her leg further.

Jonni cried out. Probably, she felt a terrific pain as my fabric abraded exposed bone.

The spurting blood was no longer obvious. But it might still be oozing out at a high rate from under the fabric.

The second rule was to elevate the wound.

I tried to turn her body so her injured leg was above her heart. It wouldn't solve the problem. But it might slow the speed at which her remaining blood escaped her body.

Third rule: Apply pressure to the artery upstream from the wound.

I wasn't especially knowledgeable about anatomy. But I knew the femoral artery came down the thigh on the inside and then moved toward the back of the thigh as it approached the knee. If I could apply enough pressure in the right area, I might help slow the bleeding.

But I didn't have any time. I had to get her to the hospital immediately. I didn't even have time to check my phone for cell reception. And if I had reception, I probably didn't have time to wait for an ambulance. I could try calling as I drove.

I lifted Jonni up in a fireman's carry, her body across my back with her injured leg over my left shoulder and her left arm over my right. I tried to shift her so her left leg was highest and her body hung down a bit to my right. That would minimize the blood pressure to the wound. Perhaps it would also increase the blood pressure to her head. Maybe that was good. Or maybe there were negative aspects to that position I didn't know about.

A fireman's carry has the advantage of allowing the person doing the carry to use just one arm to hold the injured person in place. I took my free hand and put my light in my mouth, lighting my way as I clawed and scrambled and fought my way up the slope to the path.

My right hand was holding her leg and arm over my shoulders, keeping her in place. My left hand was gripping the back of her left leg, squeezing hard to apply pressure to her femoral artery.

I'd only climbed a few yards and her rollerblades had already caught on the bushes. But I didn't think I could dare take the time to set her down and try to get the laces untied and the blades off. Instead, I shifted sideways a bit, leading more with her head and upper body so that the brush was deflected away from her rollerblades and less likely to catch in the mechanism.

Jonni couldn't have weighed more than 80 or 90 pounds, yet I was immediately winded hauling her up the slope. I knew it wasn't just the physical effort, but the psychological strain of knowing she was dying from blood loss.

Because my mouth was holding the light, I could only breathe through my nose.

I shifted the light into my right hand, holding her limbs and the light at the same time. With the light out of my mouth, I could breathe better. I gasped for air as I nearly ran up the slope.

I hit bushes. My feet hit loose rocks, making me stumble. I fell to my knees. Got up, pressed on.

And then I came through into open space. Hard surface.

I was on the path.

I turned and ran. Jonni's body was bouncing hard on my shoulders. If she had any shred of consciousness, she'd be under severe stress not just from the open wound and exposed bone, but from the bouncing motion.

I tried to lower my body, tried to run in a smoother motion.

My lungs burned. I couldn't get enough air. I worried I might collapse to the ground. I couldn't afford to let that happen. If Jonni struck her head on the asphalt, that could kill her even faster than bleeding to death.

I focused on breathing. It became a mantra. One deep, fast breath for each running step. I was no longer going up a steep embankment, yet it felt like I was working harder than before. The path was a dark tunnel. My little light seemed to waver everywhere but down the path.

Breathe, run.

Breathe, run.

After 100 yards, something seemed to leap out in front of me.

It was my Jeep.

I jerked open the back door and carefully shifted Jonni from my shoulders onto the seat. I positioned her on her back so her head was on the right side of the seat. I draped her wounded left leg up and over the seat back to keep it elevated. The weight of her rollerblade helped hold her foot in place. Through my pushing and pulling to get her into position, she didn't even moan. While I was glad she wasn't conscious to experience agonizing pain, I knew it was a bad sign. She'd bled too much, her life ebbing away with her loss of blood.

I shut the door and opened the front passenger door.

"Spot! Into the seat."

He'd done it before and knew the only positions where he could fit. He sat sideways, his butt down on the floor, elbows and upper body on the seat. His back was pushed against the door as I squeezed it shut to latch it.

I ran around and got in the driver's side. Started the engine. Threw the shifter into Reverse and stomped on the accelerator.

I shot backward out onto the highway, thinking about hospitals. There was one in South Lake Tahoe and one in Truckee.

I knew that Sugar Pine Point was midway between the two. Both directions had many areas that forced slower driving. But going south entailed the switchbacks of Emerald Bay. I thought going north might be faster.

I shifted into Drive and raced up the highway. The road surface was still dark, but the surrounding area was visible in the dawn. I flipped on my high beams and emergency flashers and ran the Jeep up to 70.

I got out my phone and dialed 911, unaware of whether or not I had cell reception.

"Nine, one, one emergency," the dispatcher said, her voice exuding a professional calm.

"This is Owen McKenna, heading north from Sugar Pine Point, approaching Tahoma. I have a passenger who is severely wounded from a fall. She cut an artery on the inside of her knee. I've got a compress on the wound, but she's unconscious from major blood loss. I'm heading toward the hospital in Truckee. If paramedics with blood could meet me part way, it might save her life. If you can also contact Placer County Sergeant Santiago, he can possibly arrange for an escort. I'm in a dark-green Jeep, my flashers on."

"Hold the line, sir. Let me contact the hospital, first. Stay on the line."

The line went quiet. The silence seemed like death. I realized I'd been shouting into the phone. My throat felt raw. Maybe it was from gasping for air as I hauled Jonni up the embankment. Maybe it was from yelling at the dispatcher.

The road had several curves. I took them at the highest speed I dared. I went past the turnoff to Chambers Landing at 65 miles per hour. After another curve, I popped out into the gathering light next to the lakeshore. To the east, the lake reflected the dawn. The water was placid, as if everything was just right in the world.

Headlights appeared ahead. I flashed by them like a rocket ship at escape velocity.

"Sir," the voice said in my phone. "I've got an ambulance enroute. They will be coming south from Truckee down eighty-nine. I've told them you are in a Jeep. I've also got a Placer County officer on the line. I'll patch him through to you."

"Deputy Baker, here. McKenna?"

"I'm here."

"I'm heading south from Sunnyside. Where are you?"

"I'm heading north, approaching Homewood."

"You know Eagle Rock?"

"Yeah," I said, barely able to hear the officer over the roar of my engine.

"I'll turn around there. Look for my lights and pull up behind me. I'll be in contact with the ambulance. I'll give you escort."

"Got it," I said and hung up to concentrate on my driving.

"You can do it, Jonni," I called out to my unconscious passenger. "You've just started in this life, so there's lots more to come. I know you've seen some ugliness, but it's not all bad. There's lots to live for, lots to explore. I've heard how you like that book by Ann Radcliffe, 'Mysteries of Udolpho.' Brie told me your favorite quote from the book, that 'a well-informed mind is the best security against the contagion of folly.' That's you, Jonni. You're one of the smart ones. One of the well-informed minds. We need you to fight on against foolishness. We need you..." I stopped as I lost my train of thought in my upset. So I just repeated the words. "We need you, Jonni."

After a minute, I added, "Brie and your father will be with you in the hospital, Jonni. And then they'll be waiting for you to get better. They need you to be strong. The sun will shine again, Jonni, and the night sky won't represent threat, but a sense of wonder and possibility."

And as I said it, I realized I too would be waiting for Jonni, rooting for her.

I saw the sheriff's deputy's flashing lights in the distance. But the reds and blues were blurry through my tears. I wiped my eyes as I slowed and approached the patrol vehicle. I flashed my headlights and tapped my horn. The sheriff's vehicle sprayed gravel as the driver raced away. From behind him, I could see he had turned on his oscillating headlights. His high beams flashing down the road, left side, right side, left side...

The man sped up to 80. I stayed a half dozen car lengths behind him.

Oncoming headlights appeared. I heard a faint hint of the deputy's siren turning on, then off. The oncoming vehicle veered onto the shoulder as we raced by.

The sheriff's vehicle slowed a bit as we went past Sunnyside and the sharp curves just to the north of it. Then the deputy sped up as the road straightened out and we approached Tahoe City.

There were more vehicles going both directions as we flew over the Truckee River and headed north. But they all gave way to his lights and siren. The deputy slowed down from 80 mph as we went by the turnoff to Alpine Meadows ski resort, then sped back up to 85 on the straight sections of highway. He slowed again at Squaw Valley and then began slowing more, even though the road was straight and empty.

In the distance ahead came more flashing lights. As the ambulance approached, it slowed to a crawl, then turned 180 degrees, pulled onto the northbound shoulder, and stopped. Its rear flood lights turned on.

The sheriff's vehicle stopped well back and turned on its flood lights.

I pulled between the vehicles and parked on the shoulder behind the ambulance.

I jumped out and opened the back door as the paramedics were rolling the gurney out of the ambulance.

I stayed back to let the pros work without my interference.

One called out. "Where is the wound located?"

"The cut artery is just above the back of the left knee on the inside. The exposed bone is lower, her tibia, I think."

Jonni was motionless as they transferred her onto the gurney, fixed her head position, and strapped her down.

With ballet-like precision, they ran with her to the ambulance, folded the gurney's leg supports, and slid the gurney into the ambulance in one smooth motion. Two medics jumped inside the back with her. One of them positioned an IV bag above the gurney as the other shut the rear door. The third got into the driver's seat, and the ambulance raced away.

EPILOGUE

"The reason I want to be a doctor is so I can save people the way you saved me," Jonni said. "I'm just a big pile of bandages," Jonni said. "But I'm alive, thanks to you." She looked up at me from her wheelchair, squinting against the brilliant summer sun bouncing off the water at the Commons Beach in Tahoe City.

"You're more alive than most people with no injuries at all," I said. "Anyway, it was Spot who found you. He gets the credit."

Spot stood behind her. His head came over her shoulder from behind. His jawbone rested on her chest. His eyes were closed. He looked blissfully asleep. But his tail was doing a very slow wag. Jonni had her arms up, one hand rubbing his nose, the other fingering Spot's faux diamond ear stud.

The left leg support of the wheelchair was raised, and it had a large U-shaped bracket that kept her lower leg in position. Her knee and leg were surrounded by a thick bandage. There were several bandages on her head. Her upper right arm was encased in bandages.

"Even after I got down to you, the reality was I didn't know how to save you," I said. "It was only after I remembered your rules for treating a lacerated artery that I got a grip on myself and started doing something."

"What rules?" she said, frowning, as Vince and Brie walked up. Vince had bad bruises on his forehead and jaw and looked unsteady. He sidled up next to Spot and leaned on one of the wheelchair handles for support. Spot didn't move. He knew when he'd found prime real estate. Brie stood to Jonni's side.

"When I first saw you from outside the fence at Stone Lodge, the guard cut his thumb," I said.

"Oh, that's right! I forgot about that."

"You explained how to treat cut arteries. So I repeated what you had said to focus my brain. Apply pressure with a compress. Elevate the wounded limb. Apply pressure to the artery upstream of the wound."

"Wow, you are a good student," she said.

"No, you are a good teacher. How long do they think it will take for the skin grafts to heal?" I asked.

"On my arm? A few weeks. My leg is worse. I was told the bone and muscle surgery has to heal more before they fix the skin. They say it will be six months to a year before I'm all better." She made a wry smile. "I was feeling so good having escaped the guard on his bike. I forgot how that kind of speed can tear your body apart if you hit the rails. But as one doctor told me, 'as long as you've got fluid in your pipes, you can do almost anything.'"

A group appeared on the stairs leading down to the beach from the street. Lucy LaMotte and her mother Emily Taylor, William Lindholm, and Anders Henriksson. Lucy looked stressed, as anyone would after finding out their spouse had been murdered. But she seemed to be holding up okay.

I held out the cooler as they walked up. All took Sierra Nevada Pale Ales except for Lucy who took a seltzer water.

I knew that Lucy and Emily had visited Jonni in the hospital. I made introductions to William and Anders. They chatted with Jonni and her parents. Spot held his ground and didn't move from Jonni's embrace.

I walked over to where Street and Blondie stood with Sergeants Bains and Santiago and Martinez.

"Did your little project go okay?" Diamond asked.

I nodded. "Agent Ramos got the FBI computer pros on it."

"Did it turn out as you suspected?"

"Yeah. The Tahoe Robotics software is safe."

As we talked I watched Jonni. She still had her hands on Spot's head. But she was ignoring her visitors and was staring across toward Blondie. In classic rescue-dog fashion, Blondie looked both happy but also very aware of every little detail around her. Unlike Spot who thought everything in the world was designed and created for his pleasure, Blondie was always on the lookout for unseen hazards. I worried that Jonni felt the same way.

I saw another man coming down the steps.

I waved at him. "Tapper Logan, our Tahoe Robotics guest of honor has arrived," I said.

He scowled. "I've never before had a picnic invitation feel like a subpoena. Did you invite me so you could throw me into the lake?" he said.

"Not quite. But I do have a little surprise for you."

"Well, make it fast. I have work to do."

"Sorry, but you won't be going back to work just yet."

He looked at the men next to me.

"I want you meet Sergeant Santiago of Placer County, Sergeant Martinez of Douglas County, and Sergeant Bains of El Dorado County. I have some questions for you, and they're all interested in your answers."

"I don't understand. You're plotting something against me?"

"You'll find out shortly."

I put my arm around his shoulders and forcibly walked him over to where Jonni sat in her wheelchair.

"Hey, everybody. I asked you here because I wanted to break some news. In case some of you don't know, of the four men who were involved in Jonni Cooper's abduction, one died up on Job's Sister. We caught two of the others up at Stone Lodge, which sits on a high ridge to the southwest of here. Stone Lodge is where Jonni was held prisoner. We found the fourth man at the Hellman Mansion. Jonni got away from him, and he made the mistake of trying to chase her. He was on a bicycle, and she was on her rollerblades. The man never had a chance. She blew him away, and he is now rotting in a jail cell."

There were some chuckles and a cheer or two and a general sense of awe.

"And if any of you heard about the man's German Shepherd, the dog has already been placed in a good home here in Tahoe City."

I saw Street pet Blondie.

"I know you'd all like to know why Jonni was kidnapped."

Everyone went silent.

"The kidnappers' initial crime was to steal Yardley LaMotte's robotics software. However, that software was protected by a password, and they couldn't use the software."

I looked at Tapper. "Everyone, this is Tapper Logan. He is what they call the Concertmaster at Tahoe Robotics. Tapper is more familiar with Yardley's work than anyone else. As such, he knows Yardley put password protection on everything he created."

Tapper shot me a frightened look. He jerked himself out of my grip but didn't try to run away. In addition to me, there were three athletic sheriff's sergeants in the group.

"So my question for Tapper is this: How would someone like yourself attempt to break Yardley's password security?"

"Well the principles of cryptography are straightforward," Tapper said. "We have encryption and authentication. We have hash functions and various keys. All of these can be complex. It's not something average people would understand. So there's no point in me playing professor, here. Actually, most professors are pretty stupid about this stuff, too."

"Have you ever tried to figure out one of Yardley's passwords?"

Tapper looked infuriated. "What is this, a court of law?"

"No. But if you don't answer my questions, these law officers might argue over who gets to haul you in first. Answer the question."

"No, I haven't tried to figure out Yardley's passwords. Of course, I probably could. But Yardley was a clever fellow. It would take a long time, and I have better things to do."

"Then what would you do if you needed to get into Yardley's computer files?"

"I'd go phishing. The movies always show fancy tech devices for uncovering passwords. But that's fiction. The truth is that almost every time a password is compromised, it's because the password owner fell for a fake website or fake email attachment and then entered the password onto a page that was controlled by a thief. If a password owner is very careful, it's almost impossible to get their passwords."

"Was Yardley one of those careful people?"

Tapper made a big sigh as if frustrated with how dense and slow I was. "In general, yes. But Yardley periodically went to local schools as a sort of outreach teacher. He called it giving back to the community. He always came back saying the kids were so dialed into their phones they were worthless. They knew everything about their favorite musicians and their Facebook friends and nothing about anything smart or useful."

"He thought that about all kids?" I asked.

"Well, no. He said there was one kid in one of his classes who was different. A real standout."

"And did he tell you the name of that kid?"

"Yes. He said her name was Jonni Cooper."

Everybody turned and looked at Jonni. Vince and Brie were still next to her. They both beamed. Spot's eyes were closed, appearing to sleep with his head on Jonni's chest, but his tail was still wagging.

I asked, "Did Yardley say what it was about Jonni that made him think she was a standout?"

Tapper made an exaggerated nod as if Yardley had told him a hundred times. "He said he liked to tell the kids about password protection in conceptual terms, and he purposely made some of his comments almost transparent as to his own passwords. He always wondered if he'd ever come across a kid who paid enough attention to figure out what he was getting at."

"And Jonni Cooper was that kid?"

"Yes."

I turned back to the group. "When I realized the only way for the kidnappers to get the password would be to force it out of Jonni, I re-examined which people were close enough to Yardley that he would have told them about Jonni. And which people knew enough about Yardley that they could send someone to pretend to be Anders Henriksson's brother."

I held Lucy's eyes. "I could only think of five people who had close access to Yardley and his ways and would have heard Yardley talking about Jonni. One was your mother, Emily Taylor. She lived with you both, and she no doubt heard Yardley brag about how he'd finally met a child who could figure out his password hints. The second person, of course, was you, Lucy."

She looked shocked.

"You knew these things, too. You were very frustrated with Yardley. As you stated, he was a jerk. And he was impulsive about money, never consulting you, the better money manager. You also believed you were about to lose your house to foreclosure all because of foolish things Yardley had done. Your life hadn't turned out the way you wanted it, and, more than anything else, Yardley was to blame.

"Of course, the whole idea of losing the house was an illusion," I said, "created by the mastermind of the theft and the kidnapping, a ploy put over on Yardley by a good actor who convinced him Anders Henriksson was dead, an actor who was good enough with his story that Yardley invited him into the helicopter with the notion that he could change his mind about the supposed foreclosure. That man was Lucas, who is now in jail."

Lucy was shaking her head and looking horrified.

"The third person who knew Yardley well was Tapper Logan."

He jerked and stared at me.

"As Tapper just explained, he knew Yardley's password techniques. And Tapper, more than anyone, knew the value of Yardley's software.

"The fourth person was William Lindholm, Yardley's first investor and, as Lucy said, the one person who had a better big-picture view of Yardley's business than anyone else."

Lindholm snorted like a bull. "You're on thin ice, McKenna. I have a team of lawyers. You say one more thing, and I'll take everything you care about."

I ignored him. "And of course, who better than Anders Henriksson to provide the kind of information so an actor could know the perfect things to say to Yardley?"

Anders turned bright red.

I said, "How did the actor know the details of Yardley's loan from Anders? It all came from someone that actor had never actually met. Someone he corresponded with over an anonymous criminal network."

I paused and watched the group. Accusing looks competed with guilty looks.

"A few days ago, I arranged a meeting at Lucy's house. William Lindholm was there along with Anders Henriksson. Emily Taylor lives there with Lucy, so she was there, too. Tapper wasn't there, but all of the assembled people knew him. I'd learned how the men who took Jonni associated with the Brotherhood gang network, and the gang used bitcoin for their payments. But I didn't have a clue about who could be involved until Emily asked the simple question, 'What is bitcoin?' Both Bill Lindholm and Anders Henriksson gave good explanations, using Paypal as an example, not realizing Emily wasn't familiar with Paypal, either. However, Emily sort of gave up trying to get the nuances of bitcoin, saying she'd just accept it was a digital currency."

I took a sip of my beer.

"And that's when I knew who had ordered Yardley's death by having him tossed from the helicopter. But things often go wrong. And Yardley went to his death along with his computer and flash drive with the software."

"Then the killer ordered Jonni Cooper kidnapped for two reasons. One, to force her father Vince to take men up to find Yardley's body and get the flash drive, and two, to force Jonni to reveal Yardley's password.

"Of course, we now know Jonni isn't easily manipulated. Not only did she refuse to unlock Yardley's software, she used one guard's phone to get into the security alarm they'd installed at Stone Lodge and crashed it, so it couldn't be used. Because of that, we were able to make our entrance without being immediately noticed. One man, Lucas, got away, taking Jonni down a zip line. But we caught the other two."

The people still looked unsettled.

"We found Jonni at the Hellman Mansion, which had the same backup entry as the Stone Lodge. And when the last man chased Jonni, her rollerblade skill exhausted him, and we caught him as well."

"So you're saying someone helped these men?" Lucy asked.

"Not helped. Ordered. There was a general who planned and orchestrated the crime. That general was your mother."

Emily made a little scream and raised her hand to her mouth. "What are you saying? You're crazy."

"I wish it were so. But I knew it when you described bitcoin as a digital currency, words that neither Bill Lindholm nor

Anders Henriksson had used. It showed that you did, in fact, know about bitcoin. We've got you several different ways. The FBI has searched the Brotherhood computer server that runs its website. They found an archive with the original ad you placed for an enforcement team that included a helicopter pilot. They've traced your bitcoin payments back to the man who responded to that ad. You've committed many crimes in multiple counties. But I think the murder pulls rank, and the murder took place on the cliffs of Job's Sister, in El Dorado County. So Sergeant Bains gets first dibs on you."

Sergeant Bains unhooked the handcuffs from his belt and walked over.

"Emily Taylor, you're under arrest for ordering the murder of Yardley LaMotte and for ordering the kidnapping of Jonni Cooper. There are a host of racketeering laws you've broken, but we've got enough for now." Bains proceeded to give her the Miranda warning.

As Bains pulled Emily's hands behind her back and started putting the cuffs on her, she began screaming. "He was a bastard, Lucy! He was everything bad you thought and worse! He made you sign a prenup. Your support made it so he could be a success. But he was unfaithful to you. He might have made billions and then divorced you, and you wouldn't have gotten a penny. I was looking out for you. I was going to make sure you got what was owed to you!"

Bains walked Emily toward the stairs up to the street. His path took Emily past Lucy.

"No, mother," Lucy said in a low voice filled with sadness. "Now you're getting what is coming to you."

After Bains had taken Emily Taylor away, we redirected our attention to the sunshine and the lake and the beer.

I turned to Jonni whose wheelchair was in the shade of a tree. "Jonni, are you going to tell us what you figured out about Yardley's password?"

"If I told you, that would counter the whole point of a password, right? I told Lucy, and she reset the password."

Street and Diamond and Santiago and the two money men

joined us.

I raised my beer. "A toast to Jonni's recovery," I said.

"To Jonni," Street said.

Everyone clicked bottles.

"How are you going to celebrate?"

"Because Lucy now owns Stone Lodge, I asked her if I could go back there and fix my bad memories. It's an amazing place. So Lucy's letting me and dad and Brie go up there to have a little vacation. I'm going to sit out in the yard and read a good book."

"Speaking of which," I said, "I almost forgot. I found an antiquarian bookseller who had a book I liked. It was produced in eighteen ninety-four as a one-hundredth anniversary special edition." I handed her a package. I hadn't been able to find wrapping paper, so I put it in a paper sandwich bag and tied a string around it in the loose shape of a bow.

Jonni opened it up. Her motions made Spot wake up enough to lift his head. He started panting.

"The Mysteries of Udolpho!" Jonni said. "Ann Radcliffe's masterpiece. And this one is bound in leather!" She turned to Brie. "Do you know why I always liked this book so much? Because your last name is Du Pont. And the character Monsieur Du Pont in the book helps Emily escape from the castle."

Brie nodded but didn't speak.

Spot sniffed the leather-bound book and reached for it.

Jonni snatched it back from his jaws. "This isn't a leather slipper, Largeness! This is literature! You don't eat it. You - I don't know - I guess you live it."

About The Author

Todd Borg and his wife live in Lake Tahoe, where they write and paint. To contact Todd or learn more about the Owen McKenna mysteries, please visit toddborg.com.

A message from the author:

Dear Reader,

If you enjoyed this novel, please consider posting a short review on any book website you like to use. Reviews help authors a great deal, and that in turn allows us to write more stories for you.

Thank you very much for your interest and support!

Todd